WHAT READERS ARE SAYING ABOUT PREVIOUS BOOKS BY DIANNA CRAWFORD

"I loved your book so much that I read it over and over. I thank you for writing such wonderful books that have to do with God, romance, and our nation's history."

› Kim Hanson, Maine ›

"I can't begin to tell you how much I enjoyed your book. Please keep up the great work."

› Jo An McNiel, Texas ›

"You don't just tell a story; you make it live. I look forward to each evening when, once again, I laugh with true enjoyment and get to know the oh-so-interesting family of characters you have created."

› Deborah Jones, Maryland ›

"I could not put your books down! I have highly recommended them and passed them around to my friends."

› Mary Lou Hess, Illinois ›

"Your stories have been the refreshing oasis that I so often need but can never quite find."

› Kathryn Soulier, Louisiana ›

"So real, exciting, and funny. We have problems every day, and it's so much fun to see how God will help us. Your story shows this in a big and wonderful way."

› Sherrie Sumner, Texas ›

"I used to laugh at my mom whenever I'd see her crying over something that happened in the book she was reading, but now I understand why she does. Now it's her turn to laugh at me, because I have been crying over your books."

› Quimbly Walker, Texas ›

"Definitely the best books I've ever read."

➤ Jasmine Madson, Minnesota ➤

"Your books have turned many a boring night into a wonderful evening and a trip back in time."

➤ Stephanie Bastion, Illinois ➤

romance the way it's meant to be

HeartQuest brings you romantic fiction
with a foundation of biblical truth.
Adventure, mystery, intrigue, and suspense
mingle in these heartwarming stories of
men and women of faith striving to build
a love that will last a lifetime.

May HeartQuest books sweep you
into the arms of God, who longs for you
and pursues you always.

D

Romance fiction from
Tyndale House Publishers, Inc., Wheaton, Illinois
www.heartquest.com

Visit Tyndale's exciting Web site at www.tyndale.com

Check out the latest about HeartQuest Books at www.heartquest.com

Copyright © 2003 by Dianna Crawford. All rights reserved.

Illustrations © 2002 by Victor Gadino. All rights reserved.

HeartQuest is a registered trademark of Tyndale House Publishers, Inc.

Edited by Susan D. Lerdal

Designed by Ron Kaufmann

Scripture quotations are taken from the *Holy Bible*, King James Version.

Library of Congress Cataloging-in-Publication Data

Crawford, Dianna, date.
  Lady of the river / Dianna Crawford.
    p. cm. — (Reardon Valley series ; bk. #2)
  ISBN 0-8423-6011-5
  1. Women pioneers—Fiction. 2. Frontier and pioneer life—Fiction. 3. Mothers and daughters—Fiction. 4. Mentally ill women—Fiction. 5. Tennessee—Fiction. I. Title.
  PS3553.R27884 L33 2003
  813'.54—dc21   2002014502

Printed in the United States of America

08 07 06 05 04 03
9   8   7   6   5   4   3   2   1

*I dedicate this novel to Sue Rich and Sally Laity,
my two writing buddies,
who have been with me through all the thicks and thins
and especially through those sagging middles.*

Acknowledgments

I would like to acknowledge Helen Moore, who kindly journeyed with me to and throughout her native state of Tennessee; Sue Lerdal, my editor, whose conscientious edits always improved the manuscript; and Louise Cox and the other gracious librarians at the Nashville Library.

I would also like to extend my appreciation for the hospitality and tour guidance of Bob and Faith Murray, Bill and Opal McCoy, Stan and Connie Melhorn, and Roger Lowrance.

Chapter One

JULY 1804

The hair prickled at the back of Belinda Gregg's neck despite the sticky noonday heat. She felt a strong presence of others.

She was being watched.

Hiking her chin, she refused to show concern as she picked up her olive plaid skirt and mounted the steps to Bailey's General Store. Her mother needed more ginseng and figwort, or some other herb that might begin to soothe the tormented woman's soul. Without delay.

Still, Belinda kept her head down, making sure her own eyes could not be viewed from beneath the floppy brim of her sunbonnet.

But it was hard to be inconspicuous with the soles of her shoes tapping like drumsticks as she strode across the porch planks to reach the open doorway. Stepping inside, cooler air brushed her cheeks, giving her an instant of relief—before she spotted those who had been watching her. Two young misses stood gawking out the front window. Obviously a couple of busybodies.

Instead of turning to face Belinda, they continued to stare at the dusty street outside. Someone else must have captured their attention.

Glad for the reprieve, Belinda started past the sacks and barrels for the counter at the other side of the store, where the short stocky proprietor leaned over a ledger. Gripping a quill in his stubby fingers, he seemed unaware that she'd entered his establishment. Against her better judgment, she'd developed a special affinity for the middle-aged storekeeper the few times she'd been in the store during the three years since she and her parents had moved downriver of this Tennessee Territory settlement. Mr. Bailey always had a ready smile, and though graying like her father, he had the same shade of red hair as the Greggs.

"From the way Max is a-hobblin'," one of the girls at the window said to her companion, "I cain't imagine how he got hisself this far from his house. Nursing a broke arm whilst hoppin' along on that crutch."

Her own interest piqued, Belinda couldn't resist turning back to look, but the two calico-clad misses blocked her view.

"Why don't y'all run on out there and help him, sissy?" the one with long sandy hair urged, giggling. She elbowed her taller friend.

"Not me." The neatly bunned brunette stiffened. "He thought he was too good to settle down with one of the valley girls back when he run off to go explorin'—near broke poor Sally Sue's heart." She tilted her head. "Now, the way I see it, we're too good for what's come draggin' back. His ma told mine that his leg is so busted up, only a miracle of God's mercy will put it to rights again."

"You gotta admit, though," the smaller one said, "he's still one big hunk of man. Even all busted up."

"Liza, I'll swan. You'd take on over a stinkin' ol' polecat iffen he wore pants."

"I would not." Liza whirled around, her hair sailing out from her back as she stalked to the door. "You're just jealous," she tossed over her shoulder, " 'cause the twins sat next to me at church last Sunday, 'steada you."

The dark-haired one chased after her friend. "That is *not* so. I don't give a fig for . . ." The girl's words became lost in the pound of bare feet as the two bounded down the steps and out of sight . . . leaving Belinda with a clear view of the subject of their conversation.

Even hunched over his crutch, he appeared to be an exceptionally tall, broad-chested man. Hatless, his thick thatch of blond hair shone like ripened flax in the noonday sun, especially against the deep tan of his squarely etched face. He truly must have cut quite the stalwart figure before he suffered his injuries.

A wave of compassion washed through Belinda. Poor man. Like a gut-shot wolf, he was no longer the brave hunter but reduced to the hapless role of victim. And, as usual, town hypocrites were circling for the kill like the vultures they were. Belinda glanced up the street to the white spire of the community's church. Those heedless girls, like the rest of small-town dwellers, were given the privilege of hearing the love of God preached from the pulpit every Sabbath, yet they never bothered to listen. They were much too busy looking for something to condemn. Townfolk were worse than vultures. At least the scavenger birds never pretended to be other than what they were.

Thank You, Lord, for the reminder, lest I weaken and fall prey again to their town-talking lies. She swung back to the business at hand.

3

Mr. Bailey looked up from his ledger, his round blue eyes crinkling with a ready smile. "Miss, can I be of help?"

"Yes, sir, I have my list right here." Pulling a scrap of paper from her skirt pocket, she handed it to him, then took a last peek at the injured man. He'd turned off the road onto a narrow path that trailed into a thicket of trees tangled in vines and brush. It probably led to some bluff overlooking the river. If the fellow was smart, he'd go down to the dock instead, get in a canoe, and paddle as far from this town as he could . . . just as she would be doing as soon as the storekeeper filled her order.

~

Grunting with pain, Max Bremmer set his crutch aside and lowered himself onto a sheared-off boulder above a smooth stretch of Caney Fork. Sweat beaded his brow and not merely from the heat. It had taken all his strength—what there was left of it—to reach this hidden spot. But here for a little while, maybe, he'd be allowed to relax and breathe a bit of unused air. Get away from his mother's smothering concern and the solicitous pity of the neighbors.

A sharp pain shot through his throbbing leg as he eased his heel onto the ground. Sighing, he adjusted the sling holding his splinted arm. Resettling it upon his linen hunting shirt, he absently massaged his dangling fingers. What a broken-up mess he was. Helpless as a newborn pup.

How much longer was the healing going to take? Five weeks had already passed since the attack. Five wrenching weeks, with the first two spent laid out in a canoe, only half-conscious with fever, as his friends brought him from up St. Louis way.

Max focused on the dark shadowy depths along the far bank where the sun, even at its zenith, couldn't reach. A twig broke free from a skimming branch, caught in the current, and swept out to the center of the wide fork.

His gaze followed the twig's journey downstream. Max was aware that within a day or two, it would reach the Cumberland, then travel on till that river fed into the Ohio then the mighty Mississippi. Farther upriver of where the Ohio fed into the Big Muddy, the Missouri merged. The Missouri . . . the river that came from the far west, cutting through vast reaches of virgin land—open prairies as far as the eye could see and mountains so high, their peaks floated above the clouds. And beyond? No white man knew for sure what lay on the other side. Only rumors of great wealth in furs and land so fertile that, if planted, even a broomstick would sprout leaves.

Ah, but this was the year the mystery was destined to unfold. President Jefferson had assigned that task to the Lewis and Clark expedition. At this very minute the surveying party was on its way up the Missouri. While he sat here in a miserable heap, left behind.

Such a cruel trick of fate to have the dream of accompanying the expedition dangled before him, to be given permission to join them, only to have his chance snatched away by thieving river pirates before he rendezvoused with the team.

Max rubbed a spot on his leather breeches to relieve a nagging ache in his upper leg. One good thing, he thought grimly, the curs who attacked his group wouldn't be ambushing any other unsuspecting travelers. They were now six feet under, pushing up daisies, if any flowers would bother to grow over them.

Noticing his teeth were clenched, he relaxed his jaw. No sense getting all hot over lost chances. Or much of anything else, for that matter. From what Widow Smith said when she examined him, too much of his thigh muscle was damaged along with the bone for him to ever do much trekking off into the wilderness again.

He sucked in a breath. "No, I'll be stuck here the rest of my life, pounding iron for Pops. Sweating away in his smithy just like him and Mama always wanted."

Max's eyes fell shut at the throat-clogging thought. He'd be like one of those miserable ferry mules that spent its life harnessed to a pulley wheel, trudging around in a never-ending circle.

"Lord, will You please tell me, what did I ever do that was so bad You'd let me fall to this dull, boring state?"

Loud cawing shattered the stillness.

Max opened his eyes and snapped his head around, taking in his surroundings. War parties imitated ravens when signaling one another.

War party? Feeling foolish, he relaxed. There weren't any tribes within a hundred miles of here. Never had been. Black Bear was the closest thing to an Indian he'd ever seen set foot in Reardon Valley. And he was only Shawnee by adoption.

A pair of ravens swooped high above the river in a playful dance. Max then caught another flash of movement upstream. A birch-bark canoe came sliding out from behind a bend. As it floated into full view, he saw a lone woman down on her knees, paddling from inside the sliver of a craft.

She glanced behind her as if she was being followed, then settled back and pulled the oar from the water. She laid it inside the canoe, letting the slender boat glide with the current.

Max guessed that her wariness had been unfounded, and she now felt safe to rest a bit. From a distance he couldn't place her, especially with a sunbonnet covering her hair and most of her face.

As if she'd read his mind, she reached up, ripping loose the ties and tearing the bonnet from her head. And tumbling down in a mass of curls came the brightest red hair he'd ever seen. Redder than fiery flames.

Not a single young woman in the valley could he recall who had wildfire for hair. She must have moved here after he left to join Drew Reardon at a new Shawnee village north of the Missouri.

The woman shook her head, and the blaze flew about her like a spreading forest fire.

Breathtaking.

She retrieved the paddle and redirected the drifting canoe downriver again.

Max hoped she'd look his way. If her face held even a hint of the beauty of her hair, she'd purely be a sight to behold.

The black birds swept down toward the canoe, cawing loudly, spiraled up and swerved in his direction. The woman's attention followed their lead, and she turned toward the high bank where he sat.

Though more than a long stone's throw away, he could easily see the saintly perfection of her face, made blessedly human by her startling blue eyes. Suddenly he realized she had caught sight of him.

Startled, she quickly recovered and gifted him with a slow smile, hesitant at first, then more friendly.

Gorgeous.

She lifted a hand and waved.

Before he could think to return her greeting, she'd sliced past, heading away . . . to where, he knew not.

Then, to his surprise, both of the large black birds landed on the canoe's rim. Even more astonishing, just before the small craft rounded the downstream bend, he saw the woman reach out her hand and give them each some kind of tidbit.

Max squeezed his eyes shut for a second to clear away any blur of his vision, any distortion. When he opened them again, he caught naught but a last brief glimpse of the flame-haired lady and her ravens as the current swept them from his sight. Although he was sorely tempted to dive into the water and swim after her, his body refused to respond.

Almost instantly, he began to doubt what he'd seen. A flame-haired beauty with a pair of pet ravens? The walk to this secluded spot had obviously been too much for him. He must be hallucinating . . . falling into some sort of delirium.

Tales came to mind of sailors being lured into the depths of the ocean by strange, illusive sirens of the sea. Was this merely his imagination, this lady of the river whose smile had beckoned him to come to her? to follow her deep into the dark tangled reaches of Caney Fork?

He shook his head to clear it. He must be coming down with another fever. She was far too radiant to be real.

But what if she was?

Grabbing his crutch, Max hauled himself up on his one good leg and started to hop-skip toward home. If anyone would know about the mysterious redhead, his father would. Brother Bremmer was pastor to everyone in Reardon Valley as well as to those living in the surrounding hills and coves. He'd know if she existed.

Max slowed to a stop. Why bother? No woman would ever look twice at a man with a game leg.

But this one might. She just might. Hadn't he seen it in her smile?

The corners of his mouth curled with his own meandering grin.

Chapter Two

The walk back from the river seemed twice as long and three times as hard. Perspiration slid down Max's face, stinging his eyes, tickling lips that were no longer protected by a beard. With one hand in a sling and his other on the crutch, he couldn't even swipe it away.

He gave his head a fierce shake, sending some of the droplets flying. He hobbled by the church, staying away from the main road, and took the path along the back side of the buildings. By rounding the far edge of the kitchen garden, he gave his parents' two-story log house a wide berth, hoping his mother wouldn't spot him behind the corn rows and come running.

Safely past, he crossed the clearing that separated their place from his father's rambling blacksmith shop and corrals. The odor of the hot furnace began to assault him before he'd come within twenty-five yards. Exhausted, he stopped to rest in the shade of a lone oak, letting the smell take him back to his first memories.

During all his growing-up years, he'd watched his pops work, muscles bulging with the strain of pouring and bending hot iron into tools and horseshoes and various kinds of hardware. And not once had the man complained about the grueling labor. He'd always just gotten up each weekday morning and done it. He never seemed to have any other dreams or desires. Except, of course, that of being a husband and a father and a servant to the Lord. That had always been enough for his father.

Now Max listened to the steady pounding of iron on iron. Even in the summer heat his father never wavered in his duties. Never questioned. As Max leaned against the rugged trunk of the sprawling tree, a weary smile lightened his mood at the remembrance of a conversation the two of them had had when he was twelve or thirteen.

"This is America, Papa," he'd said, walking past this very oak. "You can be anything you want. Why work so hard at smithing? Lots of ministers don't do nothing but preach on Sunday and call on sick folks the rest of the week. Wearing a fine suit, their hands all lily-white."

His pops had burst out laughing, that gruff but warm rumble from deep in his huge chest. He clapped a big hand on Max's shoulder. "Folks round here, dey don't haf da time for sitting around *mit* da sickness, vaiting for me to come by in da fine suit. Ve all got food to put on da table, clothes on da back. Da goot Lord put us all here to do our part. *Und* mine is to put shoes on da horses, make hinges for da doors, *und* help put God's goot song in da hearts of mine neighbors."

"That's all?"

"All? I am never getting up in da morning dat I don't haf more to do dan I haf da hours for."

Max had wanted to say more, try to make him understand, but knew his father never would. As for himself, he had the need to get up some mornings not knowing where he would lay his head that night, the need to go where no white man had set foot before, to feel the rush of blood at knowing that danger might meet him over the next hill . . . all totally foreign thoughts to his stubbornly steadfast father.

Nonetheless, Max couldn't help loving the old man. His hulking father was a rock. Home.

Max pushed away from the rough tree bark and headed for the yawning entrance to the barn-sized smithy. Carefully making his way into the shadowy structure, which provided no relief from the summer heat.

Rolf Bremmer, wearing a smudged leather work apron, stood to the side of the furnace door, stoking the coals.

"Working hard, Pops?" Max called, announcing his arrival.

His silver-headed father looked over a shoulder, his heavy cheeks flushed from the intense heat. "Max!" A grand smile took years off the face of a man in his sixties. "Is goot. You are up *und* out of da house."

"Barely." Max managed a strained grin of his own as he lumbered toward the nearest bench. "I went to the river, and I almost didn't make it back. I'm that weak."

"But make it back you do. Soon you vill be as strong as before."

Max resisted the urge to contradict his father. He didn't have the energy to get into the subject of his damaged leg. He eased down on a short bench near a barrel of water used for cooling iron and switched to his reason for the visit—the woman on the river. "A passel of folks must've moved hereabouts since I been out in Indian country."

"Not dat many." Rolf reached into an apron pocket and pulled out a rag to wipe the sweat from his faded blue eyes. "Mostly da folks, dey go on out past Nashville. Out toward Fort Pickering *und* da Mississippi."

"Well, I just saw someone paddling downriver I couldn't place. A young woman with a cartload of red hair."

Creases pinched the brows above his father's nose. "I am not remembering anybody like dat. Vhich vay you say she is going?"

"Downriver from the dock."

"Hmm. I don't recall . . ."

Max felt his spirits sag. She really was just some crazy kind of vision. He must have broken more than merely his arm and leg.

"Vait a minute. I t'ink—you say she vas alone?"

"Aye, in a canoe." Max started to add that she had a pair of ravens with her but decided it would be better to find out if she was real first.

"Hair of red *und* bright blue eyes on da face?"

"That's her."

"Und you say she is alone? Dis surprises me."

There *was* such a woman. She was real. But, of course, Max berated himself, she would be married. "I take it her husband is usually with her."

"Nein. She is not da vife. Her papa is da one dat alvays comes to da store for t'ings. Not her."

"I take it, then, he keeps a tight rein on her. I can understand. She's real fine-looking. But she looked full growed."

"Fräulein Gregg? *Ja,* she is. Da Greggs, dey don't mix *mit* da udder folks. Dey keep to demselves." Frowning, his father untied his apron. "I better ride out dere. Her coming to town alone *und* in a canoe . . . dat sounds like she didn't vant to take da time to hitch up a buggy. Somet'ing is not right. "

His father's concern proved contagious. "But if they need help, wouldn't Miss Gregg have asked for it when she was here?"

"Like I say, dey is real private folks."

"If you wouldn't mind saddling up ol' Kaiser and giving me a boost up, I'd like to ride along with you."

"You sure you're up to it? Dey live on da udder side of da river. 'Bout t'ree miles down."

"I'd like to give it a try." His leg be hanged—the thought of seeing the red-haired beauty sent his heart racing. "I've been cooped up for weeks."

Unexpectedly, his pops gave Max's shoulder a squeeze. "Plumb pleased I am to haf your company. Plumb pleased."

At the look of joy on his father's face, Max realized what miserable company he must have been since being carried home, sulking and whining. He'd make a special effort to be more like his old self.

Starting to follow his father, a pain shot fire up his leg. Gritting his teeth, he ignored it. Miss Gregg awaited him at the end of the ride.

Mounting his father's gray workhorse had been harder than Max had imagined. But with the help of a bench and Rolf, Max had managed to gain a seat high up on the animal's back while gasping for breath. After that, the going had been somewhat easier on the plodding, surefooted gelding. Max remained mounted as they were ferried across the river, then followed his father's big black saddle horse down a wagon road along the far side. Still, the three miles through the woods would feel like a hundred, since every step of the horse jarred his leg.

During the long ride, Rolf pointed out each of the farmsteads that newer settlers had hacked out of the wilderness, but mostly, he talked about each family's walk with the Lord. As usual, nothing else seemed as important to this man of God.

After fifteen minutes or so, he fell silent. They came across no more clearings or trails leading away from the river. Now, only forest crowded in on one side, with the river below on the other.

When his father had said the Greggs lived off to themselves, he hadn't been joking.

Max hoped to glean more information about the family. "You say the Greggs don't come to church," he called to his father just ahead. Max tried to sound casual, careful not to seem too interested.

"*Nein,*" Rolf tossed over his shoulder. "Dey is alvays polite ven I go to da place. But dey never talk about much of anyt'ing. *Herr* Gregg, he talk *und* talk about da heat or da cold or da price of crops, even ven dey don't grow nut'ing more dan a kitchen garden."

"What business are they in?"

"Dey make da bowls *und* jugs from da clay dey dig from da creek bank. Tings like dat. Sometimes real fancy ones. Den *Herr* Gregg floats dem downriver to da merchants at Nashville."

"Surely, they have hired hands or maybe a slave or two."

His father frowned back at him. "You know ve don't abide no slaveholding in da valley. A crew of men he hires from Nashville to build da house *und* da udder buildings. A fine profit dey must make from dem bowls. *Herr* Gregg alvays pays *mit* cash money too. *Und* he don't skimp on nut'ing for his vomenfolk."

Max wouldn't have thought a man living so far from the eastern cities could support a family making nothing but pottery. But what did he know about such things? He was an expert only on the price of deer and buffalo hides and beaver pelts or reading the tracks and Indian signs.

Riding through these quiet woods, without the smell of chimney smoke and with only the sounds of the river and an occasional bird, Max felt as if he were out past the frontier—if it weren't for the gnawing ache in his leg.

A dock came into view below where the river receded from the cliffs, leaving a strip of beach. Tied to one of its jutting pilings, a raft bobbed gently in the current. On the bank nearby, a canoe lay beached. On its upward side, the word *Gregg* had been daubed boldly across the rough birch bark with green paint.

"Dis vay." Rolf guided his mount, Pitch, onto a crossing path that led from the river where a stand of young hazelnut trees arched over, causing his father to duck beneath the light airy leaves. "Dis is da Gregg cutoff."

Max, on Kaiser, followed his father's big black, hoping the trip would soon end. The pain in his bound and splinted leg had steadily increased. "How much—"

A strange screech wended its way through the trees. A cat of some kind. A big one. "Pops, I didn't know there were still panthers in these parts."

His father turned back with his own confused expression. "Big cats? Not dat I know of."

Max felt extra vulnerable astride a horse he couldn't dismount without help. And considering old Kaiser's ears twitched back and forth, nervously trying to detect any other sound, Max wished he had thought to bring his rifle.

"Da Gregg place, ve be dere soon," Rolf assured. "Maybe dey know somet'ing about da wild animal."

A moment later, his father emerged from the tree shadows into bright sunlight. He reined Pitch onto a small bridge, and the horse clunked loudly, crossing over.

When Max reached the top of the bridge, he saw a posted sign saying "No Salesmen or Tinkers Welcome." Then a full view of the Greggs' clearing lay before him. He pulled Kaiser to a halt and stared, utterly amazed.

This was where the woman in the faded sunbonnet lived?

In the middle of an expansive pasture stood not the usual log home but one of sparkling white clapboard with light green shutters. For an area that had no sawmill, that was most impressive. But even more so were the four rounded pillars that held up a veranda and a balcony above, both stretching across the entire face of the house. A white picket fence enclosed the front yard to keep livestock from eating an array of colorful flowers. And an arbor of pink roses arched over the front gate. If Max didn't know better, he'd think he was at one of the merchants' houses in Nashville.

"You are surprised, *ja?*" his father said with a laugh. He'd stopped on the other side of the bridge. "Grander dan you t'ink, *nein?* I vanted to see your face."

Gravel covered the drive that led to the gate then circled around to the outbuildings in the rear. The crumbled rock was also in use on pathways that led to the various structures. Everything very tidy, like in a picture book.

Max clicked his tongue to start his horse moving again. "This all looks real genteel. I thought you said it was just the three of them."

"It is. *Herr* Gregg, he hires Nashville men to come a couple times a year to do da heavy vork."

That seemed odd. Max brought his mount alongside his father's. "Why not hire valley men? There's always a shortage of cash around here."

Rolf lifted his rumbling voice to be heard over the crunch of hooves on the gravel. "Like I say, dey don't haf nut'ing to do *mit* folks around here. Dey don't even vant me coming. But God, He gifs dem to me, so I come."

A horrible howl rang out again. From the house!

Exchanging glances, Max kneed Kaiser into a leg-jarring trot and followed his father.

Had the cry come from the beautiful one? Was she being assaulted? tortured?

Two cawing ravens added to the noise as they circled above.

Rolf reached the gate first and swung down as another scream rent the air.

"Wait, Pops. Help me down."

Shooting a glance toward the house, Rolf wheeled back and eased Max and his splinted leg from the saddle, then took off, tripping the gate latch and hustling up a brick walkway.

Max felt incredibly hampered as he untied his crutch, then hobbled toward the house at a useless pace.

Rolf, usually a man of decorum, didn't bother to knock as a screech changed to an excited "No! No!" He burst through the front door while Max was hoisting his bad leg up the first of the wide porch steps.

They were needed. Desperately.

"Come back!" a male voice shouted. Someone was being pursued.

Finally reaching the entrance, Max heard the pounding of feet from the second floor. The sound then moved to the top of the stairs that ran along the back wall.

A woman in a flurry of pale blue chiffon raced down the stairs. She halted near the bottom, and Max saw that it was not the redhead. He took a relieved breath as this frail-looking woman stared wildly at his father. In disarray, strands of her light brown hair flew across her face.

From the second step up, she flung herself into Rolf's arms. Clinging tight, she glanced back toward the open-railed stairs. "They're trying to kill me."

At the top of the steps a tall but gaunt man came into view. Seeing Max and Rolf, he stopped, his eyes widening. The flush on his face caused his red hair and freckles to stand out.

"Brother Bremmer! What a pleasant surprise," he said,

breathing hard. "But as you can see, we are not able to entertain visitors at this time."

"Save me!" The woman, still frantic, clawed her way up Rolf's massive chest and clasped her hands around his neck. "They're trying to poison me."

Max stepped inside and caught sight of the redheaded woman he'd seen on the river. She descended the stairs behind the man at a hurried pace, her hair now pulled back by a black ribbon, exposing a scratch down her cheek that oozed blood. A sleeve was torn from the shoulder of her green plaid dress, the high-waisted bodice and skirt dotted with moisture.

She, too, stopped.

Max was sure that her first reaction upon seeing him was one of pleased surprise, and he detected the beginning of a smile. But then her gaze darted to the older woman; and her mouth, her eyes, both widened into an expression of horror.

Chapter Three

They took my Johnny from me," cried the woman, still clinging to Rolf. "And now they're trying to poison me. Make 'em give me back my Johnny."

"I'm here, mine *frau*. You're safe now." Max's father held the woman far enough from him to see her face. "Who is dis missing fellow?"

"My son. My baby—they hid him in the woods," she railed, low and angry. "He's all alone. He needs me. I heard him crying for me all last night. Terrible cries. They're ripping my chest apart." She gripped Rolf's shoulders. "Take me to him. *Now.*"

Max didn't remember his father mentioning a baby. And poison? What was going on here?

His father cupped the back of the woman's head in his huge hand and pulled her close. "Don't you vorry yourself. Everyt'ing ve make right." As he spoke, Max caught him exchanging helpless glances with the thin-framed, red-haired man. "Ve go out dis minute *und* find da lost baby. But you look plumb tuckered out. I t'ink you should go lie down. Rest. Strong you haf to be for da baby ven ve bring him back."

The wildness disappeared from her soft gray eyes along with the tension in her thin arms. "Yes. I am most weary, and I should rest. My Johnny will need me more than ever. He's so little, you know."

"*Ja*, dat he vill." Pops turned her toward the stairs. "Come. I help you up da long stairs."

The woman's husband stepped aside as Max's father helped the shaky woman on the return trip to the second floor. The man looked as haggard as the woman. "The room at the end of the hall," he directed quietly, then followed them.

Max felt rather useless. For him right now, mounting those stairs with his crutch to help with the unstable woman would be like trying to climb to the top of a mountain. His gaze gravitated to the young woman.

She stared back at him, not seeming to take note of his injuries as she studied his face.

He wondered if she recognized him from the riverbank. Or had she heard talk of the minister's crippled son?

Her lips parted as if she were about to speak. "I . . ." She ran her hand across the wet spot on her gingham bodice. "I'd better fetch my mother some more brew."

Not only did Max admire her looks, but he could listen to the velvet smoothness of her voice all day. . . . *Brew?* Perhaps the husband and daughter really were trying to poison Mrs. Gregg.

Redirecting her gaze, the lovely one reached the bottom landing with the sure grace he knew she would have. Her bright curls, still caught at the nape of her neck with the black ribbon, bounced across her back as if they had glorious lives of their own.

Max took his own crutch-assisted steps deeper into the room toward her, hoping his awkward gait wouldn't appall her.

But she wasn't even looking at him. She'd turned toward a doorway across from the staircase.

He felt suddenly deprived. He wanted to see her eyes up close, the arch of her brow, those wonderful cheekbones. "You're bleeding," was the only thing he could think to say.

She did gaze at him then, but with a puzzled expression.

Puzzled or not, it failed to deter him from memorizing her astonishing eyes. They were starbursts of blue, fringed with dark lashes and framed by arching brows a few shades darker than her hair. "Your cheek," he said, coming to his senses.

Reaching up with long slender fingers, she ran one down the scratch. Withdrawing it, she stared at the blood that now stained her fingertip. She looked at Max then—really looked at him. "My mother is normally a very kind and loving person. But sometimes her memories get the best of her. And that's *all*," she said fiercely. "I must have your oath that you will not repeat to anyone what you have witnessed here today. This is our own private business. No one else's." She continued to pin him with her splashing blue eyes. She expected—*demanded*—a reply.

"You have my word," he answered. "Bandying it about would be like kicking a fella when he was down."

She continued to look at him, studying his face as if she was judging his words against the honesty in it. Then a smile slowly spread across her full lips. "From the look of you, it would seem you've had your own experience with being kicked while you were down."

He answered her with a smile of his own. The lass had a sense of humor. "That I have."

Her gaze deserted him for the stairs, and all signs of pleasantry fled her features. "I need to hurry back with the soother." She turned and sped across a nearby threshold . . . to the kitchen, Max assumed.

Not wanting to be left behind, he jammed his crutch into what he now observed was a plush Oriental rug of mostly beiges, gold, and coral. Suddenly, he realized he hadn't noticed a single thing about the rather large room. He glanced toward the fireplace and found the parlor to be more beautifully appointed than any other home this son of poor immigrants had ever been in. Like the rug he stood upon, all the furnishings were in those same hues, from the damask drapes at the tall windows to the velvet chairs and the brocade settee. And every piece of highly polished furniture was obviously professionally made.

But the one item that most held his interest sat in front of the staircase . . . a harpsichord in a casing of finely crafted inlaid woods. His father's congregation had donated money for several years before they'd been able to save enough to buy one for the church, and this family had a far more expensive one for their own personal use.

The lady of the river was accustomed to being surrounded with beautiful and expensive things. She and her parents probably considered themselves socially far superior to the more common folk of the valley.

His spark of indignation was quickly doused by his sinking heart.

Then reason returned. It wasn't as if he was in the market for a wife. If, by some miracle, his leg was sufficiently restored, he'd be out of here for parts west anyway.

But in the meantime, a pretty face should never be neglected.

Max leaned on his crutch and swung his bad leg forward. Reaching the opening through which the young woman had disappeared, he spotted her at the hearth across the room, holding a steaming kettle. She was pouring a pungent, brown-tinted liquid into a large earthenware mug.

He couldn't identify the smell of it. "What do you have brewed there?" he asked. "Does it merely calm your ma or does it bring on sleep?"

She slanted her blue gaze up to his. "I have figwort and ginseng, along with some squawberry Mr. Bailey at the store recommended. I've never tried them together before, but they're all reputed to calm folks and help them sleep." She straightened and took a sip. "It doesn't taste half bad either. Now, if I can just get her to drink some of it . . . ."

"Let my pops help you. He has a way with folks. His prayers alone can calm most troubled seas."

Mug in hand, she moved past him, leaving him with too short a whiff of some sweet fragrance. "I do hope that's so."

Max maneuvered around as fast as he could to reassure her. But the lovely redhead was already halfway up the stairs. Then she disappeared, leaving him and his useless leg behind.

Belinda watched out an upper window as Brother Bremmer helped his son to mount, then watched the two ride away while Jacob and Esau, her two overly curious ravens, circled above. She remained there until the men disappeared into the distant woods, unable to take her eyes off them. Off *him*.

How odd that the very first man she'd allowed herself to daydream about in years had actually arrived at her doorstep on the very same day. Oh, but at such an inopportune time. Nonetheless, he had come. Somehow he'd known she needed help.

Had he seen it in her eyes when she glided by him on the river? He must have. And he'd cared enough to fetch his father and come to her aid . . . and he in such a debilitated condition himself.

A true hero if there ever was one.

And the way his sunny hair feathered boyishly across his brow . . . quite endearing, especially for such an otherwise tall and sturdy fellow.

"I'll never forget the moment," she heard her father say quietly to her mother, drawing Belinda back to the present, "that I first knew I loved you and wanted you with me forever."

Belinda turned from the window to view her father lying on the bed with her mother, his arms cradling her, her head resting on his shoulder, her eyes peacefully closed. Such a change from a mere half hour ago. *Thank You, Jesus.*

"Remember, love? The day you read your poem in our little classroom."

Her mother gave an almost imperceptible nod, and the smallest of smiles moved her lips. The herbal mixture, along with Brother Bremmer's soothing yet powerful praying, had done wonders.

Mr. Gregg began speaking quietly:

"Last night I had a dream.
In it I became light as a leaf, a feather on the fly.
I whirled and soared far above the mournful cry.
My shackles, their chains, they fell by the by."

Once before, Belinda had heard him recite the poem, and when she'd asked its meaning, he'd told her it had been his beautiful Felicity's way of pouring out her horror when she lived on her domineering father's plantation with over a hundred downtrodden slaves . . . a poem he would keep in his heart always to remind him of the source of her later suffering.

"No more whispers of hate, no more dark watching eyes.

24

No more snarls of anger or deserting good-byes.
No more bombarding heaven with wails of why.

I am gossamer silk rising above the sky,
Lifted by His light to the fragrance on high.
I am shimmering hope, forever free to fly.

Last night I had a dream,
And now I am no longer afraid to dream."

Belinda studied the two of them lying there in the big, lace-canopied four-poster. Her father had made such great sacrifices for his beloved. He'd left South Carolina and his family for her sake, and because of her dark days, they'd been forced to move three more times. He could have been a respected minister and teacher like his father before him, but his life had, out of necessity, been devoted to his wife and daughter. Particularly after little Johnny had died of yellow fever.

Belinda had hoped to find a true love for herself one day. But she knew her chances were slim at best. The daughter of a woman who had spells of madness was not considered an acceptable choice for marriage.

Sighing, she reminded herself of what a fine life she and her parents had made for themselves right here in this lovely spot. To be content, they truly didn't require anyone else. They had each other, plus their pottery business. She had the care of the house and gardens, and she had her ravens and her baby fox upon which to lavish her affections.

Still, her wayward mind refused to stop picturing the man with the most charmingly playful smile she'd ever seen.

But could he be trusted with today's secret?

Belinda moved to the side of the bed, where her father still lay, his short red lashes fallen to his cheeks. She reached over and touched his arm.

His dark blue eyes opened, questioningly.

She motioned for him to come downstairs as she quietly made her exit. They needed to talk. She needed to know what his thoughts were about the two Bremmer men. Especially the younger one.

Chapter Four

The ravens followed Max and his father even past the Greggs' bridge. They hopped from one treetop to another, their little yellow eyes watching, their heads cocked to listen, as if they could actually understand anything the two of them said.

Max shrugged. Perhaps they could. He'd heard they were bright little scamps . . . Miss Gregg's busybody pets. The lovely Miss Gregg. Even his aching leg couldn't stop him from thinking about her.

"Pops." He turned to his father riding beside him. "Perchance, did you catch Miss Gregg's Christian name?"

Rolf cracked a one-sided smile. "Ah, da pretty young *fräulein*. *Herr* Gregg, he calls her Belinda."

Though Max didn't repeat the name out loud, he did let the syllables roll slowly across his tongue several times. The name felt pleasing, lyrical, and he decided it suited her perfectly.

"Everything seemed quiet by the time you came downstairs. I assume Mrs. Gregg drank the tea mixture."

"*Ja*, dat she did. Den ve spend time praying for da baby *und* for her. She vas sleeping peaceful vhen I leave."

"That must've been some powerful praying. The woman looked completely mad when you took her up to her room. Her wandering eyes . . . lost."

"Son, vhat I am saying to you, ve don't speak of dis even to your mama. Folks need to know dey can trust da pastor *mit* da deepest secrets."

"I understand. I agree. Besides, I made Miss Belinda a promise that I wouldn't mention what happened either."

"Is goot. Folks, sometimes dey can be mighty cruel. Back home in Bavaria, my cousin marries a voman who sometimes sees t'ings dat are not dere. Da neighbors, dey start calling her a vitch. Pretty soon, dey get all excited *und* vant to burn her at da stake. My cousin, he haf to run avay *mit* her *und* da *kinders*. Ve never hear from dem again. I pray for dem every morning."

"I wonder what makes some people go mad."

Rolf snorted. "Your mama, she vould say it is mad blood in da family. *Und* maybe it is, sometimes. But from vhat *Herr* Gregg says to me after his vife is sleeping, I t'ink bad tings happen vhen she is young, *und* dey come back to haunt her."

"Indian attacks?"

"*Nein*. Da Greggs, dey look like rich folks dat come here from da East. But cruelty can be lurking anyplace, not only in attacks from da Indians."

"That's true. Even here in Reardon Valley. And now I reckon we know why the Greggs have kept to themselves." Something he hoped to remedy . . . at least when it came to his seeing the lovely Belinda.

~

Slowly Max came awake the next morning on a cot his folks had placed under the stairs for their invalid son. His first thoughts were of red curls and freckles sprinkled across a pert nose. A grin started but ended in a yawn as he stretched his one good arm.

And those startling eyes . . . how free and enchanting she'd looked on the river with her pet ravens. Then to learn how trapped she really was, living an isolated life with a mad mother.

Ah, but the beauty did have fire . . . such fervor had been in those eyes when she demanded he keep the family secret.

Well, since he was already privy to their secret, he saw no reason for them to object to *him* visiting. With that thought firmly lodged, he sat up and eased his injured leg off the cot. The day held real promise. But he'd better not merely show up unannounced without some kind of a reason.

Hearing his mother rummaging about in the kitchen and catching whiffs of bacon and coffee, he struggled into a clean linen overshirt and some loose-legged trousers she'd sewn to fit over his splints. Not very dashing, he noted, wondering what the affluent young lady might think. He'd never paid much attention to his attire before. But now he had the urge to spruce up more. Belting the overshirt and replacing his arm sling, he collected his crutch and made his way toward the back door to take care of the remainder of his morning needs.

"Ah, my son, I see you are up early," his rosy-cheeked mother said. In a faded calico apron, she swung up from the hearth across the kitchen. Using her arm instead of a doughy hand, she shoved a stray strand of silver-threaded blonde hair from her brow. "Goot. Every day you are feeling better. Da breakfast I haf almost ready. You go shave *und* vash up. A clean towel I put by da vashstand outside."

Max chuckled to himself. His mother must think he wouldn't know how to take care of himself if not for her. He wondered what she thought he'd done these past six years when he'd lived away from home. True, he hadn't shaved all that often out west of the Mississippi, but neither did most of the hunters and trappers he'd run across.

Working his way down the rear steps, he looked across the yard to the outhouse. Ever since he'd been up and shuffling about, he'd purely wished it was closer.

After a few minutes of mulling over plausible excuses for calling on the Greggs today, one finally took root. He returned to the kitchen, whistling. He had a plan.

"You sure is sprightly dis morning," his mother, wearing her usual crown of braids, beamed as she came to the gingham-covered table with a heaping plate of fried potatoes, eggs and bacon.

"Me and my leg are feeling so good today," he said, lowering himself onto a simple homemade chair, "after breakfast, I think I'll ride on out to the Smith place." Ma Smith kept quite a store of healing herbs and other remedies. He'd pick up something to take to the ailing Mrs. Gregg.

"To see da mama of Ken? I t'ink dat is goot idea. Haf her look at dat leg of yours. See how it heals. But I t'ink ve get her to come here instead."

"No. I'm through being laid out in the parlor like a dead man."

"Humph. *Ach*, if you are insisting . . ." She set down a steaming cup of coffee. "You eat first. I am coming *mit* you. But I need to change into a fresh dress." Swinging away in a rush, she replaced the coffeepot on the hearth, shoveled the hot coals to the back, and started for the stairs, but stopped at the doorway. "Ve take da buggy. No more straddling da horse for you. Not after how you come dragging in here yesterday like some eighty-year-old man."

There was no arguing with his mother when her mind was set. And she had seen how he barely made it through supper yester's eve before he headed to bed.

Less than an hour later, Max and his mother rolled past Ken Smith's wheelwright shop, with Max holding the reins of the long-legged black, Pitch.

The Smiths' spotted hound started raising a racket, announcing their arrival to anyone within a mile.

Despite the yapping noise, Max felt considerably more comfortable in the buggy than he had yesterday on horseback. Glancing around, he didn't see Ken Smith coming forth, but plenty of evidence of their neighbor's trade was strewn about. Wagon wheels of various sizes, some new and some in need of repair, were stacked against his shop, along with an axle or two.

Passing the shop, Max brought Pitch to a stop a bit short of the family's log home, where Ken's mother, wife, and daughter were outside doing the week's laundry. The two older women knelt over washboards, scrubbing steaming clothes, while Betsy's only daughter, Liza, hung clothes on lines strung between poles.

The very second Liza spotted Max, she ripped several wet undergarments from a line and dropped them back into a basket near her feet, no doubt to hide them.

Max couldn't stifle his amusement. With a mother and two older sisters, it wasn't as if he'd never seen the contraptions women wore beneath their clothes. But Liza had reached that age. When he left for Indian country, she hadn't been more than eleven or twelve.

His mother elbowed Max in the ribs. "Don't you shame her. She is pretty young voman now, yust like her mama."

Inga was right. Liza had her mother's same light brown hair and eyes that had a way of tilting downward even when she smiled. "She isn't much bigger than Betsy either. You'd think she would've inherited some of Ken's size."

"*Na ja,* da boy is big like his papa, *und* dat is vhat counts."

"Max Bremmer, what you doin' out ridin' so soon?" Ma Smith, whose size made up two of the younger womenfolk, eyed Max while wiping her hands on an apron already splattered with water. "I ain't give you permission to be up an' traipsin' about. I already put too much time in on that leg a'yourn."

"Dat is vhat I say to him," Inga said, climbing down from the rig.

"Well, since you're here," the white-haired grandmother groused, "I reckon you might as well get on down." The tall, stocky woman turned back to her daughter-in-law. "Betsy, come give us a hand getting this hulk of a man down."

"I can manage myself."

"Not with me here, you ain't. Them bone pieces won't knit back together iffen you start jerkin' 'em around," Ma Smith said.

Max felt even more helpless as the womenfolk crowded around, all of them trying to grab hold of him. It was particularly embarrassing to have one as young as Liza helping, those sad eyes of hers filled with concern as he reached the ground and hooked the crutch under his good arm—the one that was functioning at the moment.

"Y'all come inside," Betsy invited. "I'll fix us somethin' cool to drink."

"*Nein.*" His mother started forward purposefully. "First I help you *und* Liza finish *mit* da wash, so Alice, she can look at da leg of mine son."

Betsy halted. "No, Inga. I don't want you doin' our work for us."

"Don't be da silly goose." His mother was already rolling up her sleeves. "You got a goot fire going under dem tubs."

A hearty laugh rolled out of Ma Smith, jiggling her bosom. "Well, looks like Max is all mine." She shot him a prankish smile and nodded toward a hut a dozen yards from the house. "Come with me, said the spider to the fly."

"But, Grandma . . ." Frowning, Liza glanced from her to Max. Then her pretty features turned sheepish, and she whirled away toward the washtubs.

Inside the small cabin, various plants hung drying from the ceiling, and labeled jars lined shelves attached to the walls. A small iron stove took up one corner and metal instruments cluttered a table, while more jars and a basin sat under one of two windows. Another long table took up the center. Obviously Ma Smith took her doctoring seriously. If anyone would have something to help Mrs. Gregg, it would be Ma Smith.

The elderly yet robust healer always seemed to have a sense of humor, though. From what his mother had told him, Ken's mother had arrived here last year to live after her husband died and had been a blessing to the valley ever since with her medicinal plants and nursing skills.

"Up on the table, big boy," Ma Smith ordered with a mischievous lift of her brows.

Embarrassed more for being almost helpless than because of the woman's teasing remark, he scooted onto the surface and sat there in silence.

She pulled up a tall stool and unbound the leg wrappings and removed the splints. Then with care, she pulled away the thick bandage and poultice covering the entering and exiting wounds from where he'd been shot.

"Looks a sight better than it did t'other day. Healin' from the inside out just like I want." Leaning down, she sniffed. "An' I still don't smell no rot settin' in. You just keep prayin' the crushed bone is knittin' just as good."

"Believe me, I am." If it didn't, he'd be a lot worse off than just losing a chunk of muscle.

She looked up, her smile serious now. "If prayin' will make it right, you ain't got nothin' to worry about. Ever'body in the valley's been prayin' for you since you was brought in. I'll redress this and you can be on your way. But don't you be gettin' too frisky, now. I don't want you undoin' all my hard work here."

Be on my way. There was only one place he wanted to go. "Ma, you sure got a lot of healing plants and potions. You know of one that's potent enough to stop folks from getting crazylike? Something stronger than, say, ginseng or figwort or squawberry?"

"Who is it that's havin' the problem? Maybe I oughta go pay 'em a visit."

"I'm sorry. I can't say. I'm bound by a promise."

"I see." But from the way she said it, Max could tell she wasn't satisfied.

He hoped he hadn't said more than he should. But if this healer could help . . . "I'd like your word that you won't mention what I told you to anyone."

"I wouldn't anyways. It's my business to fix folks, not cause more hurt. Tell me more about the symptoms, and I'll see what I can come up with."

Max fervently hoped she'd come up with something that worked. If she didn't, his mystical lady of the river would have no spare time for him. And he knew the beautiful redhead was interested. He'd seen it in her eyes, in that brief unguarded welcome she'd given him just before she realized he'd seen her mother.

Chapter Five

After an interminable hour enduring tea and gossip at the Smith table, Max and his mother finally drove back to the settlement. He did, however, have a pouch of ground, pink lady-slipper root tucked safely inside his belted shirt. He reined Pitch to a halt in front of his parents' German-style house with its every window and railing box in full bloom.

His mother caught her somber gray skirt to one side and climbed down from the buggy.

"Mama." He stopped her before she started around to help him off. "I'd like to drive around a spell. I'll be back in a couple of hours."

She opened her mouth to object, then sighed. "You be careful. *Und* you keep dat horse moving slow."

"*Ja*, Mama. I ain't going to do anything foolish. Too much is at stake."

Max waited until she walked into the house before he

snapped the reins over Pitch's back. If she caught him heading toward the ferry dock, she'd raise a ruckus. Horses were always nervous when aboard a raft, and with him and the buggy attached . . .

He passed the church, its white spire bright in the late-morning sun. Then just as he reached the saddler's shop, the local gathering place for the men, one of them lounging in the shade of the deep overhang called to him.

"Howdy, Max." It was Mr. Hatfield, the owner of the business and neighbor for many years. "Good to see you up and about. We been prayin' for you."

Max raised his good hand, the one holding the reins. "Thanks. I 'preciate that. See you after a while." Normally, he would've stopped for a short visit, but he had pressing business . . . the business of seeing Belinda Gregg again.

Once the trees beyond Bailey's General Store blocked the view to his home, Max relaxed. But just as he started down the slope to the ferry dock, a familiar voice rang out behind him.

"Max! Max Bremmer, hold up."

Glancing back, Max wondered which Dagget twin had yelled. Their voices were as identical as their looks. Reluctantly, he reined in to wait. They'd all been friends since they were six years old.

The only perceptible change in his rawboned friend with a mop of black shaggy hair was that his frame was no longer as rangy; he appeared more solid. He wore the same baggy workaday homespun as most all of the other men in the valley. "Been meanin' to come by," the long-toothed fellow said with a grin as he reached Max, "but your ma's been like a hen with a lone chick."

Max saw the small scar on the chin and knew it wasn't Peter. "How's it going, Paul?"

His childhood friend propped a booted foot on the running board. "Things could be better. Pa sent Pete to fetch back our bull from up Knoxville way, an' I'm havin' to take on all the chores. But you . . ." His brows dipped like ravens' wings.

Ravens . . . Belinda.

"You sure look a sight," Paul finished. "Like you been in a war."

Max glanced down at his slung arm and splinted leg, then grinned. "Would you believe I came out the winner?" He set the brake stick with his good foot. He knew he'd have to visit a bit. "Still at home, you say. And from the way you're talking, I'd say neither you nor Pete has settled on a bride yet. Or am I wrong?"

Paul actually slid his dark blue gaze away on an embarrassed grin. "Maybe. That's the other reason I ain't been by. I gotta get in my licks whilst Pete's away. You know how he always wants whatever gal I take a likin' to."

And vice versa. When it came to courting, like everything else, the twins spent all their time trying to outdo each other. They'd push and argue till the one they'd set their sights on would send them both packing. "And who are you sweet on at the moment?" Max asked.

"Liza Smith. You remember her, don't you? Ken and Betsy's daughter."

Max grinned. "Fact is, I just come from their place. Ma Smith checked my leg."

"Ain't Liza turned out purty? Silky hair . . . and those eyes. You didn't flirt with her, did you?"

"No." Not that she hadn't sent him enough coy glances from across the table. The lass obviously didn't hold the same affection for either twin as they did for her. "I ain't in the market for no wife. If I can ever get this blamed leg working again, I'll be on my way up the Missouri."

"Glad to hear it. Anyways, I figure if I put on all my charm,

I can get her to promise to wed up with me before Pete comes traipsin' back and messes up my chances again with his loud, clodhopper ways."

"Sounds like the best plan," Max agreed, stifling a grin. "The two of you together could scare off a wounded bear."

Paul tucked in his long chin. "Pete's the one what always starts it. Not me." He lowered his foot to the ground. "You never did say, where you headed?"

"Oh, just out for some air." Max had no intention of telling Paul. Although he'd promised not to speak about the family to anyone, he had a much more compelling reason not to mention them. If the other bachelors in the valley got a good look at the reclusive Belinda, they'd be just as taken with her as he was. And who needed that kind of competition? Especially as slowed up as he was.

"I ain't been out for a pleasure ride in a long time," Paul mused. "I'd love to come."

Everything in Max balked. If Paul climbed aboard, he wouldn't be able to go out to the Greggs'. He racked his brain for something believable that would dissuade his pal. "I . . . uh . . ."

"But I gotta get this flour home to Ma." Good-naturedly, Paul slapped Max on the shoulder—the one attached to his broken arm.

A pain shot through, but Max didn't complain. Paul couldn't come.

"Ma was fixin' to make dumplin's for noonin' when she opened a new sack and found it was chock-full of weevils . . . too many to sift out."

"Well, maybe I'll take a drive up your way later on." Max hoped that would mollify Paul.

"Yeah, do that. If you come, I'm sure Pa'll let me off from the evenin' chores." Paul's expression then turned chipper. "Then you an' me, we could saunter on out to Liza's for a visit. What d'ya say?"

"Sure, why not?" Max returned Paul's grin for his own reason.

"Well, reckon I better get on back, make myself look useful, so Pa will let me go early."

As Paul headed to the store, Max shook his head . . . a grown man still under his father's thumb. Clucking his tongue to start Pitch walking, Max had an unpleasant thought. If he had stayed here with his own parents, would he still be acting like some overgrown kid, asking Pops's leave every time he wanted to walk out the door?

He glanced down at his splinted leg. Even if it never healed properly, he'd never fall back into that humiliating life.

~

Belinda heard a distant rumble. She saw no clouds. Her gaze chased to the bridge.

Someone was coming! In a buggy. She couldn't imagine who, or why. And twice in two days.

Had the Bremmer men betrayed her confidence, spread word about Mama? Mayhap a delegation of townsmen was coming to test her mother for evil spirits. Or some other equally vile purpose.

Well, not if she had anything to say about it.

Standing in the vegetable garden, a pail of green beans in her hand, she whirled around past the end of the row and toward the house. She had to get to the gun cabinet before they reached the gate.

Running up the back steps, she snatched off her sunbonnet, wondering whether or not to wake her father. She knew he'd want to face them himself. But he'd been up most of the night with Mama, and they were finally peacefully asleep.

She shot a glance up the stairs as she hurried to the gun cabinet in the parlor. She plucked out the shotgun. It would speak the loudest, especially if more than one man had come. Grabbing the box of fixings and the powder horn, she loaded the barrel and primed the flash pan in record time.

The cawing of the ravens came through the open front windows along with the sounds of wheels and hooves on the graveled drive.

As the creaks and crunching came to a stop, Belinda set her chin and headed for the door. Swinging it wide, she brought up the heavy weapon and marched out to intercept the intruders before they stepped into the yard.

She was halfway down the veranda steps when she spotted the head of ruffled blond hair shimmering in the sun overhead.

Max Bremmer. The injured frontiersman who was so pleasing to the eye. He'd come back.

He held up his good hand and hollered, "It's just me."

Placing a finger to her lips, she nodded up to the second floor.

He followed her gaze and returned her nod; then he spoke in a loud whisper. "I see your birds are still watchdogging."

She sent what she hoped was a disparaging look to the noisy ravens, then leaned the shotgun against one of the columns and strolled out to meet him. All the while, she wished the dress she wore wasn't one that hung so limp and plain. And her hair! She had no idea what kind of mess it was in. She'd done no more this morning than catch the curls back with a ribbon.

But there was nothing she could do about it now. "I'd ask you in," she apologized quietly, "but my folks are finally asleep. I don't want them disturbed."

"That tea you brewed did work then," he said, still in a whisper.

"Not nearly as well as I'd like."

"Well, just in case, I've dropped by with some pink lady-slipper root. Ma Smith said it might work better."

"How *could* you?" Instant rage flamed her blood. She caught hold of a wheel rim. "You vowed to keep silent about my mother."

"I have," he defended with equal, though quiet, vigor. "I asked Ma Smith what she recommended for hysteria and sleeplessness while she was dressing my leg this morning. When she asked who it was for, I told her I wasn't at liberty to say. And she understood completely. She's a fine, honorable woman, and she knows all the ins and outs of healing real good. You might think about trusting her with your mother's ailment."

"I see," Belinda rasped through clenched teeth. His defending words had done little to appease her. Too much was at stake. "And who do you plan to not tell next? Why don't we just throw a party and invite the whole blamed town? What a grand show we could put on for them." She flung an arm out. "Go. Get out of here."

Max caught her hand on the fly. His grip was unexpectedly powerful. "No harm whatsoever has been done." He lowered his voice again and softened the gaze in his clear blue eyes. "But if you want the whole truth, I felt I needed an excuse to come see you again. And trust me, the last thing I want is to be joined by the 'whole blamed town.' " His last words ended with a hopeful, endearing grin.

"Oh." She stared up at him in the buggy, unable to think of anything to say. Again, she wondered at the sight she must be . . . her unruly hair and dirty dress. She glanced down to her muslin shift, gathered haphazardly at the waist by her spotted apron. "I'm really not dressed for company."

She then realized he still held her hand, his so much larger and darker than hers. And such heat fed from it into hers . . . and traveled all the way up to her cheeks.

Deftly, she slipped her fingers free.

He watched them go, then looked down at her. "I didn't expect you to be."

"What?"

"Dressed for company. I ain't exactly dressed for Sunday-go-to-meetin' myself."

No, he wasn't. But simple undyed linen went so well with his flaxen hair and deeply tanned skin.

"I just hoped to come by," he continued softly, "and if things had settled down, I thought maybe you and me could visit a spell. Nothing formal."

Suddenly the raw realization struck. She would be considered unmarriageable because of the insanity in her family. Most likely, he figured she'd be desperate for whatever attention she could get. Even the unsavory kind. "Do you take me for a simpleton? No man would want to come visiting a woman whose mother has spells of insanity. Leastwise, not one with any kind of honorable intentions."

He settled back in his seat, any vestige of his good humor gone. "You sure ain't making this easy for me, are you? I admit matrimony ain't something I ever gave much thought to. I'm a man used to being on the move."

Being correct gave her no pleasure, but she had no intention of letting him know it. She arched a brow. "Your wings are clipped for a while, so you thought you'd have yourself a little dalliance."

His lips drew into a hard line—she'd ruffled his feathers. He exhaled heavily. "No, that was not my aim. I thought we might be friends. Someone to talk with now and again. I had an idea you might need that too. Besides, you intrigue me. I never met a woman with two pet ravens before."

"My ravens?" That was unexpected. And completely disarming. "I-I found them last year on one of my walks. Something had knocked their nest down from a tree. Two of the chicks were dead, but I managed to keep these two scamps safe and fed. Now I've got myself a couple of real mischief makers. Always stealing things from me. Right out of my hand. A spoon, a hairpin . . ."

He chuckled, a low pleasing sound. "I know what you mean. I raised an orphaned coon when I was a kid."

"Really? I have a raccoon right now. Out in one of my hutches. He's getting over a broken leg. Like you."

The square-jawed man grinned again, showing a mouthful of straight white teeth. "So you take in orphans and hurt animals. Then I should fit right in."

His smile was much too appealing. Belinda's heart gave a crazy little kick. "I also have a fox kit at the moment."

"You don't say. I'd like to see them . . . if you'd be kind enough to invite this dangerous fellow to stay a spell."

She tried not to smile at his wheedling charm, but she couldn't help herself. "All right, you're invited."

He hoisted up his splinted leg and moved it toward the buggy's edge.

"Wait. Stay seated," she offered. "We can ride around to the back. It's a ways." Circumventing the black horse on her way to the other side of the vehicle, she couldn't believe how easily she'd been persuaded. But, then, he obviously didn't present much of a danger to anyone in his injured state. Still, she would have to watch her tendency to always want to nurse the needy. Max might not be much of a physical threat at the moment, but he could still easily break a lonely gal's heart.

Chapter Six

Yes! Victory was his! He might be crippled, his leg aching, but the old Bremmer smile still worked just fine.

With his good arm, Max reached over and took the delicately slender hand of his "lady of the river" and helped her aboard the buggy. Considering the rather narrow width of the seat, she would have no choice but to sit fairly close.

Once she was settled beside him, he reluctantly released her and threaded the horse's reins through his fingers . . . though he would have much preferred to be untying her hair ribbon and freeing her captive curls.

Acting like the typical female, she primly smoothed her skirt and sat ramrod straight. But she was still near enough for him to breathe in the lavender-scented soap she must have used this morning.

"Take the drive around to the back," she directed in a rather husky whisper. She didn't sound any less affected by him than he by her.

Max liked that. Making a clucking sound, he guided the horse along the curved path around the house. It led past a roofed well and a chicken pen to what must have been the pottery shed. A number of jugs and pots were stacked on its deeply recessed porch. Beyond stood a carriage house, a stable, and a couple of lean-tos, but nothing else. Except for a milk cow munching grass in the back pasture and a springhouse down near the stream, none of the other things that made a farm self-sustaining were present. They kept no pigs or cattle, no sheep, no corncrib or smokehouse. The Greggs would be required to purchase a great many of their needs. Still, he found it hard to believe that a simple pottery business could have provided such a fine house and furnishings, not to mention their fine clothing.

But it was no business of his.

"Pull around to the back side of the chicken coop," Miss Gregg directed.

That gave him another excuse to look directly at her—up close. Her nose had a slight upward tilt. Cute. And the sprinkle of tiny freckles took just enough edge off her perfection to make her approachable. Yes, he did love those freckles.

She turned to face him, her starburst gaze colliding with his. "The hutches are behind the coop."

It took all his willpower to turn his gaze forward again, make himself focus on directing Pitch to a row of roofed cages at the rear of the chicken house and to bring the horse and buggy to a stop.

"I'll bring my charges to you so you don't have to get down." Her kindness matched her beauty.

Although he'd planned to somehow get himself out, then do the gentlemanly thing and help her to the ground, she'd already stepped onto the running board and lowered herself to the ground . . . in a most becoming manner.

It was probably for the best. Plus, it gave him the pleasure of watching the lovely Miss Gregg stroll around the horse to the hutches. Though she was a pleasingly proportioned woman, her legs and arms and her neck had just enough added length to lend her an extra touch of grace.

Reluctantly, he pulled his gaze from her to the row of cages and the furry creatures inside two of them—not that he was the least interested in them at the moment.

The tame ravens landed on an empty cage next to the one that held a tiny ball of orange-brown fur.

"You boys be good," she said to them. "Don't scare my baby."

She opened a cage, where a raccoon looked at her while sniffing and glancing around warily.

As she did, Max had an odd thought. "How do you know the ravens are male?"

She glanced back at him with an expression as lively as her copper curls. "As much mischief as they get into, they have to be boys."

"I see." He couldn't help grinning.

"Besides," she said, pulling the stripe-tailed coon into her arms, "since I named them Jacob and Esau, it would be bad manners for one of them to start nesting. Wouldn't you say?"

"Absolutely." He turned to the ravens, whose keen eyes didn't seem to be missing a thing. "Both of you are forbidden to ever lay an egg."

"Stop trying to make me laugh," Belinda said softly as she brought the raccoon forward, her arms wrapped firmly around the good-sized animal and his splinted and bandaged back leg. "Ben here isn't all that tame."

"You've named him too?" He reached down and ran his hand over the long coarse fur.

"After Ben Franklin, because he looks like he's wearing

spectacles. Isn't that right?" she said to the creature in a soft crooning voice, her mouth moving closer to its ear.

And all Max could do was wish that he were that raccoon.

One of the inquisitive birds flew into the vacated cage, picking among a bed of rags, distracting Max. Yet he managed to come up with something casual to say. "Looks like you did as good a job fixing ol' Ben Franklin's leg as Ma Smith did on mine."

He must have spoken too loudly. The raccoon started squirming, trying to break free.

Miss Gregg whirled back to the cage.

The raven flew out, flapping its wide span of wings close to the panicked animal.

Belinda managed to hold tight yet not get herself scratched by his sharp nails; she deposited the creature back inside and latched the door. "Ben is having a hard time understanding he has to stay put till he's mended."

Max chuckled. "I know how he feels."

Belinda unlatched the next cage and brought out a ball of orange fluff. She placed the tiny kit on her shoulder, and it skittered under her hair. A second later, Max spotted a nose and two big eyes peeking from beneath her curls, watching him.

Belinda nuzzled her cheek against its fur. "This is my little Downy, because her fur is as soft as the down on a duckling. She's still such a baby, I keep her with me when I'm not busy. She likes to curl around my neck and nest in my hair."

"That's one lucky kit." Max wouldn't mind doing that himself.

"I know I spoil her. But if I hadn't found her when I did, she wouldn't have survived." She plucked the fur ball from her shoulder and handed it up to him.

The tiny creature fit easily in the palm of his hand. And sure enough, the baby fox did feel soft as down. Max lifted it up and smoothed the fur across his own cleanly shaven cheek . . . all the while wondering if the lady's cheek would feel as smooth. He glanced at Belinda and found her watching him.

"I admire seeing a big man like yourself having such a gentle touch."

Feeling a little embarrassed, he handed back the fox. "I ain't never been accused of that before."

"It's something you should take pride in." She replaced the kit in the cage and turned back to Max. "Gentleness is a virtue."

"I reckon." He warmed to the thought that this girl had taken a particular liking to him, regardless of his crippled state. He'd be a fool not to take advantage of his good fortune. "I was wondering . . . I mean . . . I'd be honored if I could come by with the buggy Sunday morning and escort you to church."

"No." Her brows flared. "Absolutely *not.*"

He clamped his mouth tight. The woman couldn't have been more convincing if she'd slapped him in the face. What did one say to such a rejection besides farewell? Contrary to what he'd thought, he was not welcome here.

"Oh, please forgive me." She reached up and caught his arm. "My answer was not directed at you."

"You could have fooled me."

"It's going to church I object to, not you personally." Slowly, her fingers released their grip on his arm.

"I see." But he didn't. What kind of person was she? A heathen? Were these folks actually in Satan's camp? That would explain her mother's tormented state.

"No, from your expression, I don't think you do. I—my parents and I—have found that churchgoers are the most cruel of all people when it comes to my mother's melancholy spells. They have accused her of being possessed by the devil, or worse, of being a witch. We refuse to ever expose ourselves to such ruthlessness again."

Max was greatly relieved that she hadn't dismissed him, despite her feelings about church congregations. "I do understand your reluctance. Even folks who profess to be followers of Jesus sometimes forget to keep their eyes on Him." Max decided to chance that Miss Belinda knew something of the Bible. "Just like the apostle Peter did when he started walking across the water to Jesus. And this was one of Jesus' own disciples. The second Peter took his eyes off Jesus and glanced down, he began to sink. It sounds like some of them folks you was talking about got scared and started sinking into fear, too, instead of looking to the Lord."

"I never thought of it like that." The lady seemed to be softening.

"I reckon with me living these past years among heathens who didn't know the light of God's love and mercy, I saw plenty of evidence of the suffering what comes from that kind of darkness. The Shawnee tribe Drew and Crysta Reardon now minister to, west of the Mississippi, considered the beating, the torturing, and ofttimes the killing of outsiders to be a community celebration. Terrible cruelties . . . even the women and children took part in them. Them Indians thought if their enemies feared them enough, they wouldn't attack and do the same to them. A mountain of evil is born out of fear."

Max thought he'd persuaded her. But Belinda brushed away his words with a rather condescending smile. "I have no doubt what you say is true. And I also understand that we're to give our fears to the Lord. As the writer of the book of Hebrews said, 'The Lord is my helper, and I will not fear what man shall do unto me.' For my family, I believe God's way of helping us was to find us a place to live and work *away* from those who would cause us harm. Particularly those who would harm us because they're afraid."

Max sensed that Belinda's own fears were much too entrenched to be removed during one polite debate. *"Patience and prayer,"* he'd often heard his father say. *Prayer and patience.*

"Well," he said, hoping his own smile was disarming, "if I can't persuade you to accompany me to church, perhaps I could come by after services. We could take a drive along the river road. Before I left the valley six years ago, nobody lived on this side of the river. It was nothing but a tangle of woods back then."

Belinda's own relief erased the small frown pinching her brows. "I would invite you to dinner at the house, but I can't be sure if Mother will be better by then. . . ." She brightened. "I know what we could do. If she's feeling herself, we'll have you here for dinner. If not, I'll prepare the two of us a picnic lunch, and we can find a nice spot in the woods to eat. And you could tell me something of your more pleasant adventures among the Indians." Her enthusiasm suddenly burned shy. "That is, if it's agreeable with you."

He reached down for her hand. "Pretty lady, it's more than agreeable." The thought of a picnic in the woods with the prettiest gal he'd ever seen—an afternoon of being with her, beholding her, listening to the soft music of her voice. He knew it wasn't the Christian thing to wish for, but he hoped her mother would not be up to entertaining Sunday. Or for some time to come.

～

Belinda felt younger than she had in years as she watched the horse and buggy leave down the drive. On Sunday she would be entertaining her first gentleman caller. A handsome man was coming to see *her*.

She remembered the pouch of pink lady slipper he'd left with her. It was still warm in her hand from where it had lain in a pocket next to his heart. She pressed it against her cheek. The man had seen her mother at her worst, and instead of being repelled or frightened, he had returned with something he hoped would help.

And he wished to see her again. She wanted to shout out the words over and over.

The unpleasant remarks she'd overheard those two girls say at the general store stole into her thoughts, reminding her that Max Bremmer was no longer considered the object of those young maidens' dreams. That he was now damaged, crippled, possibly for life. In truth, had he sought her out only because he no longer felt he was worthy to court one of the more acceptable girls?

She didn't want to think that. In his eyes she had seen genuine admiration.

She was almost sure of that.

But he said he'd never given marriage much thought. Was he considering it now? Or was he merely filling time till he healed enough to return to Indian country?

Oh, how she wished she had more experience in these matters. Even a little. And her parents would be no help. They'd known one another most of their lives and had never seriously considered anyone else.

Just before the rig crossed the bridge, Max Bremmer leaned to the side of the canopy and waved.

With a broad sweep of her arm, she waved back. He really was interested. No more room would she give to the girls' unpleasant comments.

Her step felt lighter as she walked back to the house. She had a beau! And such a handsome one, at that. Perhaps she could trust God even for this unexpected blessing?

Returning inside to start dinner, Belinda spotted her father descending the stairs. He looked much more rested, his thin face no longer so sallow or hollow-looking.

"Is Mama still asleep?" she asked in a whisper while diminishing the space between them.

He nodded. "Let's go out on the veranda where it's cooler, and you can tell me about our latest visitor."

Belinda's chest tightened. Daddy had seen them outside together. Had she said anything when she and Mr. Bremmer said good-bye at the front gate that he might have overheard? Had her expression given away how she felt about her caller? She really wasn't prepared to share feelings with her father that she herself was just now experiencing for the first time.

"Let's sit over there," he said, meaning the end of the veranda farthest from her parents' upstairs windows.

Belinda settled on the swinging bench cushioned by floral chintz, while her father chose a nearby wicker armchair. A bit nervous, she took the initiative, not waiting for him to begin. "If you saw Mr. Bremmer drive up, you should have come down and greeted him yourself."

A one-sided smile lifted a freckled cheek. "You two seemed to be doing just fine without me. Besides, I really don't think he came here to call on me."

Heat rose from her neck—a silent confession that what he said was true. She looked away. "I'm sure Mr. Bremmer would have been pleased to see you too."

"There's nothing to be embarrassed about, Carrots. I'm purely pleased to see someone taking an interest in you. You're a lovely young woman inside and out. You'd make any man a wonderful wife."

"Daddy! A man rides up and talks to me, and you have us married already?"

"Romance has to start someplace."

"*Daddy*. I . . . uh . . . to begin with, he's not the marrying kind."

Her father's grin widened maddeningly. "Most men don't think they are till they find that one special miss. And this one seems quite capable of carrying the extra, shall we say, baggage."

She couldn't believe her father was speaking thusly to her. "Our situation here is more complicated than mere 'baggage.' Even if he did have thoughts of marrying one day, it cannot be to me. I could never leave you here alone to care for Mama when she's in one of her direful periods. It takes both of us to watch her."

The humor fled her father's face. "I've been much too selfish, keeping you here. I should've sent you back East to school years ago, given you a chance for a more normal life."

"Oh, Daddy." She reached across and caught his hand, rough and dry from years of working with clay. "I didn't want to go then, and I'm surely too old now. Don't fret. You've always done the very best for us that you could. Don't you ever think you haven't."

He squeezed her hand. "I don't want you to fret either. Young Bremmer saw your mother at her worst. If he's still interested in you after that, we should admire him all the more and not go worrying about me and your mama. It's past time you started thinking about your own future." He stood up, leaned over, and kissed her cheek. "Enough said."

She rose right after him. "Not quite. I invited Mr. Bremmer for Sunday dinner—if Mama's better. If not, I thought I'd make us a picnic lunch to take to the falls upstream . . . if that's agreeable with you."

His narrow face creased with a questioning smile and a lift of his sun-bleached brows. "So you invited him to dinner, did you? I wouldn't have thought you'd be so bold."

Her cheeks flamed again. She caught them between her palms. "Oh, dear, I was, wasn't I? But he asked me to church, and I was so blunt in my refusal, I felt I needed to make up for it."

Her dad turned serious. He stepped close, took her shoulders. "Belinda, we've talked about this before. You must not condemn all Christians for what a few have said or done. The Bible teaches us to not forsake the gathering together as a church. For all you know, that man was sent here by the Lord for the very purpose of bringing you back into the fold."

"What about you, Daddy? You and Mama?"

"I reckon we're supposed to be our own little church. Belinda dear, your mother and I knew we were destined to lead a different kind of life from the first time we were driven from a church. My only regret is the isolation that has been thrust upon you."

She reached up and touched his face. "As you've always said, Daddy, we all have a cross to bear in our life's journey. And I wouldn't have chosen any other parents to take that journey with."

"Yes, but this is only the beginning for you. There's a lifetime waiting for you out there. On Sunday, use the good china. Let's make it a festive day."

Chapter Seven

It wasn't until Max had the buggy on the ferry and was halfway across the river that he recalled his promise to visit Paul. But at the moment, the idea was nothing but an intrusion in his thoughts about Belinda, and he wasn't ready to give them up. Besides, he told himself, his injured bones and muscles ached in several places.

As the ferry docked, he looked up to the main street to find someone who lived in the Daggets' direction and spotted Marvin Lowe at the saddlery, no doubt swapping stories with the other idlers. Once Max had sent his regrets to Paul by way of the lad, Pitch didn't need much urging to travel on. The horse smelled his home barn and the hope of a feed bag full of oats.

When Max reached the front of his house and drew on the reins pulling the black gelding to a stop, Pitch strained against the bit in his mouth. The animal's paddock was in plain sight. But once Max set the buggy's brake, Pitch settled down.

Then, with great care, Max lowered himself to the ground, balancing himself between his one good arm and leg. By the time he had the crutch in place, he was so shaky he wondered if he'd make it up the porch steps. He knew he'd have to go over to the shop in a little while and ask his pops to unhitch the horse. But by no means would he call into the house for help from his overanxious mother and have her start harping on him again.

Gaining the top landing, he was so out of breath he had to take a moment to restore himself. With trembling fingers, he wiped the beads of sweat from his brow. Watching them shake, he couldn't remember any other time in his life when he'd been so weak. Still, he was stronger today than yesterday. And tomorrow, he vowed, he'd do even more.

Shuffling through the open doorway, he heard voices from the big kitchen at the rear of the house. And the smell of food teased his stomach. It must be an hour or two past noon.

"Is dat you?" came his mother's call. "Come. You eat now."

"*Ja,*" his father's voice boomed. "Ve get tired of vaiting. Ve eat *mit*out you."

In spite of the colorful calico curtains fluttering at the open windows, the kitchen was much warmer than the rest of the house. Inga Bremmer had always insisted on cooking inside even on the hottest days. Needing cooler air, Max hobbled to the back door and opened it wide.

"Da flies," his mother complained.

"How much can a fly eat?" Max retorted.

His pops blustered into laughter. "Ja, how much can dey eat?"

"Sit." His mother's sharp command intimated that she was not happy about losing the argument. "Fill your plate, so I can start *mit* da dishes."

That was one order he'd never had trouble obeying. Pulling

the serving bowls and platters close, he piled his plate with her tasty Bavarian cooking . . . from knockwurst to red-cabbage kraut, salted cucumbers, and pickled potato salad. Food the likes of which he had never seen during the long months he was away from home.

Just as he was digging in, his mother wiped the residue of an apple dumpling from her mouth. "Son, I vas telling your papa about our trip to da Smiths' dis morning. How dey invite us in for tea *und* sveet biscuits."

Taking his first mouthful, Max looked at his father with a grunt and a nod.

"*Und* I am telling him," she continued with a curiously happy expression—her round blue gaze as bright as her cheeks—"how dat dear little Liza had eyes for you da whole time ve are dere."

"Mama, she's just a kid."

His mother leaned forward. "Dem Dagget twins don't t'ink so. Liza is seventeen years old. Plenty old enough to be t'inking about getting herself a husband."

Max glanced at his father . . . who was suddenly very occupied with his dessert. Pops would be of no help. "Ma, every time I come home, you start up with your matchmaking. Besides, if Pete and Paul are courting her, I wouldn't want to butt in."

"Dem Dagget boys?" she scoffed. "Dey don't know da first t'ing about courting a *fräulein*. Dey scare all da girls off. One word from you, *und* Liza is yours."

"Will you stop it? If my leg will just start working even half-way, I'm headed back up the Missouri. I want to catch that expedition if it's not too late."

His mother's eyes narrowed, and she set her strong if sagging German jaw. "Alice Smith says you is not going traipsing off nowhere for a long, long time. If ever. You got to t'ink about udder t'ings now. A life here *mit* us. You get dem fancy dreams out of your head, *und* you vill see it is a goot life ve haf here."

Had Ma Smith told his mother something about his leg she hadn't told him? He didn't think so. "If my leg is as bad as you say, why would you want your dearest friend's granddaughter to be burdened with a cripple?"

"*Nein, nein,* you do not understand. Your arm vill be goot as new. Big *und* strong like your papa's. If one leg, it is not so goot, no matter. You can still be da fine blacksmith."

Back to him smithing with his father again. The woman never gave up. Max filled his mouth with food to keep himself from telling her to stop trying to run his life.

"I tell you vhat," she said, her tone more placid. "I invite da Smiths for dinner after church. I vill not say nut'ing. I let you decide for yourself vhat you t'ink of Liza."

"That'll be hard to do since I won't be here. I've accepted a dinner invitation elsewhere."

"Out to da Daggets'," she sniffed with disdain. "Dem boys, dey is nut'ing but wort'less pranksters. I don't—"

"Ma, that ain't very charitable of you," Max said, cutting her off. "Actually, a Miss Gregg has invited me to her family's home for Sunday dinner."

"Miss Gregg . . . ?" She swung her attention to her husband. "Rolf, who is dis *Fräulein* Gregg?"

"I t'ink you haf not met dem. Dey live 'cross da river. Dey keep pretty much to demselfs."

"Do dose people t'ink dey is too goot to mix *mit* da rest of us?" She turned back to Max. "Dey don't even come to church."

"Inga, dear." His father placed a hand over hers. "Da Gregg family seem like God-fearing folks. Dey probably keep der worship services private too."

"Humph. If dey worship at all. *Frau* Jessup tells me dey is up to no goot, living secret lifes like dey do."

Max had heard enough. "And I say Mrs. Jessup is up to no good with all her fool gossip. I'll be having dinner at the Greggs' Sunday. And that's all there is to be said."

It was no mystery that his mother was angry as she lunged to her feet and started clearing plates with a loud clatter.

Max glanced at his father.

The stout old man sat there, fork in hand, toying with his dessert . . . and with his own very private grin. It would seem the good Brother Bremmer had his own thoughts about his son and the redheaded beauty.

Not quite sure what to think of his father, Max, too, sat back and grinned.

~

"I am feeling so proud of you dis morning." Max's mother beamed up at him on this sunny day in mid-July. Standing below, she waited for him to reach the porch steps.

Inga, of course, wore her black summer day gown for church rather than her heavier winter black one. The woman had always considered it her duty as the minister's wife never to seem frivolous on Sunday. But over the years, she had given in to the vanity of placing a few satin tulips on her black straw bonnet. "You alvays vas mine bright *und* shining penny."

Max woofed a strained laugh as he hopped down the first step. "That's not what Pops used to call me."

She held out a hand in case Max stumbled.

As he reached the bottom, her alert blue gaze softened, turning misty. "I am talking about da beautiful baby boy you vas. *Und* da vay you look today. Such a handsome man you are. So beautiful in da new Sunday clothes I make for you."

She was getting downright mushy. And repetitive. "I know, Ma. You already told me."

Her round-cheeked smile vanished. She stepped in front of him and tugged down the beige brocade waistcoat she'd made for him to match the buff-colored breeches. "*Und* I vill tell you again in front of your friends if you don't show your mama more respect."

Her swift fingers then fluffed out the white cravat at the throat of his bloused white shirt. "Vhen I t'ink how dem river pirates came up on you *und* Drew in da night, shooting you in da leg *und* busting your arm . . ."

Max brought up a hand to ward her off. "Ma! Everyone over at the church can see you. Stop fussing over me."

"*Und* don't you use dat broke arm," she chided and started out the walk. "Taking off da sling . . . I don't like it."

"I know, Mama. You already told me that. But having my arm wrapped all the time in this heat kept it swollen. Besides, it's had six weeks for the bones to knit back together. Plenty of time." Besides, he told himself, he wanted to look halfway whole when he showed up at Miss Belinda's door this afternoon. And, if he did think so himself, the clothes his mother had fitted to him did look rather fine. His face might be a bit too tanned for polite society—whatever that was—but it did set off his blond hair and made his smile seem all the brighter. Hadn't his mother said so not ten minutes ago?

And he did have to admit—but only to himself—it really did feel good to be doted on for a change. He hadn't had much of that these past six years, living mostly in the rough-and-tumble of the wilds. Too bad his knee-length breeches were marred by the bulge of bandages beneath them and splints lashed over the one legging.

His mother stayed close as they slowly made their way toward the congregation gathering in front of the church. She leaned her bonneted head toward him. "Dere is dat sveet Liza girl. See? She is standing *mit* da udder young *fräuleins*. Such a pretty girl she is, *mit* da yellow ribbon in her hair."

"I'm sure the Dagget twins think so," he said, countering his mother's matchmaking attempt. "I see Pete's back." The two rangy fellows were fast making their way past the parked wagons and toward the petite lass.

"*Und* dat is vhy dey is never getting a vife. No *fräulein* vants to be da bone dem two is fighting over."

Max grunted. "If those boys really wanted to get married, you'd think they'd learn."

"Dem two blockheads learn? Bah. Dey is having too much fun fighting."

Again Max realized how much he'd changed since leaving the valley. Living on the edge of danger day after day had made him realize how fragile life could be. Those two had yet to comprehend that their being here on earth was not forever and should not be frittered away by drifting aimlessly through the years like they were the endless waters pouring down the Caney Fork. A verse from Job came to mind: *"Man that is born of a woman is of few days, and full of trouble. He cometh forth like a flower, and is cut down."* Just as he himself had come very close to being.

"But you," his mother was saying, "any *fräulein* here vould be proud to call herself your vife."

Mrs. Skinner, one of the most prolific gossips in the valley, stood with her husband no more than a few feet away. And the pinch-nosed woman was looking straight at him.

"Ma, keep your voice down."

"Ah, dere is Annie Reardon. *Und* dat must be da sister I hear about. I need to go velcome her. She comes here to live after much sorrow."

Wondering about his mother's last remark, Max glanced to where the Reardon women circled near the church steps. An extra woman similar in looks to Ike's wife stood with them.

His mother shouted back one final order. "Go pay your respects to da pretty Liza. Keep dem Daggets from bothering her too much."

No, sir, the woman never gave up. If his leg didn't recover enough for him to escape soon, she'd be bringing gals home in droves. She was that set on tying him down.

But in the meantime, he had some of his own visiting to do this afternoon—on his own terms—with his lady of the river.

$\sim$

"Mama, let me do that." Belinda attempted to take the big spoon from her mother's hand. She and her parents were together in the summer kitchen preparing the special meal.

"Don't be such a clucking hen." Felicity resumed stirring the pot of roiling turnips and potatoes. "Surely I'm equal to this simple task. More than equal. From the moment your father told me we were having a young man to Sunday dinner, my spirits have been rising to the sky, shaking me free of the dark clouds. My little girl entertaining her first beau." Her thin face fairly glowed.

"Don't get your hopes up too high, Mama," Belinda warned. "This is not a man who usually lives around here. He's just home recuperating from some severe injuries. I do believe he'll be heading out west when he recovers."

Her mother turned to her dad, who was slicing the ham he'd bought especially for today. "Chris, you didn't mention he was merely visiting when you said he was Brother Bremmer's son. I assumed . . ." The light faded from her dove gray eyes.

Belinda could've kicked herself for stealing any part of her mother's joy. "Then, again, Mr. Bremmer may not be leaving. From what I heard, his leg may not be up to any more long treks."

"We'll hold on to that thought," Felicity said, her thready voice regaining lightness. "Everything's about ready here. Belinda, you go up to your room and put on something pretty while your father and I go into the house and set the table."

Belinda glanced at her dad. "Are you sure you two can manage?"

"We've been doing it since before you were born, Carrots. Wear that gown with the roses sprigged across it. It's my favorite."

"And tighten the strings on your corset," her mother added with an upraised brow.

Belinda had such a mix of feelings as she took one last look at her parents before running back to the main house. She was exhilarated that Max was coming, happy that her mother was so much improved; yet the way her father talked, she got the feeling he wanted her to leave them. She'd always thought they couldn't manage without her, especially after her baby brother died when she was five. Mom had fallen into one of her melancholy moods after his death and didn't come out of it for almost a year.

Not wanting to think of the dark times—not today—Belinda raced upstairs to ready herself for her gentleman caller. She also refused to think about whether he would or would not be remaining in the valley. No past, no future . . . just this one glorious day.

Belinda dashed into her mahogany-furnished room that she and her mother had decorated in blue-and-green paisley, trimming the canopy with Belgian lace. Stripping off her apron and muslin work dress, she ran to her wardrobe and pulled out the garment her daddy had mentioned. The cream-colored silk picked up the light flooding into the room; the material some-how always made her skin seem to glow when she wore it. She adored the huge roses painted haphazardly down it. The mauve velvet ribbon that tied just below the empire waist added just the right touch to the slim but easy-flowing skirt.

Smoothing a hand down the silk, she hoped Mr. Bremmer would think she looked as pretty in it as her father did.

After she finished with her toilette and dressing, Belinda was shoving the last tortoiseshell comb into her cascade of ringlets when she heard the creaks and rattles of a vehicle, the crunch of wheels across gravel. Her heart pounding as hard as any drum, she hurried to the partially opened glass-paned doors that led onto the balcony and peeked out across the meadow.

She was certain it was him—the buggy was the same single-seater. But today he wore a rather tall and narrow-brimmed hat that hid most of his blond hair and shaded his eyes. But the fawn-hued waistcoat stretching across his broad chest and pris-tine shirt were easily viewed. And if she wasn't mistaken, there was even a ruffled cravat at his throat. His clothing would all go so splendidly with his coloring.

That was when it came to her. The man wore no arm sling today. He was as interested in looking his best for her as she was for him. Her heart skipped a beat.

He pulled to a stop in front of the arbor.

Not wanting him to climb down unassisted, Belinda started to swing away from the balcony doors when she heard her father's voice.

"Good you could come," he greeted as he came into view from beneath the veranda roof. The silver in Christopher Gregg's red hair gleamed in the noonday sun as he strode out to the buggy in his own white shirt and gray knee breeches.

"Welcome to our home." Words she had not heard her father speak in years.

Her sentimental thought quickly vanished as she turned all aflutter. She whirled back to the tall oval mirror beside her dressing table. Did her bodice still fit smoothly? Was her bow looped evenly? Her hands shook while tucking in one of her springier curls. She had too much hair, simply too much. And so bright. A body would think she had a forest fire on her head, burning out of control.

And those wretched freckles.

She stepped closer to the mirror and glared at them, but it was useless. Nothing could be done about them or the brightness of her hair. She sighed . . . then realized they must not bother Max Bremmer too much. He'd come calling three times in one week.

Taking a deep breath, she turned to go greet him with a smile that she couldn't have stopped even if she'd wanted to.

Chapter Eight

Mr. Gregg looked considerably more calm and much more welcoming than the other time Max had seen him—that day the man had been struggling with his hysterical wife.

"We're so pleased you could join us for Sunday dinner. We've all been looking forward to your visit most eagerly."

"Thank you. Me too."

Still, Mr. Gregg's cheery greeting gave Max a moment for pause as the skeletal older man gave him a hand down. First, disappointment surfaced, since Mr. Gregg's words, "join *us* for dinner," didn't sound as if he and Belinda would be going into the woods alone for their picnic. Then he had another thought, an uncomfortable one—that he would be seated across from the woman who had been quite demented the other day.

He shook off that unkind thought as he leaned on his crutch and moved beneath the arbor. The air was fragrant with the perfume of pink roses. He inhaled deeply and glanced around.

Mrs. Gregg's family was much too protective of her to expose her infirmity to the scrutiny of outsiders.

One thought remained as Max walked alongside Mr. Gregg. The man was truly, overwhelmingly, glad to see him. He grinned unabashedly—that matchmaking gleam was all too familiar. Max strongly suspected that Belinda's father saw him as a possible husband for his already grown daughter.

"Felicity and Belinda are both upstairs freshening up a bit. Let me help you up to the veranda." He caught hold of Max's arm. "Then I'll get you something cool to drink. Mighty hot even for the middle of July, wouldn't you say?"

"And muggy. It's not as sticky up the Missouri where I normally spend my summers." Max added the last to let the man know his life was usually a far distance from here. He didn't want to play false with Belinda's father.

"Ah, yes. Belinda told me you've spent time with the Shawnee west of the Mississippi. I thought that tribe was mostly in the Ohio Valley."

"Several of their Indian towns have moved farther away from our settlements."

"I see. I reckon we have pretty much homesteaded most of the hunting grounds in Kentucky and, I hear, north of the Ohio too."

"Aye. The tribes aren't real happy about it either," Max said as they got him up the last step.

Mr. Gregg clapped Max on the shoulder. "Too nice a day for such serious talk. Have a seat. I'll get us something to drink."

As his host went inside, Max took the opportunity to peruse the wide veranda. He noted that the floor was milled board sanded smooth and painted a shiny green, a few shades darker than the shutters at the windows. The wicker furnishings were painted to match the boards beneath his feet. Plump floral pillows had been added for their beauty as well as for comfort. He'd never thought of such refinement for just an old front porch. But then, he'd spent most of his life on the woodsy side of the Appalachians, living in rough-hewn cabins like most of the people he knew.

Maybe it wasn't such a bad idea for the Greggs to keep to themselves. If folks across the fork saw this place up close, they'd probably start coveting what they couldn't afford.

Easing down on the cushion of an armed wicker rocker, Max settled back and let his gaze wander the meadow that rolled gently down to the stream before the woods took over again. Several horses grazed peacefully in the lower field . . . two of them stylish long-legged bays. Covetous or not, this was a view a man could easily get used to, sitting here in this comfortable chair, not to mention a cool drink and the loveliest of women both on their way.

He heard the swift patter of footsteps and turned toward the open doorway with anticipation.

Miss Belinda swept through in a shimmering bouquet of mauve roses. A bounty of curls danced about her upswept cascade. Belinda the beautiful.

"There you are," she said breathlessly, her cheeks flushed to just the perfect shade of pink. "I'm so pleased you could make it." Only a faint mark on her cheek reminded him of the first day he came here.

Max gripped the chair arms to assist himself up.

"No, please. Stay seated. Let me get you something to drink."

"Your father is doing that."

"Oh. Then I'd better check on dinner."

Before he could stop her, she disappeared.

Max frowned and glanced around, feeling rather foolish sitting outside alone.

But that soon changed. Mr. Gregg returned with two tall glasses of lemonade . . . *with ice*. Such extravagance, spending precious winter ice on mere drinks. It was mighty hard, cold work, sawing blocks of ice from frozen ponds in January, but from the Greggs' look of prosperity, Max figured they could afford to hire it cut and stored underground for them.

Just as the man was about to hand Max the thirst-quenching treat, Mr. Gregg turned back toward the entrance. "Wonderful. Felicity is coming down now." He returned his attention to Max. "Come inside. Meet my lovely wife."

Max hoisted himself up, feeling a twinge of apprehension. Would Mrs. Gregg truly be a lovely hostess today? If so, would she be self-conscious, remembering him from before? If she did, introductions could prove awkward.

Still holding Max's coveted glass of iced lemonade, Mr. Gregg led the way into the tastefully appointed main room with its highly polished furniture and Oriental rugs and drapes in coral, gold, and beige.

Coming toward Max strolled a whisper of a woman, her light brown hair swirled gracefully atop her head. A wispy muslin of powder blue molded softly to her slight figure. Even her welcoming smile looked fragile enough to break on a face that was still quite lovely in a helpless sort of way.

She extended a painfully thin hand. "We're so pleased you've accepted our invitation . . . our first dinner guest in our new home." Then she turned her questioning gray eyes to her husband. "He *is* our first, isn't he?"

Mr. Gregg slid an arm around her shoulder. "You're absolutely right, my dear. Our first guest."

Steadying his crutch, Max took her proffered hand and bowed over it. "It's my honor, Mrs. Gregg. You have a charming home."

"We enjoy it. It's rather small by some standards, but we

prefer the intimacy." She glanced past Max. "And where, pray
tell, is our Belinda?"

"Bringing the food in from the summer kitchen," Mr. Gregg
said.

At that moment, a set of double doors to one side of the
entrance opened wide, bringing a mix of delicious aromas . . .
and Belinda. "Dinner is ready," she said lightly and stepped
back. "If you please."

Max allowed the Greggs to precede him to the dining area
and a lace-covered table that stood beneath—of all things—a
crystal chandelier. He had to remind himself it wasn't polite to
gawk. Still, he'd only heard of that kind of twinkling extravagance. He'd never actually seen one. He felt all the more clumsy
as he crutched his way to the table alongside the rather tall,
lithe Belinda whose head rested on the most gracefully turned
neck he'd ever recalled seeing. The creamy skin looked
smoother, even, than the dress she wore. And fragrant . . . she
smelled better than any flower he could remember.

Again, he had to force his gaze elsewhere . . . to the dining
table. His drink had been placed at one of the place settings.
These he made himself memorize in case his mother questioned
him later. The china was rimmed with green and white squares
trimmed in gold. A bouquet of roses that stood at the center
reminded him of Miss Belinda. The utensils, all of matching
silver, verified these were not common folk. Even without
servants, these people seemed quite wealthy.

But, as Mrs. Gregg had mentioned, the home really wasn't
that large. The downstairs was split into only the two big rooms.
Separating the dining area from the hearth and less attractive
work area were two Oriental silk screens . . . as elegant as they
were functional.

He wondered if, once they came to the realization that he

was nothing more than a loose-footed hunter, they'd want to screen themselves off from him. Or, at the very least, from their daughter.

"Shall we serve ourselves?" Belinda asked and plucked two plates off the tablecloth, one from where his as yet untouched drink sat. Her coquettish glance up at him more than assured him she had no intention of placing him behind a screen.

"Do try some of the cinnamon peas, Mr. Bremmer," her mother said, coming alongside him. "It's one of Belinda's specialties. You'll find our daughter is quite an accomplished cook. We've come to prefer our own cooking to that of servants. Haven't we, dear?" she added, including her husband.

"Yes," he agreed. "And, Max, do try some of the sweet potatoes. They're Felicity's specialty."

The food, the hospitality, the setting were all perfect. Overwhelmingly so. Max was beginning to feel like some doe-eyed rabbit being lured into a snare by a dangling carrot—one as tempting as Belinda Gregg and her flame-haired beauty.

Max awkwardly filled his plate with the ham dinner, but not as heaping as he might have, had he felt more comfortable. He did congratulate himself on remembering to hold out Belinda's chair for her as she moved past him, her fragrance teasing his senses while her silky neck and her slender arms, mostly bared in the summer frock, teased his eyes. He even noticed the soft rustle of silk as she settled herself on her elegantly carved chair.

He barely gathered enough composure to take his own seat. He leaned his crutch against the wall, noticing that it was the only crude-looking thing in the room.

They each sat on a different side of what by most farm-family standards would be a small table. But for only four, it was more than adequate—and really rather cozy. At least, it would have been if Max hadn't started to feel as if he were playing the dupe—like the turkey who came to the Pilgrims' Thanksgiving dinner.

It all seemed much too perfect to be true. Doubts started surfacing. What did he really know about these people?

Living among the Indians, he'd witnessed some pretty strange things. Once he'd seen an otherwise strong and sensible man reduced to groveling on the ground, eating dirt. All because of some medicine man's incantations.

Now that Max allowed his thoughts to go in this direction, he began to wonder if these people had indeed hidden a baby from Mrs. Gregg. Or was she the evil one? the one possessed by the devil?

Ridiculous. Max took a long sip of his lemonade, directing his attention to the icy coolness as the liquid traveled downward. He knew his imagination had run amok, but still he remained tense.

"Shall we give thanks?" Mr. Gregg asked, bowing his head.

Max's gaze surveyed the table. The women had folded their hands, along with Mr. Gregg, and closed their eyes. Another wild thought came to him. Exactly to whom would they be giving their thanks?

"Our dear and gracious Father, You have again provided us with a bountiful meal beneath this roof You gifted us with. You never fail to pour out Your blessings upon us. Let us never forget to count them. And, Father, during our times in the fiery forge, never let us forget to praise You, for You are in the testing fire with us. Just as You were with Shadrach, Meshach, and Abednego. Again, You brought us out unscorched. For as You know, You have already conquered death and freed us from fear."

Max saw Mr. Gregg place his hand over his wife's and give it a gentle squeeze. His own heart contracted at that private display of tenderness. Regardless of his wife's affliction, the man deeply loved her.

"We thank You in particular, Lord, that we can enjoy this Sabbath meal as a family today. And let us not forget that we are blessed with a guest who has shown us Your love and compassion through his thoughtful gift of the healing root."

The pink lady slipper must have helped. Max realized he'd forgotten to ask about the medicine. For him, the primary purpose for bringing the root had been to see Belinda Gregg again.

As Mr. Gregg closed his prayer in the name of Jesus, Max had to make his own silent heavenward plea, begging God to forgive his own selfish scheme and for doubting these good people.

The dinner went so well, Belinda felt as if she was filled with far more than merely food. Max Bremmer and her father seemed quite relaxed conversing with one another, and her mother looked radiantly pleased merely to be at the table with the others. Her appetite had also returned. Her emaciated mother ate almost everything she'd placed on her plate.

Talk had centered on Max and his adventures in Indian country. Belinda had noted, though, that her father had been impressed mostly by the fact that Max had spent much of his time in the company of Drew Reardon, one of the valley's founding brothers. The fellow had become a missionary to the western tribes, and, amazingly, his wife had accompanied him.

Her father always enjoyed hearing about the latest workings of God's mysteries, His miracles, and His healings. Belinda, though, ofttimes wondered why her own family had not been thus favored by the Lord. Was it possible that God had a purpose in allowing her mother's condition to remain unchanged these many years?

But this was not a day for dwelling on such thoughts. As they finished their dessert of raspberry flummery, Belinda rose to clear the table.

"No, dear," her mother said with a wave of her hand. "Your father and I will do the dishes. Why don't you take our visitor out on the veranda? I do believe a cool breeze has come up."

"Are you sure, Mama? Do you feel up to it?"

"Of course, child. I'm not an invalid, though you two try to treat me like one." Her attention left Belinda for her husband. "Besides, your father and I would like some time to ourselves. Wouldn't we, dear?"

Belinda knew her mother's ploy was to give her daughter time alone with Max. So why was she hesitating? "If you don't mind then," she said, picking up her and Max's goblets, "we'll take our lemonade with us."

They settled on the veranda, he in a chair and she lounging on the bench swing with one foot tucked beneath her, the other braced against the floor to rock herself. They were finally alone. Alone, and Belinda realized she had no idea what to say. At twenty-one years of age, she had absolutely no experience entertaining a caller.

She took a sip of her drink, trying to think of some snippet her mother had mentioned of her own courting days. But nothing came to mind.

He was staring at her! His very steady, sky blue eyes. Waiting, expecting. Surely he wasn't as inexperienced as she.

Still, he was her guest, her responsibility to entertain.

From the corner of her eye, she caught a flash of black, then another as her ravens landed on the porch railing just behind her. "Sorry, fellas. I didn't bring out any scraps for you." She spread the fingers of her free hand to show them it was empty. "Later."

Her thick-feathered birds pranced along the porch railing,

cocking their heads this way and that, giving Max the once-over. Then with raucous cawing, they took flight again.

"You talked to them," Mr. Bremmer said, his voice deep, reso-nant, startling, "just like they could understand what you said."

"That's because they did. They really are quite clever. Because I showed them my empty hand and said, 'Later,' they will now go and perch nearby to wait. I always keep a store of dried meat for them. They're quite partial to it."

"That's amazing." He grinned that friendly grin of his. "I knew a Shawnee boy once who had a pet hawk. It rode on his shoulder."

"Jacob's and Esau's claws are too sharp for that. If I want them to come to me, I hold out a stick for them to land on."

He settled back in his chair with that comfortable smirk. "And the rest of the time you wear a baby fox around your neck."

"They do keep me company."

"Speaking of company, I've enjoyed yours so much today, I'd like to invite you to our house for supper next week. You and your parents could ride over in the cool of the evening. I know my folks would love to have y'all."

"My parents? I thought you understood how impossible that is. My mother can't—it's simply impossible."

He leaned forward. "Miss Gregg, I'm going to speak frankly. You and your folks cannot spend the rest of your lives hidden away with only wild creatures for company. Especially you. Your folks at least have each other, but you—you're wasting the life the good Lord gave you."

Don't you think I know that? she wanted to scream as she had during her most desperately lonesome times. "Sir," she said instead, pulling in her emotions, "we never know for sure when

one of my mother's spells will come on. For her to merely see
a woman with a small child could trigger one."

He stared at her a moment, his square chiseled features deadly
serious. "Very well." He pulled himself to his feet and picked up
his crutch.

He was leaving? She'd offended the only man to ever come
courting. And he was leaving.

"I concede that it might not be wise for your mother to go
visiting," he said flatly, as he swung toward the steps on his
crutch. "But you have no such problems, do you?"

She came to her feet. "No. Of course not."

"Good, then you have no excuse. I'll be here next Saturday
about an hour before sunset to fetch you. And I'll not take no
for an answer." He stopped and looked over his shoulder. "One
more thing." A grin cocked into place. "I'd purely appreciate it
if you wore that dress again. I'm real partial to it on you."

Again she'd been rendered speechless. She couldn't think.
But that didn't stop the warmth of a blush from rising to her
cheeks. Max Bremmer was down the steps and heading for his
buggy before she found that her mouth was open.

After he hoisted himself up and retrieved the reins, he looked
back. "Give your folks my warmest thanks. I had a wonderful
time. And don't forget. Saturday, about six." He released the
brake, and with one last wave, he was off.

Belinda remembered, then, to wave. But she doubted he saw
it. He'd left so abruptly. But one thing she did know. He was
partial to her dress. And he wanted to see her again.

Chapter Nine

Max had felt pretty good about himself as he drove the buggy home after his visit with the Greggs. But when he'd arrived at the house, no one was there. Instead he found a note on the kitchen table. His father had written it, but the words, no doubt, were his mother's. Bossy.

Son, we are spending the day at the Reardons'. When you get home, take a nap, then join us for supper.

He was in no mood for more visiting after going to church and then dinner at the Greggs'. But here he was, the sun hanging low in the western sky, guiding Pitch and the buggy onto the Reardon cutoff that was marked by a lightning-struck tree. It was easier to comply than to listen to his mother harry him about it later.

But there was one positive aspect in going to the Reardons'.

His mother would be hesitant to ply him with too many questions about his visit with the Greggs in front of the other family.

From the cutoff, he drove through lush acreage of ripening corn, beans, and cotton. Aside from their gristmill, the two Reardon brothers and their crop of boys maintained a productive farm—not to mention that Ike's wife, Annie, had her own beehives and a cheese-making business. They'd done just fine since settling here back in '86.

Max remembered well when he was nothing but a tyke, his family coming overmountain with Ike and Annie Reardon. For a boy of five, it had been a great adventure. They would travel for days at a time not seeing another soul, as if their little group were the only people on earth. He'd felt like he was going into some great unknown and claimed for his own everything he saw, as if he were the lord of all he surveyed. The lure of discovery . . . that was something that had stayed with him from that time on.

On the other hand, the Reardon brothers had been weary of the long war, and Max's own family were at last free of a seven-year indenture—one that had funded their trip from Bavaria. Both families had had all the adventure and uncertainty that any of them wanted. Their own land to settle, a home for their families—that's what they desired.

He smiled at the irony. He'd grown up with the mundane everyday chores of settlement life, and during all that time, he never ceased to hunger for more of those magical few weeks of wilderness travel.

Max neared a trio of log homes standing fairly close together around a central yard. These housed the two brothers' families and their mother. Near the facing barn, Max spotted the familiar team and wagon that belonged to the Smiths. They were the other couple who'd made the trip overmountain from North Carolina with his family years ago. A bond of close friendship had been forged at that time, and regardless of how many other settlers they'd later welcomed to the valley, these first ones were as close-knit as a family of blood relatives.

Kids were running about, laughing and wrestling like a litter of half-grown pups, and all of them he'd known since they were born. Every year when he returned for a visit, he'd have to get reacquainted, though, and meet the occasional new addition. This morning at church, he hadn't recognized Ike's oldest at all. At seventeen, the lad, like his Nordic father and uncle, was taller than Max's own considerable six-foot-three.

Max now spotted the older Smith and Reardon girls—those in their blossoming years. They sat on a quilt under a big-leafed sycamore, lined up one behind the other, braiding flowers into each other's hair.

Flowers and pretty girls, they just seemed to go together . . . Belinda and her silken roses . . .

He pulled the horse to a halt a stone's throw short of the yard shared by the three homes and sat there watching the girls' slender fingers combing and weaving. Although Belinda was a few years their senior, it was really too bad she couldn't be sitting here with them, laughing and talking, with flowers being sprinkled among her riot of blazing curls.

Marring the idyllic thought, one of the black-haired Dagget twins leaped off the steps of one of the porches and strode toward the young misses. The other rawboned brother followed almost immediately, walking fast to catch up.

The first one reached the girls and went to the back side of the colorful quilt; the other stopped at the front. Then, as one, they reached down and hauled up one of the girls. Naturally, it was Liza with the light brown hair and wearing the same yellow dress she had on this morning.

She let loose with an angry howl as the flowers that had been in her lap spilled to the ground.

"Aw, you're already purty enough," one of the twins returned. "Come on. I want to show you my—"

"No," the other brother said. "Come for a walk with me. I want to tell you about my—"

"Max!" Liza had spotted him. She jerked loose from the brothers and headed toward him.

He snapped the reins and drove the buggy the rest of the distance to the communal yard.

The twins came on Liza's heels as Max brought the conveyance to a halt.

"Glad you could come," Pete, the brother without the chin scar, said. "Paul's just itchin' to show someone his new rope trick."

Moving together, the coarse-featured brothers reached into the buggy, each hooking a hand under one of Max's arms, and swung him out—splinted leg and all—and set him down on his good foot as easily as they'd lifted Liza up from the quilt. Their attention, though, was still on their latest battle.

"Liza don't want to go walkin' with Pete."

"Well," Paul's brother countered, "she sure as shootin' don't want to watch you twirl no stupid ol' rope."

"You're both right," tiny Liza said, her tone taking on airs, her prim nose lifting skyward. "Max promised he'd tell me all the latest news about Drew and Crysta as soon as he got here." With that very convincing lie, she twined her arm through his. "Pete, would you be a dear and fetch Max's crutch for him?"

The girl was enjoying herself, that was for sure, *and* with the adults congregated on both porches watching. She was confident, too, as they strolled past several tables set up for the evening meal. Although Liza was probably four or five years younger than Belinda Gregg, she'd never be at a loss for words

84

when a fellow came calling, as Belinda had been this afternoon. Liza not only had doting parents but an entire valley of neighbors who made her feel safe and loved.

Struggling to keep up with Liza as they neared the homes, Max knew he wanted Belinda to have that too. Although he might not be staying around himself, as long as he was here, he'd work toward that end . . . to bring Belinda into the bosom of the valley.

The men had congregated on one of the shaded porches, chairs cocked every which way, while the women sat in more orderly fashion on another porch.

His mother, her hair in its usual tidy coronet of graying blonde braids, stood up and walked to the edge of Ike and Annie's porch. "Liza, bring my boy here to me. I get you two somet'ing cool to drink. *Und*, Liza," she continued to holler, "you can read to him for me da letter I get from his sister."

For once, Inga Bremmer's matchmaking had played into Max's hands. She was more interested in putting Liza at his side than in questioning him about his visit to the Greggs'. "Which sister wrote?" he asked his mother.

"Isolda." Her voice lowered to a more normal pitch as he reached the steps. "Storekeeper Bailey gives to me da letter at church dis morning. A new grandchild Isolda is giving us dis fall. But da Lord only knows when I get to see it. Dat husband of hers, dragging her so far out past Nashville to live. Mosquitoes dey got dere big as dragonflies." Her gaze narrowed on the Dagget twins.

Max noticed they started drifting away, fully aware that his mother had taken over both Max and Liza. From the time they were young boys, the twins knew better than to tangle with Max's mama. Max couldn't help grinning.

"Ven you haf *kinders*, Max, I vant dem born right here. Not a hundred miles avay."

Max's grin froze. Now the woman was planning his grand-children for him. Being laid up with injuries had certainly put him at her mercy. Didn't she know her son well enough to know he intended to return to his travels? to the life perhaps *God* had planned for him? Well, that was something to think about. "So, Isolda is having another baby? That makes five, doesn't it?"

"*Ja.* She is goot breeder." With that blatant remark, his mother walked into the house for the drinks.

Isolda, four years older than Max's twenty-three, was the nearest sibling to his age. But she'd been married and gone since he was twelve. At sixteen, she'd been even younger than Liza . . . awfully young to be saddled with a husband and a houseful of babies.

Max glanced back at Gracie and Hope, Noah Reardon's oldest daughters. They were fast approaching the age of Isolda when she wed. So young, but still they were braiding flowers in their hair to attract some young fellow. That was all any of these girls ever seemed to think about—catching a man to marry. Soon their perpetual cycle would begin . . . the men tied to the land, plowing, planting, and harvesting; and the women to the house, cooking, cleaning, and sewing for an endless stream of youngsters. Until the day they died.

Raised with older sisters who'd dragged him around by the ear often as not, Max had been immune to feminine wiles in his younger days, able to block out their winsome flirting. But since he first caught sight of Belinda Gregg, he certainly could see how the lust of a man's eye could lead to his downfall. He'd been consumed with thoughts of her ever since. And those led to a life of drudgery, didn't they?

Maybe it wasn't such a smart idea that he'd asked her to supper next Saturday.

"Max, why such a frown?" Liza said, as the slip of a girl

turned back to help him up the stairs. "Don't you want me to read you the letter from your sister?" Her lower lip protruded in as engaging a pout as he'd ever seen.

Yes, the girl was manhunting with a vengeance, and his own ma would be right there helping her, if Inga thought that would keep her last child here in the valley.

Reaching the top step, Max glanced over to where the Daggets had rejoined the men gathered on the other porch. Mayhap the twins' overzealous courting wasn't as dumb as he'd thought. For several years now, they'd both managed to avoid that deadly walk down the aisle.

Maybe he should invite them to supper, too, along with Belinda. Take a few pointers from them.

No. The thought of either of them so much as smiling at his lady of the river made his stomach churn. He'd rather take his chances.

"Max, we're purely proud to see you gettin' around so good." Annie Reardon was still as vital and capable-looking as ever, her honey blonde hair showing only a few gray strands. She rose and pointed to the place his mother had taken. "And, Liza, you take my seat. I'll get a couple more chairs from inside."

Trapped with a porch full of women. Max took another longing look at the men but knew he'd better humor his mother—for a few minutes, anyway. He glanced around. Including the two who went inside and Liza, there were eight of them!

He and Liza took their designated seats, his own injured leg sticking out, while the others kept their lower limbs tucked in even on a sultry evening such as this. But, thank goodness, he was at the end closest to the steps—better for a quick escape.

Grandma Louvenia Reardon, sitting next to Liza's mother and grandmother, cleared her throat. "Max, dear. I don't believe you've been introduced to Annie's sister. She's come to live with us since her husband passed on." The long-boned older lady's wise gray eyes moved to a woman on the other side of Liza. "Emma Jane, I reckon you already guessed this is Inga's youngest. The one we all been prayin' for."

"Pleased to meet you," the woman said without the usual accompanying smile. Somewhat thinner than Annie, she had a dark blonde bun that also showed little gray for a woman in midlife, and she had the same warm tones to her skin. But her eyes sorely lacked Annie's spark of confidence. They met his gaze for only an instant before returning to stare at the tightly clasped hands in her lap.

"Pleased to meet you too," he said, realizing he'd hesitated. He felt the need to say more, to put her at ease. "This is a rowdy bunch you've come to stay with. If any of 'em get outta hand, you let me know. I'll come over and knock a few heads together."

Her gaze shot up to meet his. But not with the expected humor in them. Just as quickly, she looked down before he could determine whether her hazel eyes held fear or horror.

Then he noticed that no one else had been amused by his attempt at levity either. "I was just sporting with you," he said, hoping to repair some of the damage. "I wouldn't touch a hair on any of them sweet heads." Blast, he wished he was over with the men. He glanced around at the other women. "Where's that letter Ma was talking about?" The sooner it was read, the sooner he could escape.

His mother walked out just then with two glasses of buttermilk. She handed one to him, then reached into the pocket of her apron. "Here." She handed the letter not to him but to Liza, along with her drink. "Read dis to him, purty girl. You sound like mine Isolda. Da rest of us, ve get da food on da tables."

Grandma Lou turned in her seat. "Noah, Ike, you men come get the chairs and carry 'em out to the tables."

Annie's sister sprang from her seat and started for the entrance as if Grandma Lou had hollered "Fire!" instead of merely summoning the men. In her haste, she tripped over Max's splinted leg.

He caught her arm as she stumbled, steadying her until she could regain her balance.

"Beggin' your pardon," she spewed, pulling her arm from his grasp without looking at him. Then she practically ran across the threshold.

A body would think someone was chasing her.

First Mrs. Gregg and now this woman. The valley was sure getting its share of strange-acting females lately. Shaking his head, he did his best to pull his stiff leg out of the way as the others followed Emma Jane inside.

All except Liza. "Max," came her plaintive cry.

"Yes?"

"You're not listenin'." She stared pointedly, holding the letter at a slant to catch the waning daylight. Did all females eventually turn into his mother?

Pete and Paul came marching across the yard toward them, now that they'd been given leave to. Neither looked too happy with him.

"Why don't you wait to finish reading the letter till the twins get here?" Max said to Liza, as much for himself as for them. "I'm sure they'd enjoy hearing you read too."

Let those two fight over Liza all they wanted. He had someone else he'd rather have meandering across his thoughts . . . someone with hair that glowed brighter than this evening's sunset. The loveliest creature to light this valley or any other. And he saw no reason not to daydream about her. Just thinking about her was safe enough.

Chapter Ten

"Vell, I am vaiting. Da dinner at da Greggs, how vas it?" Inga Bremmer sat on the buggy bench, squeezed between Max and his father as they drove home from the Reardons'. His parents had ridden over earlier in the Smiths' wagon.

Rather than face her inquisition, Max would gladly have walked home regardless of the fact that it would've been three miles on his crutch. But she'd insisted there would be room for all three of them, leaving him no escape.

"The food at the Greggs' house was real good, Ma," he said, answering her question. "They laid out a fine spread."

"Da food? Dat is not vhat I am vanting to know."

His father grunted into a chuckle, causing Max to grin. Fortunately, the lantern light was directed to the ground ahead and not on his face as they rode through a copse of young trees.

Inga ignored her husband. "Vat do you t'ink about da people?"

Max relished his next words. "I think that Mr. Gregg gave one of the most heart-stirring blessings before the meal that I have ever heard. I have no doubt that the man has a very close walk with the Lord."

"Is dat so? *Und* all dis you learn from dis one prayer?" His mother wasn't letting go.

"*Ja*, dat is so," he replied, mimicking her Bavarian accent.

She reached up and yanked his ear. "Don't you make fun of me."

"Ow!" He pulled her hand away and returned it to her lap. "I think they had a bad experience the last place they lived and are wary about making new friends."

"And vhat is da cause of dis bad experience?"

He felt her eyes boring into him.

His pops stepped in. "Inga, dat is da business of da Greggs. If Max feels dey is good Christian folks, he has been out in da vorld long enough to know."

Max leaned forward slightly, directing his next words to his father. "I invited their daughter, Miss Belinda, to our house for supper next Saturday, if that's all right with you and Mama."

"Son, you know your friends is alvays velcome at our house."

"A young voman, you say?" his mother piped in. "From a God-fearing home . . . I make somet'ing goot to eat. Not as goot as I make vhen you invite Liza."

The woman was like a dog with a bone.

"Speaking of unsociable people," Max said, changing the subject, "Annie Reardon's sister sure is standoffish. She acts like she's scared of everyone, even of her own shadow."

"Only dis ve can say," his father said for both of them. "*Frau* Thompson, she has suffered many trials. She needs us to show her much kindness."

"*Und*, Max, don't you go stirring up questions about da poor

Emma Jane," his mother ordered, coming to the woman's defense. "She needs da time to find her old self."

The fact that his mother was treating him as if he didn't have any better sense irritated Max. "That's fine by me, Ma. But I'll expect you to give Miss Gregg the same courtesy when she comes on Saturday."

"Oh? Has her papa beat her down like da husband of Emma Jane?"

"*Inga.*" Rolf's tone silenced her. "Enough talk about private matters."

Max had rarely heard his father speak harshly to his mother. An uncomfortable quiet followed, with no sounds but those of the horse and the creaking buggy and the occasional cry of a night creature. The three of them sitting so close made it even more strained . . . and they wouldn't be arriving home for another fifteen minutes.

"Forgif me," Inga finally offered—a rare apology from her. "I promise I take better care of dis unruly tongue."

Pops wrapped an arm around her and hugged her close. "Da people must be able to trust secrets to us. I be a poor pastor if dey cannot. Ve must never forget dis commission da Lord gives to us."

She rested her head on his shoulder and spoke softly, just to her husband. "I know. It slip out."

Pops kissed her temple. "I know."

Max sat there, feeling as if he were eavesdropping on a very private moment. He rarely thought of them as husband and wife, usually just as his parents. This love and quiet understanding between them was such a departure from their everyday activities.

He thought about this commission given to them by God. Max's first memories were of his father preaching on Sundays, and he knew the old man visited the sick and needy, but he'd never before thought of all the secrets he must have been told over the years . . . secrets, troubled or sad, that he'd kept locked away as he ministered to the people God had placed in his care.

How audacious he had been last week when he urged his father not to tell others about Felicity Gregg. Next Saturday, when his lady of the river came, he was just as sure his mother would be as gracious as he knew she could be.

As for himself? He'd go out of his way to make sure Miss Belinda had a good time. She'd been without friends much too long.

~

Belinda descended the stairs late Saturday afternoon, trying to let the music her mother played soothe her. She placed unsteady hands over an even more turbulent stomach. Aside from the emergency trip to the general store last week, she couldn't remember the last time she'd gone amongst strangers without her father's company. Years.

Glancing over the banister to her mother, who was playing one of Mozart's more lyrical arias on the harpsichord, Belinda sought to draw courage from the bravest woman she'd ever known.

Without her fingers slowing, her mother smiled up at her— a reassuring smile that told her again that going to supper at the Bremmers' was the right thing to do. "You look lovely, sweetheart." Felicity glanced at her husband sitting in a nearby wing chair. "Doesn't she, dear?"

"You always look gorgeous."

Of course he'd say that. He was her daddy.

"The gown is lovely, Belinda," her mother added. "But perhaps you should've worn something that Mr. Bremmer hasn't already seen?"

Belinda glanced down at the rose-strewn silk. "He asked me to wear this one again."

Her mother stopped playing. "He did, did he?" A fine brow arched with a knowing smirk. "I don't recall you mentioning that earlier."

Heat flooded Belinda's cheeks. "Perhaps I should change into something else." She glanced at the tall clock near the dining-room doors. Seven before six. He'd be here any minute.

"Darling, if Mr. Bremmer requested you wear that particular gown, then by all means, you should."

Her dad rose from his chair and walked toward her. "You'll have a wonderful time."

"But what will I talk about? And Mrs. Bremmer is sure to ask questions."

Her mother swung her legs around to the back of the bench, pulling her own indigo-dyed batiste gown with her, and faced the room. "It's really quite simple, child. Compliment Mrs. Bremmer and her home, her food. Share a recipe or two. Ask about the latest news from back East. I'm sure there'll be no reason to—"

"But, Mama, we've been here three years. You know she's going to ask why we've never come to any of the social gather-ings. Their Fourth of July celebration was just three weeks ago."

"Don't put yourself on the defensive by acting guilty. Simply tell Mrs. Bremmer that we've been entirely too occupied with our enterprises to socialize. And that's not a lie. With just the three of us to care for this place and fill our pottery orders, we don't have much spare time . . . especially since I don't always feel well enough to do my share."

The ravens started cawing.

Belinda looked past the tied-back drapes and saw the birds

take flight from the veranda's railing. Her gaze flew with them to the drive below the house.

Max Bremmer. Right on time.

Her heart fluttered more wildly than her stomach. She placed a stilling hand over the spot.

Her father wrapped an arm around her waist. "One breath at a time. One moment at a time." He pecked her cheek. "And this, my belle, is the moment to go out and greet our guest." With Mr. Gregg providing the courage, they went through the door and down the steps.

Her mother followed close behind. "Flowers," she exclaimed when they all reached the brick walk. "Most women like to share seeds and cuttings." She hurried over to a bed of zinnias along the picket fence and broke off spent blooms of three different colors.

As Max's buggy drew ever closer, Felicity tapped the zinnias against her palm, jarring loose a sprinkle of seeds. Then, plucking a large hydrangea leaf from a nearby bush, she folded the seeds into it and handed the impromptu envelope to Belinda.

Feeling Max's eyes on her, Belinda glanced back at him.

A flash of white. He was smiling.

"Put the seeds in your purse." Her mother referred to the small mauve bag dangling from Belinda's wrist.

Belinda did as she was told, all the while sneaking peeks at a man who looked so vital, so manly, it was hard to believe he required a crutch to walk. As Max reined the black horse to a stop, she moved beneath the rose arbor to reach him.

"Evening, Mr. and Mrs. Gregg," he said, his sky blue gaze leaving her for them. Unlike last Sunday, he was hatless and merely nodded to them. But all else was the same. He wore the same taupe-and-beige paisley vest and white shirt.

"Good evening, Mr. Bremmer." Mr. Gregg stepped to the side of the buggy.

"Please, call me Max."

"Would you care for some refreshment," her mother asked, "before you go?"

It was strange watching her parents acting so hospitable. For so long they'd made it a practice to discourage any passersby. Everything had floated along the same—and now, how quickly it was all changing.

"Better not, ma'am. My ma gave me very strict orders not to dally. She's purely looking forward to meeting Miss Belinda."

Belinda's father drew her forward. "Then we shouldn't keep your mother waiting." Without warning, he lifted her up beside Max.

Too quickly, she was sitting beside him. He smelled of something quite heady that he must have splashed on after shaving. They were so close, her filmy skirt lay against his splinted leg.

"I expect you to get her home at a decent hour," Mr. Gregg said, as if she weren't a grown woman.

Max returned her dad's steady gaze. "Of course, sir. And I'll see, no harm comes to her."

"I'm counting on it." Her father slapped the horse's rump.

The animal lunged forward.

And off they went, just like in one of Belinda's romantic novels. She'd read them over and over but never believed anything like this could actually happen to her.

Although she didn't look back, she knew her parents were still watching and probably smiling. As the buggy rattled and clattered over the bridge and onto the road that would soon be enclosed by the woods, she realized she shouldn't have worried so about what to say to Mrs. Bremmer—not when she had close to an hour to fill before even getting there. She mustn't forget that last week when she hadn't been able to make conversation, this handsome man had soon left.

She breathed in to quell her rising panic. The weather. Mama said that was always a safe topic. Then she remembered. "I've brought some flower seeds for your mother. Does she like flowers?"

"Yes, very much." He glanced at her, and his own shoulders visibly relaxed. "Mama grows petunias every year in her window boxes."

Belinda loved the low timbre of his voice . . . a voice with the kind of confidence that told her he was quite able to keep his promise to her father. This stalwart fellow would let no harm come to her this evening—or to her mother.

A warm glow chased away any lingering fears she might have as they turned onto the river road. The setting sun had turned Caney Fork into a shimmering golden ribbon. Lovely. She sat back to enjoy its momentary glory. "Mr. Bremmer—"

"Max, please. You being so formal makes me feel as old as my pops."

He truly did want to be good friends. "Max, then. I was just wondering, since you've traveled far and wide and spent time on the Mississippi, is it true?"

"What's that?" His gaze traced her face and her upswept curls, telling her he thought she was pretty.

She almost lost her train of thought. "I . . . uh—" her own gaze wavered—"I heard the Mississippi would make four or five of Caney Fork."

He barked a chuckle. "More like twenty or thirty."

He began to expound on the great river and its many tributaries, and the last vestige of unease left Belinda as she let his words pour over her like warm sweet honey. For this one special evening, she had her very own, very handsome, very charming beau.

~

As Belinda rode up the incline from the ferry dock with Max, the spire on the church glowed glaringly white even in the fading daylight. The threatening sight caused her chest to tighten—this symbol of her greatest fear—the building that housed all the condemning hypocrites every Sunday morning.

She sucked in a breath, assuring herself that no one would be inside this evening.

Max laid a big square hand over hers and squeezed. "Don't be nervous. I won't leave you alone with anyone."

"*Anyone?* Who else is going to be there? Do you have younger brothers and sisters at home?"

"No, I'm the last. The anyone I spoke of is Mama. Sometimes she speaks without thinking. But if she does, I'll see you through."

Belinda searched his eyes. "How did you come to be such an understanding man?"

"Me?" He looked at her with disbelief. "I've never been accused of that before. Must be this game leg has slowed me up a mite. It's given me more time to think about life. My mortality." He moved his hand from hers to his splinted leg and rubbed where the bandage bulged beneath his buff breeches. "But it's getting better every day. Stronger."

"That's wonderful. I'm most pleased for you." But not for herself. From the way his face lit up whenever he spoke of the West as he had earlier, she knew he'd leave the minute he was fit to travel again. A warning, she reminded herself, not to get too dependent on his company.

They drove past the line of stores, then the church, its windows looming dark and silent. Max reined the horse toward a two-story log house. Its lower windows and front doorway glowed, shedding light on narrow boxes of lushly blooming petunias suspended just below each sill and on the porch railings. A happy house.

The woman who planted the flowers must be a happy soul, too, particularly with a husband as kind as Brother Bremmer and a son any mother would be proud to call her own.

As Max drew the horse and buggy to a halt, the light streaming from the front door became blocked; a silhouetted man and woman walked out onto the porch. They came down the steps. Hulking Brother Rolf, with that broad friendly grin, and the woman he dwarfed.

She wore a white apron with a matching dust cap, both adding to her bright welcoming smile that was made even more friendly by her round plump cheeks. With lines on her brow and crow's-feet at her eyes, the older woman looked to be a decade or so older than Belinda's own mother yet much stronger and healthier. Her strength showed in her straight shoulders and sturdy hands. Compared to Belinda's own smaller-boned family, these were certainly hardy people.

"Velcome," Brother Bremmer called as he and his wife strolled to the buggy. He reached out his arms and swung Belinda down, using little of his blacksmith's strength. He then walked around to assist Max.

As he did, Mrs. Bremmer extended a work-hardened hand. "Pleased we are, Miss Gregg, dat you could come. Mine Max, he is not one dat slows down long enough to invite many pretty *fräuleins* to supper. Dis is a pure treat." Her sure but accented words were confirmed by her firm grasp of Belinda's hand.

Belinda wasn't accustomed to shaking hands with a woman. Probably a German custom—one she found herself liking as much as she did the straightforward woman. Max must have been over-cautious when he hinted at some concern about her. "Mrs. Bremmer, I'm most pleased to accept your kind hospitality."

~

Max couldn't have been prouder of his mother. Although he knew her curiosity about Belinda and the Greggs was at a high pitch, she had hidden it beautifully during the meal. The conversation had mostly centered on a discourse his father had recently received comparing the Calvinism differences between the English Puritans, the French Huguenots, and the Reformed Churches of the Rhineland. Considering the depth of the topic, Belinda's comments had been few, but informed enough to convince his mother of her Christianity—Inga's most vocal doubt earlier in the day.

To add further to the enjoyment of the evening, his mother had shoveled all the hot coals out of the fireplace, providing them with a much cooler room than normal for the end of July. She'd also laid out quite a spread: bratwurst, sauerkraut, cooled cream of corn, potato salad, salt-soaked radish slices, and a pickling of onions, cucumbers, and beets, along with a loaf of wheat-flour bread.

Max had pretty well stuffed himself, and Belinda across from him had eaten a goodly share once her shyness had dissipated.

His father shoved his chair back from the table and rubbed his bulging belly. "A fine supper, Inga. Anot'er bite I cannot eat."

Inga rose from the table, grinning playfully. "Goot. Dat leafs more peaches *und* cream for da rest of us."

"Peaches *und* cream?" Pops sat forward again. "I t'ink maybe I got enough room for dat."

"I t'ought so." Chuckling lightly, his mother swung around toward the dish shelves above the sinkboard.

"Let me help you," Belinda offered, starting to rise.

His father laid a staying hand on her arm. "No, you are da

special guest tonight. Dat you haf been here is a fine treat. Max must invite you again. Soon."

Max had no doubt his pops was totally serious. Though Rolf never uttered the words, Max knew his father hoped he would marry and remain in the valley, probably as much as his mother did.

And perhaps he would return . . . a dozen or so years from now, when his parents could no longer see to their own needs, and he had tired of life in the wilderness. But in the meantime, while he was still here and recuperating, Max saw nothing wrong in enjoying the company of a beautiful woman. "I'd be pleased to keep on asking Miss Belinda to meals as long as she'll put up with me."

"I t'ink I hear somebody coming." Inga turned from scooping sliced and honeyed peaches into individual bowls.

Disappointment caught hold of Max. Couldn't his family have this one evening without someone riding in with a crisis that needed the attention of the only minister in the valley?

"Most likely, dat is da Dagget boy. I vill get da door." Rolf shoved back his chair and hefted his bulk up to his feet. "Pete, he come by vhen you vas gone. He vas vanting you to go visiting da Smith girl *mit* him. He said he might stop back by later."

It was all Max could do not to groan audibly. He couldn't think of anything he needed less right now, except maybe *both* twins showing up. He glanced across to Belinda and saw panic stirring in her expressive eyes. "Let me go." Hanging on to the table, he got up on his one good foot.

"I better put out anot'er bowl," his mother said, reaching for one.

Pete wasn't coming in if Max could help it. Leaning on his crutch, he made his way to the front entrance by the time the rider had dismounted and walked up to the porch.

And sure enough, that swaggering stride coming within the light beaming out the threshold could only belong to one of the twins.

"Pete." Max tried to sound cheerful. "My pops just told me you'd been by. Where's Paul?" Max remained directly in the doorway, blocking Pete's entrance.

A long-toothed grin plainly displayed Pete's joy in his brother's absence. "Now that Pa's rheumatiz has set in strong, me an' Paul take turns tendin' to Pa's errands and such. I had to go last time, so there was nothin' Paul could do but go."

"Where?"

Pete lounged against a porch post, looking even more pleased with himself. "To my pa's brother's place, ten or fifteen miles the other side o' Nashville. Uncle Amos has come down with some kinda wastin' sickness, and since his own boys has taken up the flatboat trade over on the Big Muddy, Pa had to send Paul to take care of his place till he's up on his feet again." He shrugged happily. "And, who knows, it could take quite a spell."

Max nodded, adding his own knowing grin to Pete's. "So, now it's your turn to have Liza all to yourself."

"Yeah. I know she likes me best. But she's still holding back. I ain't lettin' up, though. Not till she gives in. If Paul will just stay away a month or so . . ."

Poor Liza. Small wonder she'd turned her sights on someone as unlikely as a banged-up hunter.

"Speakin' of courtin', your ma said you went downriver to fetch some young miss here for supper. That sounds mighty serious. I didn't think you was leanin' that way."

"It's just supper," Max found himself defending.

"Is that so? I don't recall you doin' that since you was a pup. Sounds to me like you're fixin' to give up your roamin' and settle down."

"Not if I can help it." Max glanced down to his slow-healing thigh. "But whilst I'm laid up, I don't mind a little feminine company." *With the most beautiful woman in any valley*, he could've added but didn't.

Pete craned his neck, trying to look past Max into the house. His friend was blatantly curious. "Your ma said it was a Miss Gray, or somethin' like that. I don't recall no Grays hereabouts. They must live farther down toward Nashville." Then he widened his stance and crossed his arms as if he weren't planning to budge from that spot. He tipped his head to one side. "You are gonna invite me in so I can make her acquaintance, ain't ya?"

Max stared back. "No."

Pete's chin jerked up. "You ain't?"

"No." Max knew how rude he was being, but no way would he risk ruining Belinda's first social outing. "Maybe another time."

Though Pete's eyes remained narrowed, his mouth slid into a knowing smirk. "You're scared I'll take her away from you. Ain'tcha?"

Max patted his injured leg. "Let's just say I'm not as fast on my feet right now."

Pete burst out laughing. "You never was. Tell you what—the Underwoods is havin' a cornhuskin' party next Saturday. By then I should have Liza talked into a yes to my marriage offer. And—"

"No one'll ever accuse you of lackin' confidence."

"That's right. And since I'll be betrothed, I won't be the devilishly charmin' threat you seem to think I am tonight. So I'll expect to see you and the little missy there." Again, he tried to look past Max.

"I don't know," Max hedged. "Don't you think we're getting too old for them kinda gatherings?"

"I ain't in my dotage yet. And neither are you, whether you think so or not. But if you ain't up to joinin' us, then I reckon I'll just go on in the house and introduce myself to your Miss Gray right now." He started forward.

Max grabbed his arm. "Hold your horses . . . all right. I'll ask her if she wants to go to the cornhusking." He purposefully didn't use Belinda's true surname, preferring to keep Pete in the dark a while longer.

Pete eased back and cocked a smug grin. "If you don't show up, I'll track you both down. Hear?"

Chapter Eleven

Belinda waited at the Bremmers' table for Max to return, all the while trying not to show her apprehension by peering too often through the kitchen doorway that directly lined up with the front door.

Max, with his back to her, blocked the entrance, and she could hear only the rumble of male voices but no distinct words.

Thus far, he hadn't invited the visitor in. To be entertained by a couple she'd never met was already strain enough without adding another person.

"Miss Gregg, here is da peaches for you." Mrs. Bremmer set a plain wooden bowl on the red-checked cloth in front of Belinda, the fruit swimming in sweet cream.

"Thank you. It looks delicious." She drummed up a smile for the rosy-cheeked woman then scooped a peach slice. She forced herself to concentrate on it and its tangy sweet taste.

The clomping of Max's crutch finally echoed across the parlor floor. He was returning to the kitchen.

Belinda tried not to look obvious as she strained to see beyond him.

Brother Bremmer, not a subtle man, leaned forward for a better angle from his end of the table. "Max," he called out, "Pete is not coming in?"

"No." Reaching the kitchen, he looked straight at Belinda, a reassuring warmth in his eyes. "I didn't want to interrupt our evening with Miss Belinda."

"*Und* you should not haf to," Mrs. Bremmer said, dropping into her chair. "Sit. Eat your peaches."

Max leaned his crutch against the table and retook his seat, not taking his eyes off Belinda. "It took some talking and a promise to get rid of Pete."

"Vhat you mean?" his mother asked, putting voice to Belinda's own question.

Max glanced at the older woman. "Pete was real persistent about wanting to get a look at Belinda." His smile was warm as he returned his attention to her. "I promised him that if he'd go quietly, I'd ask Miss Gregg to accompany me to a cornhusking party next week at the Underwoods'. That seemed to satisfy him."

"But, I—," Belinda started to protest, her heart pounding. Visiting here was one thing, but being thrust into an entire party of people and all the questions they could ask? She wasn't ready for *that*.

Mrs. Bremmer rested a wide hand over hers. "It is time you meet more young people. You *und* Max vill haf da goot time dere. *Ja?*" She looked at her husband.

Brother Bremmer was watching Belinda. "It is goot for you to start *mit* da mixing. Dere is a party of some sort every veek or so, depending on da season. Lots of hands make for da quick vork, den dey clear da floor *und* haf a frolic. Lots of laughing *und* marches to da music. Your papa, he vill t'ink dis is goot, *ja?*"

That was true. Still, Belinda knew her father would understand her reticence. Even if he was pushing her to start socializing, she couldn't feel comfortable with the prospect. Her mother was just now climbing out of her latest bout with melancholy. Although it had been more than a year since the episode before this latest one, she could fall into another at any time. And what if Belinda's appearances at social gatherings made people think they could reciprocate by dropping by the house unexpectedly? She could not forget the time her mother had spiraled into the depths merely by seeing a babe in its mother's arms.

"Belinda," Max said, capturing her with his china blue eyes, "if you'd like to accompany me, I'd see that you enjoyed the evening without disclosing anything you would prefer to keep private. Pete don't know a thing except that you live somewhere downriver. Don't even know your name. He referred to you as Miss Gray."

"*Und* you do not tell him he is wrong?" Mrs. Bremmer reprimanded.

Belinda suspected she wasn't all that happy, considering her own lack of knowledge about her guest.

"All in good time." Max picked up his spoon. "The peaches sure look good."

His mother shot him a disgruntled look then eased her expression as she turned to Belinda and smiled. "You go *mit* Max. He needs to mix more *mit* da young people too. 'Specially da *fräuleins*. Get da rest of dem woodsy edges shaved off."

A smile crawled along Belinda's lips. If nothing else, Mrs. Bremmer was forthright in her desire to have her son settled in civilization again. A desire Belinda certainly wasn't averse to.

She took a fortifying breath. "I'll speak to my parents first. Though I don't foresee any objection."

Brother Bremmer slapped the table. "Goot. Now, ve stop da talking *und* eat before dis here cream curdles."

Laughter erupted from Max, and his parents joined him.

It was music to Belinda's ears. What a joy to be in the midst of this happy, boisterous family. Of course she'd had to say yes to the invitation.

And after being here with them—with *him*—how would she ever return to her lonely life again? But hope as she might, she must never let herself forget: Max Bremmer, explorer and hunter, did plan to leave for the West once he was well.

~

"That German blood of yourn is purely showin' itself here," Ma Smith remarked as she studied Max's unbound leg.

"It's bleeding again?" Would the vexing wound never heal? He sat on her examining table, enduring her twice-weekly prodding.

"No, that ain't what I meant." The white-haired woman walked around her examination table and eyed the leg from another angle, pressing here and there with a flat, smooth stick. "You're going to have some nasty scarring, but the flesh has knit itself together real fine, from the inside out as it should. And if the shattered bone has been doin' the same, you oughta be able to start puttin' some weight on it in a few weeks."

"A few *weeks*." Max sat up and looked at his exposed wound—and winced. The top of his upper leg looked like a half-chewed piece of fish in several shades of pale pink. But as Ma had said, there was still no sign of infection. "I never seen a leg this tore up without rot settin' in.

"You have Black Bear to thank more'n me. Whatever he put

on it kept the poison from settin' in. Next time you see him, find out what it was. Now, roll over so I can get a look at the back side." Ma supported his injured leg as he rolled. "Careful now." When he was on his belly, she grunted.

"Something wrong there?" Max craned his neck to see over his shoulder.

"No, sonny, it's just fine. This side is completely healed. I won't have to put no more salve on it. Yessir, you're a mighty lucky lad. Don't never let anybody tell you prayer don't work." She slapped his rear. "Sit up, and let's get you bandaged and splinted again."

As Ma Smith sat on her stool tying the last strip around the wooden splints, she glanced up at him. "Did that pink lady slipper I give you do that person any good?"

He'd forgotten about that. "The family seems to think so. They added it to them other plants I told you about."

"It's not always good to mix things. But it sounds like it didn't do her no harm. I'm glad to hear it." She rose from her stool. "One of them Dagget boys was by here last night to see Liza. Again. He said you was takin' some lass from way downriver to the cornhuskin'." She gave him a slanted look. "I know it ain't none of my business, but you know you don't have to go so far outta the way if you're lookin' for a young miss to take places. All you gotta do is be the one what asks Liza, instead of them two yahoos."

"Ma, I know you mean well, but if my leg is healing as good as you say, I'll probably be outta here by fall. On the other hand, Pete and Paul are planning to stay right here in the valley. They may be loud and pushy together, but if you take 'em on one at a time, they really ain't half bad. And if Liza does pick one of 'em, I know they'll provide a real good home for her."

"I see. So what you're sayin' is, you got your sights set on that other lass from downstream. Pete said her name was Gray. I know I ain't been here more'n a year or so, but I don't believe I ever heard that name mentioned before."

He couldn't lie to Ma. "Her name ain't Gray. It's Gregg. Belinda Gregg."

The comfortable-looking woman crimped her brows. "I still ain't heard of it."

"They keep pretty much to themselves."

One of her brows arched. "I see."

Had she put two and two together as Belinda feared she might? The pink lady slipper and Mrs. Gregg? Well, he wasn't about to ask and stir the pot any further. He pulled a silver coin from his pocket and folded it into Ma's hand. "Thanks for all your fine nursing."

Hobbling out the door of her herb shed, Max headed straight for the buggy. If he had anything to say about it, he wouldn't be taking tea with the younger Smith women today. There'd been too much scheming going on between his mother and them.

He hoisted himself up to the seat and was pulling up his crutch when he heard the dreaded sound of the door at the main house squeak open.

Out came sweet-faced Liza. "How's your leg a-comin'?" she called, hurrying across the clearing toward him.

"Fine." He snatched up the reins and clicked his tongue to start Pitch moving.

She stopped. "You can't stay awhile?" The lass sounded disappointed.

He felt like an ogre. "I promised Pops I'd get back to help him as soon as your granny finished with me." It wasn't a lie.

She shaded her eyes against the sun as he moved past. "Then I reckon I'll be seein' you at the cornhuskin'."

"Wouldn't miss it."

She still looked as if she'd lost her favorite puppy.

Feeling guilty, he reined in. "Bring some of those cookies we had the last time I was here. I sure was partial to 'em."

Liza smiled, and even her down-slanted eyes brightened. "I will. Just for you, Max."

While driving the rig into town, Max had the nagging inkling that he shouldn't have led Liza on. In the end it would be crueler, especially when she saw how close he would stay to Belinda at the party—protecting her from hurt as he wouldn't be doing for Liza. But just the thought of walking onto the corncrib's lower floor with the most beautiful woman in Tennessee on his arm . . . how could he not be elated? And attentive . . . lest the other bachelors in the valley started circling.

Reaching the blacksmith shop, Max had started guiding the horse and buggy around to the back when he spotted a half-grown girl riding bareback at a gallop and coming fast upon him.

Her long hair flying, she yanked on a halter rope, bringing the sweat-foamed plow horse to a dust-kicking stop. "Where's Brother Bremmer?" Out of breath, she stared into the dark hollow of the large building.

"He should be in there."

She kicked the brown animal's flanks with her bare feet, and the horse took a few more laggardly steps toward the open doors. "Brother Bremmer! Come out! We need you! Now!"

By the time she finished hollering, Rolf came walking out, wiping his hands with a kerchief as grimy as the rest of him. "Dolly May. Vhat is da matter?"

"It's Pa. He's been drinkin' again, an' he's gone on a rampage. He's breakin' up the place, threatenin' to kill us all. Come on. We gotta go now."

His father turned to him. "Goot, you're back. I take da buggy.

Tell Inga I am going out to da Allen place. *Und* Max, vould you finish da hammerhead?"

"Sure, Pops. But if he's on such a rampage, don't you think I should go with you?"

"*Nein*. He alvays settles down vhen I get dere. He is goot man in da heart. 'Cept when he starts drinking dat devil brew."

Max eased himself to the ground, then watched his father climbed aboard.

Rolf snapped the reins across Pitch's back several times, sending the horse into a gallop. He and the young girl then charged off in the direction from whence she'd come.

Too late Max realized his father had not taken a rifle. What if the man was drunk enough to try to shoot Pops?

Max chuckled. Unlike him and his hunting friends, the only thing Pops ever went armed with was his faith in God. Two weeks ago he'd calmed a mad woman with a few verses of Scripture, and now he rode out to a man who was crazy drunk. Only the Lord knew where he'd be called to next week . . . into whatever tragedy that he would not hesitate to go.

For as long as Max could remember, he'd seen his father leave suddenly on these missions of ministry. He'd never thought much about them in the past, because his father had always kept the details to himself, never making much of the trips. Just as he hadn't talked about Mrs. Gregg and just as he wouldn't about Mr. Allen either.

Leaning into his crutch, Max saw a truth that had been there all along, yet revealed to his "blind" eyes for the first time today. All those daring exploits he rushed into pell-mell couldn't hold a candle to his father's everyday bravery. Or integrity. This lumbering, stick-in-the-mud old man was the real hero of the family. And the reason Max's leg was healing so well had nothing to do with his "German blood": *"The Lord heareth the prayer of the righteous."*

Max started for the smithy, feeling uplifted by his revelations. This had been one fine morning. And soon he'd be having another fine evening. He grinned, knowing it would be only two more days before he again drove out to fetch Miss Belinda Gregg.

On the ride home the other night, he'd suddenly been struck by the thought that he hadn't yet worked up the nerve to kiss those tender lips of hers—she'd been too skittish and he hadn't wanted to scare her off. But next time, he just might get a kiss from his lady. *There wouldn't be any harm in that, would there, Lord?*

"Belinda Gregg." He still loved the way her name rolled off his tongue.

Chapter Twelve

Belinda sat in one of the green wicker chairs on the veranda, her fingers clutching its arms, preventing them from clasping together on her lap. She'd already caused some wrinkling of her blue gingham plaid, not that anyone except Max Bremmer would see it. She had no intention of going to the cornhusking party with him. There would be too many people there, too many questions.

Nonetheless, she did want to look adequately groomed when he arrived—which should be any minute now. The tall clock in the parlor had already chimed three times.

The fingers she used to recheck the ringlets cascading from her crown felt quite numb, she was so tense. She hated the idea of disappointing Max, but she simply had no choice.

She listened for the sound of footsteps or voices in the house and thankfully heard none. For the first time, she really understood the old saying "sitting on pins and needles."

She watched the drive. If only Max would arrive and leave before her parents finished work out in the pottery shed. She could send him away without them ever knowing about his invitation. She would not give them the option of sacrificing their privacy, jeopardizing the safety of this home, just so she could attend some frivolous gathering. Young people, especially, would not be easily put off when they sought to know more about the strangers in their midst . . . strangers who'd shunned every attempt at neighborliness the valley folk had made.

The ravens, hopping from picket to picket of the flower-laden fence, suddenly took flight, cawing loudly.

Max's black horse. The buggy. He was crossing the bridge.

Belinda came to her feet, her heart racing. She smoothed down her plaid empire-cut skirt, flicked down a turned-up spot on the white ruffling at one of her shoulders. She couldn't help wanting to look nice for him.

Max would understand why she couldn't go. He just had to.

But would he ever come back again? Who would want to keep company with someone so averse to mixing with his friends—not to mention a young woman who might one day inherit her mother's affliction.

She closed her eyes. *I can't think of that.* "Lord God, I know I'm not supposed to worry. I give all my worries to You."

Ignoring the tightness of her corset, she took a deep breath and put on a smile, then sauntered down the veranda steps.

Within the shade of the buggy bonnet, Max's delightfully cocky grin gleamed forth before the rest of his face could be distinguished . . . that absolutely mind-stealing grin.

He did always seem such a cheerful man, regardless of the severity of his injuries. A fine quality. She felt even worse, knowing she would be disappointing him, stealing his cheer.

Reaching the rose arbor, she waved.

He returned her greeting, then glanced beyond her and raised his hand again in salutation.

She looked behind her. Coming alongside the house, her parents walked briskly. Hands caked with clay, they still wore their clay-spattered smocks.

The blood drained from Belinda's face, and she caught hold of the gate for support. Her plan had failed.

"My, don't you look pretty in blue," Max managed to say to her before her parents converged on the small carriage.

Belinda lagged behind, dreading what would come next.

"If we'd known you were dropping by," her father said, rubbing the clay from his hands, "we would've cleaned up first."

"Oh?" Max eyed Belinda, his grin fading.

"I didn't want to bother them," Belinda said lamely.

"Bother us about what?" Mr. Gregg asked.

Belinda had no choice. Shifting so she wouldn't have to see Max's expression, she said, "Mr. Bremmer asked me to accompany him somewhere, and I've since decided not to go." Not seeing Max didn't hurt any less as the words spewed forth. She swung to him.

His smile, of course, was replaced by a frown.

Belinda caught her lower lip in her teeth. "I do apologize for your having to drive out here for nothing. I should've found a way to send you a message."

Her mother turned from Max to Belinda, lines bunching her brow. "Sweetheart, you were so pleased with your visit to the Bremmers. Why ever would you renege on another of this kind man's invitations?"

"It's to a party, Mrs. Gregg," Max answered in her stead. "A cornhusking. Your daughter is afraid to meet new people. Afraid of their questions."

"I see." Her mother's fragile features slowly disintegrated into

those of despair. Tears sheened in her soft gray eyes as she
looked away.

Fear for her mother's well-being gripped Belinda. "Mama, truly
I don't mind missing the party. Please, don't be sad." She caught
her mother's hand, praying this wouldn't toss her into another pit
of melancholy. She'd just climbed out of the last one.

Mr. Gregg came at them in an unexpected rush, his jaw
clenched, his auburn brows forming a low shelf over his eyes.
Before Belinda knew what was happening, he scooped her up
and plopped her down on the buggy seat. "Have her back here
by midnight," he almost growled to Max.

Speechless, Belinda caught hold of the side. Her father was
not given to such outbursts. "Daddy?"

"And we want her brought back here happy and laughing," he
announced before giving the horse's rump a hard slap.

Pitch took off with an abrupt jerk, throwing Belinda back on
the tufted-leather bench seat.

"Looks like you're coming to the party after all," Max said
while frantically collecting the reins. He turned to her, and his
boyish grin was back.

"It would seem so." Her heart tumbled over itself. Her first
party. She took a breath. Would it also turn out to be her last?

An hour or so later, Belinda drove with Max through a field of
corn and into a clearing with a scattering of farm structures to
the rear of a log house.

"This is it, the Underwood place," Max informed her with a
pointing nod.

Belinda tried not to show her disappointment. The pleasant
interlude they'd shared, chatting mostly about the antics of
wildlife and, notably, stories about her ravens, now came to an
end.

Her stomach knotted as she surveyed the many carts, wagons, and saddle horses already parked before a lofted corncrib, with the ground level open at both ends. A huge pile of corn filled the center of the bottom floor, and no less than a score of young people sat around it, frantically tossing yellow shucked cobs of corn onto piles on either side and the husks haphazardly behind them.

Belinda's throat clogged. So many people, so many questions they could ask.

One of the fellows, an ungainly sort with black wavy hair, scrambled to his feet. With a toothy grin, he headed toward the buggy. "You brought her," he crowed much too loud.

"I said I would." Max spoke as if there'd never been any doubt.

The young man, about Max's age, was upon them, on Belinda's side of the buggy, staring boldly. "Now I see why you been tryin' to keep the little lady to yourself. She's a real looker. 'Specially for a redhead." He started to pull a hat from his head, but then remembered he wore none. "Pleased to meet you, Miss Gray."

Miss Gray? Then she recalled that he'd heard her name wrong. "Do call me Belinda," she replied, not correcting his error either. *Especially for a redhead, indeed.*

"Miss Belinda," Max insisted gruffly. "And this here is Pete Dagget. We went to school together."

"And everywhere else," Max's friend said, "till he lit out for Indian country with Drew and Crysta Reardon. Here, miss, allow me to help you down." Without waiting for her to even make a move, Mr. Dagget reached in and swung her, skirts and all, in a wild flourish to the ground. While the blue plaid still wove about her legs, he walked to the other side of the buggy and assisted Max down.

Pausing while Max joined her, Belinda noticed that all the

talking had ceased inside the barn. Without turning to face them, she sensed every eye was on her. Her stomach tightened into a knot. How would she ever withstand such an onslaught of curiosity?

Max reached her on his crutch, his gaze demanding hers; then he leaned down to her ear. "Honest, they don't bite."

Pete followed with a large covered crock that Belinda had not noticed behind the buggy seat. When they walked within the wide opening, he veered off to one side, where a long board-on-barrel table already held a number of other food offerings.

"Which side do you want us?" Max asked, addressing the rudely staring group.

"Ain'tcha gonna introduce us to the purty lady first?" a fresh-faced lad said, coming up to his knees.

"Miss Belinda, that there's Ezzy Underwood. This is his family's farm. As for the rest of you, she'll be more apt to put your names to memory if we take it more slowly."

Belinda relaxed slightly. Max would see her through as he'd promised.

He scanned the piles on opposing sides. "Looks like that side could use our help," he said, pointing to the one with the smaller stack of shucked corn. "Any red ears found yet?"

"Nope," several of the young people chorused together.

"Lessen you count the ones on ol' Pete's head," a dark-haired lad with deep brown eyes joshed.

A loud guffaw broke forth as a lad standing next to Pete butted him with his shoulder.

Belinda noted that Pete and Max were several years older than many of the fellows, and she, the oldest miss.

"No red ones yet . . . good," Max said with real enthusiasm. "How many we looking for?"

"Ten!" Pete hooted as he dropped down on the opposite side

beside a pretty oval-faced girl with wide, down-slanted eyes that were the color of honey. "And I plan to find 'em all."

"Not if I have anything to say about it," shouted another fellow.

And the race was on. Belinda was all but forgotten as everyone dove into the task with as much gusto as before.

Max eased to the floor, with the help of his crutch, then reached up and tugged Belinda down beside him. "Hurry up. The side with the biggest pile of shucked corn wins a special dessert." He raised his voice. "What's the dessert this time?"

One of the younger-looking girls in looped braids and a round face resembling Ezzy Underwood's yelled back without looking up from shucking. "My ma made a orange cake with cinnamon and cloves. And it's got boiled icing on it too."

Now that was something worth working for. Belinda grabbed an ear and started stripping the green husk, joining Max and the rest in the race.

Once she had a rhythm going that matched the other girls', she could keep up with them. But the fellows' enthusiasm at the prospect of the dessert, plus their added strength, gave them a decided advantage.

Belinda's presence soon seemed all but forgotten, and within a few minutes the others started chatting amongst themselves again.

Remembering something Max had asked them, Belinda leaned close to him to whisper a question, not wanting the others to learn how really ignorant she was about the contest. "What about the red ears?" she asked. "What's the prize if I find a red ear of corn?"

His fast-working fingers slowed to a stop. He leaned even closer. "Whoever finds a red ear gets a kiss from anyone they choose."

"Oh." The heat of a brush fire rushed to her cheeks. She ducked her head and grabbed another ear of corn.

∽

Belinda's face had turned almost as red as her hair.

A burst of laughter pushed up from Max's chest. Holding his breath, he blocked its escape. His lady was already close to bolting. But still, a full-grown woman who'd never been kissed by a beau? Such a beautiful woman at that. Just the thought of giving her her very first kiss sent his hands and his lips to tingling. Max reached deep into the pile, renewing his quest for a red-dyed ear.

Belinda's shucking efforts, though, had slowed considerably. Her long agile fingers, he observed, even trembled slightly as they tore down an outer layer.

Extending mercy, he leaned close to her again and whispered, "It'll be a while. The red ones will be buried near the bottom. The farmers want to make sure we don't quit before all the husks are off."

Still not looking at him, she took a shuddering breath. "Gives me a little time to get used to the idea." She glanced up at him then, and her starburst eyes nearly shattered his own composure. And those full, soft lips . . .

Catching himself staring, he quickly turned back to the contest. Before this day was over, he'd know what they felt like touching his.

He wasn't the only one hard at work. Minutes passed in near silence as the pile of unhusked corn shrank; then unexpectedly Jacob, the Reardon clan's oldest, broke out in song.

" 'Enraptured I gaze when my Delia is by,' " he warbled, his hands still stripping away the coverings. He leaned toward the Clay girl, staring into her doelike eyes as he sang her name. " 'And drink the sweet poison of love from her eye.' "

Gracie, Jacob's flaxen-haired cousin sitting next to the dark-haired Delia, elbowed her in the ribs, and both of them fell into each other giggling.

" 'I feel soft passion pervade every part,' " Jacob sang even louder.

Several other fellows then lifted up their voices and joined him for the last phrase. " 'And pleasures unusual play round my fond heart.' "

Patting his hand over his own *fond* heart, Jacob brought from behind him the first ear that had been dipped in red dye.

A roar went up, the lads hooting and the girls squealing.

"Who ya gonna kiss, Jakie?" Gracie teased as she nudged Delia again.

The tall skinny lad rose up on his knees, his chest puffed out till his ribs showed through his chambray shirt. "Well, I reckon it ain't no secret." In one swift motion, he hauled the brunette girl named Delia up to her knees and kissed her square on the lips.

Another round of laughter exploded along with some loud clapping.

When he released the tanned miss, her cheeks had gained a tinge of extra color. Shrugging, she pretended nonchalance as she sank down and went back to shucking.

But Max had no doubt that the cobbler's daughter was pleased as punch. He stole a peek at Belinda next to him and saw that she was smiling along with everyone else. His own heart gave a little kick. He hadn't considered the immense pleasure he'd receive by merely watching Belinda enjoy herself.

And suddenly it became more important than ever that he make this a night to remember, one she could relive in the years to come . . . the night of her first party. And her first kiss.

Chapter Thirteen

All these young people, laughing and teasing . . . Belinda couldn't believe what a grand time she was having. Her hands were grimy, and the front of her skirt was covered in dust from the field corn. And she didn't care one whit.

" 'The higher up the cherry tree . . .' " The lilting tune came not from the lads this time, but from the lass Delia, the blonde next to her, and a fine-boned girl with eyes as light as her hair was dark. The three girls grinned boldly as they serenaded the others. " 'The sweeter grows the cherry. The more you kiss and hug a gal, the more she wants to marry.' " The last words they sang while wagging corn ears at the lads next to them.

Tall, skinny Jacob clutched his chest in mock horror. "La, no. Never!"

Belinda laughed along with the younger girls. Peeking past some escaped ringlets, she beheld Max and his jolly grin. With his sun-bleached hair and bronzed face, his gleaming teeth and the bluest of eyes, he could set any gal's heart to singing.

Another few moments brought a shrill cry of triumph and a waving red ear. But this time the shout came from a feminine voice—the slip of a girl with the startlingly light eyes.

"Who ya gonna kiss, Hope?" everyone started chanting. "Who ya gonna kiss?"

The delicate-limbed miss looked around the circle with a coy smile, her eyes moving from one male to the next.

When Hope's gaze stopped at Max, Belinda tensed. She hadn't thought that one of the girls might pick him to kiss. And she found herself not particularly liking the idea.

To Belinda's relief, the ebony-haired lass's gaze moved on around the circle until it stopped again. It settled on a lad sitting next to her. He had even features and light, ginger brown eyes, and looked scarcely old enough to shave. Sixteen, maybe seventeen. Hope's smile suddenly turned shy. "Well, I reckon since you are the closest . . ."

The young man rose up on his knees and cupped her delicate heart-shaped face in his hands while he looked at her, a long quiet moment. Then he kissed her—not fast like the first fellow had Delia, but gently, tenderly.

Belinda began to feel somehow embarrassed at watching what was clearly a very meaningful moment. She looked down to the corn in her lap and started shucking again.

A near-grown lad with the same dark eyes and hair as Delia began another lively song. " 'In Reardon Vale there lives a lass more bright than a May-day morn.' " He swung a flirty gaze at the girl beside him, the silky blonde with a sweet dimpled smile.

She gave him a playful shove.

" 'Whose charms all other maids' surpass, a rose without a thorn.' "

Belinda recognized the tune as "The Lass of Richmond Hill," not Reardon Vale, but it surely did turn the lass's head.

" 'The gal so neat,' " he continued with a cocky grin, " 'with smiles so sweet, has won my right goodwill.' "

Belinda expected him to do as the first singer had and produce a red ear. But he didn't. He continued to dig and shuck as he sang.

Instead, a wild snatching and grabbing scramble between Pete Dagget and a lad several years his junior took place across the diminishing pile. Pete broke free and leapt to his feet with the prize. He held a red ear aloft. Ripping off the outer layers, he tossed the cob onto the pile behind him, then plucked the light-haired girl to her feet.

She didn't seem all that pleased. Or was it just her naturally sad-looking eyes?

In one swift move, the coarse-featured fellow bent her back and kissed the helpless miss with a noisy smack, finishing with a triumphant bellow that was louder than that of his cheering companions.

As he drew her up straight again, the girl shot a glance at Max, one wrought with meaning . . . a meaning Belinda could only guess at.

And she didn't like how it made her feel.

Pete must have noticed, too, because he shifted his attention from one to the other then, unsmiling, pulled her down beside him. Almost immediately though, his long-toothed grin returned. "Max," he called across the green heap, "Liza here says your leg should be healed in another coupla weeks. I reckon that means you'll be chasin' off again, leavin' all of us behind."

" 'How swift the hours did pass away,' " the lad with brown eyes piped in, singing, " 'with the girl I left behind me.' "

"The girl I left behind me"?

All attention again centered on Belinda.

Her own gaze dropped, and she stared at her hands frantically ripping away husks. Had the others seen how disappointed she'd be when Max left?

"Ma Smith ain't sure about my leg yet," Max said in an even tone that gave no hint of his feelings. "But she's pleased with the progress so far."

"I know you," Pete blustered. "You'll be outta here in no time." He seemed determined that everyone knew, especially Belinda. "You always said you wasn't gonna end up tied down to an anvil iron like your pa."

"When we're young we're apt to say most anything, Pete. For now, I'm just—," Max stopped speaking so unexpectedly that Belinda looked over at him to learn why.

Lips parted, he was staring at her hands.

And so was everyone else.

Belinda cringed. *What now?*

"Well, Miss Belinda," the flaxen-haired miss, Gracie, called out, her eyes bright, "who do you choose?"

"Choose?" What did the girl mean? Then Belinda looked down. In her hands, she held a red ear.

From the expression on her face, a body would've thought she had hold of a panther's tail, not an ear of corn. When she finally quit staring at it, she turned panicked eyes to Max.

If he hadn't been so happy at the prospect of kissing her, he would've tried to sympathize. "I promise, I won't bite," he said, spreading his hands—the most disarming thing he could think to do at the moment. He reached over and took the red ear from her. Shucking it, he tossed the clean corn behind him, then took her hands in his and captured her gaze. "Do you choose me?"

"Yes." Her whisper was barely audible but unmistakable.

Just to make sure she didn't change her mind, he moved his hands to her shoulders and lowered his lips to hers . . . those full, beautifully shaped, slightly trembling lips.

And he was not disappointed. Though the kiss lasted no more than a few seconds, he came away with his lips buzzing and his lungs filled with her lavender scent, his heart banging helter-skelter. Then, while he steadied his breathing, he drank in the wonder expressed in her eyes.

It was a moment before he realized the noise wasn't just his pulse pounding in his ears but the clapping of his friends. Reluctantly, he released Belinda and, smiling sheepishly, went back to work.

She did, too, her lithe yet trembling fingers moving fast.

Once Max noticed everyone else doing the same, he stole a sidelong glance at his lovely lady, his gaze gravitating to her lips. How he wished he could reach out and touch them this very instant. How he wished their first kiss had not been here in front of his neighbors, but alone, where he wouldn't have to pretend it meant nothing more than a mere prize in a game.

Even after the last ear of corn had been husked and the last kiss witnessed by one and all, Belinda could not forget the one she'd received. And just as Max had promised, he hadn't left her side from the moment they arrived. He now took a place right beside her at one end of a keg-and-board bench to give his splinted leg room to stretch. They sat at a long eating table set up on grass in the dappled shade of a maple, both attempting to brush the corn dust from their clothes.

The other young ladies, their own dresses just as dirty, had not seemed to mind. They'd merely laughed at each other as they washed their hands at the well then set the table and placed the serving bowls, platters, and several beverage pitchers on it.

Now, with a moment to ponder as the other merrymakers took their places, Belinda couldn't stop wondering what it would have been like if Max had given her her first kiss on the ride home instead—without a passel of strangers looking on . . . within the haven of the buggy bonnet . . . his arms around her, holding her close, his heartbeat mingling with hers. The thought caused her lips to tingle again.

The soft breeze was filled with a mix of delicious aromas. But Belinda couldn't find her appetite for thinking of the man beside her . . . so powerful of build, yet his touch was always so gentle. Always so considerate . . .

"I say the oldest man at the table should have to say grace," Ezra Underwood, their host, said, sidestepping his duty.

Max and Pete eyed each other from across the table, the two obviously older than the others.

"Wasn't you born a couple months before me'n Paul?" Pete asked. "Anyways, you're the preacher's son. You must'a had a lot more practice."

Max's thick brows dipped into a V. "Pete, you know perfectly well you two are older than me by half a year. But no never-mind. Let's bow our heads." After a couple seconds' pause, he began. Max was a born leader. "Lord, we thank You for the fine harvest of the Underwoods' early August corn. And for all the good food and fun You've provided in this gathering of old friends. And new," he added. "We ask this in the name of Your Son, Jesus. Amen."

Before the *amen* was out of Max's mouth, Pete had snatched up the nearest bowl and was scooping potato salad onto his plate. "Let's get them vittles a-movin'," he ordered in a loud voice. "I got me a powerful hunger."

Beside Pete, Liza shot him a disgusted look.

All evening the girl had seemed put out with the boisterous fellow. Belinda wondered why she'd bothered to come to the party with him at all. Especially since most of her smiles had been directed at Max.

"Would you care for some corn bread?" Max asked. He held a platter of cut squares in front of her.

"Why, yes, thank you." Feeling a bit abashed for thinking jealous thoughts while he'd been thinking only of her, she took one then passed the plate down the table.

"Miss Belinda," Howie, the dark-haired lad who had an enthusiastic love of singing, called from down the table. "Max told Pete you and your folks live downriver 'twixt here and Nashville."

"Yes, that's true," she answered with a polite smile, hoping he wouldn't get any more inquisitive.

"My pa makes shoes for most everybody between here and where the Caney Fork feeds into the Cumberland, and we never got any orders from no Grays. Whereabouts do you folks live?"

"You trying to cut in on my territory, boy?" Max asked, chuckling.

But Belinda knew his intent was to protect her. She reached over and squeezed the top of his hand.

Liza noticed—her gaze latching on to Belinda's gesture.

Belinda quickly withdrew her hand and picked up her glass, as much to block herself from Liza's stare than anything else. She took a sip of chilled cider as the lad spoke again.

"We already got more territory than we can handle." He flashed his expressive brown eyes at the girl he'd kissed earlier, the dimpled blonde, Gracie. "I just ain't heard'a no Grays."

"That's because my family name isn't Gray," Belinda said, jumping in before she forced Max into the compromising situation of having to lie or expose the truth. "My last name is Gregg. We have a place on yon side of the Caney."

Liza sat up straighter. "You're the ones with that fancy milled-board house. The one with the green shutters."

The young folks around the table stirred, their eyes all turning on Belinda. The cat was out of the bag.

"We been expectin' to see you folks in church for quite some time now," Liza continued, her voice sweet but deadly. "For nigh onto three years."

Feeling as cornered as she'd feared she would be, Belinda's belief that she shouldn't have come was being confirmed.

"Belinda's mother is in poor health," Max provided in her place. "Perhaps if we all keep Mrs. Gregg in our daily prayers, she and her family might one day be able to attend. Fact is, this is a rare outing for Miss Belinda. Let's not spoil it with a lot of—" Max stopped short and looked over his shoulder.

Belinda followed his lead, hearing the clop of an approaching horse.

On a gray workhorse Brother Bremmer rode in, his usually comfortable expression now grim.

~

What could possibly bring Pops to this gathering?

Max hoisted himself up and grabbed his crutch. His father wouldn't be riding out here at suppertime unless something was very wrong.

Rolf swung down from Kaiser before the animal had come to a standing stop. "Sorry I am to bust in on da party, but I come to fetch Peter home."

In a boot-scuffling scramble, Pete dislodged himself from his bench and strode around the table. "Why?" His voice sounded harsh with alarm.

Max's pops wrapped an arm around the shorter Pete and guided him away from the group at the table. Max kept pace. Whatever the bad news, he was certain Pete would want him close by.

"Peter," his father said in a quiet rumble, "I am sorry to tell you dis, but your brother, Paul, had da accident. He is cleaning da hoof of a plow horse, *und* he vas kicked in da head. He never wakes up. I am sorry."

Max's old-time friend turned sallow white. Absently, Pete pushed a strand of wavy black hair from his forehead. Then he backed up a step. "No. Paul'n me, we do everything together. Always have." He jerked away from Rolf. *"No!"*

Max couldn't believe Paul was dead either. It was impossible. All their growing-up years, the three of them had been inseparable.

Rolf filled the space Pete had created between them and took the twin by the shoulders. "I know dis is hard to belief. But try to hear vhat I am saying. Now is da time for you to ask God to give you all da strength you can handle. *Und* His comfort. Grab on to His comfort. Can you do dat?"

Pete looked up with bleak blue eyes and crumbled against Max's father.

Rolf hugged him close. "I pray *mit* you. Come, ve pray on da ride home. Your mama is asking for you."

Max's own insides felt like they'd been punched with a fist. Paul, gone. He squeezed Pete's shoulder. "I'll go with you." Then, remembering his lady, Max turned to his father. "Is it all right if I take your horse? I'll go with Pete if you wouldn't mind seeing Belinda home. And Liza," he added in afterthought.

"Are you sure you can handle it?" his pops asked, a pastor's concern in his voice.

Max nodded. He glanced back at the table. His beautiful Belinda had come to her feet. He started toward her.

She met him halfway, her lovely features etched with a mix of confusion and concern.

"I'm sorry," he said, memorizing the curve of her cheekbone, her lips. "This promised to be the most wonderful evening, but I must leave you. There's been a death in Pete's family."

"Oh, la." Her gaze gravitated to Pete, still being supported by Pops. "Is there anything I can do?"

"No, I don't think so. Go with my pops; he'll see you and Liza home."

In his grief, Max ached to hold her and never let go. Instead, he placed two of his fingers to his lips, then touched them to hers.

Her lips parted, and her eyes held even more questions as he turned and left her.

Chapter Fourteen

Sitting crowded between Liza Smith and Brother Bremmer in the buggy was definitely not the leave-taking Belinda had planned. The glances Max had slipped her during the party had set her heart to humming with anticipation of the ride home alone with him. But now, all had changed. If Paul Dagget had been half as lively as his twin, such a huge hole his passing would make.

The gloom of death now rode on every breath of air as they traveled the east road to the Smiths'. In the glow of the long summer twilight, the younger but more worldly Liza had lost her haughty air. Those tilted, honey brown eyes looked all the sadder as she leaned forward to glimpse the pastor beyond Belinda.

"I feel sore guilty," Liza bemoaned. "I was snippy with Pete all afternoon. I treated him like he didn't mean nothin' to me. He was bein' so pushy, tryin' to get me to say I'd marry up with him before Paul got back. And now . . . ." Her thin voice trailed off.

Brother Bremmer nodded his massive silver head. "The Daggets, dey is going to need all our sympat'y now. *Und* I know you vill do vhat you can for dem. Pete, more dan da udders. Him *und* Paul, dey vas two peas in da same pod. Like two halfs of a whole. Pete is going to feel mighty lost *mit*out his twin."

"I know. And what's worse, the last time I saw Paul, I wasn't nice to him either. He was trying to get me to say yes to him before he left. I wouldn't even let him kiss me good-bye. And now he's gone forever. What harm," she said, her voice rising with emotion, "would a little kiss have done? His last kiss before he died."

Belinda wanted to speak up, tell the girl she'd done nothing to feel guilty for. She herself couldn't imagine being bombarded by one, much less two, Petes. But she didn't feel it was her place.

The minister sent Liza a comforting smile as he drove the black horse around a chuckhole.

"Liza girl. Dem lads vas yust having fun—more *mit* each udder dan you. If you had said *ja* to either of dem, dey probably be struck dumb." He reached across Belinda and patted Liza's knee. "A body can only do da best dey can *mit* each day da Lord gives to us. Alvays ve expect tomorrow to come. Ve need to be living *mit* da knowing dis could be da last day for me or you or somebody else ve love. Like da goot Lord says, don't let da sun set on your anger . . . *und* your kindness."

"You're right, Brother Rolf." Liza sat up straighter. "I have another apology to make. To Miss Belinda here."

Surprised, Belinda swung her attention to the younger girl.

"I didn't treat you with the kindness I should've today. I never met you before, yet I treated you like you wasn't welcome, like you'd come to steal what didn't belong to you. Please forgive me."

Belinda was rendered speechless by the girl's naked apology.

So completely unexpected. "I, too, owe you one. I thought you were a rather uppish young miss. But now I know your true feelings run deep and pure." How many other souls, Belinda wondered, had she also misjudged during these past years of isolation?

"From now on," Liza said in a faltering whisper, "I'll try to live up to that. Deep feelings, pure and true." Then those sad eyes spilled over with tears. "Poor Paul. Poor Pete."

"Paul, he is in da far better place. For all da pranks dem two boys pull, dey haf strong belief in Jesus Christ. Da family, dey need our prayers. Ve pray God is giving Max da right vords to say." Max's father glanced over his shoulder in the direction his son and Pete had ridden.

After Brother Bremmer's request that they pray for Max and his mission, Belinda began to feel unworthy again. While she'd been experiencing disappointment at being abandoned by him as much as feeling empathy for Pete and his family, she'd not considered the solemn task that lay before Max. She'd been no less shallow and unfeeling than Liza Smith.

She took the weeping girl's thin hand. "If you are willing, I'd like for us to be friends."

~

Max rode with Pete toward the Dagget farm without either of them speaking. Never in his life had he seen Pete more distraught. Max knew he should be giving Pete some sort of comfort, as his father surely would have, but he was having a hard time with his own struggle over the sudden death.

He rubbed his aching leg while also realizing that by usurping his father's position, he would be required to furnish spiritual comfort not only to Pete but to his parents as well. But what could he say about such a fickle turn of events? If anyone should be dead, it should surely be himself. He'd been the reckless one, riding deep into Indian country with Drew and Crysta Reardon, then far beyond, facing the myriad dangers of wild animals, unknown terrain, radical weather, not to mention Indian war parties that would've loved to have had his blond scalp hanging in their lodges.

But as the Reardons had staunchly believed during that first long journey to Black Bear's encampment, the Lord had sent them on their mission, and they were merely following His all-knowing lead. Although Max's friends had faced their own danger from time to time, the Lord had always kept them safe. As his father did, they lived their lives in God's hand.

Drew's and Crysta's faith had been wonderful to watch, but as time went by, Max's lust for adventure had caused him to leave them *and* the Lord behind, in many respects. He'd followed his own dream of hunting and exploring, never asking if these life-risking forays were God's will for him. The most he'd ever done was pray for deliverance whenever he found himself in a tight spot.

And not only had he lived a wholly selfish life, but he'd left his parents at home to wonder if they'd ever see their youngest child again. Then for him to be brought home near death . . .

Max could hardly believe he'd survived. He should've died of fever and infection if not from the wounds. But now, here he was, this selfish sinner, riding to the Daggets as if he had the right to bring God's comforting words to their grieving souls.

How could he explain why Paul, who'd dutifully gone to help a sick relative, had been killed and not him? Or why their youngest son had been taken before his parents?

By the time they neared the Daggets' place three miles north of the settlement, Pete, in his hurry, was a good fifty yards ahead. When Max rode in, lamps were lit on the porch and Pete's horse had been left to wander toward the barn.

Max spotted Pete on the front step, his arms wrapped around his mother, who stood above him on the porch. His head lay on her shoulder, hers on his, both of them shaking with sobs.

Never in all the years Max had known the twins had he ever seen either of them cry. Panic rose up in Max. He shouldn't have come. He pulled the reins of his mount hard to turn him around. Escape.

But he couldn't do that. He loosened his grip. It wasn't as if he'd been dragged here. He'd volunteered. Swallowing down his panic, he guided Kaiser back toward the Daggets' home.

Mr. Dagget saw Max and stepped past his wife and Pete to greet him. As Max brought Kaiser to a halt, the older, still-rangy man also stopped. "I thought you was Brother Rolf." He scanned the road behind Max. "You're ridin' his horse. Ain't he comin' back?"

"I wanted to be here for Pete, Mr. Dagget. Pops said he'd be by again in the morning. Before church. He took Liza and my lady friend home for us."

The angle-faced man glanced back at his weeping wife. "Not till mornin'? We could sure use him tonight."

Feeling even more inadequate, Max leaned forward while straining to hoist his lame leg over the horse's rump. He didn't want to ask for help and seem any more useless than he already was.

Lord, I'm doing it again, Max prayed as he lowered himself to the ground. *Waiting till I'm in trouble before I pray. Forgive me. But please don't make them pay for me thinking I had to be here instead of Pops. Please give me the words You want them to hear.*

~

"I want to thank you for carrying me home, Brother Bremmer." Belinda remained beside the buggy as the minister climbed aboard again after helping her down to the gravel drive. "And do forward my condolences to Mr. Dagget and his family when you next see them."

"*Ja,* dey vill 'preciate your concern." He spoke in the dim light of the lone carriage lantern. "Nicer it vill be, I t'ink, if you tell dem yourself . . . tomorrow at church."

"I . . . uh." She didn't want to give him an outright no after all his kindnesses. "I'll speak to my parents."

Holding her in his gaze, he nodded. "I am holding you to dat." He'd obviously known she'd just been placating him.

"I promise."

As the old German minister drove away, Belinda started up the walk, noticing that the parlor was still well lit. Realizing it was no more than an hour or so past dark, she knew her parents were still up. But was she ready to answer the questions she knew they would ask?

"Belinda, you're home early." Her father's voice came from the darkness of the veranda, startling her.

"I didn't see you there."

"We're out here watching the lightning bugs," her mother's feathery voice added.

Walking up the wide steps, Belinda saw their heads silhouetted as they sat side by side in front of one of the windows.

"Since it's still early," her father said, continuing his probe, "you should've invited Max to come up and sit a spell."

Belinda dropped down on the bench swing. She wouldn't get away without telling them everything. She explained about the death of Paul Dagget, and both her parents commiserated a moment, expressing how devastated they would be if she were suddenly taken from them.

"My heart goes out to the Dagget family," her father said. "And my prayers."

"Yes," her mother agreed. Then after a reflective moment, she asked, "Tell me, dear, up until Brother Bremmer came with the tragic news, were you enjoying yourself?"

Caught off guard, a blush burned Belinda's cheeks. She was grateful the only light came through the windows. "Yes, Mama, I had a fine time." Trying to appear nonchalant, she started the bench swinging with her foot. "But you never told me a kissing game was part of a cornhusking contest."

Both her parents chuckled softly.

Then her mother leaned toward Belinda. "If you recall, you never gave us a chance."

"I reckon I didn't. But after the way Daddy literally tossed me into the buggy . . ."

"Well?" her persistent dad asked. "Did you get kissed?"

Belinda swallowed down her embarrassment; then, lest she be teased, she decided on the bold answer. "That I did."

"And it's about time." Her father gave his knee a resounding slap.

"Speaking of that—," Belinda began.

"Of kissing?" her mother piped in.

"No. That maybe it's time—" She placed her feet on the floor, stopping the gentle sway of the bench and faced them more directly. "Brother Bremmer invited us to church tomorrow. He understands the reason for our reluctance, and he still wants us to come."

"Darling," her mother said, "you know that long ago we decided the only way we could live in peace—"

"I know, Mama. But Brother Bremmer is fully aware of our

situation. And after getting to know him and Mrs. Bremmer and some of the valley's young people—they all hold him in the highest regard—I think this man is a godly leader who would not let any of the bad rumors start."

Her mother sank deeper into her chair. "We've built this lovely home here. The thought of having to move again . . . I couldn't bear to have to start all over again."

"Mama, I don't want to push you into something that would cause you distress, but I know how often you've said you missed going to church services on the Sabbath."

"Oh, I do. But—"

"And you and Daddy have often told me that we can trust God with our greatest hopes and fears. Can't we trust Him to protect us and provide for us now, with these people?"

"Ladies." Her father folded one of his wife's hands in his own. "I say we chance venturing forth, but by taking only one step at a time . . . very careful steps. So why don't we get up in the morning, feed the animals, put on our finery—"

"Not too fine, Daddy. Folks hereabouts dress more simply than city folks."

"Not too fancy." A smile was in his voice as he draped an arm expansively across the back of her mother's chair. "And we drive in to church, enjoy the services, and offer our condolences to the grieving family. After that, we can decide if we want to take any more steps into the valley's life. And, sweetheart—" he bent and kissed his wife's temple, this loving, ever-patient man—"we'll not take a single step you can't handle."

Felicity ran fingers down her husband's cheek then turned back to Belinda. "I am getting better. I've had only two bad spells since we moved here. And, besides . . ." Her eyes sparkled in a shaft of light as she turned a smile on her daughter. ". . . our daughter has had to wait to get her first kiss until she was twenty-one years of age. We certainly don't want her to wait that long again for another."

~

Near midnight, Max rode past his family's house on his way to stable Kaiser. To his surprise, he saw that the parlor lamps were both glowing strong. His father must still be working on tomorrow's sermon.

Or waiting up to learn how his son had fared at the Daggets'.

He heard the front door open. Glancing back, he saw his father's shadowy form move down the porch steps, no doubt to learn if Max had been successful.

"Son, vait up," he called as he hurried to catch Max. "I help you put avay da horse."

As weary as Max was from the draining evening with the grieving Daggets, he was grateful when his father first steadied his descent from the tall plow horse and then handed him his crutch before beginning to question him. After lighting a lamp from some furnace coals, Rolf started loosening the saddle cinch while Max removed the bit and bridle.

"*Na ja,* so tell me," his pops said, sliding the saddle from the horse's back, "da family, dey vas better vhen you leaf?"

Max vented a heavy sigh. "I think so. I hope so. It's hard to say. I'm sure you would've done a better job. I should've left it to you."

"You vas gone a long time." He dropped the saddle over a wooden horse. "I t'ink dey like you being dere to share da grief *mit* dem."

"I hope so." Max handed him the bridle. "Remember back when we were in school, you'd come over every day and give us kids verses to learn?"

"*Ja.*"

"I must've learned hundreds over the years. But when it came time to lend the Daggets some comfort, I could only come up with a couple."

"*Und* what did you remember?"

"I can't remember where the first one came from, or the exact words, but it goes something like, No one knows what'll happen tomorrow, for what is a life? Nothing but a vapor that appears for a little time, then vanishes away."

"It sound somet'ing like a verse in da book of James."

Max shifted his weight off his bad leg. "It didn't seem quite right for what I wanted them to hear. But I thank God for bringing another passage to my mind. This one fascinated me when I first learned it as a kid. I think I got these words right: 'I would not have you to be ignorant, brethren, concerning them which are asleep, that ye sorrow not, even as others which have no hope. For if we believe that Jesus died and rose again, even so them also which sleep in Jesus will God bring with him.' " Max shrugged. "I was hoping to help them think of Paul as just gone away for a while but not forever. Of course they can't help but miss him. But hopefully they won't think of his death as quite so final."

"You did goot. Dat is part of da great hope ve haf as Christians."

"Then I mentioned a few passages in Psalms. I'm afraid they comforted Pete's folks more than him. He kept blaming himself for all the pranks he'd pulled on his brother, the ornery things he'd said. But you know how they were. I tried to tell him he never gave more than he got. The two were always having fun with each other."

"*Ja.*" His father opened the stall gate for Kaiser to enter. "Dose two. Dey been togedder before dey is born. Pete don't know nut'ing about living *mit*out Paul. It vill be hard."

Max grunted. "He must feel like I did when I thought I might lose my leg, only worse—if that's possible."

"*Ja,* somet'ing like dat." After stabling the gray gelding, Rolf clapped a hand on his son's shoulder. "You know da Daggets goot as me. I'm sure you tell dem vhat dey need to hear. Losing a child, dat is a hard t'ing."

"I hope you're right. And now there's something I want to say to you. I never really understood or appreciated all you did as the valley's minister. As a kid, I knew you spent a lot of time reading the Bible and your books on theology so you could come up with a different sermon each week. But I never really thought just how difficult those emergencies you got called out on could be. Having the right words for every situation."

"Da brilliant genius I am not. If you vant to know da secret, read da book of Proverbs. I pray for da visdom of God before every place I go to visit." Grabbing the lantern hanging from the post spike, his father started for the door. "Is late. Let's go back to da house."

Max joined him, remembering he had some questions of his own about the evening. "Speaking of places, when you took Liza and Belinda home, were they all right? This whole thing must have been very upsetting for them."

"Dey talk some. I t'ink tonight gives dem time to become friends."

"Friends? That's wonderful. I hated deserting Belinda after I'd promised I wouldn't leave her side all evening."

"Mayhap you can make it up to her tomorrow. I ask her to come to church."

"Oh, I doubt she'll come. She turned me down flat last week." But his father did have a mighty persuasive way about him. "Did she say she would?" The idea of seeing Belinda so soon again started his blood pumping harder. "You did say I'd come by and fetch her, didn't you?"

"*Nein.* I ask her to come *und* bring her folks. *Und* I t'ink she vants dis too. Ve add da Greggs to our nightly prayers, *ja?*"

Nightly prayers . . . something Max had pretty much left behind along with his home and family. "Pops, on the ride home tonight, I had a crazy thought."

"Dat your accident come right as da Daggets need you to be here for dem," his wise father interjected as they strolled across the open field. "You know da Bible says dat God, He takes da bad dat happens to us *und* turns it into goot for dose who are called to His purpose."

"Aye, that's part of it. But I was thinking of the Greggs. That maybe God allowed me to survive not just for my own selfish purposes, but so that I could befriend Belinda and her family. That the Lord wants me to help bring them back into the fold. You know, it could be that the Lord chose me to be here for them. *Me.*"

A heavy arm dropped across Max's shoulders. "It does dis old heart goot, knowing you vant to do dis kindness for dem folks. But even more, dat you are listening to da call of God. 'Specially," he added, his gravelly voice crumbling into a chuckle, "if it gifs you more chance to spend time *mit* da beauty of da flaming hair. *Ja?*"

Chapter Fifteen

Max wondered if perhaps he'd splashed on too much of the mint water after shaving. He wasn't accustomed to bothering with such civilized niceties. Dressed in his brocade waistcoat and buff breeches, his shirt bleached to an eye-hurting white, he stood on the top landing of the church steps awaiting the Greggs' arrival. A morning breeze teased his hair, making him wish he'd put on a hat—even though he'd always thought it foolish to wear one just to walk from the house next door to the church and then hold it on his lap for an entire service.

Hearing the clop and rumble of another outfit coming from the direction of the ferry dock, he leaned forward for a better view of the road. At the same time, he tugged down his waistcoat.

Realizing the family coming was not the Greggs, he eased back on his crutch and noticed that a cluster of women gathered nearby were watching him. Obviously, they'd heard about him and the lovely lady he took to the cornhusking the day before.

And here he was, putting on a grand show for them.

How many years had it been since he'd stood at this very same spot, waiting for some young miss to arrive? Fussing over the fit of clothes he usually never gave a second thought? Or how pretty he smelled. There could be no doubt to anyone watching that he was besotted.

And today of all days.

Any minute now, his pops and the Daggets would be riding in together for church. His mind should be on the family and their loss.

The cravat at his neck was already too hot. He pulled it away from his skin and glanced up to the sky. Fluffy clouds floated overhead on a warm breeze up from the gulf. It would be a muggy day.

More conveyances arrived with families aboard, prompting him to offer greetings to neighbors he'd known for years. Some of the older folk passed on by to wait in the cool of the high-ceilinged sanctuary, while the younger people joined various groupings, and the kids romped about. Their mothers, of course, yelled at them to keep their good clothes clean.

But today an extra tension filled the air. Not quite so many smiles, the conversations more subdued. News always spread fast, and no one seemed surprised this morning to hear the news about Paul Dagget. Today would be particularly sad for the close-knit community.

The Reardon clan arrived in two wagons with Ike's oldest, Jacob, riding horseback alongside. The lad probably planned to go visit Delia Clay after church. He'd certainly enjoyed kissing her yester's eve. Twice. Both Delia and the lad had been lucky enough to find a red ear.

Max rubbed his fingers over his lips at the thought of

Belinda's kiss, and his mind started to drift in that direction again.

But the newest member of the Reardon clan caught his attention.

Mrs. Emma Jane Thompson did manage a smile as she allowed her brother-in-law to help her off the back of his farm wagon, but her eyes continued to have that hunted look. She glanced around as if danger might lurk behind one of the trees shading the churchyard.

He wondered how long it would take for her to feel safe again. Then he wondered if Belinda's mother would be as anxious, leaving the tranquil haven they'd created for themselves.

Newly arrived, Liza Smith left a company of several young misses and, looking straight at him, strolled toward him in a froth of pink summer muslin. She looked rather grown-up today, with her hair pulled up beneath a flower-bedecked straw hat and short white gloves. "How did it go with the Daggets last night?" she asked when she reached the porch landing.

"I'm not sure. Paul's death is such a sudden blow."

"Aye." Her golden gaze wavered. "Pete without Paul is like . . . I don't know. I can't figure out how to feel. They were so much alike. I'm not even sure which one I'm mourning. It's very confusing." She lifted a delicate shoulder and quirked a helpless smile.

"It is hard. I think, in the end, we'll be mourning both of them. Without Paul, Pete will have to become his own new person."

"I never thought about that." Her gaze drifted away, then returned. "Me and Miss Belinda had us a fine talk on the way home last night. She seemed real nice for bein' a spinster lady and all. I know fellas don't usually warm up to gals with red hair and freckles—them bein' known for their bad tempers. But I don't find them unbecoming on her. Not at all. Do you?"

"No." Was that how others saw Belinda? Or just Liza? Was this just a sneaky way of bad-talking her, trying to make him think less of his lady?

A hurried exchange of whispers drew Max's attention.

The Dagget wagon came rolling past the smithy, with his father, already garbed in his Sabbath black, riding alongside on Pitch. The three Daggets sat crowded close on the driver's bench, Pete and his father on either side of the solemn-faced older woman, and all of them wearing the black of mourning. Their mouths were drawn into tight lines, their eyes downcast.

As they pulled to a stop in the hitching area, church members converged on them, helping Mrs. Dagget down, hugging each of them in a circle of comfort . . . the church family sharing their sorrow, trying to absorb some of the pain.

And these were the same people who'd been praying for his wounds, who'd come visiting . . . the neighbors, whom in his arrogance, he'd pretended to appreciate for his mother's sake. For all their little quirks and foibles, these were good, God-fearing folks who deserved far more credit and respect than he'd ever given them in word or deed.

Perhaps when he returned to the frontier this time, he'd have enough sense to know all that he was leaving behind. Friendships of great value. And Belinda.

He glanced toward the river.

"Liza." Betsy, her slightly graying mother, stood at the bottom of the steps. "You, especially, need to go say somethin' comfortin' to Pete."

The girl glanced back at Max. "I reckon I better. He does look plumb beat down."

Watching her descend, Max sent a plea heavenward. *Lord,*

give her a tender heart. And words that'll fill Pete's soul with Your peace. More than what I managed last night.

Max's father lumbered up the steps, flushed and looking hot in his preaching suit. He paused at the top. "Did da Greggs come?"

"Not yet." Max glanced toward the river.

Frowning, his father drew a timepiece from his vest pocket. "Da hour is past for da service to begin. Ring da bell. Ve start now."

Max shot one last glance down the road, then let out a lungful of air. Neither Belinda nor her parents were coming.

And why should he think they would? Why should he think one word from his father or one kiss from him could erase years of keeping to themselves? He'd been standing here all this time, just making a fool of himself.

∾

After refreshing his memory by rereading the apostle Paul's first letter to the Thessalonians Monday morning, Max left the house determined to lighten some of his father's many burdens. He might not be much good at ministering to people's needs, but he could bend iron with the best of them.

After he and his pops had the furnace roaring and were feeding in some pig iron, the older man started whistling a lively hymn, a sure sign he was pleased that his son was working beside him.

For a change, Max didn't mind. His father had spent his whole life giving to others—he deserved to have something helpful come his way once in a while.

A couple of hours later, the two stopped pounding the rough edges off an order of nails, long enough for a replenishing drink of springwater. Sweat beaded on Max's face and neck, but he hardly noticed. The talk between them had been good, especially the discussion on varying interpretations of the second coming of Jesus.

As Max downed the last of his water, he noticed a shadow in the wide doorway.

Mr. Gregg came walking in. "Whew, it sure is hot in here," the lean-built man said with a congenial smile on his gaunt face. "Makes me glad, especially in the summer, that I took up working with clay instead. Our kiln gets just as hot, but it's outside and off to itself."

The man sounded unexpectedly cheerful. Max took that as a good sign, though he wasn't ready to completely relax. He pulled a kerchief from a pocket of his leather apron, wiped his brow, then extended a hand. "What can we do for you?"

"I don't mean to interrupt, but I was wondering if you and Brother Bremmer could spare me a couple of minutes?"

"Sure t'ing. A break out in da cool air vill do us bot' goot. Max, you take *Herr* Gregg over to da house. Have Inga bring us out some lemonade. I come after I pour dis last batch of nails to cool."

By the time a still-on-edge Max and Mr. Gregg were settled on the petunia-scented porch with their drinks, his father joined them. The senior Bremmer collected a third tall glass his wife had left for him on the railing and took his place in one of the crude homemade chairs, cushioned by feather-filled pillows.

"Ah," Rolf sighed after gulping down half his citrusade, "I can never get enough to drink in da summer."

The few wispy clouds held little promise of blocking the sun, but the heavy shade of the surrounding elms offered some relief from the August temperature.

Rolf's chair groaned as he placed his glass on a side table and settled back. "I vas hoping to see you *und* your vomenfolk at church yesterday, *Herr* Gregg."

"Yes, that's why I've come."

Max, growing impatient with the pleasantries, wanted to shout, "Spit it out." But he bit back the words, knowing he'd have to wait for Mr. Gregg to continue.

"Actually, my wife, Felicity, and I," he finally said, "would like to rejoin a community of believers more for our daughter's sake than our own. Our isolation has deprived Belinda of having friends her own age. Beaus. A chance to marry."

Marry. Of course that would be what he'd want for his daughter. Had he come to ask Max his intentions?

Max's hands went clammy. A wife would change everything, his entire life . . . not that the thought hadn't crossed his mind, especially in his weaker moments.

"But Felicity has serious concerns," Mr. Gregg continued. "You two already have some idea of her problem." The man stalled again by placing his own drink on the table that separated him from Max. "And we've decided to trust you with more of an understanding of her illness. My wife and I were raised on the same plantation. I was the son of the farm's teacher and minister. Felicity was the daughter of the owner. The kindest thing I can say about her parents is that they had a loveless marriage. Felicity's mother spent most of her time staying with friends in Charleston."

Max leaned back in his chair. This had the markings of a long story. But already there was an interesting thought he knew he'd want to mull over later . . . Mr. Gregg and he had similar beginnings, both having had a minister for a father.

"When one of her younger brothers was eleven, he recklessly dove into a dangerous spot at their swimming hole. He hit a boulder and broke his neck. Not only did my Felicity have the misfortune of witnessing his death, but she watched her father beat to death the boy slave who'd been with them for not keeping better watch. In that one day, my wife lost two people she deeply cared about, and she lost all love and respect for her father.

"This had a profound effect on her. During the next few years she teetered between bouts of rage and melancholy. My dad and I tried to help her, but her father, Mr. Durant, considered her behavior as a betrayal of the family and an embarrassment. Rather than allow her to, as he called it, 'sully their name and her other brother's future,' he planned to send her to an asylum for the insane.

"I'd grown to love Felicity over the years but had always thought a union between her and the son of lowly Irish immigrants was hopeless. But when I learned that Mr. Durant was going to have her locked up, I went to him and convinced him to let me take her far away, where no stain of insanity would ever darken the family name."

"I've seen your devotion to your wife," Max said. "It's clear you love her very much."

Mr. Gregg's skeletal features softened with a smile. "My Felicity is very easy to love . . . most of the time. But it's those other trying times that I'm here about. We left the Durants', and I took a position north of Columbia on another plantation teaching and ministering, as my father had trained me to do. Regardless of the fact that Felicity had lived in a grand mansion, she was quite happy in more humble surroundings. And the yearly allowance her father sends has always provided extras my own income never could.

"But after Belinda was born, Felicity fell into her first period of melancholy since our marriage. It lasted only a short time. But three years later when our son was born, it happened again. Thinking it would be better if she were away from the cruelties of plantation life, I took a position as schoolmaster in a village up in hill country. For the next couple of years she did fine. One couldn't ask for a gentler mother or kinder friend to the ladies at the local church.

"Then our son took fever and died. After that, she fell into a mourning so deep, she began to have periods of hallucination. And since that time, every year or so, she will fall into these pits of despair, sometimes for a month or two. You two saw her at her worst, during one of those times when she thinks our son is crying for her.

"On two different occasions, Felicity has actually taken babies from their mother's arms, thinking they were hers. Each time we were forced to move because our neighbors turned on us, accusing Felicity of being possessed by demons. The second time it happened, Belinda was thirteen, at an age where she was greatly affected when even her closest friends at church shunned her."

Max's heart went out to Belinda as he pictured her as a colt-ish, freckle-faced young girl with bright hair and a terrible sadness in her eloquent eyes.

"Since that time," Mr. Gregg continued, "Belinda has been overprotective of her mother and our privacy—at her own expense. Her mother and I would like to try again to have a more normal life. But only if we have the understanding and good wishes of the community." He leaned forward and looked intently at Rolf. "Can you give me some assurance that we won't be faced with the same kind of vicious hysteria we have suffered in the past?"

Max looked at his father, waiting to hear what this man who'd spent his life serving others would say.

Rolf filled his massive chest with air and tilted his silver head. "I cannot gif you da guarantee you ask for. I learn years ago not to try to outguess da Lord. But I vill give you dis assurance. I serve a God who is as merciful as He is mighty. *Und* if He is leading you to come again to vorship *mit* fellow believers, I say ve trust Him to know vhat He is doing. Perhaps God is sending your family to our little church to test our own wort'iness to be called His children."

A slow grin softened Mr. Gregg's severe features. "I knew I was right about you." He stood and held out his hand.

Rolf pushed up from his chair to take it. "*Und* I t'ink you *und* me, ve are going to be goot friends."

"I think so too." Mr. Gregg then turned to Max, who was rising awkwardly on his sound leg. "We'll look forward to seeing you all next Sunday."

Max wanted to invite himself to their home before then but hesitated. He didn't want to seem overeager. "We'll be expecting you. Do give my regards to Miss Belinda."

Mr. Gregg's grin widened as if he was privy to some secret. "I'll surely do that."

The kiss. Belinda must have told him about the kiss. Max's mouth slid into its own self-conscious grin.

Max spent the next few days trying to convince himself that if he went to visit Belinda before Sunday, he would be taking on the appearance of a bona fide suitor. One with serious intentions. And that he was not quite prepared to be. His leg improved with each day—bringing him closer to his departure from the valley.

But after spending half of last night dreaming about canoeing on a golden stream with the flame-haired vision and her ravens, he threw caution out the window. He talked his mother into making him a picnic lunch. After working the early hours of the day with his father, he hitched the buggy and set out for Belinda's house. Picnicking in a secluded spot far from her folks might very well get him that kiss he'd hoped for last Saturday night. One he could take with him after he said good-bye.

Chapter Sixteen

Perspiration beading Belinda's brow began slipping down to her eyes as she kneaded a large lump of dough. With her hands covered with the sticky mess, she swiped at the moisture with her sleeve. She knew she should've had the loaves in the oven long before eleven o'clock, but she'd gotten caught up in making pies for Sunday.

Max simply had to accept her invitation to come here to eat after church.

She gazed out a window of the summer kitchen where the two chocolate pies cooled, their meringues golden. Not a cloud remained after last night's rain. Yet the valley was even more humid than before. "A breeze," she said out loud to the sky. "Couldn't you send even a little cool air in here?"

After forming the dough into loaves, she wiped her hands on her apron and slid the pans into the heated brick oven next to the hearth, then turned back to the table. She needed to get it cleaned so she could start preparing the noon meal.

As she poured hot water into her dishpan, she heard her watchdog ravens began to caw.

Was someone coming? Max? At the thought, her pulse quickened. Every evening this week she'd hoped he'd drop by, but he hadn't. Now, of all times. She was a sweaty mess.

Without delay, she stepped out the summer-kitchen door and moved to a rear corner of the main house and peeked around. It was him!

Ripping off her apron, she ran to the washstand by the back door and splashed cool water on her face and neck. Drying off, she found that a number of stray curls had spilled from the knot she'd haphazardly pinned up this morning. And she was wearing nothing but a waistless shift. Frantically she tucked in the willful strands as she ran up the steps and into the house, making a mad dash up to her room, where she grabbed a ruffled shawl collar and a matching white sash.

Why couldn't he have come last evening when she was in a fresh gown, her hair tidy?

She tied both the collar and the sash as she rushed back down the stairs, then tried to even out the tucks at her waist. As she reached the mirror near the front entrance, she paused long enough to make a few more adjustments to her hair and shift. She took a couple of calming breaths and walked in measured, ladylike steps out the door.

The horse and buggy were already stopping in front of the gate. Upon seeing her, Max flashed that wide infectious grin of his.

She couldn't help doing the same, even after her mother had told her just yesterday that she shouldn't seem too eager. Men loved the challenge of pursuit.

"I know I'm always dropping by unannounced," he called as she headed out the brick walk. "Almost unannounced, anyway," he added, tossing a glance at the ravens now landing on the rose arbor. "But since I planned to pay a visit to the Dagget family this afternoon, I decided to drop by here first."

"It's always a pleasure to see you," she responded, trying to make her voice sound leisurely. "Fact is, this gives me the opportunity to extend my family's invitation for you to join us for dinner after church Sunday." She moved toward the buggy to help him down.

He warded her off with a wave of his hand. "I don't need help. I'm getting quite good at this." He used his lone crutch for a brace and vaulted down.

Every time she saw him, he'd gained more use of his limbs, grown stronger. Soon he'd be fit again. Fit enough to travel. To leave. Soon he'd be gone—for a year, maybe two. Possibly forever. She might never see him again. But that was to be expected. He'd told her as much. Besides, no man would seriously consider the daughter of a woman who suffered spells of madness.

"What happened to that gorgeous smile?" Max asked as he reached her, toting a cloth-covered basket in his free hand.

"I was just marveling at how much your leg has improved since last Saturday. You're putting some weight on it now."

Although her own gaze danced about a bit, his looked nowhere but at her, as if there was nothing else to see. "Ma Smith said we'd try it without the splints next week."

"So soon?" That was terrible news.

"So soon? It's been splinted for going on three months now." His gaze lowered to her lips.

She felt her lips begin to tingle. Was he thinking about the kiss he'd given her at the cornhusking?

He looked down at the basket in his hand. "Ma fixed me a picnic lunch. I was hoping to share it with you." His attention came back to her eyes.

"Picnic . . . ?" Alone, just the two of them. "I—" Then sense and reason returned. "I'm sorry, but I have bread baking, and my parents will be coming in from the pottery shed any minute now, and I haven't even started their meal."

"Aye, well . . ." The ardor in his gaze diminished. "I just took a chance." He started to turn away.

"Oh, but you're most welcome to join us," she hastily offered. Now that he was here, she didn't want him to just turn around and leave. "My parents would be most pleased for the company." She plucked the basket from him before he could decline. "We can add your food to ours."

"If you're sure they won't mind."

"I'm sure." She took his arm. "Come around to the summer kitchen with me. Keep me company."

His gaze gravitated to her lips again. He expelled a breath. "Sure. Let's go."

She knew he was disappointed. So was she. And making matters worse, as they rounded the corner, she saw her mother coming from the pottery shed. Her parents, too, must have heard Max's arrival.

But there'd be another time for that kiss . . . if only he'd stay in the valley a spell longer. Why, why did she have to be falling in love with a man whose life was elsewhere, while hers could be nowhere but here, helping her father care for and protect her mother?

~

On Sunday morning Belinda's spirits soared as she walked down the stairs dressed and ready for church. She hoped Max would admire her in the nut brown linen jacket cut short to show off the long, slender skirt, both piped with shimmering satin. The costume was supposed to be the latest style. But mostly she chose it because she thought it would go so nicely with Max's Sabbath attire. Her matching bonnet did add a little flair, though, with its stylish egret plume.

Her tall, almost too lean, father walked in the front door, looking distinguished in his charcoal waistcoat and knee breeches. "The horses are hitched to the four-seater." He paused halfway to the kitchen entrance. "La, but you are really quite elegant this morning. I can guess the look in young Max's eyes when he first sees you." Her father sported a teasing smile.

"Daddy, don't you dare do or say anything to embarrass me. Or him."

"Ah, but that's half the fun of having a beautiful daughter. By george, I do feel good today." He glanced past her. "Where's your mother?"

"I suppose she's still getting dressed."

He frowned. "She was ready before I went to the stable." He brushed past her and hurried up the stairs.

Panic knotted Belinda's stomach. *Please, God, not today.* She lifted her skirt and hurried after her father.

When she reached her parents' oversized room, she glanced toward the bed at the far end. Her mother lay in it, curled into a ball with the velvet-trimmed floral counterpane pulled up to her ears.

Her father strode across the Oriental rug to the massive canopied bed. Several feet short of her mother, Belinda slowed to a stop, the joy of the day dropping away.

Mr. Gregg sat down beside his wife, leaned close, and kissed her temple. Then he whispered something that Belinda couldn't hear, but the tighter ball her mother curled into needed no words.

Tears stung the backs of Belinda's eyes, tears she could not afford to let flow in front of her mother. What had happened? Just a short time ago, her mother had seemed fine—a little edgy, maybe, but fine.

"Belinda, come here." Her dad motioned for her. "Sit on the other side of your mother. Hold her hand." He lifted his wife's chin. "Join us in prayer, my love. Show God you're ready to take this one small step."

She raised her lashes, her soft gray gaze finding him. "I'll try," she whispered.

Kissing her again, he reached across and took Belinda's free hand, completing the circle. "We're here before You, Lord. . . ."

Yes, Lord Father, again. Belinda's tears would not be stopped. Tears of futility streamed down her cheeks.

Max deliberately chose to wait for the Greggs down among the incoming conveyances this Sunday. Much less conspicuous than last week. But again, as the number of arriving wagons and saddle horses grew, there was still no sign of Belinda and her parents. Gripping the brake of the Clay wagon, Max knew he should have followed his instinct and ridden out there to check on them two hours ago.

The Smiths pulled their wagon into a vacant spot nearby.

He nodded and smiled in greeting to his friends, though he wasn't pleased to see Liza staring intently at him. Every time he saw her, she became more blatant in her pursuit of him.

As big-boned Ken and his sturdy half-grown son helped their womenfolk alight, Liza never took her eyes off Max. Looking petal fresh in her summer pink, she made a beeline for him the instant her feet touched ground.

Max braced himself for her next feminine assault, though he

was obliged to be polite. "You look as pretty as ever this morning, little missy."

That didn't seem to please her. She frowned, tilting her gaze up to his. "I can't help it if I took after my mother 'stead of my pa. I am taller than her, though." She lifted her chin.

"Height ain't no true measure of a person," he said, hoping to pacify her. He redirected the topic. "I was over to see Pete yesterday. He was still looking down in the mouth. Nothing like his old self. Have you seen him lately?"

"No. And I don't intend to either." The pint-sized girl seemed in a real huff. "Me an' Ma rode over to his place on Wednesday, and Pete shunned me. Treated me like I weren't even there."

"That don't sound like him."

"If you don't believe me, ask Mama. It was downright humiliatin'." She shot Max a coy smile. "I can't imagine you ever treating me like that. No matter what."

Max was starting to feel boxed in again . . . wagons on two sides, a thicket behind, and her in front. "Pete's just feeling a little guilty right now for being alive with Paul passed on. Pete mentioned something about how Paul had been set on marrying you, and that it would seem like he was robbing the dead if he came calling on you right now. I tried to tell him—"

"That's just stuff an' nonsense," she blurted, anger flashing in her amber eyes. "Paul had no claim on me. Why, I turned both of 'em down at least a dozen times." She whirled around, her pink muslin swagging after her. "Where is Pete? Is he here yet? It's time I set him straight."

"He's over by the steps." Max pointed toward the church. "He's kinda hard to see with all the gals around him, trying to give him comfort."

"They're what?"

Max had to turn his head to hide his mirth as she trounced toward Pete and the gaggle of girls. Liza, marching off to defend her territory.

Someone rang the church bell. The congregation was being called to worship service.

Max took one last disappointed look toward the river . . . and saw a carriage coming. A stylish one with yellow spokes and trim. Red hair shone from beneath the driver's tall hat. The Greggs were actually coming!

Hooking his crutch beneath his arm, Max couldn't stop the grin as he sallied forth to meet them.

None of the Greggs seemed nearly as glad to see him.

From the seat behind, Belinda smiled, but it didn't reach her usually lively eyes. Mr. Gregg's smile was even fainter as he nodded a greeting while guiding their stylish pair of bays to a vacant spot among the other plainer rigs.

And Mrs. Gregg didn't even acknowledge him. Beneath a hovering blue bonnet that matched her fitted linen costume, her eyes were lowered, and in her lap her gloved hands were clinched tightly together.

Max reached the carriage as Mr. Gregg was wrapping the reins around the brake stick. "You're just in time," he told them and reached for Mrs. Gregg first, in deference to her age. "My mother is saving a place for you near the front."

Instead of taking Max's hand, she shrank back, her gaze fleeing to her husband.

The reason for their tardiness was becoming unmistakably clear. Urging them to come as he and his father did—had that been a big mistake? He thought he'd been following God's will. Now he felt like a meddler.

"Assist Belinda," Mr. Gregg suggested. "I'll help her mother."

Belinda smelled of honeysuckles this morning. Lilacs or

honeysuckle, she was just as wonderful to hold in that moment
when circumstance gave him permission.

"Thank you." Her words came out in a breathy rush. She
further treated him by threading her gloved hand through the
crook in his arm. Then she did smile up at him, though it
seemed a bit forced. "I've been so looking forward to hearing
your father preach."

Those of the laity who had yet to enter the church glanced
back and nodded politely. Some, though, continued to stare not
quite so politely.

But Max didn't mind. The loveliest woman he'd ever seen
clung to his arm.

As Max and Belinda headed toward the church, she leaned
closer and said for his ears only, "My mother became frightened
about coming this morning. But Daddy insisted she brave it
out."

Max's own anxiety heightened. He'd seen just how demented
Mrs. Gregg could be.

"Please pray for her," Belinda finished with an urging squeeze
to his arm.

For some odd reason, just the fact she'd said those words sent
a calm over him, and he knew that God would surround this
morning with His protection. "Everything's going to be fine," he
affirmed. "And, by the by, I don't think I've mentioned yet just
how exquisite you look this morning."

"Despite my red hair." A hint of her humor had surfaced.

Max grinned. "Most particularly *because* of it. That's the first
thing that attracted me to you. Flaming hair and black ravens
. . . who could resist that picture?"

She graced him with her first unrestrained smile today, wide
and free.

His heart gave one of those crazy kicks. Then just as quickly, it died when Max saw that Belinda stared across the grass to the church steps.

Following her lead, Max spotted Annie Reardon's sister on the top landing, watching Belinda's parents. The woman's mouth was twisted down, and she wore a scowl as fierce as any she-bear's.

Lord, Max reminded himself as much as he did God, *You promised us a peaceful morning. I cling to that promise, knowing that You are faithful.*

Still, as he neared Annie's sister, he decided to divert her. He stopped with Belinda directly in front of her, blocking the woman's view of the Greggs. "Good morning, Mrs. Thompson."

After that, he took a longsome time, introducing her and Belinda, explaining in drawn-out detail where each lived, while giving the older Greggs the time needed to pass by and enter the sanctuary without being offended. Then, tucking Belinda's arm more securely, he escorted her through the arched church-house door . . . and breathed a relieved sigh.

Yessir, the wilderness was not the only place wrought with danger. It lurked about, waiting to pounce, right here in peaceful Reardon Valley. But why? What possible grievance could Mrs. Thompson have with the Greggs?

"Thank you," Belinda whispered as they stepped into the cool of the vaulted room.

"Anything for you." And he realized he'd never said truer words. Like it or not, he was falling in love, helplessly in love. No call of the wild had ever come close to matching this call to his soul.

And it scared the stuffing out of him.

Chapter Seventeen

He *would do anything for her?* Belinda couldn't help wondering if Max was just acting the gentleman or if he actually meant those words as she accompanied him into the sanctuary of the unadorned country church.

Her parents had taken seats in a rear pew that held only two other people, a young couple with no children.

"Please," she whispered to Max, "could we sit here with Mama?"

Max nodded and paused while she took her place on a hard, straight-backed bench beside her mother.

Before Max could take his own seat, the middle-aged woman to whom Max had introduced Belinda came into the building, still looking as severe as her charcoal gray day gown. She walked down the aisle almost to the front, before entering a pew beside the two Reardon girls Belinda had met at the cornhusking party.

For all Mrs. Thompson's glowering, when Max literally

confronted her, she'd had nothing to say. Still, the woman was most unsettling.

Max obviously thought so too. He'd remained standing to keep his eye on Mrs. Thompson until she had taken her seat; then he took his own beside Belinda.

A plump older lady at the front struck a few introductory chords on a harpsichord, and the service began with a melodious song of praise.

Scanning the large room, Belinda spotted what she thought was the black wavy hair of Pete Dagget; then she saw pretty little Liza sitting next to him. Belinda prayed he would let the dear girl share in his grief and draw strength from her.

It had been so long since Belinda had heard a hymn sung by an entire congregation. She settled back against the hard seat and let the strains wash over her as the music filled the room to the rafters.

Max, sitting next to the aisle, joined the singing, his deep bass a match for his father's up at the front, though not nearly as loud.

Belinda began to sing along, hoping to bolster not only her own confidence but his as well. He did have a most enjoyable voice to complement his tanned good looks. She smiled up at him—always a pleasure.

After several songs, marred only slightly by a few curious glances in their direction, Brother Bremmer called them to prayer with a stirring invocation. And, as with every time Belinda had been in the man's presence, his words came forth as from a man who no doubt walked humbly yet boldly with the Lord.

He stepped up behind his simply built pulpit, pretty much dwarfing it, his huge hands gripping the sides. A plain wooden cross hung behind him on the back wall, completing the picture of a man of unhidden truth.

And his son was so like him.

"Dis morning, I vill continue talking on da book of Romans, beginning vhere ve leave off last veek. Ve begin today on chapter twelve."

Of course Brother Bremmer didn't have the lofty pearl-shaped tones of Reverend Varner back in South Carolina. This was not a man of eloquent speech but of eloquent heart. He held Belinda's complete attention . . . particularly since the message seemed to be meant specifically for her and her family. If the minister hadn't said he was continuing from the prior Sunday, she would have sworn he'd chosen the topic because he knew they would be in attendance.

The Scripture passage concerned the holy call of believers to belong to one another, each needing and sharing the needs of their fellow believers. That all were called to minister to one another with the gifts of the Holy Spirit.

Belinda's own soul felt a tremendous conviction that she should no longer be so distrustful of other believers, but she should reach out to them, trust in their mercy and love. And begin to trust God more too.

She took her mother's thin hand and held it during most of the sermon to lend encouragement. At first, she'd felt a tremor in it, but gradually the shaking subsided, and she knew her mother had relaxed. Her beloved, needy mother.

But threaded through everything else, she could not forget that Max sat right beside her. Big, strong, capable. And gentle. Someone who could be as loving as her father had always been and, she was sure, his own father.

If Max was disposed to give up his wandering ways. Still, even if he was, would he be willing to live with her family and take on the added burden of her mother? She doubted any man would. And she could never leave her father to care for their dear one alone.

By the end of the service, Belinda's dilemma had stolen her initial joy in coming. But when they rose to leave, Max bestowed that charming unabashed grin on her, and she forgot all else.

"Sir," Max said to her father, "would you mind if Belinda walks over to the stable with me? I need to saddle a horse to ride back home from your place."

"Sure, son. We'll bring the carriage over to collect you."

He'd called Max "son." Belinda couldn't bring herself to glance up at Max to see how he'd reacted to such a familial expression.

Whatever his reaction had been, Max wasted no time taking Belinda's arm and escorting her out the door ahead of the rest of the congregation. He glanced back. "I know Pete and his folks will be surrounded by well-wishers like they were last week and won't miss us. So I hope you don't mind us not lingering. With you on my arm, we'd be in for quite an onslaught of introductions. And I'd really like to have you just to myself for a few minutes."

A tickling sensation shot from the pit of her stomach straight to her heart. "Not at all," she barely managed past her relief. The man wasn't scared off yet. Not yet. And he liked her red hair. "Perhaps we could speak to Mr. Dagget afterward."

Max congratulated himself on managing to whisk Belinda out the church door ahead of his nosy neighbors and their questions. Not allowing his crippled gait to impede his progress, he set a fast pace past the horses and rigs. This could very well be his only chance to get her alone today.

"Max!" someone called from behind.

"Ignore it," he said to Belinda, not slowing.

"You don't want to introduce me to your friends?"

"Not at the moment. I'd much rather have you to myself."
Particularly away from a couple of young bucks he'd noticed
stealing glimpses of her during the service.

"I see." Those starburst eyes glanced up at him, along with
a knowing smile.

But, knowing what? What did she expect from him? What
would any other woman in her place expect? Every time he
opened his big mouth he sounded vitally interested in her. As if
he were courting her. Her father must think so. Mr. Gregg had
called him "son." Even he himself thought so when he wasn't
thinking so clearly—which was most anytime she was in close
proximity.

He decided on prudence and changed the subject as they
walked past his house and headed for the smithy and corrals.
"How's Downy, your baby fox, doing? And the injured coon?
Benjamin Franklin, wasn't it? I forgot to ask the other day."

"Yes, I released Ben yesterday. But my little Downy will probably be with us for a long time. Daddy built her a little house. I
put her blanket in it, and we set it under the front porch just
behind an azalea. She's so much fun to watch, playing among
the stalks in my flower garden when I'm out pruning dead blossoms."

"That's a picture," he said, beholding her cute freckled nose
as they neared the smithy.

"Downy curled up in her house?"

"No, you among your flowers."

Oh! He'd done it again. Brought the conversation straight
back to them. "Speaking of blossoms, beyond the Mississippi
there are grasslands that stretch as far as the eye can see. And

every spring they're alive with wildflowers and butterflies, the likes of which I'd never seen."

"They say there are no trees to close you in. You must be able to see lots of sky. Like looking from atop a mountain."

"Pretty close." Though he was grateful they were on a safer topic again, he knew he needed to be more honest with her . . . but not too honest. He certainly didn't want to tell her that he'd thought of little else but her and her mouth since that kiss more than a week ago. Maybe just a subtle reminder of his future plans. "The next time I come home for a visit, I'll bring you seeds from the prettiest prairie flowers."

For a second or two she didn't say anything. Then, "That would be most thoughtful of you."

Thoughtful? If anything, he was a thoughtless knave. He should never have toyed with her feelings . . . never become infatuated with everything about her. Never have become so utterly confused.

They'd reached the smithy with its stalls in the rear. She hesitated as he started to escort her inside the cavernous building.

"The tack is near the back door that goes out to the paddocks." He pointed with his crutch to a saddle and blanket draped over wooden horses and then to the bridles hanging on the rear wall.

"I'll take the blanket and gear, if you can manage the saddle," she offered, her words and tone as measured and subdued at they were a moment ago. Her steps, though, were quite clipped as she headed for the items.

His guilt mounted. "Are you sure? I don't want you getting the smell of horse on your handsome outfit."

"I'll be careful." She plucked a bridle off its spike, grabbed the soiled blanket, and headed out the back door before he was half-way there.

If there had been any doubt, none remained. He'd upset her.

Despite the chasm he'd managed to put between them, he knew it was the honorable thing to do. Years from now when he was ready to give up his travels, there'd be other women to court, women perhaps even as lovely as she. If that were possible.

"Which horse?" she called back sharply.

"The gray, Kaiser." He hoisted the saddle up under his arm and followed. Perhaps he'd been too blunt.

She unlatched the second of four gates and swung it wide.

He halted just short of its crashing into him . . . and he an injured man with a crutch. She wasn't merely upset—she was furious. Folks always said redheads had tempers to match their hair.

He closed the gate to the stall behind him, tossed the saddle over the rail next to the blanket Belinda had brought, and went to help her loop the bridle over Kaiser's ears.

She rammed the bit into the animal's mouth. "I can do it myself." Her tone rang with petulance.

Max was glad it wasn't his mouth. He probably would've lost a couple of teeth. He patted Kaiser's neck, then reached for the blanket.

Belinda had beat him to it. She slapped the smelly thing over the horse's back. She sure was in a mighty big hurry.

Max made a point of grabbing the saddle before she got to it. Stirrups flying, he tossed it on top of the blanket, then reached down to catch the cinch straps—and collided with Belinda, hard.

Her arms flailed and she fell back. Just before she hit ground, he caught hold of her waist and yanked her up again—too hard. She slammed into his chest. Eyes flashing, she started to step back.

He tightened his grip. "Listen, I'm sorry. About before. For being such a coward. I-I just plain get scared. I've never felt like this about anyone before. It changes everything, and—"

She sighed on a long breath then reached up and placed gentle fingers to his lips.

The touch of her fingertips sent shock waves through him. He could barely focus on her eyes, her own beautifully shaped lips . . .

"You're not a coward. You've been very brave," she said, her voice a whisper, her gaze drawing him even closer. "No other man would have returned to our house just to keep me company after seeing Mama in one of her spells."

Who could resist such a woman? His mouth sought hers, found it, and there wasn't a thing he could do, or would do, to stop himself. Kissing her tender lips, holding her close, smelling the honeysuckle in her hair, meant more to him than anything he ever imagined. His whole being cried to keep her close and never let go.

He didn't know how long they were in each other's arms before she stepped back, as out of breath as he. She looked up at him just as speechless, her lips slightly parted. Finally, she spoke. "I had no idea a kiss could be so . . . so stirring."

"Neither did I." He reached for her again.

She held him at bay with a hand to his chest. "No. We'd better not." She took another step back. "I'd better wait out front for you. I have a feeling that kissing you again could be likened to starting a forest fire."

Belinda couldn't believe the passionate feelings that had over-taken her. If Max hadn't been holding her, her very legs would have collapsed. They still didn't feel too strong as she walked through the barn-sized smithy. Her whole body still hummed from the astoundingly awakening kiss, especially her lips. It had taken all her will to pull away from Max and walk away. Everything in her had begged to stay.

But she was not so naive that she didn't know where that kind of kissing could lead . . . to a closeness that God meant only for a husband and wife.

Moving out of the smithy and into the noonday light, she took several deep breaths. As she did, she heard Max and the horse coming through the hollow building toward her. Embarrassment sent heat to her cheeks . . . a blush she prayed would fade before he reached her.

With his every step, she wondered what she could possibly say to get everything back to normal. They would be spending an entire afternoon together in front of her parents.

Max came to a stop behind her. Much too close. She could hear him breathe, smell the fresh scent of mint, a smell that would forever remind her of their first real kiss.

"I know," he said softly, wrapping her in his words, "there's more I need to say. But at the moment, the only thing that I can think to say is thank you."

She found herself turning toward him, searching his face, his sincere expression, his eyes that matched the noonday sky. "I know. Me too."

"We can talk later. In the meantime, I reckon we better start back. Your folks must be waiting for us."

Turning, she saw her dad standing beside their carriage with Brother Bremmer and another man. And, indeed, Daddy's eyes were on her and Max. He must have seen her, read her face when she first walked out of the smithy. And a girl's daddy would be fully aware of all those things poets wrote about so lyrically. He'd know the powerful forces at work between his only daughter and a red-blooded young man.

As the two of them started back to the church under the watchful eyes of her father, Belinda was grateful that both of Max's hands were otherwise occupied. One held the horse's reins; the other was working his crutch.

"Blast," Max suddenly muttered.

"What's wrong?"

"Annie Reardon's sister is talking to your mother. The woman came here to live with the Reardons recently, and she doesn't seem quite right in the head." He stretched his legs into a faster gait.

His urgency shot straight through Belinda. She hastened to keep pace.

But before they could reach the women, who stood apart from the others under an elm, several young people surrounded Max and Belinda; some she remembered from the cornhusking party and a few she didn't. They all talked at once.

Belinda tried to listen.

But Max didn't even pretend to listen as he looked over their heads. "We promised Mrs. Gregg we'd get right back to her." Dropping the horse's reins, he caught Belinda's hand and started past them. "We can spend more time talking next week."

"Tryin' to keep her all to yourself, ain'tcha?" a young man bantered with a cocky grin, someone Belinda had never seen before.

"Never could fool you, Charlie," Max returned over his shoulder without slowing.

Away from the young people, Belinda again had a clear view of her mother and Mrs. Thompson. Belinda relaxed. Her mother didn't seem the least distressed. In fact, she seemed quite absorbed in the conversation—a real treat to see.

The other woman spotted them coming, said something in parting, then walked away, and her mother headed toward the carriage, seemingly unaware they'd been coming to save her. Frail-looking as ever in tailored slate blue, Mrs. Gregg walked with the grace that the years of her privileged childhood training had taught her.

Max turned with Belinda back toward her carriage. "Your mother seems fine. I reckon I was just being too protective."

Too protective? The very idea that Max had been as intent on shielding her mother as she always was endeared him to her even more. And a moment ago, she wouldn't have thought that possible.

How would she ever go back to life as it was before he came busting in? How could she ever bear to see him go?

Reaching the rear of their yellow-trimmed carriage, Belinda waited while Max retrieved his mount and tied it to the rear. Then, together, they walked around to join her parents.

Her father, turning from helping her mother into the roomy conveyance, strode to meet them. He took Belinda by the arm and escorted them both several yards away.

An odd thing to do.

"I'm sorry, Mr. Bremmer, but my wife has had all the excitement she can handle today. I'm afraid we're going to have to postpone our dinner together. I do hope you understand. We'll reschedule for later in the week, if that's all right with you."

"Whatever you say." Max shot a glance to where Mrs. Thompson stood with Mrs. Bremmer and two other women. No doubt he blamed the sour woman for the canceled invitation. "I understand," he added with a polite nod. With one long look at Belinda, he left her standing there with her father.

Disappointment washed over her. Why hadn't Max thought to suggest she remain behind with him? Perhaps he'd had more of his second thoughts.

Max limped toward the carriage to fetch his horse, she

assumed. But instead, he stepped to her mother sitting upon the high seat and said a few words to her that Belinda could not hear.

Her mother reached out and touched his cheek. She added a rather wan smile to the kind gesture.

"Your young man has a very understanding heart," her dad said, taking Belinda's elbow. "He's a credit to his father."

"Yes, he is," she murmured absently as she watched Max retrieve his mount and walk away. So many emotions assailed her, hurt and desire, hope—and the worst—the feeling that she would soon be abandoned.

"He'll be sorely missed," her father said quietly, "if he leaves for the West again."

Belinda couldn't risk a reply to that. Her throat had begun to close as she watched Max move farther and farther away. She could hardly breathe for the emotion clogging her lungs.

Chapter Eighteen

Watching the Greggs leave the churchyard in their carriage, Max knew he should have walked over to where most of the congregation stood commiserating with the Daggets again this week over the loss of their son. He should have checked on Pete. But he figured his own mood would bleed through. And the family certainly didn't need to add his own personal disappointment to their grief.

Instead of returning Kaiser to the smithy the way he'd come, he took the quickest exit out of sight. He led the horse into a grove of trees on the back side of the parking area, then walked to the rear of his family's place. He needed to cool down, something he hadn't done since he kissed Belinda.

Hitching the gray plow horse to a peach-tree branch in the backyard, he headed down to the deeply shaded springhouse to fetch something cool to drink. Even before reaching it, he felt a change in temperature. He stopped outside the half-buried stone structure and unbuttoned his waistcoat. Removing it, he draped it across a young dogwood while reveling in the feel of the breeze playing through his shirt and cooling his back.

Opening the door, he tried to concentrate only on the chill air that filled his lungs as he stepped down into the room. A steady stream of springwater poured inside the dugout through a clay pipe and fed into a wooden trough that made a horseshoe circuit of the room before exiting out another hole.

He scooped up two handfuls of water and splashed his face while his eyes adjusted to the dim light coming from the small openings near the roof. Feeling somewhat refreshed, he checked the various crocks and jugs standing in the aboveground stream until he found a jug of cider.

Leaving the springhouse, he returned to his mother's sweltering kitchen, where she had a cauldron sitting on some banked and still red-hot coals. He shook his head. Whether she liked it or not, he was going to build her a summer kitchen before he left this time.

If he left.

That kiss had his brain so muddled, he might very well be incapable of making a decision again.

He'd kissed plenty of gals in his youth. Held their hands, smelled the perfume in their hair. But never had he been so blown over by anyone. Even the touch of Belinda's hand on his arm could steal his every thought.

And to prove his point, here he stood in the middle of the stone floor, staring at the place she'd touched on his sleeve.

He tucked the jug under his arm and snatched up three glasses from the shelf; then, juggling them along with his crutch, he limped out to the front porch. Setting the jug and glasses down, he glanced across to the church. Folks were finally beginning to disperse. But he knew his folks wouldn't leave until everyone else did. That would give him a few more minutes to himself before he had to explain his unexpected presence to his mother. Knowing her, she wouldn't understand his explanation that Mrs. Gregg had been too tired to entertain visitors. His mother had always been such a healthy, hardworking woman.

He'd been tempted to ask Belinda to stay behind and have dinner with his family. But with her mother looking so pale, it would've been a selfish request. Besides, she probably wouldn't have come anyway, with her mother in such a tenuous state . . . any more than she would leave Mrs. Gregg tomorrow, or next year. The only way he could ever be with Belinda was if he stayed here, very close to her parents.

Pouring himself a drink, he settled into a chair and took a long draft of the cider, foolishly hoping that it would fill the vast empty place in his chest, his heart, that hole only Belinda's smile could fill.

"Belinda, beautiful Belinda." He saw her again in all her fierce anger, blanketing and bridling old Kaiser, her slender femininity crashing into him. The wildness, the fire in her eyes just before they kissed. There wasn't anything about her he didn't adore. Even her anger.

Especially her anger. All because he threatened to leave her . . . only because he threatened to.

If ever he could be talked into staying, made to want to stay, it would be for her.

"Max, see you next week," came the call from Buster Hatfield, one of the leatherworker's sons. He rode by with his young wife, her hands supporting her very round belly.

He mustered a smile and waved, but his gaze quickly returned to the young woman beside Buster. Belinda . . . the thought of his Belinda one day having children intrigued him. There couldn't be a more loving and responsible mother than she would be. She'd more than proved that by caring for her own mother and her stray creatures. And even his German mother couldn't fault her housekeeping, not to mention her gardening skills.

As if his mother had been privy to his thoughts, Max spotted her walking toward the house with Pops. His arm was around her waist as the two chatted. Pops must have said something that pleased her. She leaned her head affectionately against his shoulder. For all her fussy ways, she loved her husband very much. Max couldn't imagine either of them without the other.

He took a second look, trying to imagine them young and as foolishly in love as he was right now.

"Ah, dere you are," his mother scolded as if he'd been hiding from something . . . and perhaps he had.

"I'll pour you and Pops some cider. Come sit down and cool off. Those black clothes have to be awful hot out there in the sun."

"Ja." His father huffed as he came up the steps, removing his hat and coat. He laid them across the railing and took the first glass Max poured. "Folks, dey stay longer dan usual. All of dem vanting to offer comfort to da Daggets. Dey is hafing a hard time." He dropped into a chair and downed a quarter of the cider in one swallow. "Maybe dey should haf brought da body home for burial. Say good-bye in person."

"Pops, you know the weather's too hot for the body to keep till they could get him back here. He needed to go in the ground right away."

His mother remained standing, eyeing Max, her arms crossed. "So? Tell us. Vhat happen dat Mr. Gregg don't vant you at his house?"

Max busied himself by pouring her drink. "It didn't have anything to do with me. The strain of coming to church wore

Mrs. Gregg out. She wasn't up to being around any more people today." Bracing for more questions, he held out her glass.

"Humph. Dat is not vhat I hear." She took the cider but didn't sit down. She remained directly in front of Max. "Annie's sister talk to *Frau* Gregg, *und* she t'inks da poor voman is treated bad by her husband. Dat he is keeping a mean thumb on her. *Und* probably on dat red-haired gal too. Dat is vhy he don't vant nobody around. He don't vant dem to see vhat goes on. *Und* dat is da real reason he keeps dem avay from da valley folk."

Max took a long drink from his glass. "Mama, did Mrs. Gregg tell Mrs. Thompson she was being mistreated?"

"*Nein*. She would be too scared *mit* her husband standing right dere. But Emma Jane, she says da voman has all da earmarks. Da vay she hung back vhen her husband force her to walk next to him from da carriage."

"You've got it all wrong. That's what you get for listening to that kind of gossip."

"Oh, I know how you men t'ink." She wagged her finger at him. "If a man says da very same t'ing, den you belief. You belief him."

Max sighed wearily. His mother could be like a bulldog when an idea got stuck in her head. "No, that's not true. I believe what I see, not hearsay or wild imaginings of some crazy woman."

Inga jerked to her husband. "Rolf, did you hear dat? Your son is calling poor Emma Jane bad names. *Und* the tone he uses *mit* me . . ."

Pops rolled his eyes. He'd already had a long day, up before dawn praying and going over his sermon notes before doing his morning chores, then preaching and pastoring his flock. He didn't need to be dragged into this. "Son," he said in a gravelly rumble, "you are to respect your mama . . . even vhen she is wrong."

That put fire in his mother's round cheeks. "Ah, so you side *mit* Max, do you?"

She was too old and it was too hot for her to get this excited. Catching her hand, Max gained his feet. "Please, Mama, take my seat. I'm sorry. I guess you could say I'm not having myself the afternoon I expected and I'm taking it out on you."

"*Nein.*" With a sigh, she shoved him back to his seat. "I am not being kind neither." She cocked her head. "But I still t'ink I am right." She turned to his father. "You need to go out dere, do somet'ing to save dat poor *Frau* Gregg."

"Inga, I haf already paid dem many calls. Christopher Gregg *und* his daughter do all dey can for *Frau* Gregg. But da *frau*, her mind . . . sometime it plays tricks on her. Makes her t'ink she hears t'ings, like a baby crying when dere is no baby. Sometime she sees vhat is not dere."

Inga's mouth fell open, and she caught hold of the nearest porch post. "You are saying *Frau* Gregg is a madvoman?" She looked from Rolf to Max and back again. "Our son, he is finally courting a *fräulein und* dere is madness running in her blood?" She swung back to Max. "*Und* you! You bring her here for supper. You make me t'ink you are serious about dis girl. Dat you are staying. Make me into da fool vhen all da time you know about her, know she cannot be a vife to anyone."

"That's *enough.*" Max shot to his feet. "There's nothing wrong with Belinda's blood or anything else about her. Don't you dare start spreading such tales."

Too angry to remain in her presence, he bolted past his mother and bounded down the steps.

"Max!" she yelled after him. "You forgot your crutch. Max!"

Rage boiled up in Max. Fists clenched, he stalked away from

his mother as fast as his splint-stiffened leg would allow. He rounded the corner of the house, the quickest way out of her sight. Reaching the rear, he practically ran into the gray horse before he noticed Kaiser still tied to the fruit tree.

As he untied the gelding, his first impulse was to mount him and ride as far from Mama's hateful words as he could get . . . maybe out to see Belinda, visit her awhile. But her father had asked him not to come today. He'd said they'd send him another invitation.

Max looked longingly toward the river. When he woke this morning the day had held such promise.

Kaiser nudged him in the back.

"I know, ol' boy. You want to go back to your stall." He scratched the gray's cheek. Better to get the animal unsaddled and put away before he followed his heart instead of his head. At least the smithy was one place his mother rarely butted in.

As he took Kaiser back to his stall, the memory of the kiss he'd shared with Belinda rushed back full force. He could still make out her footprints in the soft dirt . . . and his own facing hers, only inches apart.

Max didn't realize how slowly he was unsaddling the horse until Kaiser, impatient, pulled his blanket off with his teeth and slung it to the ground.

"Think it's time for me to leave, do you?" Max slipped the bridle off him, then gathering up the equipment, carried it back to the tack room.

Slinging the saddle over a wooden stand, he stumbled across a protrusion. His splinted leg unbalanced him even more, sending him down in a sprawl. In the smeltery dust. In his good clothes. He could hear his mother now, harping at him about it.

His rage at her resurfaced, and his ire spread to his injured leg. "I'm through being a trussed-up mess," he railed, the sound bouncing off the blackened walls. Still sitting in the dirt, he started ripping at the ties holding the hated splints. "I'm through coddling you, leg. And I'm through being coddled. Through letting Inga Bremmer talk to me like I'm some overgrown kid."

But he remembered her calling after him. Deep inside, he knew she only wanted the best for him. She was his mother.

With a sigh, he closed his eyes, trying to remember the last time he'd allowed his frustrations to get the best of him. More carefully now, he completed the unwrapping of the sticks around his leg. When he finished, he prudently left the bandage covering the wound in place.

As he tried to rise, he discovered how weak the limb was without support. Grabbing hold of the wooden stand, he regained his feet, then hopped to the ax handles that leaned against the wall awaiting iron blades. One would make a sturdy enough cane.

On the shelf just above his head, he noticed the beat-up old Bible his father kept out here. Picking it up, he dropped into a nearby chair. Staring at the cracked leather of the cover, he rubbed his finger over the faded lettering. He couldn't remember when his pops didn't have this Bible. Almost every page was dog-eared and smudged from years of being read while his father waited for the pig iron to heat or cool.

The evidence of his father's life lay here in Max's hands. Perhaps something in it could quench the rage and frustration burning holes in his own life.

But after staring at the black Bible a few moments, he knew the only thing he wanted to read about was found in the first pages of Genesis. Leafing through, he found the passage in the second chapter . . . the day God made Eve for Adam: "And the Lord God said, It is not good that the man should be alone; I will make him an help meet for him."

Max scanned ahead to verse twenty-one:

> And the Lord God caused a deep sleep to fall upon Adam, and he slept: and He took one of his ribs, and closed up the flesh instead thereof; And the rib, which the Lord God had taken from man, made He a woman, and brought her unto the man. And Adam said, This is now bone of my bones, and flesh of my flesh.

" 'Bone of my bones, and flesh of my flesh,' " Max repeated out loud. "It says right here that it's not good that man should be alone."

He picked up where he left off: "She shall be called Woman, because she was taken out of Man."

Yes, those were verses a man could believe in. More with each passing hour that he was separated from his lady. Gazing out the big doors of the smithy, Max saw nothing but her, on the river, her hair catching the sun . . . the burst of pleasure on her lips whenever she saw him . . . the look in her eyes when he kissed her. . . .

On a sigh, he looked down at the page again. "Therefore shall a man leave his father and his mother, and shall cleave unto his wife: and they shall be one flesh."

He read it again. "It's all there." Everything he needed to know concerning her. Everything he desperately wanted to know. He'd been a fool, thinking he could ever be happy again without Belinda Gregg. God had made her especially for him and had brought him home at just the right time to meet her. "Thank You, Jesus," Max said.

He lifted the open Bible to his chest and held it as close as he wanted to hold her.

He and Belinda were decreed to leave their parents, his *and* hers. They were meant to cleave only to one another. Become one flesh. And it was not merely his own desire but God's wish for His children. God truly was a God of love.

A smile took over Max's features, banishing the last trace of his anger, until only joy was left, joy and peace and love and . . . long-suffering? If the Lord would just help him with long-suffering, with patience, then Belinda would one day be his. . . . Flesh of his flesh, bone of his bone.

Chapter Nineteen

In the reflection of the gilded mirror above the hall table, Belinda caught an unexpected splash of color as she cleaned the looking glass with a vinegar-and-water-soaked cloth.

Coming down the stairs, her mother looked well rested and was dressed for the day in a happy floral print. A very good sign. Yester's eve she had been unusually quiet, causing concern for both Belinda and her father. They'd both thought another spell might be imminent.

"Good morning, Mama." She wore old chambray work clothes, more befitting her own mood. She'd been sorely disappointed when her father had asked Max not to join them for Sunday dinner. Though she'd known her father's motives were sincere, a thought continued to eat at her. Had Daddy also known about the kiss? A real kiss, not merely one during a game with a score of people watching. Did he disapprove? Surely he would. Max had yet to declare his intentions toward her.

Or had he already? A kiss from a maiden, then off to the wilds he would go.

"La, but don't you look serious this morning," said Mama, breaking into her thoughts. "And I do believe you've rubbed that spot as clean as it will ever get."

Belinda focused on her hand, which was hard at work, and eased off with a shrugging grin. "My mind was elsewhere."

"On that handsome young buck, I would imagine." Her mother didn't sound displeased. She glanced out the window as she reached the bottom step. "It seems a bit cooler today, don't you think?"

"Yes. There's a breeze out of the north this morning."

"Where's your father?" she asked, heading for the kitchen.

"He had breakfast and went out to the pottery shed a couple of hours ago." Belinda pulled a second cloth from her apron pocket and started drying the mirror. "I have the tea service prepared for the two of us, though. It's such a lovely morning, I thought it would be nice to treat ourselves. If you're ready, I'll go pour some hot water in the pot and take the tray out on the veranda." She stuffed the rags in her pockets. "Oh, and I fried us some raisin cakes earlier."

As Belinda started past her mother, Felicity caught her hand. "You are such a treasure. We couldn't have asked for a better daughter or a dearer one. I should tell you that more often." She pressed her lips to Belinda's cheek.

Sadly, this morning her mother's kind tribute didn't lift Belinda's spirits but seemed like one more strand of love-filled need, another tentacle that squeezed ever tighter.

"I promise to do better when we attend church next week," her mother added.

"Next week?"

"Yes. You and your father have given me so much, made such

incredible sacrifices for me, I want very much to return some of that love. It's your time to shine, sweetheart. And yesterday, I stole that moment from you. Forgive me. Your father and I both want nothing more than your happiness."

Belinda was the one who needed forgiveness. Only last night she'd been filled with unkind thoughts, berating God and His mercy.

Her mother plucked a marigold from the vase on the narrow table and, breaking off the wet part of the stem, slid it into Belinda's hair, below her dust cap and just above her ear. "There, that's better. Now, let's bring out the tea while we decide how we're going to repair yesterday's damage."

"Damage?"

"With your strapping young man. The canceled dinner."

"Yes." Suddenly Belinda felt like putting a whole bouquet of flowers in her hair. Her mother understood everything she was feeling. Wrapping arms around her thin form, she gave her mother a hug. "I do love you so. Now, go sit down. I can manage the tea by myself."

Moments later Belinda walked out on the veranda, her spirits still as high as the sky—a sky as blue as Max's eyes. Hope, warranted or not, was hers again.

As she placed the tray on the side table, she noticed her mother held the baby fox on her lap, petting the tiny creature, and Jacob and Esau perched expectantly on the railing. Belinda pulled a couple of dried-meat tidbits from her pocket and held out her hand. The birds didn't hesitate to pluck them from her palm.

"You do have them spoiled," her mother chuckled.

"I know. But you know they won't give us any peace if I don't give them something too. They think they're part of the family. And they do make good watchdogs."

DIANNA CRAWFORD

As Belinda picked up the silver teapot, her mother glanced down at the fluff of fur in her lap. "And, Downy, are you going to become our mouse catcher?"

The ravens abruptly flapped into noisy cawing flight.

A horse and rider clomped across the bridge.

"Speaking of strapping young beaus . . . ," her mother said lightly.

"No, it's not Max." Belinda hoped her next words wouldn't betray her disappointment. "It appears to be a woman."

"Oh my, a lady caller." Placing the fox kit on the floor, Felicity's fingers fluttered up to her neatly coiled hair.

"Mama, you look lovely," Belinda reassured.

"Go fetch another cup and saucer, dear. And take off your apron and dust cap," she said, standing up to go greet their first female visitor.

How swiftly life was changing. *Lord God in heaven*, Belinda beseeched, *please, make this a good time for Mama. A healing time. Please don't let it come back to bite us.*

When Belinda returned with the extra setting of earthenware, she'd expected to see Inga Bremmer, or mayhap Liza Smith. But to her dismay, the woman who'd been such a worry to Max rode up the drive. Mrs. Thompson.

But as the taller woman exchanged greetings with her mother, she wore a warm smile, and a tenderness softened her olive green eyes, giving her an unexpected attractiveness. Perhaps she wasn't the danger that Max had thought.

Still, Belinda knew to stay alert. She watched from the top step as the two women, both graying at the temples, came up the walk. By Mrs. Thompson's simple homespun attire, it was obvious she'd come from a humble household. But from the genuine pleasure on her own mother's face, a body would've thought royalty had come visiting.

"Sweetheart," her mother said as they mounted the steps, "this is Mrs. Thompson. But she's asked us to call her Emma Jane. We spoke for a few minutes yesterday at church."

Belinda dipped into the briefest curtsy. "Yes, I had the pleasure of meeting Mrs. Thompson before the service."

"How nice." Her mother turned to their guest. "Then you've already met Belinda, my help and my joy."

At such a lovely compliment, Belinda had no choice but to be gracious herself. "Do come sit with us. Your timing couldn't be more perfect. We were just about to pour tea."

The woman glanced down at her clothes. Looking up again, she seemed less confident. "I had no idea y'all lived in such a fine house. I should'a wore somethin' more presentable."

"Nonsense," Felicity scoffed. "The fact that you put yourself out to come welcome us more than makes up for anything you could ever wear. You will always be cherished as our first lady caller here on the Caney Fork."

One would've thought that little speech would put anyone at ease, but Mrs. Thompson's returning smile seemed even more tenuous than before.

Belinda angled one of the wicker chairs, making a semicircle, and offered their guest that seat.

Mrs. Thompson did sit, but she perched on the edge as if she would be rising again any second. The woman's nervousness infected Belinda as she poured the tea and set the raisin cakes on bread plates.

Once Belinda had served them and taken her own place, her mother gave the blessing, then turned to Mrs. Thompson. "And, dear Emma Jane, how is it you're up and about so early today?"

"I already done my mornin' chores. And since I don't have no husband or young'uns, there's nothin' that can't wait till later."

The woman glanced toward the doorway. "Is your husband about?"

"He must not have heard you ride in, or I'm sure he would've come to greet you too. Most likely he's busy in the pottery shed. Chris barely keeps up with orders from our regular customers."

"I hear you folks make some real purty platters and bowls and such."

"You're drinking out of one of my cups right now," Felicity said.

"Truly?" Mrs. Thompson held out the earth-colored cup and studied the apple-blossom twigs glazed on it. "It's real purty. And lightweight. Almost like china."

"Not quite," her mother demurred. "But my husband and I always try to use the best clay and glazes possible."

Mrs. Thompson glanced around again, as if someone might be listening, then leaned forward. "It's just the three of you here then? No servants a'tall? This is such a neat kept place."

The woman was being mighty nosy.

Yet her mother didn't seem disturbed. "We prefer it that way."

Conversely, the woman's sun-browned face stiffened. "My husband kept us off to ourselves too. Me'n his five young'uns. I know all about it." With her lye-reddened hand, she grasped one of Felicity's. "I know what goes on out here. What your man don't want no one else to see."

Mrs. Thompson knew about Mama's illness!

"But I want you to be sure," she continued with urgency in her voice, "I'm here to help you. You don't have to stay with him. Not one minute longer. Whatever it takes, I'll find you and your daughter, here, a safe place to live." She turned earnest eyes on Belinda. "Someplace where he can't never find you or hurt you again. I promise you that."

"Whatever are you talking about?" Belinda asked, thoroughly confused.

"Your pa. I've come to save you from him." She turned back to Felicity.

"Oh, la." Removing her hand from their guest's, Felicity touched her cheek. "So that's why you seemed so sympathetic yesterday. You thought my gallant Christopher is an ogre. My dear kind woman, that couldn't be further from the truth."

Emma Jane leaned closer, a look of desperation on her face. "Please don't do this. Don't lie for him. I saw yesterday how he practically dragged you out of the carriage. I saw his tight hold on you whilst he led you to the church. And when he whispered something to you, I saw the scared look you had on your face. Believe me, I know. My husband was just like that. Threatenin' us if we ever said anything. And nobody seemed to care. Nobody lifted a finger to help me'n his kids. The boys all lit out soon as they was old enough." She bit her lip nervously. "I thank God ever' day for sendin' the pox what finally took him and set me free."

Belinda, who'd always thought of herself as more levelheaded than her mother, had no idea how to respond to their misguided visitor.

But her mother didn't seem the least daunted. She clasped the woman's calloused hand. "What a brave and merciful woman you are. To risk what you thought might be further abuse by coming here. May God bless you for your goodness. I pray He showers you with peace and joy the rest of your days."

Felicity sat back in her chair and took a sip of her tea while studying the woman; then she set down her cup. "I have the strongest feeling, which I do think is from the Lord, that I can trust you with the reason you saw fright on my face yesterday."

Belinda panicked. Surely her mother wouldn't tell this

untested stranger about herself. "Do you really think that's wise, Mama?"

Felicity's soft gray gaze moved to Belinda. "Your father and I had a nice talk last night, and he reminded me of something Brother Bremmer told him. That we should think of my affliction as something that will give this congregation a chance to grow in mercy and compassion. Perhaps in the past, our difficulties with a church family have stemmed from our fear of sharing my affliction with the more mature Christians while I'm well, instead of having it suddenly thrust upon them. We must start being bold and fear not, as the Lord says." She turned to Mrs. Thompson. "And I would deem it an honor to have a lady of your noble character to be the first woman from the church to pray for my sickness."

When Felicity finished explaining about her periods of melancholy and the desperate days when she thought she heard her dead child's cries, Emma Jane Thompson just sat there, staring at her, the teacup in her hand long forgotten.

"More tea?" Belinda asked, hoping to get some idea what the woman was thinking. Had Mama frightened her? Was she repulsed? What?

Mrs. Thompson glanced at Belinda then down to her drink. "Why, yes, that would be nice." Her green eyes still looked as if she'd taken a blow to the head. She turned back to Felicity. "It's really true then. Your husband don't beat you. I'm so relieved."

She's relieved? That is the sum total of her reaction?

Her mother shook her head, chuckling. "No, he's the kindest of men. I can't imagine another who would've stayed with me all these years, never knowing when he wakes up in the morning what will greet him."

"La, I need to be givin' Mr. Gregg a apology. I had some sore terrible thoughts about him."

"I'd rather you didn't," Belinda inserted as she poured more tea. "Daddy doesn't need to hear someone thought he was a wife beater."

Looking away, the woman twisted her mouth down to one side. "You're right. He surely don't." She slanted her gaze back up to Felicity. "And I want to offer you my hand of friendship. I think it'd be a good thing, with both of us knowin' the bitter cup of sufferin', to have someone we can talk to about any an' everything. I've had some real down-in-the-pit times myself."

Her mother touched Emma Jane's shoulder. "It'd be my pleasure to accept your offer. And any time you feel the need to talk or just to have someone to hold your hand, I'll be here."

Unexpected tears filled the woman's eyes. "And any time you need me, you just give a holler, and I'll come a-runnin'."

Belinda handed the dear lady a napkin from off the tray. How utterly she'd misjudged her.

"Speaking of doing for one another," her mother then said, "there is a small favor I would ask. My Belinda has a note to write to her young man, and we'd appreciate it if you would drop it off at Brother Bremmer's house on your way home."

Chapter Twenty

I t'ink it is about noon," Max's father said, tossing another new hammerhead into a box beside the anvil. "Ve go eat now."

Max had little appetite. He and his mother had been avoiding each other for days, only making the necessary responses while pretending everything was as it should be. But it wasn't. They'd both made accusations, and she was still clinging to her stance as stubbornly as he to his. "I'll be along in a minute." He took a tighter grip on the prongs holding a red-hot spike over the fire pit.

"Dat can vait till later." Pops walked over to the stool where Max sat. He took the prongs from him and replaced them with the cane Max had fashioned out of an ax handle.

As they crossed the field to the house, Max was pleased with the strength his leg had gained in the three days since he'd recklessly removed the splints. He was beginning to feel more like a whole man again. A bitter smile grew when he thought of his mother's look of surprise when she saw his leg was no longer bound. But after the menacing scowl he sent her, she hadn't mentioned it, not once.

The two washed up at the basin outside the back door. Savory aromas wafted out the kitchen window, and Max realized he did have an appetite after all.

When they walked inside, his mother, her hair in a tidy coil of gray-blonde braids, stood waiting expectantly. After several days of nothing but an exchange of hard glances, she wore a suspiciously bright smile. And her round blue eyes seemed unnaturally bright as she viewed Max. She pulled an envelope from her pocket. "A letter came for you."

His heart leaped. At last. The message from the Greggs he'd been expecting.

"*Herr* Bailey, down at da store, he says it is coming all da vay from a trading post on da Missouri."

Max's joy deflated as she handed him a wrinkled and water-stained letter. "It'll be from Drew or Black Bear." He looked at the return address. "Chauteau's Post. They're probably just letting us know they've gotten that far safe and sound." The two men had waited in Reardon Valley only long enough to make sure Max would survive before they'd headed back toward the Shawnee village. They knew their wives would be concerned when the men hadn't arrived home when expected from their fur-trading trip to St. Louis.

"Read it," his pops said. "I alvays like hearing from Drew *und* how his little church in da land of da headdens is doing."

With his thumbnail, Max chipped off the wax seal and unfolded the heavy parchment.

Dear Max, Rolf, and Inga,
I pray this letter finds you all healthy and Max on the mend. I am writing to let you know about the Lewis and Clark Expedition. It has

caused quite a stir along the Missouri. Most of the tribes have never seen so many white men all together like that. They do not know what to make of men rowing and poling those loaded-down pirogues up the river, making hardly no time at all.

The expedition is traveling so slow, Max, that if you hurry back, you can still catch up to them. Black Bear said he will go with you as long as he can get back home to his family before the first snows set in.

Give our warmest regards to my family.

Sincerely,
Andrew Reardon

"Vhat you say, Son?" his mother asked, though she didn't look up from brushing imaginary crumbs from the red-checked tablecloth. "I hear da men talking at da store. Dey all say it is a very important expedition, dis mapping of da Vest. It comes straight from President Jefferson." She glanced up. "You could become famous, like dat Daniel Boone fellow."

Max could see right through her. "You sure are fiddling a different tune. Just last week all you could talk about was me settling down and getting married *here* in the valley. Now you've got me traipsing all the way to the Pacific Ocean like it was what you wanted all along."

Her stare hardened. "Sit down. Bot' of you. I am filling your plates now."

Taking his seat, he knew his mother wasn't the only one who'd changed. A few weeks ago that letter would have been reason for a celebration. Now all he could think about was how to go about convincing Belinda to leave her family *and* his behind and marry him. There was no way he was going to subject her to his mother's Old World superstitions.

Inga set a wooden trencher filled with rabbit stew in front of him without her usual, "Eat up." He couldn't recall a time when they'd been at such an impasse. She'd been bossy when it came to her children, but always in a loving manner.

And there was the matter of Mrs. Gregg. Could he ever talk Belinda into leaving her? Leaving the valley with him, maybe even going as far away as Drew had taken his wife? Beyond the comforts of civilization?

All these questions had been bouncing around in his head for days now, with no answers, and he was tired of waiting for Belinda to contact him, to let him know when it was convenient for him to come by.

Or had he scared her off by being so forward?

If she didn't send word to him by tomorrow, he'd be riding over first thing Friday morning.

If he could wait that long.

Belinda awakened Thursday morning with a ferocious headache, feeling as though she'd finally had a taste of the melancholy her mother sometimes experienced. Her sleep had been fitful naps between bouts of weeping . . . tears flowing, wetting her pillow while she willed herself not to make a sound. To have either of her parents hear her and come to investigate would have been as unbearable as the long, tormented wait they'd shared with her the evening before.

Max had not come. The note inviting him for dessert had been sent by way of Emma Jane Thompson on Monday with the hope that Belinda could make up for Sunday dinner, and he'd simply ignored the request.

He'd had two days to send his regrets if he had so chosen. But he hadn't even bothered with the most common of courtesies.

Belinda threw back the sheet covering her and rose from her

canopied four-poster. She padded on bare feet across her blue-and-green, floral-patterned rug to the washstand beside the wardrobe. Looking in the mirror, she saw that her eyes were red and swollen.

She cringed. Nothing looked worse than a redhead who'd been crying. At the sight, tears started forming again.

For simply hours she and her parents had sat on the veranda, waiting. Waiting while the flies swarmed over the cheesecloth covering the honeyed peaches . . . while the whipped cream went flat . . . and the sweet biscuits turned hard.

Each minute had ticked by with agonizing slowness. As time dragged by, her shame grew even thicker than her disappointment. The kiss. The kiss she and Max shared had meant nothing to him—or the very reason not to see her again.

Only moments before he kissed her, he'd as much as told her that he was returning up the Missouri. Why should she expect him to allow a momentary lapse of self-control to jeopardize his plans?

Her only saving grace during the tormented evening was that she hadn't told her parents about the kiss.

And they'd been as supportive as anyone could expect. During the hours of waiting, they'd tried to ease her disappointment by offering an array of excuses for him. But short of death, she couldn't think of a single one that justified this deliberate snub.

Listlessly, she dressed and started for the stairs. As she left her room, she saw that her parents' door stood open. They both must have risen before her. Reaching the bottom landing, she glanced out the windows and saw that the sun had cleared the hills hours ago. Her gaze shot to the tall mahogany clock. *Ten forty-five*. She couldn't recall the last time she'd risen so late.

The kitchen was empty. The only evidence that anyone had

been there was the dirty dishes left to soak in the dishpan. Even the coals under the coffeepot looked cold.

They'd no doubt gone out to the pottery shed, deciding to let her sleep in, probably, she thought with chagrin, so they wouldn't have to deal with her miserable rejected self this morning.

Just as well. She was in no mood to either cook or eat breakfast. Noticing the bowl of sweet cream from last night that had gone flat, she started to toss it out then decided it would make a nice treat for the baby fox. Outside, she found the kit's bowl under the azalea, with fresh food in it and the baby curled up in her little house fast asleep. Someone—most likely her mother—had already fed Downy, taken care of another of her usual morning chores because . . .

Tears started to surface again. Belinda swallowed them down and started for the summer kitchen. The least she could do was have a proper dinner waiting for them when they came in at noon.

"Something sure smells good," her father said as he strode in the back door shortly after the clock had struck twelve.

"That's peaches and molasses fried in with the pork," Belinda informed him as she placed the last serving bowl on the dining table. *The peaches that went to waste last night*, she added to herself.

"And summer squash and corn. Sliced tomatoes." He pulled her into a hug and kissed her cheek. "You sure have outdone yourself."

He sounded a bit too enthusiastic. The meal wasn't all that special.

Belinda glanced toward the door out the back. "How much longer will Mama be?"

Her dad shrugged. "I reckon I forgot to come in and tell you. Your mother went visiting over to the Reardons' this morning."

"Went *visiting?* Mama doesn't go visiting. She never goes anywhere. Especially by herself." Belinda looked out the front windows.

"Nothing I said could talk her into waiting till you woke up. She said she owed Mrs. Thompson a visit, and that was that."

"But Mama doesn't even know where the Reardons live."

"She said someone at the settlement could direct her. She was real set on doing this by herself." Her father drew out his usual chair at the table. "Personally, I'm right pleased. The two of them know each other's secrets, and they still want to be friends." He motioned to her. "Come, sit down. We'll ask God to bless their time together while we say grace over this one fine meal."

Just a few days ago she'd thought it, and now she was thinking it again. Things were surely changing fast. And Belinda's own private prayer was that her mother's adventure wouldn't ultimately turn out as unhappily as her own had.

With only a little help from his cane, Max walked out the front opening of the smithy, hoping to catch some sign of a breeze. As he pulled a kerchief from his apron pocket to wipe the perspiration from his neck, he spotted a long-legged roan Thoroughbred tied to the hitching post at his family's house . . . not the usual breed for this side of the Appalachians.

And its saddle was a lady's. *Belinda!*

His pulse started racing. Finally, she'd come. What other family in the valley would have extra to spend on such a horse?

He ripped off his leather apron and tossed it over a hitching rail, then hoofed it to the house as fast as his legs and cane would carry him.

As he neared, he saw, not his Belinda but her mother, dressed in a white blouse and a calf-length skirt of rust-brown suede and riding boots. Mrs. Gregg stood on the porch, conversing with his mother. And not in her usual feathery-light tones.

"I find that hard to believe," she stated bluntly. "Where is your son? I'll speak to him personally."

"I tell you, he is not here," his mother answered, her own voice strong.

"Yes I am! I'm here!"

They both swung toward the direction of his shout, his mother's expression even more astounded than Mrs. Gregg's.

"I was yust about to say dat you are at da smit'y," his mother amended as he came up the walk. "Now, if you vill excuse me, I must go see to my—my chickens." She whirled around as if the devil himself were chasing her and charged back into the house.

See to her chickens? At two o'clock in the afternoon?

Dismissing her ludicrous reason for leaving, Max started up the steps to greet Mrs. Gregg. "Good day. I'm real pleased to see you're out and about. Though, when I saw the horse," he added, feeling his face lift into a hopeful grin, "I was kinda hoping it was that gorgeous daughter of yours."

"You don't say?" The older lady's normally sickly features took on a haughtiness as she arched a thin brow. "That's exactly how Belinda felt last night when you didn't arrive for dessert."

"I don't understand. Why would you have expected me?"

"So I thought." Mrs. Gregg glanced through a window into the house, then returned her gaze to him with a surprising but welcome smile. "I imagine the invitation we sent you went astray."

"Are you saying that Belinda sent me a note?"

"Yes, on Monday."

He shook his head. "All week I've been waiting for word from her, letting me know when you were up to having visitors again. And you say she wrote me on Monday?" He shot his own look into the house.

Mrs. Gregg placed a leather-gloved hand on his arm. "It's probably just a comedy of errors, as Shakespeare would say. Perhaps we might expect you, say, tomorrow evening?"

"What's the matter with tonight?" He was being pushy. He backed off. "Unless, of course, your errands today have tired you out too much."

"I'm not sure Belinda will have sufficient time to prepare a special dessert, but—" The woman did have a lovely smile, a lot like her daughter's.

"Whatever's on hand will be more than fine. What time should I arrive?"

"Sunsets are always pleasant on the veranda. Oh, and, Mr. Bremmer, I do believe Belinda's father and I will have to excuse ourselves a bit early. As you surmised, I've had a rather long day. But I'm sure you young people won't miss us all that much. I need to hurry on home now." Her silver gray eyes had an extra spark in them as she started down the steps then stopped. "Would you be a dear and give me a boost up on my horse?"

Watching Mrs. Gregg ride away toward the ferry landing, Max was happier than he'd been since he kissed Belinda last Sunday. Still, he knew her mother had left a lot unsaid.

And it all had to do with his mother.

Never in his life could he recall a time when she had deliberately deceived him. Inga Bremmer, the wife of the valley's pastor, had kept Belinda's note from him.

Max nodded sagely. So that's why she'd been acting so

strangely the last few days. "Seeing to her chickens? In a pig's eye."

Gripping his cane, Max started back to the house.

His mother intercepted him just inside the door with fire in her eyes. "Come back to da kitchen. Ve don't need da whole settlement hearing you bellow."

The woman had some gall—taking the offensive. His own muscles clenched.

Then suddenly he realized that charging her like a mad bull would solve nothing. He took a long calming breath. "I could use something cool to drink," he said so quietly it even amazed him. "And we need to talk."

"I . . . uh . . . *ja*, sure," came stumbling out, the bravado in her voice fading. Her gaze faltered. "I haf fresh-squeezed lemonade in da springhouse."

Chapter Twenty-One

With his hand surrounding a glass of lemonade, Max asked the Lord for wisdom and a calm heart. He took a seat in one of the wooden-armed chairs in their simply furnished parlor. He studied the room, knowing that his mother had always done her utmost to make it pleasant and welcoming. The rag rugs, the colorful calico gathered at the windows and cushioning the seats, crocheted doilies on the plainly built side tables. He knew she worked hard, usually with the best of intentions, but this time those intentions were decidedly wrong.

His mother, brow pinched and looking tense, sat down on the edge of her wooden rocker and immediately took the offensive. "I know vhat you are t'inking. *Ja*, I did it. I keep da note dey send to you. I burn it up in da cook fire. *Und* I already know vhat you is going to say."

She was talking faster now. Max sat back, took a drink of the tart ade, and let her finish. Then he'd speak.

"You are going to say dat I sin. Dat I lie by . . . by . . . vhat is dat vord? *Omission*. But da life of mine son is more important dan da burning of one silly note. Since you are a small boy, we haf high hopes for you, for da day dat you marry. For your *kinders* dat get born. You t'ink of da *kinders* you are having *mit* dis Belinda." She wagged a finger. "No, I am not letting you marry into da house of madness." She brushed with her hand as if shooing him away. "You go ahead. You go on back to da hunting *und* tracking *mit* dem Indian friends you t'ink more about dan your own sweet papa. He is getting old *und* wore out—not dat a selfish boy like you vould notice." She lunged to her feet. "Right now I go pack your t'ings. It is time you go avay."

"Sit down, Mama." His voice was much quieter than hers, but firm. "You haven't touched your drink." It remained on the side table beside her rocker.

Reluctantly, she lowered herself into the chair again.

Max leaned forward. "Mama, I know Pops is getting older. He'll be sixty-one his next birthday. I know he works too hard. And so do you. I also know that you're married to the best man I've ever known and that he loves you very much. So, for his sake, I think it would be best if we don't burden him with your burning of the note from Belinda."

She sucked in a breath, her chin started to tremble, and for a second Max thought she would actually cry. Then she gained control. "T'ank you," came out in almost a whisper.

"Mama, you and Pops have gone on your own great adventure. You left your homeland in Bavaria and sailed all the way across the ocean, bringing your first two babies with you. Then you took another risk by selling yourselves into servitude for seven years to pay for your trip. And then, with two more little ones in tow, you trekked overmountain, facing the dangers of man and beast *and lost kids,*" he remembered, chuckling, "to carve out a life for you and your family in a virgin land. And since then, you and Pops have been living the greatest adventure of all, pastoring the flock in this valley."

"*Ja*, I know. Your papa, he gives me a goot life. I t'ank God every night for him."

"And you have been good to Pops too. God has blessed you both because you always put your love for the Lord first."

"Not alvays, your papa *und* me, but ve try." She seemed to relax a bit more, resting her back against the chair and taking a sip of her drink.

"I know you do. But I recall a few times when you balked. When Pops packed us up to come overmountain, you thought he'd gone mad. Remember? You made life real hard for him for a time."

"*And* how do you remember dat? You vas only five den."

"Renate and Isolda. My sisters never missed much. But, Mama, what I'm trying to get at is this. Sometimes what appears to be a bad idea to one person is what the other one is meant to do. Especially if that person has spent a lot of time seeking God's direction." Max took a swallow of his lemonade, giving his mother a moment to digest his words.

"I really feel," he continued, "that God allowed me to be struck down because He needed to get my attention. I was, as you said, living a selfish existence. The Lord made me take a second look at my life . . . and yours and Papa's. To see us all through more mature eyes. And, yes, I believe the Lord brought me back to introduce me to the woman I hope to make my wife."

Sucking in a gasp, his mother's eyes flared wide. But she held her tongue.

"I don't know what's out there waiting for us in the future, but I do know, if I follow Papa's example and keep seeking the Lord and what He wants, He won't lead me astray."

His mother's gaze skittered about a moment before she stared at him again, intently. "I t'ink you see a purty face *und* you start hearing vhat you vant to hear—not vhat da Lord is saying. You better stop *mit* da oogling *und* go vash your ears out."

Max expelled a sigh. The longest speech he'd ever made, and it had been for naught. Defeated, he stood up. "I'm going back to work."

~

"Belinda, the Reardons live a good half hour south of the settlement," Christopher Gregg explained, his hands forming a large bowl with the wet clay while his feet worked the pedals that turned the potter's wheel.

"But, Daddy, Mama left early this morning." Belinda stood far enough away not to get soiled by any wet residue in the shelf-lined shop that always smelled of drying ware and metallic glazes.

"Sweetheart, you have to figure the time from here to the ferry, then the wait to cross, asking directions at the settlement. Altogether, it could've taken as much as an hour and a half to reach the Reardon place. Then your mother's time visiting. And they surely invited her to stay for nooning."

"But it's after two-thirty. I'd better go hitch up the two-wheeler."

"See here, Carrots," he said, glancing up from the rising sides of the bowl, "you worry too much. Your mother's not some lost youngster."

"But, Daddy—"

"No more *buts*. I'll tell you what. If she's not back by four, I'll go look for her myself. In the meantime, I sure would like a mess of green peas for supper. I noticed they're coming off real good out in the garden." With the bowl finished to his satisfaction, he stopped pedaling and let the wheel slow to a stop.

"You promise? Not a minute later than four."

"Looks like neither of us will have to go." He nodded past her.

She whirled around and saw her mother coming across the bridge, riding sidesaddle, and the roan at a high-stepping gait.

"Thank You, God." Belinda walked to the edge of the stone-floored porch and waved her arms to attract her mother's attention a quarter of a mile away.

Her effort proved successful. Her mother returned her wave and nudged the mare into a gallop, riding up the drive and past the house to where Belinda and her father now stood. Felicity reined to a stop before her family.

"My, don't you look fine up there on Duchess," Chris said, wiping the wet clay from his fingers. "I haven't seen roses like those in your cheeks for ages."

That brought a smile. "I've had such a grand time, dear." She lifted her leg over the extended pommel and reached out to her husband. "Would you please help me down?"

Belinda had to admit that her mother did look quite fit in her riding habit and scarfed bonnet . . . not the least distressed or nervous.

"Walk with me to the stable, you two," her mother said lightly, "and I'll tell you all about my day."

Curious despite herself, Belinda fell into step beside her parents and the horse. They headed toward the small barn beside the carriage house, both neatly whitewashed.

"First, I spent a wonderful morning at the Reardons'," her mother related in a chipper voice. "They're all such nice people. And so many children. A bit noisy for Emma Jane, I think. She scarcely spoke until I suggested that she show me their farm. Once we were alone, we had a real fine time chatting. I believe she's going to be a dear friend."

Chris pulled Felicity close and bussed her cheek. "I'm purely glad to hear that."

"Thank you, dear heart."

Belinda felt like weeping at the love her parents shared, the kind she so desperately lacked.

"I've invited Emma Jane to dinner Sunday," her mother continued. "If you two don't mind."

"Of course not," Belinda managed. Then, "But there's something I have to ask. I'm sorry, but I can't help myself."

"No need, sweetheart. The answer is yes. Emma Jane delivered the invitation to the Bremmers."

Belinda's heart plummeted. Max truly had ignored it . . . ignored her.

"I rode to the Bremmers' after leaving the Reardons'," her mother said more forcefully.

Belinda gasped. "Mama, you didn't. How humiliating."

"It was no such thing." Her mother stopped and faced her. "It turned out as I thought. Max never received your note. You should have seen his face when he learned that you waited for him last night and he didn't come." She caught Belinda's hand. "To make up for it, he's coming this evening right after supper. I tried to delay him a day to give us time to prepare another special dessert for him. But he wouldn't be put off."

"He wouldn't?" Belinda felt tears ready to brim as they had off and on all day. But this time they were the overflow of her happiness. She blinked them back.

"No, sweetheart, Max absolutely would not. I do believe he'd been agonizing as well, wondering why you hadn't contacted him." The sparkle that sprang to life in her mother's eyes mirrored the well of joy exploding in Belinda.

Then a darker thought intruded, causing Belinda to ask, "If Emma Jane delivered the invitation, why didn't Max get it?"

"Oh yes, that. Apparently Mrs. Bremmer forgot to give it to him . . . simply forgot."

Though possible, Belinda found that explanation hard to believe. And from the look she caught passing between her parents, she didn't think they believed it either. Her message had been withheld from Max purposefully.

But she refused to allow herself to delve into such concerns at this gladsome moment. Max would be here in less than four hours!

She reached up to her hair and glanced down at her work clothes. And there was dinner to fix and the other chores to complete. "If you'll excuse me, I purely need to get back to the house."

All afternoon Max worked alongside his father while a fierce but secret battle waged inside him. But no matter how much he wanted to talk over his mother's meddling with his father, he knew his pops had enough weight on his shoulders with the problems of the valley without taking on this one between Max and his mother.

He was a grown man now. He'd deal with it. Somehow. If he could keep a lid on his anger.

With next to no conversation, the two were busy making enough nails to fill an order for several kegs. These were to be floated downriver on Hatfield's flatboat next Tuesday.

But despite Max's best intentions while he labored, he silently ranted at his mother, tore into her, accused her of everything from her lack of charity to being an out-and-out hypocrite. Then he'd rail at God awhile for allowing more suffering to befall the Greggs. He had no doubt that Mrs. Gregg knew exactly why his mother had kept the invitation from him.

In his worst moments, his desire for justice brought him ever closer to condemning Mama before his father. But then he'd look at the old warhorse for God, and he couldn't bring himself to add another burden. Besides, the huggable old bear was, as his mother had said, aging. Noticeably.

"Dat is da last nail I make for today, Son." With a big hand, his pops swept a pile of finished nails from his worktable into a keg just below it. "Ve go vash up for supper."

That lightened Max's spirit. Getting supper over with meant he'd be riding soon to Belinda's . . . no matter what his mother said or tried to do.

Swiping his own batch of nails into the keg beneath his bench, he heard the sound of galloping hooves coming into the crossroads from the north. He exchanged glances with his father, hoping it was just some rambunctious buck riding in, rather than some emergency his pops would be called to attend. Especially not after such a hard, hot day's work and before he'd had his supper.

Pulling off their heavy aprons, they headed out the door and looked toward the lowering sun.

Max gripped his cane hard as his good mood turned to alarm when he saw Mrs. Dagget riding on a sweat-foamed horse, her gray hair streaming out wildly behind her.

Seeing them, she pulled back on the reins, bringing the big-boned animal to a dust-churning halt. Both were gasping for air as she yelled, "You gotta come. Both of you."

"What is it?" Max asked.

"Pete. He's up on the barn roof. He's standin' up there, lookin' down at them big rocks right behind it. He's been up there more'n an hour now, and we can't talk him down. I'm scared he's gonna jump. And it's all my fault. I shouldn't have said what I did. But it just popped outta my mouth."

Before Max could question her any further, she kicked her mount into a jumping start. "Come. Now. I gotta get back 'fore my husband kills hisself tryin' to climb up there."

"Amos has da rheumatism in bot' knees," Pops explained. "Dey stay swole up most of da time."

Max barely heard the words as he rushed back through the shop for the horse pens. Not taking the time to saddle Kaiser, Max merely bridled him and took off for the Dagget place on the gray's wide back, leaving ahead of his father.

Along the way, he noticed folks standing outside their houses and barns, curious about the commotion on the road and wearing concerned expressions. Everyone knew women of Mrs. Dagget's age didn't race to and fro for no reason, especially at suppertime. Then, to see Max following soon after with the same urgency . . .

Max passed Mrs. Dagget and her fatigued horse just before he reached the family's turnoff. As he rode into the clearing, he saw Pete standing high up on the barn's ridgepole, the low-hanging sun at his back. Max released a long breath. His friend was still alive.

Seeing a tall ladder propped against one side of the barn, Max guided Kaiser toward it, praying that his own weak leg wouldn't prevent him from reaching the top.

As he slid off the horse's back, he noticed Mr. Dagget standing near the jumble of boulders at the rear, his arms akimbo, looking helplessly up at his son. Poor man.

A pile of shingles lay beside the ladder. Max realized that Pete had probably been repairing the roof before he became suicidal. He grabbed on to a rung, asking the Lord to get him to the top; then he started to climb, pulling hard with his arms every time he used his recovering leg.

When he reached the edge of the roof and crawled on top,

his injured leg was shaking like it belonged on a palsied old man.

Pete glanced down at him from the ridge. "Max! What are you doin' here?"

Max looked up with a painful grin. "Your ma's gettin' worried about you." His leg too weak to trust, he started crawling toward Pete. "She wants you to come down for supper."

"No she don't. Not really."

"What d'ya mean? Sure she does." Max tried to sound casual as he made his way up the steep roof. "You know women take it personal when their cooking goes to waste."

"I ain't hungry." Pete turned back toward the rear edge. "Go on down. Eat my share."

Max kept moving, the splintery shingles digging into his hands and knees.

Pete scowled over his shoulder. "I know you mean well, but I'm really not up to company today."

"Pal, I thought you was getting better. Getting back to your old self again."

"Don't you know, I ain't got no old self to go back to. And Mama cain't take lookin' at me no more. Pshaw, I can't take lookin' at myself neither."

When Max finally got within a few yards of Pete, his friend thrust out a warning hand. "Don't come any closer."

"I thought—"

"Thinkin' don't do no good. You should know that by now. Thinkin' just makes things worse. An' lookin' in the mirror . . . do you know what that's like? It ain't me lookin' back; it's Paul. Him wantin' to know why he's dead and not me."

Max sat, bracing himself with his good leg before looking at Pete. "You're just letting your imagination get the best of you. Do you really think your mama would be happier if that ornery ol' horse had kicked you in the head instead of Paul? Of course not. And now she's down there . . ." He peered off the roof and saw that Mrs. Dagget had arrived, with a couple other riders coming close behind. "She's down there scared half to death that she's gonna lose you too. How could a mother endure losing both her twins?"

"Aw, Max, you just don't know."

Pete dropped down beside him. "Max, she pushed me away when I tried to hug her. Said she couldn't stand to have me touch her. My own ma." His head sagged.

Max draped an arm over Pete's shoulders. "You know she didn't mean it. But just for the sake of argument, let's say it was you that was killed instead of Paul. Don't you know she'd be grieving for you just like she is for him?"

"I always thought so. She never yelled at me any more than she did Paul."

"If it was you up in heaven, would you be sitting there wishing a horse would come and kick Paul in the head, kill him, just because it happened to you?" Max leaned down, trying to get a better look at Pete's face. "No, he'd want you to go on and live for the both of you."

Pete shrugged his bony shoulders. "You just don't understand. I'm all tore up inside."

"You're right. I don't. I never had to lose a member of my family. All I know is, it's up to you now. To remember the good times you two had together. Times nobody else knows about but you. It's up to you to keep his memory alive. And you gotta start learning how to have good times without him. It's what Paul would want. You know it."

Pete finally looked at Max, his dark blue eyes blurred with tears. "But that's the trouble. They won't let me talk about anything that happened, good or bad. Whenever I mention Paul's name, my folks just up an' walk outta the room."

Max squeezed his shoulder. "You can talk to me about him. I ain't going nowhere."

Chapter Twenty-Two

Belinda watched the last light of day fade away, and with it, her last hope of Max Bremmer coming. Two evenings in a row. She'd sat here on the veranda, her heart tearing more with each tick of the big clock . . . with every excuse her parents offered . . . with every overture they made, trying to include her in some tidbit of idle conversation.

One thing she wouldn't repeat on this night was sitting here and counting every new star that appeared, the blink of every lightning bug, turning expectantly toward each new sound from the darkening woods.

Abruptly she stood up. "I'm going up to my room. Good night."

Her mother came quickly to her feet and caught Belinda's arm. "I promise you, Max Bremmer would be here if he could. Something must have happened."

"Obviously." Belinda pulled free. "Last night his mother saw to it he didn't come, and most likely she had something to do with his not being here tonight. And that's the way of it. Now, as for me, I'm through with this courting business. It's too—much too humiliating."

She brushed past her father, feeling preposterous in a frilly, pale blue day gown, hoping Max would think it looked pretty on her. Well, that wouldn't happen again. Neither would she spend this night swimming in tears.

For all her bravado, she'd made a liar of herself before she even reached the stairs. Her eyes had pooled, blinding her, till she stumbled into the first step. But she refused to wipe them away lest either of her parents was watching her through the front windows.

"Never again," she vowed. Never again would she blithely hand her heart over to some stranger to have it stomped on. Before she took such a chance in the future, she'd have to know a man very well.

Reaching the safety of her room, she took a ragged breath. The truth of the matter was that no man would ever seriously court her, and somehow she would have to make peace with that fact, once and for all.

She didn't bother lighting a lamp. It would only add to the stifling heat that had ascended to the upper floor. She opened wide the French doors to let in some cooler air. In the moonlight, she stripped off her outer clothing and the strangling corset, then splashed tepid water over her face and burning eyes.

She walked toward the lace-canopied bed. But weary as she was, she was too agitated to lie down. On the nightstand beside it, she saw a romantic novel she'd been reading—one she'd read several times before. She knew the homeless waif would at long last be united with her true love. Her chest tightened. That was just some silly storybook, not real life.

Telling herself it was the stuffy room that was suffocating her, she moved out onto her balcony. The evening breeze did feel good on her damp face and ruffling through her thin cotton night rail. What difference would it make if she wanted to sit out here in the dark? Who would care?

A few minutes later, she heard her parents leave the porch and come upstairs and walk past her room to their own. Soon the entire house fell into complete darkness as she sat in the lone chair on her balcony . . . gazing across the lower meadow where her attention kept returning to the bridge.

Her thoughts, too, kept straying to the one thing beyond all else she could not fathom. Why hadn't the Lord simply left her as she was? Why had He allowed this torment to come into her life? She might not have been overly happy before, but she'd carved out a peaceful existence for herself . . . one with moments when she was of real service, bringing help and even a little joy to her parents and any needy woodland creatures she rescued.

Why, God?

The unshed tears now trickled down her cheeks.

Darkness had descended more than an hour ago, and still Max didn't feel he could suggest to Pete that they climb down from the roof of the barn. During the last couple of hours, Pete had done most of the talking. Max's old friend had laughed and sobbed, and Max had joined him often as not. Pete seemed bent on remembering every antic, every sad moment he and his twin had shared. For Pete to start recovering from his profound loss, Max sensed he needed to do this.

But the further into the evening hours that they remained on those miserably hard shingles, the more Max wanted to rise up and shout, *Enough. I have my own need to pursue, my own love left waiting. For a second night.*

But he didn't. He tamped down his own desires and stayed at his friend's side. All the while, he recounted the numerous occasions his father had also been called away from his own loved ones at the most inopportune times.

" 'Member the day," Pete was saying, "when Paul knocked me clean outta that tree, and I broke my arm?"

Max murmured, "Yes," as Pete rambled on.

"I sure had Paul over the barrel after that. I kept threatening to tell Ma on him. I—"

"Halloo."

Pete and Max swung toward the feminine salutation. It came from where the ladder reached up to the roof. Max had seen folks straggling into the Dagget clearing a few at a time all evening—a prime reason Pete didn't want to climb down. Until now, though, no one had tried to join them.

"Halloo. It's me, Liza."

"*Liza!*" Pete's voice rang with panic. "What's she doin' here?"

"I sure could use some help gettin' the rest of the way up."

"I ain't helpin' her off the ladder," Pete whispered fiercely. "She keeps tryin' to push herself off on me."

Max was not pleased either. She'd spurned Pete in the past, and now he cringed every time she came around. Max prayed she wouldn't make things worse. Still . . . "Somebody has to go get her. Or she might trip over her skirt and kill herself."

"You go."

"My bad leg. You can get there a whole lot faster."

"I know you're up here," Liza called. "I can hear you whisperin'."

Max tugged at Pete's shirtsleeve. "Go on. Face her like a man. She's your girl, not mine."

"All right, I'm comin," Pete hollered. He stood up and made his way toward her.

Max started scooting after his friend, all the while wishing it had been Belinda coming to find him. Belinda . . . would she ever forgive him for not showing up *a second time?*

"Oh, Peter." Liza's shadowy figure clasped Pete around his neck as he lifted her onto the roof. "You had me so scared. I came as soon as I heard."

"I reckon ever'body in the valley knows by now."

Pete sounded so upset again. Max wondered if he'd rather jump than face the crowd waiting below.

"Dear, dear Pete. Don't fret about that," Liza continued, clinging to him. "The thought of losin' you, too, has ever'one in a frightful state."

"They are?"

"We are. *I am.* If you don't care about yourself, think about me and our children. All the babies we'd never have."

"Babies? I never thought about . . ."

"If the first one's a boy, I thought we could name him after Paul. Somehow it comforts me to think about that. Doesn't it you?"

"I never . . . aye, I reckon it does, a little."

Max heard a thread of hope in Pete's voice. "See here, you two," he broke in when he reached the pair. "If Pete will promise not to do anything stupid while I'm gone, I'll climb down and send everybody home."

"Aye, you do that," Liza answered. "Pete an' me has some things we need to get said, private-like. Ain't that right?"

"Pete?" Just to be sure, Max needed his promise.

"I reckon. If Liza's willin' to risk comin' up here for me, the least I can do is listen to what she has to say." Yes, there was a definite hint of optimism in his voice.

Fortunately, it was too dark to read anyone's features, because Max couldn't stop his grin. The crisis was over, and Pete was about to get himself betrothed . . . standing on the roof of a barn.

Now that would be a story to tell their grandchildren.

As Max descended the ladder rungs to the light of many lanterns below, he wondered if he, too, would get engaged this night. That had been in the back of his mind. Determined to think positively, he was sure that once Belinda knew the cause of his delay, she'd forgive him and seriously consider his suit.

Lord, I do know this is Your will for me. . . . It is, isn't it?

Max managed to send everyone home except his father and Liza's parents. Then, as he'd expected, Pete and Liza descended the ladder a betrothed couple, hugging and kissing, not caring that their families witnessed their open display of affection for one another.

Rolf clapped a powerful hand on Max's shoulder. "Proud of you I am. You haf become a fine man since you been gone dese long years."

"Thanks, Pops." Remembering the last conversation he'd had with his mother, Max wondered if his father would think he was such a fine man if he knew of the enmity that now existed between the two of them. "But I'm late. I accepted an invite out to the Greggs' to join them this evening for dessert. I've really gotta go."

His father glanced toward the western hills, where not a hint of twilight remained. "You are late. Unless you told Billy to vait *mit* his mule, you vill haf to pull yourself across da river *mit* your own hands."

"I'll do whatever I have to. I promised I'd come."

His father shrugged helplessly. "Do as you vant. But dey probably had dessert hours ago."

Max knew Pops thought it was foolish to go calling so late. But the old man had no idea this was the second night he'd left Belinda sitting there waiting for him.

Since Billy Stanley hadn't been forewarned, Max did have to haul himself across Caney Fork. And even a quarter hour later as he rode the gray plow horse toward the Greggs' place, his hands still stung from the rope burns. In one he held the reins, and from the other he lifted aloft the lantern he'd borrowed from the Daggets. Shadows danced crazily in its light along the tree-crowded path. He followed the trail, studying each cutoff, fearing he might miss the one leading to the Greggs'. He couldn't afford to lose an extra minute.

Practicing and rewording what he planned to say to Belinda— his apology and, hopefully, his proposal of marriage—he prayed again that she would be understanding, gracious, *and* receptive. And when her father knew the reason for his tardiness, Max was sure he wouldn't oppose his offer either. The problems concerning his mother and hers could be worked out later.

Max recognized a particular stand of young hazelnut trees that grew on either side of the Gregg cutoff. His pulse quickened. Just a few more minutes. Turning onto it, he nudged his mount into a faster pace.

But when he reached the foot of the bridge, he saw no lights glowing from the Gregg house. Not even one.

They hadn't waited up for him.

Disappointment welled up in his chest. But what could he expect?

"Belinda, Belinda . . ." Undecided about what to do, he sat there, his thoughts bouncing between going on to the house and waking up the family or riding back home and returning first thing in the morning. Which would be the best course to take?

Finally, he decided upon the morning. Folks were always in a better mood when they'd gotten a good night's rest. He reined Kaiser around and started back to the ferry.

One thing he had to admit: life had been much simpler before he first caught sight of his lady of the river. Courting her had certainly proved difficult. And confusing.

~

Belinda strode into the kitchen in time to start breakfast the next morning, determined not to allow a person she'd known scarcely more than a month to steal her daily routine from her. She would neither mope nor lie in bed as she had the day before.

Still, her mother had beaten her downstairs again. Felicity turned from the hearth. "Good morning, darling. Coffee's almost ready." Her accompanying smile was much too sympathetic. "I'll start the biscuits if you'll go out and collect the eggs."

Belinda made a point of sounding just as cheery. "I won't be long." Heading out the back door, she hoped neither of her parents would ruin the day by mentioning anything about last night. Ever.

After tossing feed to the chickens, she collected eggs from inside the smelly coop and returned with them caught up in her apron. Then, as she'd wished, she helped her mother fry pota-toes and pork in silence.

As Belinda was setting butter and plum preserves on the table, her father came in the kitchen door, drying his hands on a towel that he'd forgotten to leave outside at the washstand.

"La, but you were quick," Felicity said, sounding just as sunny as she had earlier. "You have the stock fed and watered already?"

Belinda wished her mother would speak with a less obvious lilt to her voice. Her pretense at cheerfulness merely reminded the others that there was something else really on her mind—on all their minds.

Her dad tossed the towel over a hook near the back door, also in a nonchalant manner. "I see everything's about ready. I hope there's extra, because a rider is coming up the drive. Max Bremmer, I would assume."

Belinda almost dropped the plates she was carrying to the table. She peered out the front window.

Max's bare head shined silvery gold in the morning light. Shoulders wide, chest broad, back straight . . . no one could deny he was a handsome figure of a man.

It only made her want to hate him more, if she could hate him at all. "Father, you go out and speak to him. I—I can't. No excuse is . . ." Tears threatened as she fled the kitchen and headed for the stairs.

∼

Max had seen Christopher Gregg hurry from the stables to the house. He was sure Belinda's father had informed her of his arrival. He'd expected Belinda to come outside to greet him . . . everything in him wanted her to walk through the front entrance with that expectant look in her eyes, that smile that would tell him she was glad to see him.

But as he reached the hitching post near the rose arbor, it was Mr. Gregg who came out onto the veranda, not Belinda. "Good morning, Max." The tall, bone-lean man strode down the walk to intercept him. "What brings you out so early?"

Max had assumed his presence was self-evident. "I came by to explain why I didn't get here last night till after you all retired." He swung down from the saddle.

"So, you did come after all."

"Of course." Scarcely taking his eyes off Mr. Gregg, he looped the horse's reins through the hitching ring. "I want to extend my apologies to you as well for my extreme tardiness. My friend was intent on ending his life yester's eve, and I was obliged to stay with him until I knew he was back to himself again."

"Your friend," Mr. Gregg said, shifting to an easier stance, "the one who lost his twin?"

"Aye. Pete Dagget." Trying to look more relaxed too, Max managed a strained smile as his eyes darted past the older man to the front door that stood slightly ajar.

"I know how that can be," Mr. Gregg said.

Max was sure he did, considering his wife's own history.

"In some of her bad times, my Felicity has considered ending her life too, in order to free Belinda and me from the burden of caring for her."

Still, Mr. Gregg didn't make a move to invite Max inside.

"Is Belinda up yet? I'd like to explain why I spent four hours on a barn roof when I was supposed to be here."

"Barn roof?"

"Pete had been repairing it, so it was a real handy place to throw himself off of when he started thinking about kicking the bucket." Max shot another glance to the door.

"I'm glad to hear everything turned out all right, son. But I'm afraid Belinda's not up to receiving a guest just now."

"Aye, I reckon I am awful early. I don't mind waiting till she's dressed."

Mr. Gregg paused a moment, then—"Max, that's not the problem. You see, Belinda's really not all that used to this court-ing business. Your absence again last night was a great disap-pointment to her."

Tension started building in the back of Max's neck—the man was hedging. "I'm sure it was, but—"

Placing a freckled hand on Max's arm, Mr. Gregg seemed to be trying for a sincere look. "The truth is, she's too upset to see you."

"But once I explain—" Max sidestepped Mr. Gregg and charged past him—"she'll understand. If anyone would, she will."

Chapter Twenty-Three

The man did have gall. Max had bowled right past her father and was coming up the veranda steps. Having crept downstairs again, Belinda watched from the fringed edge of a parlor curtain, wondering if he'd be so bold as to burst into the house and chase after her if she made another dash for the stairs.

Well, she wouldn't give the bounder the pleasure of having her run from him.

She intercepted him at the door—her chin high, her tone icy. "Good morning, Mr. Bremmer." She hoped he didn't notice that she'd had to wind her hands and fingers around each other to keep them from trembling . . . from her anger at his boldness, she told herself.

"Good morning, Miss Belinda." His presence overwhelming her, he looked down at her with disarmingly beseeching eyes. "I was just telling your pa the reason I couldn't get here last night in time for dessert."

Belinda observed her father sneaking around the side of the house, presumably going to the back door, since she blocked the front. She couldn't believe he hadn't stayed nearby to lend his support should she need it. When she looked back at Max Bremmer, he seemed all the more imposing.

But once he started talking and swiftly explained his hours of barn-sitting with Pete, all of her anger dissipated, and she nearly sagged with relief. She couldn't possibly fault him—another man's life had been at stake.

Her mother had been correct last night when she'd said only a dire circumstance would've kept Max away. Belinda had an almost uncontrollable urge to brush his wind-tossed locks from his brow, trace her fingers along his square jaw.

Feeling that her mother and, most likely, her father were watching and listening from inside the kitchen, she stepped farther out onto the veranda, drawing Max with her. "Of course you had no choice. I'm just pleased to hear Mr. Dagget is unharmed and, as you say, betrothed to Liza Smith. I'm sure she'll make him a fine wife. She has a good heart." She started down to the walk, sure he would follow.

"That she does." Max followed no more than a step behind her. "Liza comes from wonderful people. It was purely wonderful to see her and Pete kissing and hugging, with my pops and their families circled round, giving them their congratulations."

Suspicion struck like lightning. Belinda stopped on the walk and faced Max. "Liza was there? And your father and both their families? With such a crowd in attendance, it seems a bit odd that you were needed at all."

"No, it wasn't like that." A frown pinched his brow. He caught her hand. "The others didn't show up till later. When Mrs. Dagget rode in to fetch me and Pops, folks along the road saw her and figured something was wrong out at their place.

They just sorta started straggling in. There must've been thirty or forty people waiting with the Daggets by the time I climbed down. Fact is, having so many folks tarrying below was part of the reason it took me so long to get Pete to come down." He still held her hand, his thumb pressing uncomfortably on hers in his apparent desire to have her believe him.

And she did. But his words only brought more concerns. Belinda led him farther away from the house, her anger resurfacing, but this time not at Max. "I reckon Pete's time on the roof will be all the talk at church Sunday. Won't it?"

Max's expression went blank. He dropped her hand. "Most likely. That and their betrothal."

"If that's so, I wouldn't blame Pete if he refused to go."

He tilted his head, seemingly more leery of where her comments were leading. "Pete's used to taking a little joshing. He's going to be all right."

She took in a strengthening breath. Though she knew she was going to hate his next answer, she had to ask one more question. The one that meant everything. "You're a good friend, Max. Pete's a lucky man to have you. But since we're on the subject, you haven't mentioned why you failed to come for dessert the night before last."

Max shifted the weight off his injured leg. "I'm sorry. I thought your mother would've explained. I simply never received your invitation. You know wild horses couldn't have kept me away if I'd known." His tension collapsed into a grin. "Maybe a man on a barn roof could, but never wild horses."

He so much wanted everything between them to be all right. But it wasn't.

"And, pray tell, why didn't you receive my invitation?" Belinda had to continue her probe.

His gaze shifted away.

He was brave enough to fight off river pirates, to save a friend from suicide, but was he brave enough to face the truth?

"My mother neglected to give it to me."

"And why is that, Mr. Bremmer?"

"She . . . uh . . . and" His gaze faltered a second time, then returned to her, his own expression turning as hard as hers surely was. "Mama has learned of your mother's lapses into . . ."

"Hallucinations? Madness? Is that what you're trying to avoid saying?" She refused to let him mince words, avoid the terrible reality.

"Aye," he finally admitted.

"And," she said, finishing what he doubtlessly couldn't bring himself to say, "your mother doesn't want you courting someone with insanity in her family."

He released a breath. "I'm afraid so. But that doesn't have to change anything between us."

Abruptly, he caught her hand again and pulled her along with him, not stopping until they were beneath the shelter of the rose arbor. "This isn't the way I had in mind of asking you, but I reckon it'll have to do. Marry me. I love you more than I ever thought possible. And nothing my mother could ever say or do will change that."

He'd proposed marriage! Here. Now, at this most impossible moment. If she'd been reading this in a novel, she'd have burst out laughing. It was that ludicrous. Still, Belinda knew she'd never forget that he'd asked her . . . as they stood here among the roses, his deep blue eyes desperately pleading with her.

It broke her heart. She brought his hand up to her lips and kissed it. "I'm sorry, but I must refuse. I don't see how a marriage between us could ever be, not with the way your mother feels. I am truly sorry."

He caught her shoulders. "Sweetheart, I would never subject

you to her old wives' tales or her ill will. Come with me up the Missouri. We could live with Drew and Crysta Reardon, those missionaries I told you about. She's a real lady like you, and yet she's doing just fine with the Shawnee. I know she'd love the company. And with your kind heart, we could be a real service to the Lord there, helping them."

"But, Max—"

He placed a finger over her mouth. "We wouldn't have to go there. We could go anywhere. You just name the place. I've saved a considerable amount of cash money over the years, trapping and hunting. I can provide for you no matter where we go."

"Max, dearest Max." She cupped his face in her hands. "I will treasure your proposal always. Always. But don't you see how insurmountable a marriage between us would be? I can't abandon my mother to the consequences of my actions. Not only would my father be left to solely care for her when she's in her bad times, but if your mother is capable of deceiving you to keep you from me, what else is she capable of doing? Especially if she thought we might marry against her wishes. Who knows, she may already be planning the next witch burning."

He jerked his head up. "That's ridiculous. She would never dream of doing such a thing. Besides, my father would never allow it."

"Yes," she said, lowering her hands to her sides, "he is a kind and honorable man. Like you. But some things cannot be stopped. My only hope is that once your mother sees I'm no longer a threat, she'll allow us to remain living here in peace. I couldn't bear it if I was the cause of my family having to uproot and start over again. We've worked so hard to . . ." A wave of self-pity choked off the rest of her words.

Suddenly she was in his arms, and he was speaking to her, his lips against her hair. "Please don't give up. I don't know how, but we will be together someday. Somehow. I promise. I won't lose you. I can't."

Then his mouth found hers in a searing, desperate kiss . . . one that she knew was, in truth, good-bye.

Belinda couldn't bear to watch Max ride away. As soon as he stepped out the gate, she spun around and ran into the house and up the stairs. As much as she'd wanted to believe Max, believe in him, she knew the reality of their situation. Unlike her, he'd never experienced firsthand the righteous wrath of a group of "good" people—or the evil that could be brought down on the unsuspecting.

Shut in her room, she gave way to her tears and fell across her bed. She would've been better off if he hadn't come this morning. She probably could have recovered if he'd merely ridden off for his beloved West, leaving her without a word, as she'd expected. But to know he loved her so much he'd been willing to go against his mother and everything else he held dear for her . . . to know he loved her as passionately as she did him, and knowing they could never be together . . . how would she ever find a moment of peace again?

And pain upon pain, she and her parents would probably have to leave their lovely home here by the river, start over yet another time. One way or another, Max's mother would see that Belinda was no longer around to tempt her son.

With tears soaking her pillowcase, she curled up her legs, trying to stop the terrible ache that consumed her.

"Belinda . . . Carrots . . ." Her father sat down behind her, tilting the mattress with his weight. "Why are you crying? Didn't you believe Max? Sweetheart, he couldn't help not being here last night." He put a hand on her shoulder. "Talk to me."

She knew he wouldn't leave without an answer. Taking a ragged breath, she wiped her eyes on her sleeve and rolled over.

He reached out and brushed aside a damp strand of hair caught on her lashes. "Talk to me," he repeated more gently.

"It's not about last night, Daddy. Mrs. Bremmer doesn't approve of me. She's against Max marrying me because of Mama. Because of my *tainted* blood."

He sat up straight. "I see." His narrow face stiffened.

"No, Daddy, I don't think you do. Max doesn't share her animosity. He's willing and ready to defy his mother. He wants to marry me regardless of how she feels."

Mr. Gregg's features relaxed. "I knew Max was a man of integrity." He wiped a stray tear from Belinda's cheek. "So tell me then, why did he leave? And why are you crying? I could've sworn you were as smitten with him as he is with you."

"Daddy, not you too. Surely you can see it would never work. Everything would end up just like before when the whole town came against us. We should've left well enough alone. Stayed to ourselves."

"No. I don't agree. Your mother's spells have been getting further and further apart. And the almost miraculous recovery she had with this last one . . . I'm sure it was because Max and Brother Bremmer added their prayers to ours. Like the pastor said, I think it's time we gave some good compassionate Christians a chance. Share our suffering with them as we would theirs."

Belinda's ire returned, full force. She bolted up straight. "That all sounds quite lovely. But from what I hear, Mrs. Bremmer is definitely not interested in sharing anything with us. Most particularly her son."

Her dad stared at her a moment, sighed, and rose to his feet. "Child, instead of lying here in your room, fuming with hatred and blame, I think you should get on your knees and do some serious praying. Your mother and I will be attending services on the Sabbath. We would like you to accompany us."

Belinda's mouth fell open. "You can't ask that."

"Nonetheless, I am."

Chapter Twenty-Four

Although she hadn't said the words, Max was sure Belinda loved him. And he definitely loved her. This should be the happiest day of their lives.

If it weren't for his mother.

On the long ride home, that was all he could think about . . . seethe about. His deceiving, interfering mother.

Almost forgetting to place a coin in the ferry tender's hand as he walked Kaiser off the raft, he mounted and nudged the gray gelding up the embankment, heading straight for the house. Passing the church, he spotted his mother out back in her kitchen garden, hoeing weeds—an early morning chore.

He glanced up at the sun and realized it was still hours before noon.

He'd left for Belinda's at the first light of dawn. He hadn't even had breakfast, though at the moment, that was the last thing on his mind. He reined his horse past the small graveyard at the rear of the church and headed straight for his mother.

She glanced up at him, and her plump cheeks turned a darker shade of pink. Then, as if she hadn't seen him, she returned to her weeding with renewed vigor. Nowhere to be seen was the smile she usually had for him upon his arrival home.

His own wouldn't be showing itself anytime soon, either. She'd seen to that.

He dismounted and tied his horse to a low branch of a nearby apple tree and limped down the row in which she worked. "You've won," he accused bitterly. "Belinda refuses to marry me as long as you think she's some kind of untouchable creature."

His mother straightened. Her eyes narrowed. "I never say I do not like her. She is nice *fräulein*. Fine girl . . . from vhat she shows me. It is da blood from her mama dat is bad. Tainted *mit* madness. *Und* dis is vhat Belinda Gregg passes on to your *kinders* if you marry her. Do you vant dat for your babies?"

"If there's any bad blood to be passed on, I'd say my children—if I ever have any after your meddling—are in more danger from our side than from hers."

Inga nearly choked on a breath. "Dere ain't no madness in our family."

"Maybe not, but I'd rather my children have Mrs. Gregg's occasional malady than to be stiff-necked and conniving like you."

His mother's nostrils flared, and she wielded a stinging slap across his face. "How dare you speak to me like dat! I am still your mama. No matter how old you t'ink you are."

Her eyes then did a rare thing . . . they pooled with tears. She jerked around, facing away from him, and attacked the weeds again with a vengeance.

Max stepped back, feeling like a real heel. Twice in one

morning he'd been the cause of a woman's heartache. But, he tried to tell himself, his mother deserved hers. Rubbing the sting from his cheek, he turned and walked away.

"You act like I am da villain," his mother suddenly called after him. "But if da papa of *Frau* Gregg pays her husband lots of money to keep her far away from da rest of his family—her own papa—you know dere is a goot reason." She wagged a finger at Max. "You t'ink about dat."

She was right about one thing: he did need to think. And at the top of the list would be how she'd managed to get hold of that last bit of information. Had she somehow wheedled it out of Pops? And with him not knowing the damage she'd already done.

Max snatched up the reins of the horse and mounted. Kaiser naturally started in the direction of the smithy, but Max knew that now was not the time to have a conversation with his father. His anger was much too raw. He forcibly guided the gelding back toward the river, veering off the road and onto a path that led to the spot where he'd first seen his beloved.

Dismounting just above the stone upon which he'd been sitting that day, he had the crazy idea that Belinda would be as drawn by her longing to see him as he was to be with her . . . that she would launch her canoe and paddle upstream to him. His desire to see her and hold her was that strong, and he knew she couldn't help but feel it too.

Of course, his common sense told him as he stepped down to the flat-topped boulder, that his mind was only taking a childishly fanciful flight. Yet he couldn't think of any other place he'd rather be if he couldn't be with her.

For several minutes he sat there, watching downstream for any sign of a craft. Then, feeling foolish, he leaned over and gathered some pebbles and started tossing them into the river.

One landed in a placid little cove below him, causing perfectly round rings to form. He watched as they grew ever larger.

Amazing, he thought, how one tiny pebble could cause such waves in still water. "And," he muttered, his rage reigniting, "one vicious word dropped in the right spot can do the same. Worse. Much worse."

But he couldn't let his relationship with Belinda end this way. There must be an answer. Some way to convince her to come away with him.

He swatted at a pesky mosquito buzzing around his face. Staring across to the far shore, he knew there had to be a way. "It is written," he reminded himself, "that she should leave her father and her mother and cleave only unto me."

But he knew Belinda would never leave her father to nurse her mother alone when Mrs. Gregg was in danger of doing harm to herself or someone else. The first day he met Belinda, she had a bloody scratch on her cheek and tea spilled down her dress. Together, she and her father were having a difficult time with Mrs. Gregg. He couldn't imagine only one person trying to tend her.

"No," he said, giving a flicking toss to a flat stone and watching it hop across the water. Belinda wouldn't leave her parents any more than he would've left Pete on the barn to come to her.

So where was the answer?

"Lord." Max gazed up through the broad-leafed sycamore that shaded him. "Just the other day, I thought I knew everything You wanted me to know. I really thought You were giving her to me. I reckon I should've known better—" Emotion clogged his throat, rendering him speechless. *I reckon I've never done a thing to deserve someone as wonderful as Belinda.*

She was perfect. He couldn't think of a single thing about her he'd change. Not even the fact that she wouldn't go with him.

He loved that she was kind and compassionate. And loyal. She would never take her own happiness at the expense of her parents.

There really wasn't anything he could do. Belinda was lost to him.

But if that were so, why had God brought him back here? And it had to be the work of the Lord, because he'd been unconscious most of the trip home. *Why, Lord?* His eyes stung. A grown man about to cry. When was the last time he'd— He barked a chuckle. Last night. He'd cried with Pete just last night.

He took in a lungful of the musty river air. He'd sure been on a wild seesaw ride since he came home.

Max closed his eyes. The answer was probably the one staring him in the face. The Lord had sent him here for his lifelong friend, Pete, and for Max to truly get to know the remarkable man his old Bavarian father was—the one with the funny accent and who never wore anything more noteworthy than his plain black suit.

As a kid, Max had been ashamed of his father's speech. Even the name his father had given him had been such an embarrassment that Max had insisted everyone call him by a shortened version of his middle name instead of the very German-sounding Otto. Otto Maximilian.

No, Max wasn't any more worthy of the father with whom he'd been blessed than he was of Belinda. There was nothing left to be said.

He was just sorry he couldn't say the same about his mother.

Feeling only a little better than when he first sat down, Max rose to his feet. No sense sitting here moping when he could just as easily mope while he helped Pops finish the nail order.

As he turned to collect the horse, another revelation came to him. Because he came home, he learned what it was to truly, deeply, love a woman. He doubted he'd ever be completely whole again without someone he could share that kind of love with.

But he couldn't imagine anyone else ever touching his soul or filling his eyes the way Belinda did. "Lord," he said, coming to a stop by Kaiser, "I'm sorry, but worthy of her or not, I have to give it one more try." This evening, after she'd had more time to think, more time to miss him, he'd ride over there again.

~

The minute Belinda heard her parents come up the back steps for supper, she hurried toward the front entrance and waited. "Mother, Dad," she called as soon as they walked in, "I need to get some fresh air. Please start without me."

Before either of them had the chance to respond, she slipped out the door. She simply could not sit at the table with them, assaulted by their pity. And, of course, there would've been her mother's questions.

This morning, after the confrontation she'd had with her father in her room, she'd run out to the hall to catch him before he descended the stairs. She'd insisted the two of them make a pact—one that would ensure that neither of them would tell her mother the true reason Belinda sent Max away.

Her dear mother had suffered enough through the years without thinking herself the cause of today's tragedy. Especially since it was not so much she, but the cruel and unfeeling outsiders, who'd made their lives far more difficult than they had to be.

As Belinda walked down the veranda steps, the scent from the rose arbor and the honeysuckle draped over a side fence seemed cloyingly sweet this evening. Almost nauseating. She hurried toward the gate—then caught a flash of motion as her little russet fur ball came skittering toward her from out of a stand of tall zinnias.

She reached down and scooped up the fluffy creature. "Would you like to go for a stroll with me?" Something soft and cuddly was just what she needed right now.

Belinda scratched behind Downy's oversized ears a moment, then kissed her button nose and placed the tiny fox on her shoulder. "It's such a warm evening. How about you and me taking a walk down to the river?"

Stretching her legs, she headed out the drive for the woods beyond the stream and onto the wagon trail that led to the Greggs' private dock.

For some odd reason, all afternoon she'd been yearning to take a walk down to Caney Fork.

~

Max couldn't believe his good fortune when he broke out of the trees shortly before dusk and saw Belinda.

Not thirty yards away, she sat on her riverside dock, her bare feet dangling in the water. Her hair flowed free, catching the breeze off the water as it had the first day he saw her in the canoe. She made an enchanting picture as she gazed downstream while absently petting the fox kit in her lap.

He reined in Kaiser, not wanting to disturb her just yet, and dismounted. Leaving the horse tied to some brush alongside the path, he walked a few steps closer, starting down the incline. A terrible and bittersweet thought came to him: this could very well be the last time he would ever be given the opportunity to drink in her loveliness. His lady of the river, Belinda the beautiful.

Without realizing it, he'd taken a few more steps.

She must have sensed his approach. Her head slowly turned,

and she looked up the bank at him. And odd as it seemed, she wasn't the least startled to see him. She lifted her dripping ankles from the water, then, placing the fox on her shoulder, she rose to her bare feet. Her lips parted slightly, but without a word, she stood there, watching him walk down the gently sloped incline toward her.

The setting sun cast a golden aura around her, and for some unaccountable reason, she'd never been more appealing than she was at this moment, even in the shapeless shift she wore. No ruffles, no frills to distract him from the woman before him . . . her eyes seemed darker and larger, too, with a misty quality to them.

Then suddenly they changed. They sharpened, became starbursts again, as she held out a hand, palm out as if to ward him off. "Don't come any closer."

He stopped as she bade, just before he reached the dock.

"I thought we said good-bye this morning," she said quietly.

"I know. But I couldn't let it end without giving it one more try. I was hoping after you had time to think about it . . . about us, you'd reconsider." Max prayed that every word to come from him would be the exact ones she needed to hear. "Your father— I know he wants nothing more than your happiness. Surely—"

"I'm sorry, Mr. Bremmer . . ."

Her use of his last name was not a good sign.

". . . but I cannot believe that any love that comes at the cost of another can be a good thing. As on the first day you came to our home, I must ask for your promise of silence."

"I love you. How could I be silent about that?"

On a quick intake of breath, she glanced away. "Your silence," she said as if she were speaking to the golden strip of river, "again concerns my mother. She must never know that the reason we will no longer be . . . be keeping company has anything to do with her."

"And it doesn't. My mother is the culprit here."

"Your mother's objection has to do with Mama, and we both know it. Please, let this parting be as painless for all of us as possible."

"*Painless?* I'm ripping apart." He started for her.

"Stop!" Belinda thrust out her hand again, her eyes shimmering with unshed tears. "It's important that you keep your distance. And, dear one, I know exactly how you feel. But I've given our situation a lot of thought. I've tried to put myself in your mother's place, and I hate to admit it, but if I had a son as wonderful as you, I'd probably be just as reluctant to have him marry into my family. So, please, try not to be so hard on her."

Max wagged his head. "You really are a saint, aren't you?"

Her first grin! "You wouldn't think that if you'd heard me this morning."

He returned her grin. "I love your smile. I don't believe I ever told you that."

"I've always been quite partial to yours too. But then, I'm sure you've charmed many a bird out of the trees with it. Not to mention a host of young maidens."

He edged closer. "There'll never be another young maiden for me. You've taken my heart."

Her eyes softened, and she bit her lip. "I know I shouldn't ask this, but may I keep your heart a little while longer? Since it's all I can have from you."

A lump stuck in his throat. "It's yours forever. I can't imagine leaving it with anyone else. But I must have yours in return."

"Don't you know you already do?"

She loved him! He started to reach for her but caught himself. He didn't want to do anything that would chase her away.

"Belinda, somehow we *will* be together. Speak to your father again. I know he's on our side. Let him help you come to me. Please, speak to him tonight."

Light was waning, yet the trouble that now clouded her gaze was unmistakable. Placing her hand on the fox still lounging on her shoulder, she dashed unexpectedly past him, not slowing until she reached the top of the bank. There she turned and looked back. "You haven't been listening to me, my love. This must be our farewell."

Max took several not-so-agile steps toward her. "Speak to your father. Speak to him. For me. For us."

She was running up the path now, as he shouted his last words. "Tomorrow! I'll be waiting for you! At the church!"

Chapter Twenty-Five

The church bell had rung several times, calling folks to Sunday service. Standing on the Bremmers' covered porch, Max knew he couldn't wait any longer for the Greggs to arrive or he'd be walking in late.

A variety of horse-drawn rigs and saddle mounts already filled the churchyard, with only a few straggling people left to walk into the sanctuary—just how he'd planned it. The very thought of having to converse with anyone, to answer questions about the absence of his Belinda, was more than he could bear at the moment.

She hadn't spoken to her father. She hadn't come to him.

One small plus—he wasn't using a cane this Sunday and could move more swiftly. Taking fairly long, if not quite even strides, he reached the church steps as the last few people were filing in.

"Max."

Pete and Liza filled the doorway just as he reached it.

He hadn't delayed his arrival long enough.

"We been waitin' for you," Pete said, wearing a starched white shirt with an unlikely pink ribbon tied in a bow at his throat. No doubt, a favor from Liza, since she wore her usual Sunday gown of pink. With a tender smile Max never knew Pete was capable of, Pete looked down at the petite Liza while hugging her close.

She returned his gaze, looking up at him adoringly with those big down-turned eyes.

"We're to be wed four weeks from today, on Sunday afternoon," Pete informed him.

"So soon?" Max asked, though he knew he'd marry Belinda today if she'd have him.

"We don't see no reason for a long betrothal. We've known each other all our lives," Liza said matter-of-factly.

Max smiled. She was right . . . he could remember the day she was born.

Her own lips curled into a shy smile. "And, well, we just don't want to wait." She shrugged a girlish shoulder.

Pete squeezed her waist again, then returned his attention to Max. "We're havin' a cabin raisin' at our place next Saturday. Pa says we can build our honeymoon house up on the hill overlookin' the fields."

"Where we built the tree house when we were kids? That'll be a real nice spot. If I'm still here next Saturday, I'll be there bright and early."

"What d'ya mean?"

Max motioned for his friends to turn toward the sanctuary. "We're late. The music's starting. We can talk later."

Walking in behind them to the congregation singing, "Fairest Lord Jesus, Ruler of all nature . . ." Max noticed several people still standing in the aisle near the front. In the midst of the taller Reardon men, he spotted a flash of graying red hair.

"Let me by, Pete," he whispered urgently and crowded past. He'd just seen Mr. Gregg! The Greggs were here. Belinda! How had he missed them?

As he continued down the aisle, he caught a whiff of honeysuckle. Quickly, he searched under each bonnet for Belinda's bright tresses. He found Mrs. Gregg seated between Annie Reardon and her strange sister. But no Belinda.

He wheeled around, scanning the pews he'd passed.

Folks stared back at him while they continued singing the familiar tune.

Still no Belinda.

Turning forward again, Mr. Gregg was the only person who'd remained standing—except for Max. The man shook his head almost imperceptibly and mouthed, "I'm sorry."

Before Max could question him, Mr. Gregg took his seat, leaving Max the lone member of the congregation still on his feet . . . exposed for the jilted lover he was. He stepped back a few paces and scooted into the Dagget pew beside the two lovebirds. He could not bring himself to sit with his mother up front. If not for her, Belinda would be here today. Sitting with him, holding his hand . . . betrothed to him.

Max watched dark rain clouds moving in from the south, bringing with them a welcome breeze. He'd escaped church the moment the service ended and now sat in the deeply shaded recess of the porch with a glass of cool springwater in his hand. As he had the week before, he watched the departing congregation.

Mostly, he watched the Greggs chatting with the valley folk, friendly and relaxed as if they'd been attending church here for years . . . a far cry from the first time he'd laid eyes on them.

He tried to be pleased for them. But he knew Belinda would have come to church, too, if not for— He closed his eyes, his anger just beneath the surface, then took several swallows of water. This was the Sabbath, not a day for harboring resentments.

But his rage would not be buried. He'd been right when, during the church service, he made the decision to leave for the West soon. Staying here, knowing he couldn't have Belinda, would be too painful. Perhaps they could correspond. In the privacy of the distance between them, they would be free to share something of themselves with each other. And, if nothing else, he'd have her letters to hold on to.

But before he left the valley, he needed to make sure his mother didn't continue to be a stumbling block to Belinda's well-being. If he couldn't give Belinda anything more, he would see to it that she could feel comfortable enough to come to church.

Max watched the Greggs walk to the opposite side of the church building, along with Annie Reardon's sister. Mrs. Thompson was smiling and looked quite mellow—a considerable change from the jumpy woman of a few weeks ago. Her budding friendship with Mrs. Gregg had done wonders for her self-confidence, from what Noah Reardon had said when he dropped by the smithy yesterday. And Mrs. Gregg seemed just as relaxed.

He then caught sight of the Gregg carriage as it moved onto the road. It had been parked at the saddlery. The mystery of why he hadn't seen the Greggs arrive was now solved. But had they parked there deliberately to avoid speaking to him? His feelings of betrayal rose another notch. He downed the last of his drink.

Another quarter hour passed before the remainder of the congregation departed, and his folks started walking toward the house. They weren't strolling arm in arm as they usually did. Today there was a stiffness in the way his mother held her black-garbed self.

Max wondered if his father noticed too.

He steeled himself as they started up the walk.

He and his pops had some unpleasant business to conclude. Then he'd be gone. Mr. Bailey at the store always kept a couple of usable canoes for sale. Floating along with the current until the last fork fed into the Mississippi should give his leg the extra time it needed to complete healing. After that, he'd be spending long hours in the saddle.

On a defeated sigh, Max reckoned it would be good to see his old friends again—Drew and Crysta, Black Bear and his wife, Josie. The whole world seemed to be paired off or on the verge of it.

Except for him.

The instant his mother noticed him sitting in a dark corner, she picked up the pace, her face wooden stiff.

"Son," Pops called from behind her. "Goot. You are here. Ve talk vhile your mama puts dinner on da table, *ja?*"

His mother halted on the first step—then rushed on, through the open doorway and into the house.

From the conversations he and his father'd had over the past few days, Max knew his mother had not informed her husband of the disagreement between the two of them. Her stilted behavior, though, was even more noticeable today. Perhaps she had spoken to him this morning—given him her own slanted version.

"I get myself a drink," Pops said, without his tone giving a hint of his mood.

Returning from the springhouse, his father dropped into a chair, expelling a huff. He pulled up an empty chair and propped his feet on it. "I t'ink I haf Baxter Clay make me some new church shoes. Dese sure hurt da feet after a couple hours standing." He leaned back and took a drink of the buttermilk he held, then wiped his mouth. "Hmm, dat sure quenches da t'irst."

The man certainly was taking his time getting to the point.

"Pops, I wanted to talk to you too."

"Goot. But first ve need to get dis t'ing *mit* you *und* your mama out of da vay."

He knew.

"Here it is, da Lord's Day. I even preach da sermon on Ephesians four, hoping to soften your hearts. But da look on bot' your faces? I see only anger. I ask your mama, but she is not talking. So to you I am putting it."

This was not how Max had planned to open the subject, but . . . "First, let me say how much I've enjoyed my time here with you. It's the longest we've been together since I was seventeen. I've come to appreciate you and all you do with what I hope are more mature eyes. And I have to say, you cast a pretty long shadow. I doubt I'll ever meet another man that I'll respect or admire more than you."

His father's face crumpled into a truly pleased smile. "Why, t'ank you, Son. Dem vords coming from one of mine own *kinders* means more dan if it comes from President Jefferson himself."

Max took a fortifying breath before continuing. "During the past week, I made what I thought was a decision inspired by God."

His father straightened. "Dis is so?"

"Yes. You know how over the years I've socked away quite a sum of money, trapping and hunting."

"*Ja*, you don't squander too much on foolishness. Dis is goot."

Max looked heavenward and continued. "I decided to stay here and ask Belinda to marry me. You know, maybe build a house on the other side of the pasture. I knew Belinda would want to remain in the valley in case her mother needed her. And I wanted to stay around to do what I could to help you in the shop and whatever else the Lord led me to do." Max chose to leave out any mention of his pops getting old.

"*My boy.*" The deep timbre of his father's voice turned husky. "Such a joy you bring to dis old man's heart." He placed a hand over his chest.

Max smiled sadly. "It made me real happy too. But, I'm sorry. Somehow, I must have misread the Lord. I'm afraid I won't be marrying Belinda, and I just can't stay on now."

His father's gladdened expression sagged. "Da purty young miss, she don't vant you?"

"It's more complicated than that. And—" Max sighed—"this is the part I was hoping I wouldn't have to tell you. But I must. For Belinda's sake. If nothing else comes of my meeting her, she needs to feel she can come to church again."

His father's thick brows ledged over his eyes. "You haf offended her?"

"No, Pops, not me. I'm sorry, but it's Mama. I didn't want to say anything that might cause a rift between you two—you have enough troubles to contend with without coming home to more."

"Son, da Lord, He don't put more on me dan I can bear. Besides, I am *mit* your mama for t'irty-five years. Dere ain't much about her I don't know. Keeping secrets . . ." He shook his gray head. "Dey yust make for more trouble."

Glancing toward the front door, Max felt like a tattler, regardless. "Do you recall last Sunday when we told her about Mrs. Gregg's malady, so she wouldn't go running off accusing her husband of wife beating? And remember how huffy she got about me seeing someone whose mother had spells of madness?"

"*Ja*, but ve talk about it, me an' Inga. I tell her dat Miss Belinda is not like her mama. Dat she is strong healt'y girl."

"You did? Well, Mama wasn't convinced. An invitation came for me to have dessert with the Greggs last Wednesday, and Mama burned it. Mrs. Gregg thought something smelled fishy and came by to find out why the man who'd been pursuing her daughter so avidly hadn't come. I reckon all she had to do was take one look at Mama's face and she knew the answer. Needless to say, after that, Belinda rejected my proposal of marriage. I offered to take her far away from Mama's venom, anyplace she wanted to go. But she won't abandon her own mother. And unless you can give her some assurance that Mama won't start spreading tales about them, she'll never come back to church."

"Son, you know your mama won't do dat. She is a goot voman. She knows better dan to say anyt'ing."

"I hope you're right. You know, if ugly rumors start, none of the Greggs will be back. They'll crawl back into that shell of theirs again, and that would be a real shame."

"*Ja*, dat vould."

"I realize we have to take some of the blame here. We never should've told Mama about Mrs. Gregg in the first place. Now I understand why you've always been careful to keep folks' troubles to yourself. Not even telling Mama. Especially Mama." Max picked up his empty glass and stood, his anger building again. He scarcely noticed that it had started to sprinkle out in the yard. "Pops, there's more. But I'm pretty sure you've already guessed. Not only am I not able to forgive Mama for causing me to lose Belinda, I don't even want to."

The glass Max held popped, shattering in his hand. Pieces clattered to the planks at his feet. He'd crushed it, cut his palm. He pulled a neatly folded white kerchief from the pocket of his waistcoat—one his mother had bleached and ironed so carefully to place in his Sabbath clothes. He pressed it against the blood coming from a gash . . . good blood, from sane German stock, his mother would say.

He did his best to regain control of his temper. "As you can see, I'm so full of rage that I can't stand the sight of Mama. That's the other reason I have to leave. I've lost all respect for her." A bitter chuckle ground out of him. "While I was thinking I was getting right with God again, thinking I had more of an understanding, a sense of what He wanted, I fell hard, right into the sin of not honoring my mother. Right now, all I can think to do is get enough time and distance away from her, so that, maybe . . ." He shrugged, wagging his head. "I don't know, maybe someday . . ."

"No." His father came to his feet. "I talk to Inga. Make her see da mischief she has been making." Charging past Max, he marched into the house.

Left alone on the porch, Max felt even lower than before. Now he might even be adding home wrecker to his other sins.

"Inga . . . ? Inga!" His father roared her name several times more, first in the kitchen, then in the parlor, up the stairs.

No answer came.

He returned to the front doorway. "She is not in da house. *Und* I don't see her out back. Da privy door, it is standing wide open. She ain't dere. Da food, it is not on da table. No dishes haf she put out. She is gone."

"She must've overheard us talking. She's probably hiding out behind the woodshed or something." He watched the gentle downpour outside. *Getting herself rained on,* he couldn't stop himself from hoping.

"*Ja,* I reckon ve go ahead *und* eat? If she don't come in by den, I t'ink I better go look for her." With worried eyes he, too, scanned the stormy sky.

Chapter Twenty-Six

Max and Rolf collected plates from the dish shelf above the sinkboard and dipped their meals out of the footed pots standing on still-warm coals along the hearth apron. With the lids removed, the aroma of chicken and dumplings, and vegetables flavored with bacon drippings made Max's stomach growl, reminding him he'd been too nervous to eat much this morning. Still, food held scant appeal.

After gathering utensils and napkins, they took their usual places at the big table in the center of the room.

Rolf cleared his throat. "I t'ink more is needed here, God, dan just da blessing of da food."

Belatedly, Max bowed his head—his father had started praying in an unexpected manner.

"Lord, dis is da day You haf made. Ve *vill* be glad *und* ve *vill* rejoice in it. Ve are glad because ve know You are da power. You save da leg of mine son. You bring da love of a beautiful young voman into his life. *Und* dat you did not do for nut'ing. But da devil, he comes sneaking into our midst, causing trouble *und* unforgifness in mine own household. At dis very table." Rolf slid from the chair and, using it to brace himself, kneeled down on his knees.

Max could do no less.

Rolf placed a hand on Max's head. "Fadder in heaven, creator of da very ground ve valk on, da air ve breathe, creator of our love for You *und* each udder. My son, here, needs dat peace You pour into us like a warm fragrant oil. Give him mercy for a mama who loves him *mit* all her heart, but right now she is forgetting to trust Your visdom. Help Max to see dat his mama is yust being dis poor ignorant voman. Dat she needs our help to see da truth, not our wrath."

Every word seemed to flow from his father's hand into Max's head, every truth. With them came a glow of peace that seeped through his entire body, little by little putting out the fire of anger burning within him.

"Thank You, Jesus," spilled from Max. "Thank You for my father, and yes, for my mother. I pray that I can see her through his eyes. That I can forgive her here, today, and not take it back again tomorrow morning when I wake up" . . . *aching for Belinda*, he came close to adding. "I've crossed flooding rivers, fought off packs of wolves, weathered killing twisters, but I know this will be the hardest thing I shall ever be called upon to do. But, as my papa said, You don't put more on us than we can bear. All I can do is trust You at Your word. Thank You, Jesus."

"T'ank You, Jesus," his father repeated hoarsely, then pulled Max into a bone-crushing hug. "T'ank You for giving me dis most fine son."

~

Belinda had been well aware of her father's displeasure this morning when she'd refused to attend the church service. Hoping to appease him—and to take her mind off her grief— she put considerable effort into having everything for their little dinner party ready and waiting when her parents returned home with their guest, Mrs. Thompson.

Originally, Belinda had planned to set up a table and chairs in the flower garden on the grass under the maple, but the clouds had threatened rain. She chose, instead, to keep the outdoor table on the veranda and set a bouquet of flowers on the linen covering and place more blossom-filled vases on the enclosing rails.

By the time the carriage rolled in through a cooling mist of rain, large serving bowls and platters were brimming and waiting on the dining-room sideboard, and the table had been set with their best crystal, china, and silver. Belinda wore a yellow dimity gown, hoping the cheery color would disguise her despair. Seeing the pleasure radiating from her mother's pale features as she escorted Mrs. Thompson up the walk made Belinda's efforts well worth all the extra work.

"Sweetheart," her mother said, ascending the steps. "This is delightful." Removing her feathered, pearl gray bonnet, she shook off the accumulation of moisture.

Mrs. Thompson did the same with her simple straw hat. "Oh my, yes. You shouldn't have gone to all this trouble just for me."

"It was my pleasure." Belinda stepped to her. "Please, let me take your things." Accepting the bonnet, purse, and gloves, she turned and saw her dad coming up the walk. "Dinner is ready whenever y'all are. Just take a plate from the table and serve yourselves in at the sideboard."

Reaching the veranda, her father perused her handiwork. "Looks nice, Carrots, but you should've come with us. Your young man looked mighty disappointed when we arrived without you."

Belinda steeled herself against a rush of emotion as an awkward silence followed. "Daddy," she said, filling it, "would you be so kind as to show Mrs. Thompson to the sideboard?"

She would have preferred to excuse herself from the meal, but twice in two days would be much too obvious to her mother. Once everyone was seated and her dad had given the blessing, Belinda felt absolutely cornered. She prayed that neither her mother nor father would bring up the topic of Max again.

Relief filled her when her father took the initiative and mentioned the weather instead.

"Perhaps we'll have an early fall," Mama added between bites of roast venison and potatoes. "I purely do love long autumns when the leaves turn the color of my darling daughter's hair."

"Aye," Mrs. Thompson added with a slight but friendly smile. "The lass does have a pretty color for bein' a redhead. And my, but there's such a lot of it."

Belinda wasn't sure if the last statement was a compliment or not, but she said thank you anyway.

"And, Miss Belinda," the woman added, "that was some fine deed your young man did, climbin' up on the Daggets' barn for that noisome Pete fella. And him with a shot-up leg and all. Ever'body's sayin' he's startin' to take right after his pa. Talkin' Pete down, and the way he come out here and got you folks to come to church."

Belinda blanched. The conversation had been brought back to Max.

"A son could do a lot worse," Belinda's dad said, sliding a glance in her direction, "than to take after Brother Bremmer."

"Yes," her mother added. "They're both fine Christian gentlemen."

But the same couldn't be said for Inga Bremmer, Belinda might have added if it weren't for the curiosity such a statement would arouse. Thus far, Felicity had only unsubstantiated suspicions that something was amiss. Nothing more. And Belinda wanted to keep it at that.

She sprang from her chair. "Would anyone care for more bread? I'll go fetch the plate off the sideboard."

In the dining room she took several deep breaths, trying to regain her composure. She put her hand over her laboring, aching heart . . . then remembered it was no longer hers—she'd given it away. To Max. Max, to whom she'd said her last goodbye yester's eve. A terrible, sorrowful farewell.

And her father insisted on making her sacrifice even harder to bear by touting Max's admirable qualities. Surely he should understand the impossibility of her marrying Max. Always before, she'd been able to count on him to be the sensible one, the steadfast one. But her daddy wanted her happiness so much that he wasn't weighing the consequences. And Max, he had simply refused to accept the finality of the matter. Somehow, she'd have to be strong for all of them.

Returning with the plate of sliced white-flour bread and a small bowl of butter, Belinda was vastly relieved to hear her elders discussing the pottery business.

"I saw a man," Mrs. Thompson was saying, "makin' a vase at a potter's wheel once. It just sorta grew up from a lump of wet clay. Workin' it looked like monstrous good fun."

"Oh, yes," Felicity agreed. "There are so many shapes and sizes. And the different colors. When Chris and I were kids, my daddy had a slave who knew most everything about metallic oxides, slips and glazes, and firing. The man was patient as the day is long." She glanced at her husband. "We pray for Claudius now and again when he comes to mind. That my daddy has treated him good and didn't sell off any of his family." Her voice had become thready, a sadness creeping in.

"Felicity," Chris spoke with authority, "after dinner, what do you say we take Emma Jane out to the shed and let her make some mud pies." He flashed a smile at their guest. "Or maybe a bowl or two. If that's her pleasure."

"La, yes, I'd like—" Mrs. Thompson's attention was diverted. She stared out into the light rain.

Figuring the ravens were up to some antics, Belinda followed her lead.

But it was not the birds. Someone was coming. And judging by the black skirt bunched across the horse's back, it was a woman. The horse she rode bareback looked a very familiar shade of mottled gray.

With her lace cap drooping from the shower, Inga Bremmer was riding up their drive.

In stunned silence, Belinda heard her fork clatter onto her plate. Heard a gasp. Her own. Hadn't the witch already caused enough trouble?

Belinda's father rose quickly to his feet. "I'll go see what she wants." He dropped his napkin beside his half-finished dinner and walked out to the gate only moments before the vile woman got there.

"I do hope she's not bringing sad tidings," Felicity said in a small voice. "To ride out here in the rain . . ."

Belinda had a war of emotions crashing around inside her . . . wanting to run away, to stay and fight, to hope. Frozen by indecision, she remained in her seat.

Without any of Belinda's hesitation, her father lifted Mrs. Bremmer down from her mount. He came marching up the walk with her, obviously without a single thought for the dinner party that the woman would ruin.

"Land sakes, Inga, you're soakin' wet." Mrs. Thompson didn't have an inkling of the tension the new arrival brought with her.

With her white cap soaked, her coronet of faded blonde braids lopsided, and stray hairs plastered to her damp face, the woman looked a sight. Taking in the threesome at the table, she said a few hurried words to Belinda's father then tromped up the veranda steps.

"Belinda, go fetch Mrs. Bremmer a towel," Mrs. Thompson said, taking charge.

"*Nein.*" Mrs. Bremmer turned sharply to Belinda. "I am coming here to speak *mit Fräulein* Gregg. Alone."

How dare she? Belinda stood up and glared at the outrageous woman. "Say what you have to say, here and now." Let her show herself for the mean-spirited hypocrite she really was in front of witnesses.

Inga Bremmer shot a furtive glance to Mrs. Thompson then pulled herself up taller. "I am coming here . . . I am here to say . . . I am wrong." She paused a moment, taking a bosom-filling breath, and plunged on. "I am wrong to keep da invitation from Max. I vas wrong to come between you *und* mine son."

Belinda steadied herself by grabbing the table, she was so completely caught off guard.

Mrs. Bremmer, keeping her gaze steady on Belinda, clasped her work-reddened hands tightly, turning her knuckles white. "Rolf, he alvays calls me da mama bear. *Und* he is right. I am alvays vanting da best for mine *kinders*. I vas afraid dat da madness in your mama vould be passing on to da babies of Max." She wrenched her hands apart. "But if it is da vill of God dat you two are marrying, den I am trusting God to know vhat is best. So I give you da piney woods at da back of our land—far from dis meddling old voman. Ve build you a house, *und* I give you mine best embroidered sheets *und* mine goot crocheted tablecloth. *Und* dat noisome clock in da parlor. Vhat do you say? *Ja?*"

Belinda heard her mother's chair scrape back and watched her rise, unable to tell from her bearing if she was angry or merely confused. Not that Belinda didn't have questions of her own. She doubted if Max even knew his mother was here. And for a woman who'd just apologized for meddling, she was now trying to arrange Belinda's life. Right down to the cloth she would put on her table. But still . . . *Max!*

Her father walked up behind Mrs. Bremmer. "That is unacceptable."

Belinda's resurrected hope plummeted.

Max stood in the kitchen at the drainboard, pouring hot water into a dishpan, when he heard the clomp of his father's shoes coming up the back steps. Tossing in some soap shavings, he placed the dishes he and Rolf had dirtied into the pan to soak, then turned toward the door.

Pops burst in, shirt and hair dripping from the rain. "I looked everywhere. Den I go to da corrals, and I see dat Kaiser is gone." Worry grooved his sagging face.

"Could you tell which way Mama went?" In Max's whole life, he couldn't recall his mother ever running off like this without telling anyone.

"Da hoofprints, dey circle round behind da old fort. I t'ink she don't vant us to see her vhen she heads south to da Reardons'. Da Smiths' or da Reardons'—I don't t'ink she vould go novhere else if she is upset."

"I'm sorry, Pops. Like you said, I should've told you everything from the start. Keeping secrets . . . they usually end up going bad. Everyone gets hurt worse than if we'd faced the truth and worked it out in the open."

"*Ja*, in da light of day." Rolf lowered his head and glanced out the side window next to the fireplace, then turned to the back door again. "Vhat you t'ink? I should go to da Reardons'? Or should I vait here?" Pops was in as much of a dither as Max had been in for days.

"You're asking me?" Wiping his hands on a dish towel, Max shrugged. "I have no idea." He realized that, when it came to understanding the workings of the female mind, even a man who'd been married thirty-five years didn't have all the answers.

His father stared out the window. "I don't know. Maybe I better go. Dis mess is not going to get itself fixed *mit* me sitting here." Out the door he went, looking no less confused or disturbed than before.

Max stood at the door watching him head through the gentle shower toward the stable to saddle Pitch. From the first day Max arrived home, burning with fever and all shot up, he'd been nothing but trouble to his folks. It really was time to move on. No sense prolonging the agony.

Chapter Twenty-Seven

M rs. Bremmer." Belinda's dad gave Max's mother a warm smile—a most unexpected one, since he'd just refused her apology and offer of recompense for thwarting Max's and Belinda's happiness. "Please, take a seat; be comfortable while we continue to discuss the matter."

"Continue to discuss the matter"? Had Belinda heard him correctly? Was there still hope for her and Max?

Her father motioned toward the table where they'd been eating. "Do join us. I'll bring another chair."

Mrs. Bremmer shook her head, taking a backward step. "No. I am interrupting da dinner."

"Not if you eat with us." He motioned to Belinda. "Carrots, when you bring a towel to wipe the rain from Mrs. Bremmer, do bring her a plate of food."

"I'll fetch another table setting," Felicity offered, rising from her seat, her pale features glowing as if she'd just been given a wonderful gift. "How delightful. Two dinner guests and a wedding to plan."

Wedding? Belinda whirled around. "Yes, of course. I'll be right back." Her mother must know something she didn't. Grabbing a towel hanging above the drainboard, she rushed to the sideboard where the food was laid out.

"Here let me help," Her mother stood at the buffet, gathering items for the table setting from within the drawers and doors below.

"Mama, why did you say that? Daddy said a wedding was out of the question."

"I know Chris. Be patient. Listen to what he has to say."

Belinda had never piled food on a plate more quickly. Her mother preceded her back to the veranda by only a few steps. When Belinda reached the table, Mrs. Bremmer was talking.

"Da food smells goot. I leave da house before I sit down to eat."

"Any member of the Bremmer family is always welcome to break bread with us," Mr. Gregg said, making space on the table for the additional setting.

Once the others were seated around the table and curtained in on two sides by the rain, Belinda took the empty place at a corner between her mother and dad, trying to appear calm. But when she looked across at the two visitors, she felt so fidgety, she could hardly keep her seat. *Lord, please let Mama be right.*

Her dad filled Mrs. Bremmer's goblet with iced lemonade, then finally spoke. "I do believe I was a touch abrupt a moment ago. I merely meant that it must be Max's and Belinda's choice as to where they build their home."

Belinda nearly melted in her chair, her relief was so great. The thought of going against her father's wishes in such an important matter would have been very hard. But she would have defied him for Max. Any obstacles they might yet face, such as reactions from the community, they would work out together.

"Den da marriage you are agreeing to," Mrs. Bremmer said in her blunt manner, her own face losing its lines of worry.

"Yes," Belinda's father said. "Your son is a man of sterling qualities. And I know he will be a loving husband to my daughter. But first, we must come to an understanding. My family and I had made the decision to trust the good people of your church with the knowledge of my wife's infrequent spells of illness. And if you, as the minister's wife, are willing to join your family with ours, that would be a true testimony to our acceptance."

"Like I say, I am trusting da Lord dat He is right in dis." Inga's sharp blue eyes moved from Chris. "From dis day forth, Belinda, you are mine own daughter. Max loves you, *und* I am loving you too. *Und* dat is dat."

Tears sprang to Belinda's eyes, and her throat clogged with so much emotion, she could do nothing but nod.

The stout older woman reached across the table and patted Belinda's hand. "Goot. Now I t'ink is time to get down to da business of da dowry." She sat back and took an assessing scan of her surroundings; then she sent Mrs. Thompson a happy, saucy look. "Now, vhat do you Greggs plan to bring to da marriage? My son comes *mit*—"

"Pardon me." Belinda had finally found her voice and some real reservations. "Don't you think this is a bit premature? I sent Max away, not once but twice, refusing to marry him. How do we even know if he's still interested?"

A chuckle bubbled up from Mrs. Bremmer. "Dat boy, he is interested, all right. Belief you me, he haf plenty interest."

A smile burst across Belinda's mouth, and she could no longer stay seated. "Daddy, everyone. If you don't mind, I'm not hungry." She swung to Mrs. Bremmer. "It would be my pleasure to return your horse for you. You can ride home in the carriage protected from the rain when Daddy takes Mrs. Thompson home."

Everyone grinned baldly at Belinda as Mrs. Bremmer agreed. "You are already mine goot daughter. *Und* do tell mine Rolf I am here. I didn't tell no one vhere I go. He t'inks maybe I am falling in da vell or somet'ing."

"I will," Belinda cried, already halfway down the veranda steps.

"You need to put on a bonnet," her mother called. "Something to keep off the rain."

Belinda didn't even slow. "Don't have time."

She was on her way to her beloved.

Belinda couldn't remember the last time she'd ridden bareback, but as Mrs. Bremmer before her, she hadn't wanted to take the time to saddle the big-boned gray. She'd merely pulled the horse alongside the carriage's running board and mounted from there.

But she'd certainly be smelly by the time she reached Max, her yellow gown riding directly against the damp animal's coarse hair.

She allowed Kaiser to stay at a walk, considering his labored breathing when Mrs. Bremmer had arrived at a gallop, though Belinda couldn't be any less anxious to reach her destination than Max's mother had been.

Time dragged as she made her way along the woods beside the river, catching only glimpses of the wide expanse wherever there was a break in the trees and brush. At one such opening, she caught sight of a loaded canoe being paddled downstream by a lone man. It was odd to see someone hauling goods to market on the Sabbath.

She noticed the breadth and strength of the fellow's shoulders as he sliced his oar through the water. If she didn't know better, she'd think it was Max. With the wide-brimmed hat hiding the man's hair, she was left with an uneasy feeling. But for only a second. Mrs. Bremmer said she'd left Max at home having dinner with his father. And she was coming to him.

Still, she nudge the plodding horse into a trot.

After the seemingly endless three-mile ride, Belinda reached the ferry crossing and was disappointed to see that the raft was at the far bank. But, one good thing—the rain had stopped and sunlight was peeking through in the south. She rang the big bell that hung from a sycamore branch next to the dock, praying the lad wasn't napping or off having his own Sabbath-day meal.

The skinny lad walked out from beneath a low-hanging tree and waved. Within seconds, he had his hand on the mule's bridle and started walking the animal around a big wheel-like pulley attached to ropes suspended across the river. The raft, hooked to the line, started slowly across, moving no faster than the blamed mule.

When at last it reached her and she and the Bremmer horse were transported across, Belinda realized she'd brought no coin to pay the lad. Still mounted on the tall horse, she nudged the gelding to the freckle-nosed lad. "I'm sorry, but I forgot to bring any money."

He scowled, none too happy. "And it just now came to your mind? After I brung you across?"

"Cross my heart. I'm returning the Bremmers' horse to them. If you'll give me a few minutes, I'll return to you with your fare."

"I don't see as how you can. Brother Rolf took off on the south road, and Max, he's probably halfway to the Cumberland by now, the way he was paddlin' that canoe."

Blood drained from Belinda's head. "What did you say?"

"Max went over to Storekeeper Bailey's house—wouldn't even wait till after the Sabbath—and bought a canoe off him. 'Bout half hour ago, I'd say. Then he loaded it with a pile'a his huntin' truck and shoved off. Said he was on his way back to the Missouri River. Must've been something mighty important to get him to travelin' on the Sabbath. Thought I was the only one what has to work on Sundays."

"This can't be happening."

"He surprised you too, then," the lad said, his expression brightening. "Ain't you the gal he was callin' on before he left?"

Her first thought was to take the nearby crossroad north to catch him, but she remembered it angled continually away from the Caney Fork. Besides, she'd never be able to catch Max on this old workhorse. "I really need to get back across the river again. In a hurry. Please. My father will pay you in an hour or so when he brings Mrs. Bremmer home."

The lad tilted his head and looked up at her as if to judge her truthfulness. "Well, all right. I know the pastor's wife will be good for it."

As she reined the horse around, he walked along with her to the ferry landing rather than heading for his mule. "Speakin' of comin' visitin' . . . now that Max is gone, I wouldn't mind droppin' by myself, now'n again. If that would be all right with you."

Couldn't the brash lad see how upset she was? How every second counted? She started to shout out her impatience, then thought better of it. "Mr. Stanley—that is your name, isn't it?" Without waiting for his nod, she continued. "I would be most pleased to have you come calling. But at this moment, it is vital that I return to Mrs. Bremmer and tell her that her son has left."

With the added incentive, the lad took off at a run, bent on pleasing her. By the time she had nudged the horse on board the raft again, the wheel was cranking around, and at a much faster pace than before.

Belinda's ravens came swooping in from downriver, the first time she'd noticed they'd followed her.

"La, but I wish you two could talk. How easy it would be for you to catch up with Max and tell him to come back to me." Glancing back at the mule turning the wheel, she willed the animal to go faster. Every minute, every second, Max was floating farther away from her.

Riding on the wagon trail toward the house, Belinda knew she pushed the plow horse more than she should. But she also knew that the river wouldn't run any slower just because she rode an old plug.

She patted the mottled gray hair on Kaiser's neck. "Thank goodness, it's a cooler day." Then she rammed her heels into his sides again. "Forgive me."

She didn't bother to check any openings in the brush along the bank for Max's canoe. He'd long since passed this section . . . unless . . .

He might have stopped off at her dock. Walked up to the house to say good-bye. He could be waiting for her right this minute. Sitting up on the veranda with her parents and his mother. He could be engaged in the discussion of a dowry and house building while she rode home in such a panic.

"Lord," she cried out, looking up through the web of leaves and branches overhead, "please, let it be so. Let him be there."

A wisp of new hope added a measure of anticipation to her angst . . . until she reached her turnoff. Scanning the dock area down to the right, she found only one lone canoe beached on its side. The word *Gregg* at its bow was plain to see, even at thirty yards.

In a return of total panic, she quickly searched the river in both directions as far as each bend would allow, then reined the gelding onto her family's path and urged him forward again.

As Belinda trotted over the small wooden bridge, she spotted her father in front of the garden gate, helping her mother into the carriage. He'd folded down the canopy, giving Belinda a clear view of their two guests, both ensconced in the rear seating area.

They all looked in her direction as she nudged the horse onward.

Her dad took several steps toward her, her premature return no doubt a concern. "Why are you back so soon?" he shouted before she reached them.

Mrs. Bremmer rose to her feet. Her mother remained standing up in the front of the carriage where her husband had left her.

Reaching them, Belinda briefly explained all that the ferry operator had told her, that Max had left on the river a short time before she had crossed it.

"Mine son is gone?" Mrs. Bremmer's cheeks paled. "He left *mit* hatred for me in his heart. Da fault is all mine."

Belinda had no time to spare for recriminations. She slid off the winded mount. "Daddy, quick, help me saddle Mama's roan. If I ride fast, I'm sure I can catch Max long before dark."

"I'm sorry, sweetheart, but the river road comes to an end just two miles on down. After that, the woods are too thick to make much headway at all. You'll never be able to catch him that way."

"But, Daddy, he'll be gone, maybe forever. I have to try."

He took her shoulders. "Don't fret. Tomorrow, first light, I'll saddle up and head straight for Nashville. With all the curves in the river, I'll get there at least a day ahead of him."

"Max is in a canoe, Daddy, not some draggy ol' raft."

"Take da Dillard lad *mit* you," Inga Bremmer suggested. "He knows a goot shortcut up to da Nashville road."

"And an extra horse," Mrs. Thompson piped in. "In case one goes lame on ya."

Belinda felt blessed that they all wanted to help. Still . . . "Daddy, are you sure you'll beat him there?"

Tilting his head, Mr. Gregg nodded with a smile. "Yes, child. The closer the Cumberland gets to Nashville, the more snaky that river gets. Now—" he turned her around—"go sit down and catch your breath while your mama and I see these good ladies home. Everything's going to turn out fine. I promise."

"Dear," her mother said, still standing on the floorboard, "would you prefer I stay here and keep you company?"

At the gentle concern in her mother's voice, Belinda's racing mind slowed a bit, and she took a second to survey the scene: her mother in the carriage with two ladies, ones who knew her secret and still wanted to befriend her. "No, Mother, enjoy the ride. Please do."

"You sure you'll be all right here?" her father asked, inserting a boot into a foothold. "We shan't dawdle. We'll come straight home. I'll need to pack enough food and necessaries this evening for several days."

She could get a head start on that for him. Heaven knew she wouldn't be able to merely sit here twiddling her thumbs. "I'll get some travel food cooked up while you're gone. I'll start right now."

She tied the Bremmer horse to the back of the conveyance and bolted for the house. It wasn't until leather creaks and crunching gravel faded from her hearing that she realized she hadn't bid the ladies good-bye, nor had she told her dad about the debt she owed the lad at the ferry. But she was sure they'd all understand.

Grabbing a cloth bag hanging on a spike behind the meal sacks, she hurried out to the summer kitchen to see how much food they already had prepared that wouldn't quickly spoil.

Belinda looked about her in the detached building for the most likely items to take—this morning's leftover biscuits, hazelnuts, cornmeal and some lard for johnnycakes, coffee. He'd need a pan and a pot, a cup, sugar. Potatoes from the cellar, cheese—

"No, he won't need to cook." Up on the Nashville road, there were farmsteads and small settlements along the way where he could buy meals.

She paused, her panic rising again. Most of the time the road was much too far from the river. Her father would have little chance of catching Max before he reached Nashville. And what if Max slipped through the river port without her father seeing him? Daddy could be taking a walk to an outhouse, or going to an inn for a bite to eat, or tending his horse, and Max could paddle right on by.

"And it would be more than a week before I'd know." By that time Max could be lost to her forever. She knew exactly where he was headed . . . to rendezvous with the Lewis and Clark expedition. Then they'd be off to faraway mountains in search of a route to the Pacific Ocean. Into the myriad dangers of a vast unknown with only a small company of adventurers. He could be captured by hostile Indians, fall off a cliff, be killed by an animal . . . fall sick from some strange disease and die alone in some godless place.

If her dad didn't find him, her chances of ever seeing Max again were slim at best. There had to be a better way.

"In a canoe on the water he only has a two-hour lead." If she left right this minute and took a lantern, she could continue down the river in the dark, catch up to him after he'd beached for the night. She'd never heard of any rapids downstream that she couldn't navigate for a couple of nighttime hours.

"Yes!" She could catch him . . . today . . . this very night!

Dropping only the biscuits in her tote, Belinda ran into the house and dumped the peaches from the fruit bowl into the bag, selected several strips of jerked beef she usually reserved for the ravens, and a metal cup for collecting water. That would be enough to stave off her hunger till she returned home with Max.

Then, of most importance, she checked the amount of oil in the lantern that waited on the table by the back door. The metal well was almost full, thank goodness. She started to leave with it, then remembered another essential item. Matches. Off the hearth mantel she grabbed the lidded jar of thin sulfur sticks.

A blanket. It might get chilly on the water after dark. She sped up the stairs and ran to the chest at the foot of her bed, lifting the top blanket out. Dropping the lid, she swung away and realized she'd caught her skirt . . . her stinking, horse-smelling skirt.

No time to change.

Flinging wide her wardrobe doors, her gaze landed on the silk gown with the roses—the one Max had admired so much. She draped it over the blanket, grabbed a sunbonnet to keep her nose from freckling any more, and raced down to stuff the added items in the tote.

With it in one hand and lantern handle in the other, she started out.

Then stopped.

She had to leave her parents a note. At her father's desk she dashed one off, leaving it on the hall table; then down to the dock she ran.

Before this night was over, she and Max would be together . . . forevermore.

Chapter Twenty-Eight

The rain clouds had mostly moved to the northeast, and everything looked fresh and sparkling with droplets as Max glided along between the river walls. The color of the sandstone was richer, the leaves of the plants growing out of the cracks were brighter, their branches a dark contrast, the air fresh and cool. And the river was taking on that amber sheen the sun painted it shortly before setting for the night.

A fine day to begin his journey, Max tried to convince himself . . . the first day of his trip to see the Pacific Ocean.

But it could never be the adventure he'd always dreamed of unless Belinda were here, sitting on the other cross board, looking back at him with those incredible blue eyes. Her hair alone would put all the rest of this sun-kissed beauty to shame.

He sighed, trying to dispel some of the deep sadness lodged in his chest. Thinking about her only made him hurt more.

He lifted his oar out of the water and pulled it, dripping, into the canoe. His arms and shoulders also ached from the repetitive paddling, especially the arm that had been clubbed with the rifle butt of a river pirate. But he knew those physical aches could be more easily dispelled than those of a lost love.

He rubbed his lower arm, knowing that with the exercise it would be getting on this journey, it would be as strong as ever by the time he reached the Mississippi. As for his leg, the many hours each day of not putting his weight on it would provide the extra rest Ma Smith thought it needed to further restore itself.

But his aching heart . . . that might never heal.

The abrasive sound of cawing shattered the quiet. Max looked up and saw a pair of ravens.

How could he ever forget Belinda if every time he saw a pair of ravens flying overhead he'd be reminded of his lady of the river? And he doubted that a single day would pass that he wouldn't see some. Out across the vast treeless prairies they were even easier to spot.

The black birds soared in circles above him, low enough for him to see the yellows of their eyes, as if to taunt him. Maybe they *were* taunting him. They could easily be Belinda's birds. *As the crow flies—or the raven,* he thought with irony; they wouldn't be that far beyond their usual territory.

He waved up to them. At least they were company. In the four or five hours since he'd launched the canoe, he hadn't come upon a single slower-moving raft carrying its goods to market, or passed any canoes coming upstream. But then folks didn't usually work on the Sabbath.

Still, he knew from hard experience that it was never wise to take chances, even in country that was becoming more civilized by the year.

The thought of danger brought him out of his reverie. Replanting his oar in the water, he started paddling again, searching both walls for a break carved in them by a stream. He'd take the canoe up the next likely one, deep enough to make camp in a hidden spot before dark. A campfire would be out of the question. Even the smallest breeze could carry the smell of smoke for miles.

Being that careful probably wasn't necessary, but he and his companions had been camped only a few miles from St. Louis when they'd been set upon. And tonight he'd be alone.

A few minutes later, Max spotted a fracture in one of the sandstone walls with a wide enough stream pouring into the river at its base for his canoe to navigate. He angled into it, paddling hard against the current. Twenty-five yards or so into the deep shadows of the raggedy gully, he found a sandy and fairly level spot. Looking to make sure he would not be visible from the river, he back-paddled, turning the canoe toward the bank; then he hopped out, dragging the craft onto shore with him.

After years of practice, Max easily rolled out his bed on a layer of tender pine boughs and laid out his cold meal on a brushed-off rock, with several minutes of light remaining. Viewing the dried-out corn bread from dinner and the even drier venison he'd talked Bailey into selling him, along with the canoe—on the Sabbath no less—the peach from his mother's tree looked by far the tastiest item he'd brought.

One thing he was going to miss almost as much as Belinda was his mother's cooking. *His mother.* He'd left without telling her he'd forgiven her. He pushed thoughts of her from his mind by trying to recapture some of the peace he'd received when his father prayed for him.

Picking up a stringy piece of dried meat, he caught a flash of movement behind him. He wheeled around, berating himself for leaving his rifle and powder leaning against a tree several yards away.

But it was only those pesky birds. They'd landed on the tilted side of the canoe and watched as if they expected something from him.

Then Max realized two things: one, they were indeed Belinda's ravens, and two, they expected their share of the meat in his hand.

Chuckling, he walked toward the canoe.

They both took instant flight, landing in a nearby pine. They may be pets, but they weren't his.

Not yet, anyway.

He ripped the venison into several pieces and placed them in small piles several feet apart on the side of the birch-bark canoe. He'd scarcely walked halfway back to his own meal before the birds were down and shredding the meat with their beaks and talons.

Jacob and Esau, straight from Belinda to him. Had she heard he'd left and sent her birds to him, sending him a last farewell?

"Too bad you boys couldn't have brought her with you."

The ravens stopped picking at their meat and cocked their heads toward him as if they really could understand. Then they commenced eating again.

Dumb birds. What would they care about the loss of his love?

"But, Lord, You care. I felt Your powerful presence when Pops was praying. Your cleansing peace. Your hand in my being able to forgive Mama . . ." Max sank to his knees for the second time today. "Please help me to really trust You. With Belinda, I learned how deep love can be, and I know in my mind that You love me as much as I love her. Help me to know it in my soul. Help me to love You that much. And help me to know that

whatever it is that's ahead of me in Your love is far better than
what I leave behind. Please, help me to trust You."

When Max rose from his knees, the birds were gone.

He sighed. The last remnant of Belinda had flown away.

~

"Ah, you're back," Belinda called as her pets dropped down to
land on the rim of her canoe. "It's getting so dark, I thought
you'd flown for home. La, but I do wish you could talk. Then
you could tell me how far ahead of me Max is." He would pull
over soon; then she'd catch him. Two or three hours more and
they'd be together. She smiled in anticipation.

Plowing through a wide, placid stretch of river, she drew in
her oar and laid it in the bottom of the canoe. "I reckon this is
as good a time as any to share some of my dried beef with you.
But I do wish you'd told me you were coming. I would've
brought more." She lifted the tote sagging over the seat in front
of her and rummaged through until she found the strips at the
bottom—none too clean, she was sure. She dusted them off and
fed each bird a few tidbits from her palm, though they didn't
seem nearly as hungry as they usually were.

"You boys must have found yourself something more tasty out
in the woods." Belinda chewed the rest of the salty meat herself,
then searched for the metal cup to scoop a drink from the river.

Along with the cup, she found the jar of matches. "Perhaps
I'd better light the lantern first. What do you think, boys? It's
getting almost too dark to see."

Their only answer was to prance up and down the canoe rim,
cocking their heads this way and that.

Moving forward, she unwedged the lantern from the narrow-
ing hull near the bow and made a nest for its bottom on top of
her tote—she couldn't afford for it to fall over and catch every-

thing on fire. Still, she was a bit nervous about it. She'd have to watch carefully for any rough spots in the river.

After rubbing a spot on the seat board with her already ruined yellow dress to make sure it was dry, she struck one of her precious matches on the surface. It burst into flame. Cupping the small blaze from any capricious breeze, she lit the wick. Adjusting the flame, she saw the water around her had taken on a gentle glow, one that warmed her too.

But as the last vestiges of day faded to black, she found that the lantern's circle of light didn't allow her to see into the darkness. It was impossible to search the shore for Max's canoe or even judge with certainty where the center of the fork was. Reluctantly, she blew out the light.

As soon as her eyes adjusted, she could see somewhat better, but she was forced to weave across the river from shore to shore, for fear that she'd miss Max's canoe. "At this rate," she told her almost invisible black friends, "it could be midnight before I find Max."

Night sounds—the screeches, the hoots—echoed back and forth between the riverbanks, further unsettling her. Never in her life had she been left alone at night, even in her home, let alone in an unknown wilderness.

She moved silently, now glad she'd snuffed the light. Anyone lurking along the cliffs above would easily have seen her.

With every new cry, she watched her birds for their reaction. Surely they'd let her know if any danger presented itself. After a spell, a most welcome three-quarter moon rose into the sky, casting a silvery glimmer across the water and lighting her way.

Now that the occasional sandy beaches shone bright, Belinda relaxed and started paddling in earnest again. Another hour or so and she'd find Max. Time, though, seemed to drag. Long after she thought she'd find his canoe, all was empty and still.

A dot of light above the cliff caught her eye as she rounded a bend. Using her oar as a rudder, she turned the canoe and paddled toward that side of the river. She now saw that there were three spots of light, square shafts coming from above, a dwelling of some sort. Someone had to be in attendance.

Her heart swelled. "Please, God, let it be Max."

As she glided closer to the shore, she spotted the silhouette of a dock, the first she'd seen in hours, and a raft. And on the beach lay not one, but two canoes. She could hardly contain her joy. "We've found him, boys. We've found my love."

Belinda quickly removed her stockings and slippers then steered straight for the shore, jumping off as soon as the canoe jarred to a stop.

The ravens took off into the night sky as she dragged the unwieldy craft onto the beach. Not bothering to retrieve her footwear, she ran up a rather steep incline toward the three spots of light. The largest shaft came from an open doorway.

Boisterous laughter erupted from inside the dwelling. Men's voices. Several of them.

Belinda slowed and listened.

"Gimme that deck," one of them blustered. "It's my turn to deal."

"If you'll hand me the jug'a corn," another said, even louder.

The men were playing cards and drinking liquor. Would Max be in there with them?

Belinda had her doubts. But what did she know about men when they were off to themselves? And they were drinking hard liquor. One thing she did know—she wouldn't simply walk up to the door and knock, not without checking in the windows first to see if Max was even among them.

Stubbing her toe on what she now realized was a rock-strewn pathway, she crept along more carefully, hunching low, since her yellow dressed seemed to glow glaringly in the moonlight. She approached the side of what looked like a roughly built, one-room cabin with only wooden shutters to close in case of bad weather—as if these drunken louts would notice any. Prudently picking a window nowhere near the doorway, she circled wide of the shafts of light and edged toward the opening. She could hear their drunken laughing and teasing and their loud, coarse language.

Pulling her hair aside with a shaky hand, she peeked in. Four men dressed in homespun and deerskins sat at a table in a room as crude-looking as they were. All four sported shaggy, tobacco-stained beards. Belinda's nose curled at the reek of their dirtiness. As much as she yearned to find Max, she was glad to see that he was not with these uncouth men.

She padded softly toward the front again to make her way back to the canoe. Max must still be ahead of her.

"The jug's empty," one of the men complained.

"Can't have that," another said. "I'll run down an' get more."

Belinda had just reached the corner of the cabin when she heard one of them come barreling out the door.

She leapt into the deep shade at the side of the building, praying he wouldn't see her. She could only imagine what might befall her if he did.

Not even glancing her way, the man took off at a loose-jointed run down the hill from whence she'd come.

Stepping even farther from the corner so that neither she nor her telltale dress could be seen from the dock if he did happen to look back, she realized she'd have to wait where she was until he returned inside.

In the lulls betweeen the loud yammerings in the cabin, she heard the man below, banging and clumping around on the raft, obviously having a hard time finding more whiskey. Finally his footsteps came pounding across the wooden dock, and she saw his shadowy figure ambling up the hill. Suddenly he bellowed, "Hank! Dooley! Come out here! Quick!"

Belinda shrunk back even farther. Had he seen her?

Chairs crashing, the men barreled out of the cabin far enough for her to see them in the light from the door. "What's up?" the heaviest of the men yelled.

"There's another canoe down there, layin' next to ours. Any'a you yahoos know where it came from?"

The men glanced at one another.

"Beached or just drifted ashore?" a short but compactly built man asked in a gruff voice.

"Beached! We ain't alone here. Arm yourselves."

Chapter Twenty-Nine

Hold up!" the shortest man ordered. "Boaz, drunk as you are, you're just seein' double."

"No, I ain't. Get yourself on down here, an' I'll show you. Dooley, you an' Hank get back in there an' get the rifles."

As the men took off in opposite directions, two for the cabin and two down to the dock, Belinda commanded herself to remain calm, while every fiber in her body wanted to bolt. Crashing noisily into the woods would only announce her every move. She knew, though, that she couldn't wait until the unsavory louts confirmed the presence of her canoe. Deftly, she back-stepped to the rear corner of the house.

She heard the two inside the shanty banging around, no doubt collecting the weapons meant to shoot her. What a fool she'd been to chase after Max with no thought for her own safety.

And to now make her escape, she would have to cross below

the cabin's rear window. Breath held, she ducked low and edged beneath it, with her bare feet feeling each step of ground ahead of her for any obstructions in the total darkness. Any second, she knew one of the men could look out of the opening.

She didn't breathe again until she'd moved several feet past the window. Her heart still banging in her chest, she kept low, until she reached the far corner. From there, only a few feet of open moonlit ground separated her from the inky darkness of the trees.

Glancing back to the window, she saw that no one was peering out. But soon the pair at the dock would confirm that a strange canoe did indeed exist. It was time to run or be discovered for sure.

Lord, she pleaded, *make them blind to me in this bright yellow dress.* Bunching up the skirt, she sprinted for the woods in a light-footed dash. Gravel and twigs dug at the bottoms of her feet, a thorny bramble bush tugged at her skirt, but she didn't stop. She continued into the woods until she was several yards deep.

She paused, then, and listened. Had she been heard? Her pulse pounded so hard in her ears she could hardly hear.

No one. Not yet.

Belinda started forward again then stopped. She couldn't just flee like a wild animal. She had to think. Would running farther into the forest be smart? Only the canoe could take her to Max and real safety. She needed to circle back toward the river, stay close to the beach. But which side of the dock? Upstream or downstream?

Lord, help me.

If she was forced to reach the canoe by wading neck deep in the river, it would be easier to go with the water's flow. Not knowing if her conclusion had come from God or herself, she started moving, stepping gingerly, trying not to make noise or do any more damage to her stinging feet.

"See, another canoe!" the man who'd first made the discovery shouted. "Just like I said."

Belinda almost leapt out of her skin. The voice was much too close. She dropped to the ground and looked back at the light from the cabin. By circling around, she'd put no more than twenty yards between herself and the men.

"Hank! Dooley!" the other man shouted from the dock. "Did you get my rifle and fixin's?"

"Aye!"

"Then blow out that blasted lantern! We're sittin' ducks. Boaz, you stay here. Guard the raft."

After that, all talking stopped, and the light from the cabin was quenched almost immediately. Listening intently, Belinda could still hear some shuffling around, but none that left the area. None coming toward her. Not yet.

Please, God, stop them from coming this way.

Feeling the ground ahead of her with her hands, Belinda crawled on all fours. She inched through moldy-smelling leaves and knobby twigs, the occasional lightning bug her only source of light.

If somehow she could get back to her canoe unnoticed.

But with an armed man there, guarding the dock . . .

She could take her chances. Go to them and tell them the canoe was hers and she'd simply stopped here by mistake.

Too risky. Even if they were normally trustworthy, they were full of hard drink.

A sharp thorn punctured Belinda's palm, and she came dangerously close to yelping. Easing back on her heels, she removed the offending sticker. She wiped blood and dirt from the spot with a portion of her skirt she hoped wasn't too soiled already.

Taking a minute to rest and try to clear her thoughts, she leaned back against a tree, hoping all the bugs living on its bark had retired for the night. After a moment or two, she did come up with a plan. Not much of one, she had to admit. But this she did know: men who drank heavily were supposed to fall into a deep sleep—she'd read that in one of her novels. The book's young governess of the manor was in much the same situation as Belinda herself, except the heroine had only one villain to escape from, *not four*.

If she slipped down toward the dock close enough to see when the guard fell asleep . . . if she moved very fast, pushed the canoe back into the water . . .

But if he didn't doze off and if they didn't leave for downriver in the morning, she'd— She didn't like any of her choices after that . . . walk barefooted all the way back home without finding Max, possibly even being tracked by the men once it was daylight. Or she could wait until the effects of the whiskey wore off, then appeal to the mercy of the men, who, for all she knew, could very well be river pirates.

Lord, You know I've always been a sensible girl. But, for the love of a man, I've become such a fool. Tell me what to do. I can't bear the thought of Mama suffering another loss, not after losing her baby boy. Or not seeing Max just one more time to tell him I love him. I never told him, You know. I promise, if You help me out of this mess, I'll go to church every Sunday. I'll truly trust that You placed us in Reardon Valley because You want us to share our lives with this congregation, just as Brother Bremmer said. And I'll believe You for bringing healing to Mama in Your own special time, however and whenever that may be. But right now, please, help me.

She sat where she was for several minutes, waiting for some

miraculous insight from God, some sign. The hoots of a persistent owl she heard, the rustling of tiny creatures through the fallen leaves, but nothing else.

Finally, she rose. With her hands out in front of her, her feet searching each step, she carefully made her way toward the muted shushing of the slow-moving river.

A few minutes later, Belinda saw moonlight reaching into the woods and knew she was within a stone's throw of the bluff above the river. She headed toward what would be the crumbled-down area of rock that gave way to the beach. When she again saw moonglow coming through the trees, she knew she was close. She prayed she'd be able to watch the guard from the safety of the trees.

A hulking, moving shadow blocked a portion of the light. A man was coming into the woods. Heading straight toward her.

Belinda dropped to the ground.

A twig snapped a number of yards away. He was still moving forward.

Frantically, she felt around her until her fingers brushed what felt like pine needles hanging from a branch close to the ground. On her belly like a snake, she slithered beneath the branch until she reached the trunk of the tree.

A rustling—and skittering. She'd flushed out some creature, scaring herself more than the animal.

Had the man noticed?

She heard nothing. He must have stopped, too, and was listening.

She did her best to calm her panicked breathing.

Minutes passed. No more sounds from the man.

More time. What seemed like an hour—or two.

It was as if he waited for her to move again. As with most men west of the mountains, he'd probably hunted raccoon and opossum at night since boyhood to provide meat for the table. He'd know her rustlings if she moved again.

Gradually Belinda came awake. In the dimness, she opened her eyes and realized she wasn't in her bed but in a sap-oozing, bug-crawling tangle of pine needles. Sometime during the night she'd fallen asleep.

She lurched into a sitting position, brushing a spider off her sleeve. Sunlight tinted the eastern sky. Birds were chirping, woodpeckers tapping.

Spreading two drooping branches, she searched in the direction of the dock. Scanning as far as she could in the dense undergrowth, she spotted no one between her and where the trees thinned near the beach.

Surely the searcher had returned to his friends by now. Or was he still waiting, himself hidden behind some bush? On the other hand, the men could've already started downriver.

She had to know. Max would be traveling on soon too, if he hadn't already boarded his canoe, going ever farther ahead of her. Tears started forming . . . she felt so utterly helpless.

Overhead, she heard cawing.

Looking up, she saw two birds. Were they hers? Had Jacob and Esau stayed close by?

The cawing grew more intense as the birds flew toward the river. She lost sight of them but knew they were over the water. They circled back and flew over it again, their raucous noise never ceasing.

Were they telling her that the men were leaving?

She glanced again toward the dock for any sign of the man who'd been tracking her. Not seeing him, she took a chance and crawled from beneath the pine boughs.

Still no movement.

Lifting her dingy skirt, she ran toward the bluff, upstream of the dock. She needed to know more before exposing her presence. From that vantage point, she was pretty sure she could view the beach and a considerable distance downstream.

With the ravens still cawing, she fought her way through the brambles of a last berry shrub before reaching the ledge.

And there on the water, coming downstream, floated a canoe. A lone blond-haired man paddled.

"Max!" she screamed, her voice croaking. *"Max!"*

He turned his head toward the shore. He'd heard her.

"Max! Up here!" Wildly, she waved her hands back and forth. "It's me! Belinda!"

Looking straight at her, he lunged to his feet. The canoe rocked crazily, and he sat down again. He waved with his paddle and started angling toward shore.

Warm tears rolled down her face; she was so incredibly happy. Somehow she'd bypassed Max on the river last night, and he was here! "Thank You, Jesus."

Chapter Thirty

I knew if I waited long enough, I'd get ya," the short but power-fully built man boasted, triumph in his tone.

"*Please*." Belinda tried to jerk out of his grip. "Let go of me."

"I don't think so." The man, smelling of liquor and sweat, chuckled. He was able to hold her fast, with only one arm around her waist. In the other he held a rifle taller than he was. "Tell ya one thing. You sure are a surprise. Wait'll the boys get a look at ya. All night we thought we was after some dangerous marauder, and here you be, just some sweet li'l thing— Wait a minute." He spun her to face him. No taller than Belinda, he had a slash of straight brows over piercing, deep-set, brown eyes that stared straight into hers.

This man looked capable of great violence.

"Who's Max?" Warily, he glanced quickly around.

Denying Max's presence would serve no purpose, since Max would be paddling into shore any second now. "I was calling to my companion down on the river. I lost him during the night when I beached here by mistake."

He smiled grimly. "I reckon that's as good a tall tale as any." Obviously, he didn't believe a word she'd said. He released his hold only long enough to grasp her hand in a painful grip. "Come on."

He started walking fast, and even though her scratched and bruised feet complained, she didn't care. The man was taking her straight to Max.

But had she lured Max into danger as well? If these men were, in fact, river pirates, they might set upon him, rob or kill him.

Lord God in heaven . . .

~

He'd seen her! Bright hair, yellow dress. And her ravens flying overhead, making so much racket a body would think they'd just been told they were to be tonight's supper.

Belinda had come after him. She loved him. That much. His chest swelled with such joy, he thought it would burst.

Realizing he'd stopped paddling and was drifting sideways, Max renewed his effort to pull in at the dock ahead.

One of the black birds swooped past his ear and flew above the bluff. The birds hadn't followed him; they'd been with her. But how did she manage to get this far on foot?

No, Max saw that one of the beached canoes was hers—the word *Gregg* was plain to see. She'd come downriver after him then bypassed him. He'd taken such care to hide his camp last night that his own beloved had floated right on by.

Those birds actually had tried to inform him . . . between bites of dried meat, he remembered with a grin—a grin he knew would go on forever.

He spotted two bearded men stepping onto the dock, most

likely Belinda's escorts. Surprised that he didn't recognize either of them, he reckoned them to be men who'd come to their valley in the past few years, ones he'd missed meeting on his infrequent trips home.

Regardless, they'd done him a great service.

Both, he noticed, carried rifles.

He waved as he glided to shore beside Belinda's canoe.

The two returned his greeting—one, a stringy-looking fellow with an even stringier beard and protruding eyes. The other seemed a gluttonous sort. When he hopped off the dock and headed toward Max, his barrel of a belly jiggled.

Max leapt into the shallow water and dragged the canoe up onto the bank. "Where is she?" he asked.

"Who?" the fat-cheeked fellow asked.

"Miss Gregg."

"That's the name on the canoe, Dooley," the skinny one chided, brushing a strand of greasy hair from his pop eyes.

"Right." Max glanced at his own rifle lying on his pack and wrapped in oilcloth to keep it dry. Worse, it wasn't primed and loaded. "I take it you boys ain't seen the lady who came in that birch canoe there."

"So that's why there's a purty gown in the sack," the roly-poly one said. "I thought some ol' boy was totin' it home to his ladylove. But there ain't no—"

"Hey, Boaz!" a man shouted from somewhere up above. "Come see what I found!"

A rangy fellow who didn't seem too steady on his feet lumbered out of the cabin on the hill and looked toward the woods above the bluff . . . in the direction Max had seen Belinda. Max began to realize that none of these men were with her. *And one of them had captured her.*

303

The men down on the beach with Max were also distracted by the shout. Forgetting Max, they started walking up the hill.

Max reached into his craft and snatched up his rifle, ripping away the cloth covering as he swung the unloaded thing up. He cocked the flintlock, hoping to strengthen his bluff. "Stop where you are. Drop your weapons." He spoke sharply, but only loud enough for the two nearest him to hear.

They wheeled around, their mouths gaped open.

"Drop 'em," Max repeated, pointing his rifle to the rotund one's belly while keeping the man between himself and those on the hill.

First one then the other laid their long rifles on the ground.

"Don't shoot," the skinny one pleaded. "Take what ya want and go."

"That's exactly what I plan to do. Start walking up toward your friend."

Red hair and a yellow dress flashed into view.

"Belinda!"

"Where'd she come from?" the skinny one asked.

"Max!"

Above, a long stone's throw away, a man had hold of Belinda's hand. She tried to wrench free. But couldn't. She was being held against her will.

In an instant, Belinda bent down and latched onto the man's hand with her teeth.

He yelped.

She yanked free and flew down the hill toward Max, banging past the clumsy big fellow near the cabin without missing a step, past the two Max held in his sights, and slammed into him, practically knocking him over as she flung her arms around him. "Max, Max," she cried breathlessly. "You're here. You're safe. I found you."

He couldn't ask for a more enthusiastic welcome. But this was not exactly the right moment. He eased her to one side while keeping his finger on the double triggers of his weapon. "Belinda, drag my canoe back into the water."

By now, the men near the cabin had noticed that Max held their two comrades at gunpoint. They started sauntering down. The shorter one who'd held Belinda had a rifle of his own, and unlike the two in front of Max, this one looked quite prone to using it.

"Wait! Wait jist a minute!" the bug-eyed one yelled, holding his hands out in both directions. Caught in the middle, he was understandably in a panic. "Listen, mister, we didn't know nothin' about your woman. Giff just now found her. Ain't that right, Giff?"

"Yup." He stopped several yards short of them. "We come across the canoe last night, and we thought we had a sneak thief on our hands. We been up all night, guardin' our goods and tryin' not to get ourselves ambushed. And all the time it was just this wild woman out there." The short but sturdy man shot Belinda a menacing glare and held out his injured hand. "You drew blood, missy."

"And you hurt my hand!" Belinda yelled back as Max heard her struggling to shove the loaded canoe into the water. "I have a big red spot on the back of my hand."

"That cain't hurt half as bad as my head," the big clumsy fellow piped in, his own hand rubbing his temple. "That woman cost me a whole night's sleep."

The two ravens sailed down and landed on a dead tree branch jutting out of the boulders, cawing and flapping their wings as if they were having their own say in the matter.

The whole scene suddenly seemed hilarious. Lowering his rifle barrel a degree, Max burst out laughing.

The short man joined him.

His bearded companions gawked at each other, confused.

"Don't you get it?" the short one asked, still laughing. "We been up all night, jumpin' at ever' little noise, and all the time it was just that li'l gal there, hidin' out from us."

Things were looking up. "Fellas," Max said, "you been through enough for one day. You deserve a reward, if for nothing else, for keeping my lady here for me to find." He reached into the pocket of his linen hunting shirt and pulled out a ten-dollar gold piece. "Have yourselves a good meal and a bug-free bed on me when you get to Nashville." With his thumb, he flipped the coin to the skinny one.

"The canoe's in the water," Belinda called from behind Max.

Still not totally trusting the scruffy river men, Max back-stepped toward the water. As he passed the Gregg canoe, he lifted out its paddle, and seeing a bag with the silken gown of roses sticking out halfway, he grabbed it too.

As Max backed into the chill river, Belinda stepped behind him. "Let me." She took the oar and her cloth bag, tossing them into Max's canoe. "If you'll hold the canoe while I get in, then I can take the rifle for you." Apparently she didn't trust them either.

"I take it you know how to shoot," he said, grabbing the slender boat's rim.

"It don't matter if she cain't," the rotund one called out. "With hair as red as hers, she's bound to have a whoppin' temper I sure don't want to tangle with."

This time, all four started guffawing.

Max leapt aboard. Then he and Belinda were off, paddling downstream with smooth hard strokes. Once they were well on their way, with Max on the bench behind Belinda, he looked back and waved.

Still grinning, the scruffy foursome returned his farewell.

The ravens flew down and landed on the craft's rim next to Belinda, and the picture was complete. Max collapsed into his own bout of helpless laughter.

"I really don't see what's so all-fired funny," Belinda snipped, shooting a scowl at him. "Who know's what might've happened to me if you hadn't shown up when you did?"

"You're right. I'm sorry." But he still couldn't pull down his grin. He'd never been so happy in his life.

"And that other man just plain insulted me. Talking that way about the color of my hair."

Trying really hard to curb his amusement, Max stopped rowing a moment to touch the wild mass her hair had become while trying to think of something to calm her ire. "Ouch!" Her hair bit back, pricking his finger. "You've got stickers in your hair."

"You hadn't noticed?" Her anger flamed even higher. "Look at my day gown. And my feet." She lifted a trim ankle and bare foot for his inspection, exposing a number of scratches.

"Ah, sweetheart, you really did have a hard night, didn't you? I'm so sorry." A fierce desire to hold her close overwhelmed him. But Max started paddling again—they'd begun to float backward. He surveyed both sides of the river within the jutting banks and didn't see even the smallest landing. Then— "See that log jammed up against those rocks near the right edge? Steer the canoe in front of it, and we'll rest a few minutes. I think it will hold us."

She glanced back at him, now with much gentler eyes, her slightly tipped nose starting to pinken from the double exposure of sun and its reflection off the water. "Yes, that would be nice." Her voice had lost its agitation and flowed smooth and soft.

The second he butted the canoe's bow into a V formed by the

log wedged between boulders, Max tossed his paddle in the bottom of the boat and reached for Belinda. "Come here."

Swinging her feet over her seat, she released her oar and came into his arms . . . warm, soft Belinda.

He pulled her close, feeling the greatest sense of relief. "I know I should say some nice things leading up to it, like you are the most beautiful thing I ever saw this morning. But it's going to have to wait till I kiss your cute nose—" which he did—"and your starry eyes. . . ." Much more time he took with them.

A long sigh streamed from her.

He shuddered and held her closer. "I thought I lost you."

"I know." She nuzzled his rough cheek with her smooth one.

A disturbing reality stole its way into his thoughts. He moved her to arm's length. "Surely you know the risk you took, going down that lonely stretch of river alone. How close you came to . . ." He gathered her to his chest. "Promise me you'll never do anything that dangerous again."

This time, she pulled away and slanted a gaze up at him. "I don't imagine Daddy was too happy either when he found my note. But all I have to say is I won't be so daring after this *if* I don't have to be. What do you say? Are you going to stay put and marry me?" She quirked a smile. "Or do I have to go chasing after you again?"

"Of course. You know I will. But I'm confused. Yesterday you refused me—for the second time."

"Like the storybooks go, I could say that my love for you simply couldn't be denied."

The woman was toying with him.

"But," she continued, "there was much more to it. Your mother came to our house yesterday afternoon, full of apologies and asking for our forgiveness. She said she'd let her fears overcome her instead of trusting that the Lord would give her the grandchildren He wanted her to have . . . these grandchildren that, let me tell you, she expects to be born right here in Reardon Valley."

Max chuckled. "Mama does have a hard time letting us or even God have the last say."

Belinda moved closer. "She's right, though. I learned too that I can trust God with all the cares of my life—even my parents. He is watching over Mama and Daddy just as He is watching over us, and He'll make everything work together for our good, according to His purposes for us, no matter what others—even people in church—might think or say. You'll be glad to hear, by the way, that when I left my parents and your mother, they were busy discussing my dowry."

"Dowry? You mean I get you *and* a dowry?"

As he beheld her, though, his thoughts turned solemn. From this very moment, nothing would stand between them. She was to become bone of his bone, flesh of his flesh . . . pink nose and all. His grin popped to the surface again. "Sweetheart, did you bring a sunbonnet?"

"It should be in my tote. Why?"

"Oh, I just know how you females are. You're not gonna want your nose all red and peeling when we get married next month."

Her fingers shot to her nose. "Peeling?" Then, "Married? Next month?"

He caught her hand and brought it to his lips and kissed the center of her palm.

Her breath caught.

His own became as ragged as his pulse. "Like Pete Dagget said at church yesterday, I can't think of one good reason to wait."

Epilogue

I think the curling iron is hot enough." Belinda pulled the iron rod from the coals in the Bremmers' fireplace. She blew off the ashes, then wet her finger with her tongue to test it. "Yes. Hot enough." She turned back to Liza.

"Hurry. We're gonna be late." The younger girl tilted her head, giving Belinda better access to that one stubborn ringlet that didn't want to curl.

Belinda carefully wound the lock around the hair tool. Seconds later, she pulled the strand free, and it fell to the side of Liza's cheek as springy as the one on the opposite side . . . a wonderful complement to the shorter ringlets scattered across her brow and the ones that cascaded from her crown. These mingled with creamy satin ribbons and roses.

Taking a step back, Belinda studied the complete picture. "Your wedding gown, everything is absolute perfection now. And I'm so glad we decided to match our gowns."

"They did turn out real fine, didn't they? We look like two princesses. Except . . ." Liza reached up and poked one of Belinda's less obedient natural curls into place.

With the help of their mothers and soon-to-be mothers-in-law, they'd fashioned the two wedding gowns in the same high-waisted Empire style, using yards and yards of cool, filmy batiste. The only difference between the two gowns was in their shades of beige. With the expertise of the older women, Belinda's fabric had been dyed darker with tea. And the ribbons and lace for both had been tinted to a hue somewhere in between.

Although Belinda could have afforded a much more elaborate costume, it had been important to her that she not upstage Liza. This day was just as important to the younger girl—if that were possible.

"Ladies." Christopher Gregg stood in the doorway, looking quite handsome in a black cutaway coat and ankle-length breeches. It was the latest fashion for men—or so the tailor in Nashville had told him when he and Max had gone there to be outfitted, dragging the reluctant Pete along with them. "Ike over at the church just signaled. Everyone is seated and waiting."

Liza squealed and gave Belinda an exuberant hug. "I would say age before beauty and let you go first, but I just can't wait." She glanced around her. "Where's my bouquet?"

"Your papa's got it out on the porch," Chris informed her, stepping aside as the girl picked up her skirts and dashed past him. He chuckled, watching her go.

"Don't run, Liza," Belinda shouted after her too late. "You'll muss your hair." Belinda shrugged then turned a smile up to her dear father and offered him her arm. "Shall we?"

Upon reaching the front porch, Belinda found that Liza had gotten no farther.

Her dad, a man of considerable height and breadth, stood one step down, facing her, blocking her path. "Are you absolutely sure you wanna marry that loud-talkin' ruffian? You're still just a baby."

"I'm older than Mama was when she married you. Besides, Pete ain't loud at all, not when it's just him and me." A small smile lifted one corner of her mouth. "He's just an ol' pussycat." The tiny girl smoothed her father's brow with her fingers, took his hand, and led him down the steps. "I'm gonna be just fine. I'm all growed up. You just gotta get used to the idea, that's all."

"Me too," Belinda's own dad whispered in her ear. "It just won't be the same, not seeing your pretty face every morning across the breakfast table."

"With Emma Jane coming to live with you and Mama, I think you'll still have your hands plenty full. And, besides, I'll be right up the road."

"Be sure and tell Max how much I appreciate him building you a place on our side of the river. You know, for when I need you."

"You've already told him half a dozen times." Belinda retrieved her bouquet of mums surrounded by greens and trailing with ribbons. "Now give me your best smile and take me to my groom. My big, sweet, handsome husband-to-be." She took his arm.

"You're not a bit nervous about marrying Max, are you?" Her dad wasn't handling this much better than Liza's.

"Not in the least. God brought him back home just for me. And besides, I love him so much it hurts." She gave him a tug and started him moving again.

Strolling arm in arm with her father from the Bremmers', Belinda gazed up at the church spire gleaming in the midafternoon sun . . . no longer the symbol of her fear but one of love and friends and sharing.

A soft lilting tune was being played on the harpsichord and

came streaming out of the church windows. Playing along on his flute was Howie Clay, the young fellow who'd been so musical at the cornhusking party.

And suddenly Belinda was struck by nervousness. Once she walked through the church doors, a room full of people would be staring at her, watching as her life changed forever. From this day forth Miss Belinda Gregg would be Mrs. Max Bremmer.

Walking up the steps, she held her dad's arm just a little bit tighter.

~

Max felt as much like an impostor as Pete looked in their fancy suits of clothes, his a rust brown with long fawn breeches, and Pete's navy with light gray breeches. Predictably, his mother had checked all the stitching when he had brought his tailored outfit home.

He smiled at his mother, sitting in the first row with Felicity. She beamed up at him as if the wedding had been all her idea from the start.

His pops, standing in front of him, held his best Bible in his hand, trying to maintain a solemn expression. But the twinkle in his round blue eyes was unmistakable. Max had made him a very happy father by choosing to live here in the valley and work with him.

But it had been no sacrifice on his part. He couldn't think of anyone else with whom he'd rather spend his workday. Or, he thought, his chest swelling with anticipation, anyone he'd rather go home to than his beautiful Belinda.

The church door opened. Max's attention riveted to the entrance. Liza, looking lovelier than he'd ever seen her, and her father, Ken, stood there.

Max turned to Pete and got a real chuckle at his best friend's reaction as his bride sauntered up the aisle. The poor young man was so besotted, he lunged forward when she was halfway to him.

Max grabbed his arm to keep him from going after her— which didn't make her papa any happier.

Liza, though, didn't seem the least displeased. That girl sure knew how to use her eyes. She gazed at Pete adoringly.

Just as she reached Pete and her father released her, light again shafted in from the entrance, and all else fled Max's thoughts.

There his lady came, aglow in an aura that diminished only slightly when the doors closed behind her and her father. Max could not believe this gorgeous creature was actually coming to him, to be his . . . *"and they shall be one flesh."*

He wanted to get down on his knees to thank his Lord as thanks poured from his soul. *Dearest Father in heaven, don't ever let me forget this moment . . . this day my Belinda came to me. And, Father, she's suffered with her mother and made enough sacrifices to last her for years to come. Give her a long season of joy. And I ask You to give me the love and the wisdom to make her next years full of the kind of laughter and a higher purpose that my pops always tried to give to our family.*

On an enchanting melody, Belinda reached him, her eyes soft, starlit, looking up at him with more love than he could take in. It filled the room. This gift from God he drew to his side.

His father nodded his approval. "Today ve haf all come here in da sight of God, to vitness dese two marriages of our *kinders und* neighbor's *kinders,* right here in our own beautiful Reardon Valley. . . ."

A Note from the Author

Dear Reader,

I do hope *Lady of the River* was an enjoyable, inspiring read and that you fell in love with Max and Belinda as I did. In this novel, the saying "Fiction imitates life" was sometimes an imitation of occurrences in my own life, especially those dealing with Max's growing understanding of who his father really was.

During the writing of this book, my youngest daughter and her husband were forced to live with us for six months due to financial problems. After being on her own for a time and experiencing the rigors of adult responsibilities, our daughter now saw her parents and the Lord through more adult eyes. Instead of the rebellion her father and I had experienced from her during her teen years, we were pleased and grateful to God that she had now become a loving and understanding young woman.

I knew my daughter and her husband had been relying on the Lord, and I was sad that they had been faced with some painful and humbling truths concerning the not-always-so-reputable business world. The mother in me had wanted to protect them from this time of testing. I now see that God was giving them *and* me a chance to grow in His wisdom and our faith.

Speaking of faith, in hindsight I now know that I'd had an unclear view of God's care for my daughter while looking through that proverbial glass darkly, as the apostle Paul wrote long ago in 1 Corinthians 13:12. It's such a wonderful assurance to know that God, unlike me, clearly sees every heart and knows all our lives from start to eternity.

In closing, I think I'll borrow from the apostle Paul again: "The grace of our Lord Jesus Christ be with you."

Dianna Crawford

About the Author

DIANNA CRAWFORD lives in southern California with her husband, Byron, and the youngest of their four daughters. Although she loves writing historical fiction, her most gratifying blessings are her husband of forty years, her daughters, and her grandchildren. Aside from writing, Dianna is active in her church's children's ministries.

Dianna's first novel was published in 1992 under the pen name Elaine Crawford. Written for the general market, the book became a best-seller and was nominated for Best First Book by the Romance Writers of America. Three more novels and several novellas followed under that pen name.

Dianna much prefers writing Christian historical fiction, because our wonderful Christian heritage is commonly diluted or distorted—if not completely deleted—from most historical fiction, nonfiction, and textbooks. She felt very blessed when she and Sally Laity were given the opportunity to coauthor the

Freedom's Holy Light series for Tyndale House. The books center on fictional characters who are woven into many of the real-life adventures and miracles that took place during the American Revolution.

The Freedom's Holy Light series consists of *The Gathering Dawn*, *The Kindled Flame*, *The Tempering Blaze*, *The Fires of Freedom*, *The Embers of Hope*, and *The Torch of Triumph*. Dianna has also authored two HeartQuest novellas, which appear in the anthologies *A Victorian Christmas Tea* and *With This Ring*. She has written a novella, "November Nocturne," in the anthology *Autumn Crescendo* (Barbour Publishing). She is the coauthor with Rachel Druten of the novel *Out of the Darkness* (Heartsong Presents).

Her first HeartQuest series, The Reardon Brothers, consists of *Freedom's Promise*, *Freedom's Hope*, and *Freedom's Belle*. This current HeartQuest series, Reardon Valley, includes *A Home in the Valley* and *Lady of the River*, as well as a third book due out in summer 2003.

Dianna welcomes letters from readers written to her at P.O. Box 80176, Bakersfield, CA 93380. A stamped return envelope would be appreciated.

The Reardon Valley Series

Turn the page for an exciting preview
from book #3 in the Reardon Valley series
by Dianna Crawford.

(ISBN 0-8423-6012-3)

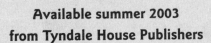

**Available summer 2003
from Tyndale House Publishers**

APRIL 1815

"Are you sure? That's downright amazin'!"

Standing outside the Bremmers' home, Hope Underwood knew it wasn't polite to eavesdrop on conversations, but from the excitement in the voice of her friend Liza Dagget, she couldn't help herself.

"And after all these years!" another friend, Belinda Bremmer, added, sounding equally astounded. "I'm surprised Max never mentioned it in one of his letters to me."

The words breezed out the parlor window, along with the hem of the ruffled print curtains. Something unusual must have happened to Reardon Valley's militiamen. They were serving with Andrew Jackson's army down in New Orleans.

Hope, on a porch step of the rough-hewn house, removed her second mud-caked shoe and scraped it across its match to knock off the worst of the muck before going inside to join the Friday afternoon sewing circle. Leaving the footwear behind, she picked up her basket of supplies and hurried toward the entrance in her stockinged feet on this first sunny day in a week, curious to learn what her friends found so astonishing.

"What all did Howie say about—"

"Shh!" someone warned in an urgent whisper. "Hope's comin'."

Secrets? From her? That wasn't like her friends . . . her closest friends.

Hope gave the usual quick rap on the door, put on a smile as if she'd heard nothing, and walked into what was normally a cozy front room. Today, though, a large worktable for the women had been set up in the middle of the polished plank floor.

Her four longtime friends sat around the table, needles piercing cloth. They all had their heads ducked, as if their minds were on nothing but stitching a set of tiny clothes for redheaded Belinda's expected baby. Then, one by one, they looked up with suspect smiles and greeted her.

"Sorry I'm late," Hope said, her returning smile probably no less stiff than theirs. "I had a hard time gettin' Timmy down for his nap, and I didn't want to leave him until he fell asleep. Ma Tilly's joints are plaguin' her what with all the rain we've been havin'."

"We can thank God that the clouds are finally gone," the very pregnant Belinda said with fervor. "Our poor beleaguered men having to trudge through miles and miles of mud to get back to us."

"Not to mention they could all come down with the ague or one of them awful Louisiana swamp fevers." A natural response from sad-eyed Liza—her grandmother was the valley's only healer, and she knew of such things.

"Does that mean the men are on their way home from New Orleans?" Hope asked, wondering if that had something to do with the secret they were keeping from her. Perhaps they didn't want it to be a reminder of the fact that her own husband would not be returning with them, now or ever. Ezra had been killed during the battle at Fort Bowyer seven months ago. Hope set her sewing basket on the table and took the empty seat next to Belinda.

Gracie, Hope's older sister with the height and blonde hair inherited from their tall Nordic father, broke into a happy grin. "I stopped off at Bailey's store, and there was a letter from my Howie. It was dated no more'n a month ago, and he said they were leavin' New Orleans in a few days, headin' north to Nashville. But he wrote that it would be slow goin' this time of year, haulin' all the army equipment and supplies, not to mention transportin' the wounded."

Almost as thrilled as Gracie, Hope reached across the table and squeezed her sister's hand. "That's wonderful. I miss Howie's jokin' and singin' as much as you do. It'll be a pure pleasure havin' the men home again."

"We should be thankin' God every day that our army had so few casualties in that last battle," Delia, Howie's sister, remarked as she looked across the table with those dark expressive eyes. "You know it had to be a miracle from God when you think that the British had two thousand casualties whilst our American boys had only eight dead and thirty-seven wounded."

"My, yes, a pure miracle for sure," Belinda said, struggling to her feet and stretching her back. Due to give birth any day, the poor woman looked hugely uncomfortable. "And we must always remember to be grateful. After three years of having our valley's men off fighting at least half of the time, we've lost only two of the valley's brave soldiers. We need to keep the Wallaces in our prayers." Her bright gaze then settled on Hope. "And you, of course, and Ezra's parents."

"Yes," Hope agreed. "It's been especially hard on Titus and

Tilly. Titus is really too old and feeble to be out plowin' like he was doin' when I left the house . . . while his youngest son dawdled on the porch."

"They spoiled Joel, that's for sure," Liza added. "From what I see, that yahoo's only got one thing on his mind—chasin' after a purty skirt."

"And at the moment—" Delia laughed—"he seems to think Hope's the purtiest."

Delia's remark hit a sore spot with Hope. "Well, it won't do him one bit of good. Not only is he four years my junior and lazy as an ol' dog, he hasn't had the decency to respect my widowhood . . . not from the day he heard his older brother was dead. If it wasn't for Ma Tilly bein' so sickly, I would've moved back home months ago." Hearing the ring of her own bitterness, Hope quickly returned to the prior topic. "This is much too fine a day for my personal grievances. The men are on their way home."

Belinda sat down again, supporting her belly. "Do pray they come quickly. This baby isn't going to wait much longer. And I've never birthed one without Max being here with me."

"Of course we will." Hope turned to her sister. "Gracie, did Howie mention in his letter how his foot was healin' from the cannon shrapnel?"

Gracie's deep blue eyes clouded despite her attempt at a smile. "He just said it was comin' along. But if his foot was still on the mend more'n two months after that last battle, I have a feelin' his wound was worse than he let on."

"That big brother of mine is such a baby," Delia said to Gracie. "If it was really bad, he'd be carryin' on like a bawlin' calf." Delia and Jacob Reardon and Gracie and Howard Clay were as close now as they'd been all their growing-up years, intermarrying the two families. They'd even built their homes facing each other across the road separating the Reardon and

Clay lands. But the reason Delia could be so flippant about her brother's injury was because her husband had won the coin toss and had remained behind to look after the two families while Howie went to fight against the British and their Indian allies in what was now dubbed the War of 1812.

On the other hand, Hope's husband had been more than happy to go—escape, would be more like it—even with Hope expecting a child herself at the time. And worse, she'd been just as glad to see him go. Their marriage had been a mistake. They never should have let their parents push them into what had been deemed the perfect solution to their separate sadnesses. It had only compounded each of their private sorrows. One good thing had come from their union, though—their son, two-and-a-half-year-old Timothy. Hope could never regret having Timmy. He was the single joy of her life.

Liza Dagget glanced at Hope across the table as she pulled a needle through a seam in a nightgown of dimity. "Hope, dear, have you heard any news from the soldiers that we haven't?" Her voice sounded too casual, reminding Hope of the secret the others were keeping from her.

Gracie, sitting next to Liza, halted midstitch. "Of course she hasn't." She lent Hope a sympathetic smile. She alone knew the depth of Hope's unhappiness . . . the long, lonely years of waiting for one man before finally agreeing to wed another—only to become a widow within three years. Gracie looped her needle through the material in a couple of finishing stitches, bit off the thread with her teeth, then held up a tiny long-sleeved blue gown. "Here's another finished one."

So tiny. Hope found it hard to believe that her own son had ever been small enough to wear a garment that size . . . her orphaned son who'd had his father at home for only a few short lulls in the war. She looked from the soft muslin gown to her older sister. "How long did you say it would be before the men return?"

"The way we figure, they could come marchin' back home in another week, maybe two." Tucking a flaxen strand of hair behind her ear, Gracie grinned. "And if I know my Howie, we'll have us the biggest ol' party you ever did see. You know how he loves to play his music."

"And we know how much you love to sing along." Delia laughed. "It'll be like old times again."

Old times . . .

It had been ten years since Hope felt like singing. Back when Ezra still had his Becky and she her Michael. Back when life had seemed so full of promise for all of them . . . before Michael had been chased out of the valley by vile accusations, and before Ezra's Becky died in childbirth. For all Hope knew, Michael was dead too. It had been nine years since his last letter.

As the other women started chatting about parties and frolics, Hope forced herself to concentrate on their words, on the baby blanket she hemmed—on anything to keep her mind from falling into that well of pain that was always there waiting for her.

"Hush!" Delia suddenly demanded. She raised a hand for silence and turned toward the window. "Somethin's happenin' out on the street."

She was right. The shouting of a male voice came from the direction of the general store.

More yells. The church bell started clanging.

Hope and the other women sprang up, their chairs screeching across the wood-plank floor. They rushed out the front door.

Danny Wilson, a lad who lived just above the river, came riding past the church. He pointed back toward Caney Fork. "The men! They're comin'!"

A thrill shot through Hope as she heard her friends cry out with joy.

The Wilson lad reached the Bremmer gate and reined his sturdy brown mare to a halt. He whipped a floppy hat from his strawlike hair. "Ma'am," he addressed Belinda up on the porch, then Gracie. "You, too, ma'am. Your men is crossin' the ferry this very minute. The militia's a-comin' home!"

Hugging and laughing, Hope's friends bounded down the steps and out the walk while she stopped to retrieve her shoes.

Gracie turned back. "Come on, Hope."

"Don't let me stop you. I'll catch up."

As Gracie took off at a run, her cheeks beaming with lively color, guilt seized Hope. She never could've welcomed Ezra with a fraction of that gladness. Surely now, though, his happiness, his joy, had been restored by his reunion in heaven with Becky and their stillborn baby.

Folks had poured out of the smithy, the leatherworks, the general store, and all the homes lining the road, filling the muddy way with excitement as they rushed to greet the returning heroes.

After banging the last of the muck from her shoes and slipping them on, Hope lifted her gray wool skirt above the muddy street and ran after all those hurrying down to the ferry landing. Reaching the splintery surface of the dock, Hope bemoaned, as she often did, that she was so tiny. Her head rose no higher than most of her neighbors' shoulder blades. She couldn't even see the river, let alone the raft being pulleyed across.

Amid the excited cries of greeting, one shout stood out. "They're halfway!"

Those just ahead of Hope stretched up on tiptoe to see, bobbing their heads back and forth. At least a score of adults and three dozen schoolchildren pushed and jostled, vying for a better view on the crowded quay.

Gracie, sweet Gracie, broke past the cheering crowd and ran to Hope. With her cheeks still aglow and sporting an unstoppable grin, she snatched Hope's hand. "Come on, little sister. Put on a smile. Be happy. Our men are comin' home."

Holding tight, Gracie pulled Hope with her as she wedged back through the crowd until they reached Delia, Belinda, and Liza.

At this vantage point, only schoolchildren stood in front of them, giving Hope a clear view of the approaching raft being drawn ever closer along a thick rope. Carrying a full load of men and horses, the flatboat dragged low in the water, swells lapping over the logs. The militiamen aboard all looked grimy and ragged, attired mostly in worn-out hunting clothes. Small wonder the British called them "dirty shirts." Scraggly beards made many of them look even more unkempt. Hope couldn't discern one from another.

"There's Max!" Belinda shouted, laughing. "Can't miss that blond hair." Holding her belly, she thrust her other arm above her head and waved wildly.

Hope's heart swelled, sharing her dear friend's joy. Max would be here for the birth of Belinda's baby.

The shouts coming from the raft and those from the landing collided in a deafening roar as the ferry banged against the dock. A couple of overeager passengers lifted the front rail from its slot and carelessly tossed it into the water, freeing everyone to converge even before the mooring lines had been secured.

Belinda's husband, Max, moved with great speed for his hulking size. Tears streaming into his golden beard, he reached his wife and buried his face in her curly red hair.

Max's father, the valley's pastor, shoved forth with his own

German bulk to reach his son. The silver-haired old gent engulfed both Max and Belinda in a burly hug.

Not to be left out, Max's youngsters grabbed on wherever they could.

Other militiamen scooped their own children up into their arms—schoolchildren who'd been fortunate to be in town at the right moment, along with Hope's sewing circle, and a few folks who had come in on other business. But it didn't matter whether or not a man's family was present—no one lacked for a hug.

Gracie's brown-eyed Howie wore his usual cocky grin. But instead of walking off the raft, he rode a sleek bay. One of his feet was swathed in bandages. He didn't remain astride for long. His wife and his sister, Delia, pulled him down into their arms while their school-age children grabbed his sleeves and shirttail, tugging and squealing. The boisterous cluster half carried him up the embankment.

Fortunately, a lone regular-army soldier in a blue uniform strode off the ferry and collected the abandoned bay's reins, adding them to those of the other horses he led.

Remaining behind on the dock, Hope took in the whole picture of Reardon Valley's returning heroes as they moved up the slope, surrounded by the happy throng. She smiled as she heard a multitude of words spilling enthusiastically over each other in an unintelligible jumble of joy. Gracie had her Howie. Liza was clinging to her baby brother, who looked years older than when he had left to join the militia last summer.

Feeling someone's gaze on her, Hope remembered the uniformed soldier. With his string of horses, he was the only one remaining on the quay with Hope.

She turned and looked up into eyes that were an unusually light shade of brown. The exact shade of her long-gone beau's. She searched his face. This man was several years older, his features more chiseled. But . . . ! "Michael? . . . Michael Flanagan?"

"Aye."

His quiet affirmation slammed into Hope, knocking the strength from her legs. Her vision fuzzed.

Hands gripped her arms.

His hands.

Hope's vision burst out of its fog. Michael Flanagan was staring at her. Intently. After all these years.

After all these years? Weren't those the exact words she'd overheard Belinda say not thirty minutes ago? Michael must have been the secret her friends were keeping from her.

But why?

Michael Flanagan squeezed her arms. "Hope? Are you all right? You're white as a ghost."

Visit www.HeartQuest.com for lots of info on
HeartQuest books and authors and more!

www.HeartQuest.com

HEART
QUEST®

CURRENT HEARTQUEST RELEASES

› *Magnolia,* Ginny Aiken
› *Lark,* Ginny Aiken
› *Camellia,* Ginny Aiken

› *Letters of the Heart,* Lisa Tawn Bergren, Maureen Pratt, and Lyn Cote

› *Sweet Delights,* Terri Blackstock, Elizabeth White, and Ranee McCollum

› *Awakening Mercy,* Angela Benson
› *Abiding Hope,* Angela Benson

› *Ruth,* Lori Copeland
› *Roses Will Bloom Again,* Lori Copeland
› *Faith,* Lori Copeland
› *Hope,* Lori Copeland
› *June,* Lori Copeland
› *Glory,* Lori Copeland

› *Winter's Secret,* Lyn Cote
› *Autumn's Shadow,* Lyn Cote

› *Freedom's Promise,* Dianna Crawford
› *Freedom's Hope,* Dianna Crawford
› *Freedom's Belle,* Dianna Crawford
› *A Home in the Valley,* Dianna Crawford
› *Lady of the River,* Dianna Crawford

› *Sunrise Song,* Catherine Palmer
› *English Ivy,* Catherine Palmer
› *A Touch of Betrayal,* Catherine Palmer
› *A Kiss of Adventure,* Catherine Palmer (original title: *The Treasure of Timbuktu*)

› *A Whisper of Danger,* Catherine Palmer (original title: *The Treasure of Zanzibar*)
› *Finders Keepers,* Catherine Palmer
› *Hide & Seek,* Catherine Palmer
› *Prairie Rose,* Catherine Palmer
› *Prairie Fire,* Catherine Palmer
› *Prairie Storm,* Catherine Palmer
› *Prairie Christmas,* Catherine Palmer, Elizabeth White, and Peggy Stoks
› *A Victorian Christmas Keepsake,* Catherine Palmer, Kristin Billerbeck, and Ginny Aiken
› *A Victorian Christmas Cottage,* Catherine Palmer, Debra White Smith, Jeri Odell, and Peggy Stoks
› *A Victorian Christmas Quilt,* Catherine Palmer, Peggy Stoks, Debra White Smith, and Ginny Aiken
› *A Victorian Christmas Tea,* Catherine Palmer, Dianna Crawford, Peggy Stoks, and Katherine Chute

› *A Victorian Christmas Collection,* Peggy Stoks
› *Olivia's Touch,* Peggy Stoks
› *Romy's Walk,* Peggy Stoks
› *Elena's Song,* Peggy Stoks

› *Chance Encounters of the Heart,* Elizabeth White, Kathleen Fuller, and Susan Warren

› *Happily Ever After,* Susan May Warren

COMING SOON (SUMMER 2003)

- *Love's Proof,* Catherine Palmer
- *An Echo of Hope,* Dianna Crawford
- *Speak to Me of Love,* Robin Lee Hatcher

HEARTQUEST BOOKS BY DIANNA CRAWFORD

A Home in the Valley—Sabina Erhardt has been lost in a hand of poker. Now she has only two choices: face the brutal gambler who has won the right to marry her, or run for her life. Sabina chooses to run. Now, as she finds herself in Reardon Valley, taken in by a widower and his four children, Sabina faces an even harder choice. Will she lose her heart to Baxter Clay, the strong loving man who has given her a home, or will she deny her feelings and her past? Only God's faithfulness and the strength of Baxter and Sabina's love can forge a straight path through the valley. . . . Book 1 in the Reardon Valley series.

Freedom's Promise—For the first time in Annie McGregor's life, she's free. *Free!* Her years of servitude drawing to a close, Annie hears there's a man in town looking for settlers to accompany him across the mountains into Tennessee country. Could this be the answer to her prayers? Isaac Reardon is on a mission to claim his betrothed— along with a preacher and a small group of settlers—and return to the beautiful home he has carved from the rugged wilderness. He is devastated to learn of his intended wife's betrayal. And now to make matters worse, he's confronted with a hardheaded, irresistible young woman who is determined to accompany his wagon train—without a man of her own to protect her! Together, Annie and Ike fight perilous mountain passages, menacing outlaws, and a rebellious companion. And as they do, both are shocked to discover their growing attraction, which threatens to destroy the dream of freedom for which they have risked their very lives. Book 1 in the Reardon Brothers series.

Freedom's Hope—Jessica Whitman lives for one hope: Reaching her mother's family, the distinguished Hargraves of Baltimore, far from the clutches of her drunken father. Noah Reardon, bitter over a broken betrothal, wants nothing to do with people. So why is he captivated by the intriguing Jessica? Despite himself, Noah reluctantly offers his protection to this feisty young woman. Together Noah and Jessica discover a shared passion for truth, for integrity, for the very ideals upon which their new nation was founded. Noah is tempted to make the biggest mistake of his life—giving his heart to a woman who doesn't share his faith. Then a shocking discovery about Jessica's family threatens to shatter her hope. As they struggle to understand God's plan, both Noah and Jessica learn who truly offers hope for each tomorrow. Book 2 in the Reardon Brothers series.

Freedom's Belle—Desperate to escape the cruel man her parents insist she marry, Crystabelle grasps at the chance of a teaching position in a remote settlement beyond the mountains. Surely neither her betrothed nor her father will be able to find her there! And she will be free to pursue the independent life of which she has always dreamed. A beautiful, refined heiress is the last person Drew Reardon would expect to be seeking passage overmountain to Tennessee Territory. But the lovely miss seems determined to procure the position of schoolmistress to Reardon Valley's youngsters. Dubious but intrigued, Drew finds himself helping her achieve her goal. Once he gets her safely to the valley, though, he'll be off again. Not even the growing threat to Crystabelle's safety can dissuade him from exploring his beloved wilderness . . . or can it? As the two join forces, they learn the *true* meaning of adventure and freedom—but a shocking betrayal threatens to tear it away from them forever. Book 3 in the Reardon Brothers series.

A Daddy for Christmas—One stormy Christmas Eve on the coast of Maine, the prayers of a young widow's child are answered in a most unusual manner. This novella by Dianna Crawford appears in the anthology *A Victorian Christmas Tea*.

MOVING FICTION

OTHER GREAT TYNDALE HOUSE FICTION

- *Safely Home,* Randy Alcorn

- *Jenny's Story,* Judy Baer
- *Libby's Story,* Judy Baer
- *Tia's Story,* Judy Baer

- *Out of the Shadows,* Sigmund Brouwer
- *The Leper,* Sigmund Brouwer
- *Crown of Thorns,* Sigmund Brouwer

- *Looking for Cassandra Jane,* Melody Carlson

- *Child of Grace,* Lori Copeland

- *They Shall See God,* Athol Dickson

- *Ribbon of Years,* Robin Lee Hatcher
- *Firstborn,* Robin Lee Hatcher

- *The Touch,* Patricia Hickman

- *Redemption,* Karen Kingsbury with Gary Smalley
- *Remember,* Karen Kingsbury with Gary Smalley

- *The Price,* Jim and Terri Kraus
- *The Treasure,* Jim and Terri Kraus
- *The Promise,* Jim and Terri Kraus
- *The Quest,* Jim and Terri Kraus

- *Winter Passing,* Cindy McCormick Martinusen
- *Blue Night,* Cindy McCormick Martinusen
- *North of Tomorrow,* Cindy McCormick Martinusen

- *Embrace the Dawn,* Kathleen Morgan

- *Lullaby,* Jane Orcutt

- *The Happy Room,* Catherine Palmer
- *A Dangerous Silence,* Catherine Palmer

- *Unveiled,* Francine Rivers
- *Unashamed,* Francine Rivers
- *Unshaken,* Francine Rivers
- *Unspoken,* Francine Rivers
- *Unafraid,* Francine Rivers
- *A Voice in the Wind,* Francine Rivers
- *An Echo in the Darkness,* Francine Rivers
- *As Sure As the Dawn,* Francine Rivers
- *Leota's Garden,* Francine Rivers

- *Shaiton's Fire,* Jake Thoene